Bei...
...
...

Falkirk
Community
Trust

Bo'ness
01506 778520

Bonnybridge
01324 503295

Denny
01324 504242

Falkirk
01324 503605

Grangemouth
01324 504690

Larbert
01324 503590

Meadowbank
01324 503870

Slamannan
01324 851373

This book is due
for return on or
before the last date
indicated on the
label. Renewals
may be obtained
on application.

Falkirk Community Trust is a charity registered in Scotland. No: SC042403

Also by Therese Beharrie

Tempted by the Billionaire Next Door
Surprise Baby, Second Chance
Her Festive Flirtation

Conveniently Wed, Royally Bound miniseries
United by Their Royal Baby
Falling for His Convenient Queen

Billionaires for Heiresses miniseries
Second Chance with Her Billionaire

Also by Stella Bagwell

The Arizona Lawman
Her Man on Three Rivers Ranch
A Ranger for Christmas
Guarding His Fortune
The Little Maverick Matchmaker
The Maverick's Bride-to-Order
Her Sweetest Fortune

Discover more at millsandboon.co.uk

FROM HEIRESS TO MUM

THERESE BEHARRIE

HIS TEXAS RUNAWAY

STELLA BAGWELL

This book is produced from independently certified FSC™
paper to ensure responsible forest management.

For more information visit: www.harpercollins.co.uk/green

Printed and bound in Spain
by CPI, Barcelona

MILLS & BOON

First Published in Great Britain 2019
by Mills & Boon, an imprint of HarperCollinsPublishers,
1 London Bridge Street, London, SE1 9GF

From Heiress to Mum © 2019 Therese Beharrie
His Texas Runaway © 2019 Stella Bagwell

ISBN: 978-0-263-27237-6

0519

MIX
Paper from
responsible sources
FSC™ C007454

FROM HEIRESS
TO MUM

THERESE BEHARRIE

For Grant,
who sees me when I can't see myself.

I love you.

CHAPTER ONE

A POUNDING WOKE her up.

At first Autumn Bishop thought it was a dream. She'd gone to bed with one hell of a headache. Unsurprisingly: she'd spent a weekend away with her parents and sister, dealing with family drama, and had then driven six hours back to Cape Town.

The familiar throbbing had come shortly after she'd arrived at home. Right on time. Her head always ached when she was far enough away from her family to brood about how different she was from her sister. And how those differences made her feel like a failure.

When she heard the pounding, she thought it was that. Perhaps the pounding headache had manifested into a drumming. But then she heard a shrill ringing, and she woke up fully. Throwing the covers off, she ran to the front door, her stomach dropping when she opened it to Hunter Lee.

Her stomach kept free-falling as her eyes swept over him. His brown hair was wild, a sign that he'd let the wind style it. The strong features of his face were tight, as if someone had attached them to a string at his nose and pulled, forcing everything to be drawn to the centre of his face. Even the muscles of his shoulders—his chest, his entire body—were tense.

Something about it sent a wave of emotion, of awareness through her. When that wave collapsed, a second one of nausea replaced it.

'What is it?' she asked. 'What's wrong?'

'Everything.'

His voice, usually steady and strong, was hoarse, the word cracking. A part of her wanted to turn on her heel and climb back into bed; another, more forceful part spurred her forward. Before she knew it, her arms were circling around his significantly larger body.

She wasn't sure why she was hugging him. They'd avoided this kind of contact since they'd made the transition from lovers to friends a year before. Besides, he wasn't the kind for contact, unless in affection, and in private. But her instinct had been to comfort him. And, though she would never admit it aloud, to comfort herself at seeing him this way.

She drew back and took a deliberate step away from him.

'What happened?'

He stuffed his hands into his jeans pockets. Her eyes automatically followed the movement, and she shoved away a kick of appreciation. It didn't matter that his legs—those powerful, strong legs—deserved appreciation. Now was not the time.

'Can I come inside?'

His voice was steadier.

'Of course,' she said, opening the door wider.

Two things happened then. One, she held her breath, not wanting to get a whiff of his cologne. The smell never failed to twist her insides, even after their break-up, and she'd become accustomed to not breathing it in when she was around him. Two was that a light breeze followed Hunter through the front door. It wasn't particularly cool—cool and summer in the Western Cape of South Africa rarely went together—but Autumn shuddered, her skin shooting out in gooseflesh. And suddenly she realised how she looked.

She was wearing a silk nightdress, a gift from her mother, since it was the first thing she'd found in her cupboard before falling into bed. She groaned softly. It wasn't demure, though she might have been able to ignore that if her breasts had played along. They currently were not, having reacted to the breeze, and, along with the silk material, she knew she'd give Hunter an eyeful if she turned around like that.

Not that it was something he hadn't seen before. It was just… Autumn liked boundaries. Preferred them, where he was concerned. Where *they* were concerned. So she closed the door and crossed an arm over her chest. She wondered how terrible it was that she was thinking about her breasts when he was clearly upset.

'This is an emergency, I'm assuming,' she said when she turned around, crossing her free arm over her chest as well.

'Yes.' It was all he said for what felt like for ever. Then his eyes sparked. 'Not so much that you can't put on something that makes you feel more comfortable.'

Her cheeks heated. Instead of giving him the sarcastic reply she truly wanted to, she nodded, and went to her room. She grabbed the first thing she found to cover up—ironically, the silk kimono that, for reasons only her mother and heaven knew, matched the nightdress—and slipped her feet into a pair of sandals.

When she returned, she found him on the patio.

'Still can't get used to this view,' Hunter said quietly as she stopped next to him.

She followed his gaze onto the city of Cape Town. When she'd moved out of her family home—the Bishop mansion, as some people liked to call it—she hadn't tried to find somewhere outside the city she'd grown up in to live. She'd merely been drawn to the Bouw Estate.

It had green fields that exploded with wildflowers; rolling hills beyond the fields; a river that surrounded the estate. The old manor and barn on the property had been renovated into what were now her home and her bakery, respectively. Every time she stood outside on the patio, at the top of the mountain that led out of Cape Town, staring down onto the city, Autumn thought that the Bouw Estate might not have been intentional, but it had been necessary.

'You didn't come here at…' She paused, frowning when she realised she hadn't seen the time. 'What time is it?'

'A little after eleven.'

So she'd had all of an hour's worth of sleep.

'You didn't come here at eleven at night to talk about this view.'

His eyes slid over to her, the brown of them a well of emotion, before his head dipped in a curt nod. 'You're right.'

'When am I not?' she muttered. She gestured to the outdoor table she'd lovingly selected when she'd furnished her house. 'Shall we?'

He nodded, pulled a chair out and stepped back. With a sigh, she sat down, thanking him when he pushed it back in. She waited as he sat down opposite her. A long silence followed. She used it to study him. To watch the emotions play over his face.

When his eyes met hers, she caught her breath, and wished she had something to drink to distract herself from how vulnerable all of this made her feel.

'I don't know how to say this,' he admitted eventually.

She let air into her lungs slowly. 'Just…get it out.'

He angled his head, as if accepting her suggestion, but didn't speak.

'Hunter.' She paused. 'Are you in trouble?'

He opened his mouth, and Autumn could almost see his lips forming *no*, but then he closed it again. Rubbed a hand over his face; took a deep breath.

'I am.'

She straightened. 'Yeah? You're in trouble?'

His eyes shone with an emotion she couldn't quite define. It disturbed her. She'd dated him for two years; they'd been friends for one more. She should be able to tell what he was feeling.

'Yes.'

After a brief moment of hesitation, she laid a hand on the one he'd rested on the table. 'What's going on?'

He took a breath, then exhaled sharply, his gaze lowering.

'I'm a father.'

'What?'

'I'm a father.'

She tilted her head, tried to process. But she couldn't. Her headache had dulled to something bearable, but it felt as if her mind had fallen out of her ear with that head tilt.

'I'm sorry, I thought you said—' She moved her head again. 'Did you say—?'

She broke off, told herself the question was ridiculous. He didn't say he was a father. He didn't say it twice. No. *No.* This was Hunter she was talking to. The man who'd gone quieter and quieter whenever she'd talked about their future together. The man who'd started pulling away from her long before they'd ended things because he'd realised he didn't want children.

There was no way that man, *this* man, was a father.

She let out a small laugh. 'You know…' she lifted her hand, though she didn't have any reason for doing it '… I thought I heard you say you're a father. Which is ludicrous, right?'

'It is,' he agreed quietly.

Relief burst in her chest as if it were a diva arriving at a party.

'Oh. Well, then, what is it? Because—'

'But it's true, Autumn.'

The diva was assassinated. The party turned into a funeral.

'Huh?' she said, inelegantly. 'What? No. You're not a father. You're… You're *you*.'

He inclined his head in both acknowledgement and acceptance, then folded his arms. 'I know. I responded in the same way,' he told her after a moment. 'I didn't believe it when she told me at first either.'

'She?' Autumn repeated through numb lips.

She tried to swallow, but the simple task seemed awfully hard. It was as if her throat had forgotten its entire purpose was to swallow. As if it, too, were stunned by what Hunter was telling her.

'She,' he confirmed with a tight nod. Though he had every right to be amused by the stupid question, Hunter spoke seriously. 'A woman I met a…a year ago.'

'A year ago.'

She was still so numb.

'After our… After.'

The words sounded distant, as if she were listening to him through a wall or through glass or perhaps under water. She blinked, trying to figure a way out, then lifted her hand to her hair, tucking it behind her ears in case it was obscuring the sound. But when he started speaking again, it was the same.

'I…was trying to deal with our break-up,' he said deliberately. 'It was hard, for both of us.'

But I didn't sleep with anyone else.

Her mouth almost said the words. Somehow, by nothing short of a miracle, it didn't.

'I wasn't dealing with it very well.'

Was she dreaming? Maybe she was having a nightmare.

'I went to the bar close to my house.'

She brought her hand to her legs under the table. Discreetly, she pinched her thigh, hard, but Hunter kept talking. She was awake.

'It was the night after we decided to end things. I started drinking. I didn't stop.' He paused. 'It was a drunken mistake. I… I made a mistake.'

Autumn sat back, her eyes sweeping over the frame of her house. She'd rebuilt it by herself, this house. It had been stately, impressive when she'd bought the estate. It had been falling apart, too, and she'd rebuilt it. The red brick outside, the balcony above them, all of that had been her.

When she'd struggled with her life, with trying so hard for people to see her, to love her, she came out here and looked at it. At what she'd built. It never failed to make her feel proud. Steadier.

Tonight, it couldn't anchor her.

She felt as if she were floating away. She wasn't quite sure where to, until she saw herself as a child, following her father around the Bishop Enterprises building. The home of their family empire. She watched as the child asked questions, was answered, but curtly, as if to brush her off. Summer, Autumn's twin sister's questions were answered patiently, though.

Then she was at home, at the Bishop mansion, listening to her mother talk about Summer. Autumn said the right things in response to her mother's concern. Waited patiently for her mother to ask about *her*. About Autumn. It never came.

Finally she saw her gangly frame at fifteen. She was standing outside her parents' house, waiting for her date to the school dance. When he arrived, he asked her where her sister was. Looked behind her—no, *through* her—to check for Summer...

The hurt that had informed her every action since those days flared again now. It asked why she wasn't enough. Why, even when she tried, people still didn't want *her*.

Even Hunter didn't want her. Of course, she'd known it when he'd agreed to break up. But they'd stayed friends. And she didn't have to try as hard with him. She felt the most like herself when she was with him. She almost felt like...like she *was* enough. As if she were the first choice.

Except she wasn't. She very clearly wasn't.

CHAPTER TWO

IT WAS AS if Hunter had been given X-ray vision and could suddenly see through flesh and bone. As Autumn sat staring at him, Hunter saw her hurt, the desire she had to scream at him. He saw how badly she wanted to run. From his news, from him. He wouldn't have blamed her.

He probably looked like a nightmare. He'd pitched up at her house at eleven at night, having got into his car almost as soon as Grace had left his place. He should have tried to get some sleep first, after he'd heard the news. He shouldn't have arrived at Autumn's house in a panic. But he doubted his ability to sleep. He probably wouldn't be able to for the foreseeable future, considering what it might hold.

What it *would* hold, he thought, Grace's words echoing in his ears.

He'd felt better when Autumn had opened the door, concern in her eyes. Something had clicked back in place when she'd put her arms around him. Now, that seemed like an appropriate punishment for coming to her with this.

Seeing how hurt she was, seeing her wanting to run, sent an unbearable ache through his body. Another appropriate punishment.

He'd thought he'd grown accustomed to her disappointment. Every day towards the end of their romantic relationship had been stained with its stickiness. She had never said it in so many words, but he'd sensed it. Every time he hadn't responded to her gentle probes about their future. Or when he hadn't added anything when she'd spoken about her dreams about having a family.

In truth, he'd been figuring out his answers. First for himself; then what he would give her. She wouldn't like them, despite the different ways he'd tried to phrase them in his mind. He'd spent too long trying to figure out what to tell her in the end, desperate for her not to have a low opinion of him.

But it had happened anyway, rightfully so. Just as it was happening now.

He could see it. In the tightness around her eyes. In the crease between her brows. More than that, he *felt* her disappointment, sharp and acute. Felt sharp and acute pangs in his chest as well. So he supposed he hadn't got used to it after all.

But no matter how much he wanted to, he couldn't say what she needed to hear: that he wanted to have a family with her. He couldn't. The desires she'd expressed when they'd been together had reminded him of how families broke. How siblings got sick. How losing them felt like losing everything in the world.

Each person involved in a family would get hurt. Would be irrevocably changed—or worse. He'd seen it with his own parents. With his own sister. He had no desire to put himself in a situation to feel that way again. Let alone with a woman he genuinely cared for.

And yet the first thing he'd done after their break-up was forget his responsible nature and get a woman pregnant. Then he'd come to her, to the woman he cared about, to tell her that their break-up had resulted in the very thing she'd wanted and he hadn't: a child.

The thing he now had and she didn't. What painful irony.

'Autumn,' he said when the silence extended long enough that even he, who was at home in silence, felt uncomfortable. 'Say something.'

Her lips parted, and for a split second Hunter remembered that they did that just before he would kiss her. But that memory was unwelcome, untimely. How could he think about kissing her when he'd just told her he was a father? When he'd just discovered he was a father?

He was a *father*.

Bile rose in his stomach. It was the same thing that happened whenever he thought about his own father. The man who'd put his feelings above his dying daughter's.

'Autumn,' Hunter said again, more insistently.

Autumn's eyes met his, and his breath did something strange at the gold that flickered in their brown depths.

'Are you okay?'

Her eyelashes fluttered. 'I— Yes.' She straightened. 'I'm okay.'

Her voice sounded strange too, as if someone had taken a hold of her voice box and were squeezing tightly.

'I'm sorry,' he said, because he needed to.

She closed her eyes, and he wanted to reach out. To brush a finger over the line where her dark lashes lay against the brown of her skin. To smooth the lines at her forehead.

Her eyes opened right then and before he could avert his own, their gazes locked. His heart stumbled in his chest, resulting in an uncomfortable beat against his chest bone. The *thump-thump* of his heart sounded in his ears, except he heard it as laughter, a mocking *ha-ha* at what he'd given up to ensure that what he'd told her tonight would never happen.

He forced his eyes away, onto the night lights of Cape Town. It used to comfort him once upon a time. Now it mocked him.

'You found out tonight?' she asked after some time had passed.

He nodded. Still, he couldn't look at her.

A voice in his head called him a coward.

'Grace, the woman I—' He stopped before he said something stupid. 'The mother of the child. She showed up at my place.'

'You didn't know before that?'

He shook his head.

'How old is the... How old?'

'Three months.'

She pursed her lips, though he'd caught the trembling long before she'd done it.

'I'm sorry,' he said again, eyes resting on her face now. She nodded.

'You're here because you're surprised.'

It wasn't a question.

'I'm here because—' he hesitated '—it's the first place I wanted to go. I needed to see you.'

Her tongue darted out, wet her lips.

'Why?'

He took a breath. 'You're my friend.'

'Not your only one.' She pushed back at some of the curls exploding over the silk band she wore. 'Certainly not the best one to deal with this.'

'No,' he agreed, but didn't say anything else. Couldn't. Because she was right.

She wasn't his only friend; not that he had many more. In fact, he had one more: his second-in-command, Ted. Most of his peak making-friends time—school, university—had been focused on other things.

Most of his school life he'd spent helping his parents take care of Janie, his baby sister, who'd had cystic fibrosis. *Ha!* a voice in his brain immediately said. He hadn't helped his parents take care of Janie; he'd helped his *mother* take care of Janie. His father had tapped out of her care early on, pronouncing himself too clumsy to help.

Hunter supposed he could understand that when it came to helping clear Janie's lungs of the mucus. The airway clearance therapy could have posed a problem for someone who was *clumsy*. But he didn't know how that prevented his father from helping to get Janie to her doctor's appointments. Or helping to keep her active. Getting her diet right. Doing anything, really, that would make Janie's life easier. Or make her feel as if she weren't a burden for the man who should have loved her unconditionally.

She was a bright kid who'd picked up on things without much encouragement. She'd noticed their father's lack of interest. Hunter had done everything he could to make up for it.

When she'd passed away, he hadn't wanted friends to know how much his life had changed. How his heart ached, all the time. How alone he felt. How...broken. He hadn't been able to tell his parents about it when they'd been fighting, all the time. So he'd stuck his head into books, reading about technology and then, after his parents' divorce, renewable energy. It had distracted him enough to survive. To thrive, even, if he thought about the tech business he'd started ten years ago during university.

But that had meant he'd spent his entire university career studying or working. And when his business had taken off, he'd spent his time making sure it stayed in the air. He'd hired Ted to help with that. He hadn't even thought about Ted when it came to this, though.

When he'd first seen Grace. When she'd told him about the baby. When she'd showed him pictures, and he'd seen a face that looked so much like Janie's his heart had flipped over in his chest. When she'd asked Hunter to help take care of the child.

No, for that, he'd immediately thought about Autumn.

'You're the only person who knows why this is...' He trailed off. He hoped she'd interrupt him. That she'd finished his sentence for him. She didn't. 'You're the only person who knows about my family.'

He didn't let her speak when she opened her mouth. Too late, he thought. Because if he didn't continue, he'd lose his courage.

'You have to help me take care of him.'

'What?'

'You… You have to help me. She wants me—needs me—to take care of him while she's finishing her articles at a law firm in Gauteng for the next three months.' His voice dropped to a whisper. A rasp. A sacrifice. 'I… I don't know how. Please, Autumn. Please, help me.'

Hunter's gaze felt like lasers pointed straight at her heart.

'I… I need a moment,' she said, and rose unsteadily to her feet. 'Coffee?'

He angled his head, looked down, and she chose to interpret the gesture as a *yes*. Though in all honesty, he could have shaken his head for *no* and she'd still have made him one. She was barely paying attention to him. She was only focusing on getting away from him.

She strode by him, through the glass sliding doors and past the stone-coloured furniture and yellow pillows she'd chosen because they made her happy. It had been the same reason she'd chosen the bright paintings on the walls, and why she'd stacked the bookshelves beneath them with romance novels.

Her kitchen looked much the same: splashes of colour that made her feel bright. Light. But the appliances were sleek and top of the range; the cupboards meticulously arranged for optimum usage; the pantry filled with every ingredient she needed for when she experimented with cakes or biscuits or cupcakes or desserts or, really, anything that tickled her fancy.

With unsteady fingers, she popped a pod in the espresso machine, put a mug where it was needed, pressed buttons and let the machine do its work. She frothed the milk while she waited, keeping her hands busy, avoiding the thoughts speeding through her mind. She placed the second mug in the machine with a new pod, added milk to the first, then did the same for the second when it finished. She set them both on a tray, fixed a plate of cookies she'd baked before she'd left for her parents' anniversary weekend, and set that on the tray.

She was ready to go out. Except she couldn't. She... didn't want to. Not yet. She braced her hands on her kitchen counter, lifting her head so she could see out of the window. She'd insisted the window be included when she'd been fixing up the house. Had insisted on the same thing when she'd built the bakery.

Usually, she'd take her coffee there in the mornings, about an hour before she'd have to be at the bakery, which was about the time the sun rose in summer. She'd watch the golden orb appear from over the hills in the distance; she'd see the faint blue of the river that ran along the edge of the Bouw Estate; and her eyes would rest on the fields of flowers she refused to cut, giving the estate a wild feeling she genuinely enjoyed.

Now, all she saw was blue-black darkness. It seemed like an appropriate representation of what was going on in her mind.

The rope that had been keeping her together since their break-up felt dangerously frayed. Which was in itself a danger, as pretending everything was fine was the only way she kept her insecurities at bay. The voices that told her it wasn't that Hunter didn't want a future, a family; it was that he didn't want one with her.

Look at how he spoke about his sister, the voice said. With such emotion. Respect, fondness, love. How could a man with so much to give not want to share that in a family?

She'd managed to dismiss it with Hunter's words. The truth, he'd assured her, was that he couldn't bear to repeat the painful experiences of his childhood. His sister had been sick, then died; his father had been physically present, but emotionally absent; and his parents had eventually divorced after Janie's death. How could she argue with that?

But she had. In silence, with herself, her insecurities

making damning arguments. Convincing arguments. Hunter's news made those arguments hard not to believe.

As she thought of it—that he had a child—a fresh bomb of pain went off inside her. She closed her eyes, held her breath, hoping it would stop the devastation. But it didn't, and she felt her insides be destroyed. Felt them crumble and lie disintegrated inside her.

As she let air into her lungs, she took the tray outside. Hunter sat exactly as she'd left him—stiff, staring out over the city—and she put the tray down in front of him.

She settled in with her coffee, but since her back was towards the city she was forced to look at Hunter. She sipped thoughtfully, waiting for him to look at her, ignoring the throbbing in her chest as she did. When he finally met her eyes, she tilted her head.

'How did it go?' she asked quietly. 'When she told you.'

He stared at her for a moment, then picked up his coffee. 'I…struggled.'

'So you were perfectly stoic, but freaking out inside.'

His mouth lifted. 'Pretty much.'

'You don't think she's lying?'

'No.'

The answer was quick and immediate, his voice hard. He was defending the woman, Autumn realised, though she didn't understand why the woman needed defending. She was only asking a question. But then, this was Hunter. Protecting what was his. And the woman was his now.

Her stomach twisted.

'She has no reason to lie,' he continued. 'And she showed me a picture. He looks…exactly like Janie did when she was a baby.'

'Oh.'

It was all she said; it was all the pain allowed her to say. All the other words that came to mind were selfish.

We could have had a child who looked like Janie. We

could have done this together, and you wouldn't have had to ask for help.

'Is he sick?' she asked.

The cup he'd lifted crashed against the table as he set it back down. 'I... I don't know.'

'You didn't ask?'

'No.'

'Hunter, why the hell wouldn't you ask if your baby was sick?'

He didn't answer her, only looked stricken. Her heart softened, though she refused to allow herself to show it. Beneath the softness was a pain she hadn't known she could feel.

He'd told her it was probably good he wouldn't have children when he was a carrier of the CF gene. There were zero chances then that he'd pass it down—the disease or the gene. Now she was supposed to believe he'd forgotten about it?

'She would have told me if he was sick,' he said.

Autumn set her mug down, her own fingers trembling too much for her to hold it.

'How would she have known? Newborns aren't tested for CF here unless it's specifically requested. What?' she asked defensively when he looked at her. 'I did the research.'

She continued so neither of them would dwell on why she'd done it.

'Besides, Hunter, what do you know about this woman?' She didn't wait for an answer. 'You met her twice. Once the night you two had sex, and tonight. Now she's asking you to take care of your child?'

'It's fair,' he said in a *back-off* voice.

'Of course it's fair,' she said, gritting her teeth. 'But you don't know her. You have no idea what she would have told you.' She paused. Saw his face. Sat back slowly. 'You've already realised that.' There was barely a second before she said, 'And you know you didn't ask because you don't want to know whether he's sick.'

Time passed. Seconds, minutes, she wasn't sure.

'You're right,' he said quietly. 'But I'll find out tomorrow.'

Tired now, she sighed. 'What's happening tomorrow?'

'She's dropping him off.' He picked up his coffee again, brought it to his mouth. When he was done, he looked her dead in the eye. 'Be there with me.'

CHAPTER THREE

THE SITUATION REMINDED him of his father.

Calvin Lee had expected Hunter to fill in where he'd lacked with Janie. Hunter knew it because his father would call him whenever he was expected to care for Janie on his own. Now, Hunter could see himself doing the same to Autumn. Treating her with that same selfishness. But he couldn't stop. Was urged forward by something he didn't understand.

'Hunter,' she said quietly, 'I can't see what either of us could possibly gain from me being there with you.'

Hunter thought about the hug she'd given him when he'd first arrived. He remembered the steadiness of her gaze, despite the news he'd told her. He could hear the concern in her voice, and, beneath it, a strength he desperately needed.

That was why he was here. He'd known she'd offer comfort, steadiness, strength. Because she was his friend. She cared about him. Even though he'd broken her heart by being unable to say yes to the family she wanted. Even though he'd seen some of the light in her eyes go out that day.

It had been part of what had spurred him to the bar the next night.

Her casual talks of a future and a family had forced him to face memories he'd been running from. Of him curling up to Janie as their parents argued in loud whispers outside Janie's door. Of distracting her when the arguments turned louder. Of almost being relieved that she hadn't been there any more when the arguments graduated into shouting.

And then, of the silence.

He couldn't imagine putting a kid through it. Through what Janie had suffered with her illness. Through what he'd suffered with his parents' marriage. Through what it felt like to have the possibility of carrying the cystic fibrosis gene hover like a noose around their necks. Or through having to make the hardest decision in his life about having a family because of it.

Now he was being forced to imagine it. He was being forced to face the fears.

He rubbed a hand over the back of his neck, over his face.

'I need you there,' he rasped, shame straining his voice. 'I don't know if I can do it.'

'Of course you can,' she said. 'You took care of Janie.'

The feeling he couldn't explain swelled, compelling him to beg.

'Please.'

The skin around her eyes crinkled in tension. She gave a curt nod. 'Fine. If it's that important to you, I'll go.'

'Thank you.'

He wanted to tell her she shouldn't have agreed. That she was being too nice to him; that he didn't deserve it. Neither did she. She deserved more than her ex-boyfriend and pseudo-friend asking this from her.

He left it at *thank you*.

'She obviously knew your name if she knew how to find you,' Autumn noted slowly, almost carefully after a bit. 'Or did you...?' She cleared her throat. 'Did you go back to your place?'

Heat curled around his neck. 'We, er, introduced ourselves when we met.' He didn't answer her question.

'So she knows your surname, too?'

He angled his head, trying to remember. The entire event was a little hazy. Another great example he'd set for his son.

His son.

'I think so.'

'Okay, then. So she looked you up on the Internet—'

'How do you know that?'

She gave him a look. 'If some guy I had a one-night stand with knocked me up and I knew his name, you can be sure I'd do an Internet search on him before finding him.'

His mug stopped halfway to his mouth and he just stared at her, his mind playing her words over and over again.

'If some guy I had a one-night stand with knocked me up...'

Purposefully, and much too violently, he brought the coffee to his lips, swallowing down the hiss when the still-hot liquid burnt his throat. But he relished the pain, since he deserved it for the criminal thoughts he'd had at Autumn falling pregnant with someone else's baby.

Selfish, selfish, selfish.

'Hunter?' she asked with a frown. 'Did you hear anything I said?'

'About the Internet search?'

She nodded.

'Yes. I probably should have thought about that.'

She studied him over her mug. 'I imagine you were... too surprised to think.'

'An understatement.'

'That bad?'

'It was fine,' he denied. Her eyebrow lifted. 'Shocking. It was shocking.'

'Enough for you to want to avoid the gene issue.'

He gritted his teeth, guilt flaring in his gut.

'Yes.'

'Enough for you not to realise what comes up when you do an Internet search for Hunter Lee.'

He didn't get what she was talking about for the longest moment, and then he shook his head.

'You don't mean—'

She wrinkled her nose. 'Afraid so.'

And he thought the situation couldn't get worse.

'Oh, no,' he groaned. 'She's seen me…' He couldn't finish the words.

'It wasn't that bad,' she said kindly.

'You have to say that,' he said, his jaw tightening, 'because you're the reason it's there.'

'Maybe,' she allowed. 'Or maybe it's there because you were having fun—'

'And you *filmed* it.'

'It was a social media challenge. I was supposed to film it.'

'I did it for you.'

'I appreciated it.'

'You utilised it.'

'A self-made billionaire doing a ridiculous dance for a social media challenge in my bakery?' She snorted. 'Damn right I filmed it. And look how amazingly it turned out.'

'For you,' he muttered darkly.

'I only used it to promote the bakery. I didn't sell your body parts on the black market.'

'It went viral.'

'Technically,' she continued, as if he hadn't spoken, '*I* didn't film it. Mandy did.'

'Yeah. We're no longer friends.'

Autumn snorted again. 'Yeah, you two looked real enemy-like when you were bribing her to make you some cupcakes last month.'

He lifted a shoulder now, refusing to be taunted any further.

'And besides the ridiculous dance, you actually did something sweet, too.' Her eyes were happy. 'You took me into your arms, spun me around, dipped me right under a wedding cake and laughed.'

'You used that on your social media as part of a *#BakeryBoyfriend* campaign,' he accused.

'An icon was born.'

She grinned at him, and—damn it—his lips twitched. How could he resist that smile? The way it softened her eyes, lit up her face. The way it widened her full pink lips, and made her look years younger than she was.

It was enough to distract him from the fact that he was smiling. It felt like a feat. Hell, it was a feat. He didn't think he could feel anything other than the pure panic that had fuelled his actions until he'd started speaking with her. He shouldn't have been surprised. It had always been part of what had drawn him to Autumn, the way she made him feel. The way she made him forget.

When he'd met her at the wedding of one of his employees—which Ted had forced him to attend—he'd carried an anchor around with him. That anchor had tied itself to his ankle when he'd been six and his sister had been born with cystic fibrosis. It had grown heavier with each of his parents' arguments. With each disappointing prognosis from Janie's doctors.

When Janie had died, he'd just about sunk into the depths of the ocean from that anchor's weight. It had felt as if he'd been living under water from that moment forward.

Then he'd met Autumn, and he'd felt as if he'd been given air for the first time in almost two decades. Which was why he'd allowed their relationship to go on for longer than he should have. After a year of dating, she'd brought up their future together. The year that had followed had been a slow decline into the realisation that he couldn't have what he wanted with Autumn.

And he'd sunk right back into the ocean, reaching the floor of it when they broke up. He could almost understand why he'd looked for a lifeline in a random woman one night.

Not that it had worked. But it had brought him here again. With her. Predictably, he felt as if he was breathing again.

'The reason I bring it up,' Autumn said after a moment, 'is because she'll recognise me.'

His mind took some time to follow. 'Okay,' he said slowly. 'We're friends.'

'Do you think she's going to believe that?'

'She won't care.'

Her eyes had gone serious, and didn't waver from his. 'How sure are you about that?'

He searched her face. Saw what she needed to hear. 'One hundred per cent. There's nothing there beside this connection. The child.'

My son.

She didn't reply immediately.

'We'll see.'

'Autumn—'

'No, Hunter,' she interrupted with a tight smile. 'It's fine. If you think this isn't going to be a problem, then I'll help you get settled with the baby.'

For how long? He didn't ask it. She was giving him something here. Because of it, he felt stronger. More in control. Not like every force in the world had turned on him. So he would give her something, too.

'I'll call you tomorrow with the details.'

'Fine.'

'And I'll leave.' He stood, then stilled when she shook her head. 'What?'

'It's after midnight. You're physically and emotionally drained. You can't leave.'

His heart thumped. 'What's the alternative?'

'You stay here. In the spare bedroom,' she said wryly, when his mouth curved. He'd been planning on teasing her—heaven only knew why—and she'd caught him in it.

Instead, he said, 'I don't have to do that.'

'Yes, you do. I'm not interested in getting phone calls about your death.' Now she stood, picked up the tray. 'Down the passage, third door to the left.' Her eyes met his. 'I'll see you in the morning.'

CHAPTER FOUR

'Was that—? Did I see Hunter's car leave as I drove in?' Mandy asked as she walked into the bakery's kitchen the next morning.

Autumn's back was facing Mandy, so she allowed herself a quick breath and silent moan that Hunter hadn't left before her pastry chef had arrived at work. The rest of her team were already there, bustling in and out of the kitchen as they prepared for the breakfast rush that would soon begin. Autumn took another breath, then turned to Mandy with a smile.

'Yes,' she said brightly. 'He came over last night for dinner.'

Mandy's eyes narrowed. 'And he's only leaving this morning…?'

'We finished late, and we'd been drinking.'

'Hmm.'

Ignoring the disbelieving tone of the woman she considered a friend, Autumn quickly changed the subject.

'Give me highlights of what I missed this weekend. Then tell me how the Thompson wedding cake is coming along.'

'Good morning to you, too.'

'You were the one who came in here without a greeting.'

Mandy sent her a look, then launched into a concise report as she got ready for work. It had been that kind of efficiency that had helped Mandy work her way up to pastry chef in the six years since Autumn had started the bakery.

If she was honest, it felt like longer than that. Perhaps because she'd spent most of her childhood in the kitchen.

At first, it had been out of curiosity. She'd strolled down to the kitchen as the staff had been preparing for one of her parents' numerous parties, and had found herself hypnotised.

The pastries had drawn her attention almost immediately. She'd loved the colours and the smell of them; wondered at the skill and caution they were being decorated with. When one of the chefs had encouraged her to join in, starting her off slowly, patiently, she'd fallen in love with the creation process. And her parents' parties had become a way for her to participate in something she loved.

Later, it had been a chance to contribute to the functions in the only way she could. When she'd got older she'd realised the parties weren't only social events, but networking opportunities. Autumn didn't have Summer's business acumen, nor did she have the professional knowledge her father had invested into her sister. She couldn't talk potential foreign or domestic clients. She had no idea about the details of global merchandise and distribution.

So she baked. And when she left the kitchen, she charmed. And felt like a failure for it.

The smell of sweetness and coffee mingled with the faint freshness of the fields around the bakery usually comforted her. Today, her thoughts turned them sour. For a moment, they even tarnished the efforts she'd put into creating her bakery. The stained cement floors and wooden panelling looked dull. The natural light and countryside atmosphere she'd incorporated when renovating the barn felt kitschy. So did the neat rock-filled paths leading to the bakery; the gardens beyond it.

She'd thought it such a good idea. A cute bakery and café with great food and even better desserts a short trip outside Cape Town that felt like the middle of nowhere. Now, she doubted it. Her memories of growing up tended to do that.

They were always accompanied by the comparisons, starting much earlier than she could even remember. All she knew was that the visits to Bishop Enterprises hadn't been for her benefit. That her questions hadn't been answered in the same way that Summer's had. That the *there, there* nature of the response to her complaints to her mother had been meant to placate her. And that being sent to the kitchen to 'bake something' had been to distract her.

Any desire she might have had to join the family business had been stifled then already. But it had been well and truly shattered after her father's affair.

When Summer had found out Trevor Bishop had cheated, she'd pulled away from him. From Autumn and their mother, too. Autumn knew now that was because Trevor had asked Summer to keep the affair a secret, which had been a burden Summer had carried with her for years. Autumn had only discovered that this past weekend, at their parents' thirtieth anniversary.

It had upset her. Not because of her father's actions, though those weren't great. No, she was upset that Summer had kept the truth from her. And she was worried about what she'd done to bring that about.

Autumn was sure Summer didn't know she harboured a tiny bit of resentment towards Summer because their parents preferred her. But what if she *did* know?

Autumn had pushed the concerns aside during the weekend. It hadn't been important then anyway. Summer had needed her. Autumn might have been jealous of Summer—only a tiny bit—but she would be there for her sister.

She'd done something similar after her father's affair. Then, she'd thought her father needed someone to take over from Summer. Someone in the family who could run the family business. There had only been her, and she'd been so damn hopeful. But she still hadn't been good enough. In fact, her father had gone in an entirely different direction. He'd trained someone new; the man who had become Summer's husband. Then ex-husband. Now boyfriend.

The anniversary weekend had…complicated things.

The point was that her father had not once thought to focus on Autumn the attention he'd spent on Summer. Even when Autumn had asked if she could help, and how she could help, he'd told her she'd be better off elsewhere. She'd realised then that whatever she achieved in her life would have nothing to do with the Bishop family business. The Bishop money would get her foot in the door—and it had, with her father's start-up contribution to her bakery—but kicking it open would be up to her.

She had her doubts about that though. Still did, if she was being honest. Despite the success of her bakery, she worried something would happen that would take it all away from her. She'd do something wrong. Or people would finally realise she didn't know what she was doing. That she wasn't good enough. Her parents had believed that, hadn't they? They'd put Summer first, so they must have.

It didn't help that that was how things had gone with Hunter, too. Their relationship had been going well, and suddenly he'd been pulling away from her. She'd tried to talk away the insecurities as she usually did, but, like always, they were valid. Despite her trying to be a good girlfriend. A perfect girlfriend.

She was still doing it. Trying to be the perfect friend. What she couldn't figure out was why. She had nothing to prove to Hunter any more. They were friends because *he'd* approached *her* after their break-up. She hadn't been desperately chasing after him. In fact, she knew a friendship with him was a bad idea. And his situation with his *baby*? This request? It proved that. Because she knew it would bring her nothing but pain.

So why had she agreed to help?

'Autumn. *Autumn*.'

Autumn's eyes widened before they settled on Mandy. 'What?' she asked.

'Did you hear a word I said?' Mandy poured herself a cup of coffee. 'Or are you too busy thinking about Hunter?'

'I'm tired,' Autumn replied prudishly. 'And not for that reason,' she said when Mandy opened her mouth. 'I didn't have much rest over the weekend.'

'Was your parents' anniversary that good?'

'Yeah,' Autumn said. 'It was touch and go for a moment. Some other time,' she told Mandy with a wave of her hand, 'but they're still in love. It's nauseating.'

'I don't think so,' Mandy said, her expression dreamy. 'I think it's brilliant. Two old people, still in love after all these years.'

'My parents are not old.'

Mandy stared at her.

'They're older,' Autumn conceded, 'and, trust me, it's less appealing when your mother and father are sticking their tongues down each other's throats.'

Mandy pulled a face. 'Ugh.'

'Exactly.' She paused, and when the thought popped in her mind, Autumn went with it. 'Could you keep an eye on things for a few hours?'

'Sure.' Mandy frowned. 'Are you okay?'

'Yeah. I thought I'd try and catch an hour of sleep before I switch the sugar with salt in a batch of cupcakes.'

Mandy winced. 'You don't have to keep bringing that up, you know. I felt bad enough when it happened.'

'Me too, considering I can still taste it.' She mock shuddered, and then laughed when Mandy mimicked throwing something at her. 'Don't worry. I'll only bring it up until you do something similarly atrocious.'

Mandy glowered at her, and Autumn grinned.

See, a voice in her head told her, *you can do this. You*

can totally pretend like your brain isn't malfunctioning and your heart isn't questioning your sanity.

Except she wasn't sure how sustainable it was. It felt as if she was offering Mandy a fake shiny version of herself that would crack if anyone stared at it too long.

'I'll see you later,' Autumn said, taking her apron off and grabbing her purse and keys.

'Don't think you got away from the Hunter question,' Mandy called after her.

Autumn's shoulders immediately tightened. She didn't bother turning around, just lifted a hand in a wave and left Mandy to speculate.

She didn't mind Mandy's curiosity. They weren't simply friends because they worked together. Mandy didn't ever question who Autumn was, or seem to expect anything from her. Autumn didn't have to worry about being *on*, though most of the time, she couldn't help it.

She was always playing a role. Perfect daughter. Perfect sister. Perfect girlfriend. And asking herself questions: what did her mother, sister, boyfriend need from her? Who did she need to be to provide it?

The problem with it was that she was consistently putting others first. More significantly, she was placing herself last. Just like with the situation with Hunter, she knew what moulding herself to other people's needs would bring her. Disappointment when they didn't see her, appreciate her. Hurt when their actions told her they didn't value her efforts.

And just like with Hunter, she couldn't figure out why she still did it.

She gritted her teeth, pausing to catch her breath. Seconds later she realised she'd reached her house. She looked up at the tall white building with the dark wooden frames. After years, it still made her happy. Her steps crunched on the white pebbled pathway, and she tried to let the roses along it calm her as she made her way to her patio.

It was a simple pleasure, standing there and looking at the city she'd grown up in. Buildings of various colours looked back at her, along with Table Mountain in the far distance, and bodies of water and houses. If she looked to the left, she could see the green grass spilling over the inclines and declines of her property. If she walked in that direction, she'd be able to see the river she could sometimes hear at night.

She took a deep breath and settled down on one of the recliners she'd bought for the pool. Her body sighed in relief. It felt as if it had been in a fight. Or perhaps it felt as if it was preparing for an onslaught. She'd barely got any sleep the night before, the thought of Hunter in the other room too much of a distraction. The memory of what he'd told her too much of a disturbance.

I'm a father.

She wanted to take those words and crumple them up. Throw them down at the city she loved so much. They filled her with so much pain, though she couldn't pinpoint exactly why. Was it because they symbolised something she would never have? Certainly not with him. Or was it because they confirmed that he'd moved on from her?

She had no right to be upset about it. He hadn't cheated on her. They'd broken up. And while she'd stayed on her couch for weeks, crying about a man she'd thought would fulfil the perfect plans she'd had for them, he'd been giving someone else everything she'd wanted.

Autumn.

She sighed, knocked her head lightly against the headrest of the recliner. She couldn't help him if she felt like this. Since she'd already agreed to it, she didn't have much choice now. She would just be…cautious. She would try and protect herself.

Though she wasn't sure how she was going to do it, she was content with realising she had to. Content enough to close her eyes and sleep as the sun's rays touched her legs.

* * *

Grace would be bringing Eli, his son, over in an hour. He paced the room, the thought of it, the realisation of it, worrying him as he waited for Autumn to arrive. He needed her with him so his mind would stop tripping over itself. So his heart wouldn't feel as if it were beating in a compressed space.

He ignored the guilt that accompanied the need.

It had encouraged him to offer to pick her up, though. She'd refused.

'Even if we ignore how silly it would be for you to drive an hour out of the city to help me,' she'd started in a tone that had brooked no disagreement, 'how would you take me home when you have a three-month-old to get settled?'

He hadn't even considered that, which had pushed his thoughts back over a cliff.

He was worried, deeply, that he wouldn't be a good father. That he'd follow his father's footsteps and act selfishly. Or that he wouldn't be able to give his son what he needed.

That fear was deeper than the ones he had about repeating his father's mistakes, though more obscured. He could see it was there, like a red light flickering under black material, but he didn't know what it said. His emotions curling into themselves, rocking back and forth, told him it had to do with Janie. But he couldn't unfurl the emotions or still their movement long enough to figure it out.

So they stayed in his stomach, making him ill. And he waited for Autumn to arrive so he wouldn't have to focus on them.

The doorbell rang then; an answer to his prayers. He nearly flung it open in his haste, and his throat went dry. Every part of him stilled, his eyes sweeping over Autumn.

There was one tiny part that began moving again though, jumping up and down, telling him he couldn't do this. He couldn't be overwhelmed by how beautiful she was. He had to pretend he didn't find her attractive. But he nearly snorted at that part because *he had eyes in his head.* He couldn't pretend the woman standing in front of him didn't take his breath away.

She was wearing a pretty summer dress, peach-coloured, which somehow stood out against and moulded to her bronze-tinted skin. Her hair had been tied back into a bunch of curls at the nape of her neck. He was sure that when she turned around, he'd see a ribbon the same colour as her dress keeping it there.

The dress scooped over her neck, giving him a tantalising glimpse of her cleavage; it ended right above her knee, giving him a generous view of smooth, defined legs. The gold sandals she wore wound around feet he'd always thought extraordinary and clung to ankles he could remember kissing.

Logically, he knew he wouldn't be able to run from the fact that he was attracted to her. Because it was simply that—a fact. And he was an adult, who could process facts and control impulses.

But he wouldn't lie: at that moment, it felt as if the universe were testing his ability to do either.

'I was going to say hello,' Autumn said slowly, 'but considering your expression, I now feel like I should ask about your fire extinguisher?'

A fierce blush hit his face.

'I have wine.'

'Hello to you, too,' she said, amusement making her even more beautiful. Annoyingly so. He nearly growled. 'Wine sounds lovely.'

She walked in, past him, and he let out a tight breath he hadn't realised he'd been holding. After giving himself a stern talking-to, he followed her into the kitchen, and poured her a glass of wine. He didn't pour himself one, though he wanted it. Or something stronger. But he couldn't drink when he had to take care of a kid. Besides, he'd been put off by drinking since it had put him in his current predicament. Abstinence—in more than one way—was his strategy moving forward.

'You've set the table,' she commented, sipping from her wine, looking around.

His eyes moved over to the dining room, which he'd decorated with the white runner his mother had sent him when she'd visited the Seychelles some time back. Since he'd opened the glass sliding doors leading into his garden—things had seemed too stifling otherwise—he'd added two citronella candles on either side of the table. He'd thrown some straw placemats around the table after, thinking it made his place look homely. Now, he wondered.

'Too much?'

'No, it's nice.' She turned to face him, and her expression softened. 'You've got to calm down, Hunter.'

'I'm perfectly calm,' he lied.

Her brow arched. 'Really? So that twitch at your right eye is because you're Zen, huh?'

'Just a tic.'

'The frown, too?'

He immediately relaxed his forehead.

She rolled her eyes. 'Why are you nervous?'

He made a hand gesture that was supposed to indicate everything. She nodded.

'Well, the upside is things can hardly go worse than the first two times you've met her. Neither of them was particular positive, I don't think.'

'Hey,' he said without heat.

'What?' she asked dryly. 'You think you're a stud when you're drunk? Because I've got to tell you—'

'You've never complained.'

'You always made up for it sober.' Her mouth curved up at the side, though the rest of her face was tight. 'She didn't have that opportunity.'

He grunted. Tried to figure out what he felt about the

casual way she was talking about him having sex with another woman. It couldn't be easy for her—or perhaps he was overestimating how much she cared about his love life. Then he remembered how she'd needed him to tell her nothing more was going on between him and Grace. And what her face had looked like as she'd asked.

Maybe not.

Except that she was dealing with this pretty casually, which was messing with his head. Did he have to tiptoe around it? Or could he talk about it freely? Not that he wanted to.

'Just ask me whatever's going on in your head instead of trying to figure it out,' she told him wanly. He took a deep breath, then let it out with a shake of his head.

'Fine, then.' Her grip was tight on the wine glass. 'I'll ask you this. Why does she trust you to take care of the child? She doesn't know you.'

'She doesn't have a choice. She doesn't have any family. She was visiting a friend here when…' He trailed off.

Her eyes narrowed. 'There's more.'

'She thinks I'm decent,' he said, unsurprised by her intuition.

'Based on what?'

'Not sure. You'll have to ask her.'

'What's available on the Internet does make you look good.' She gently swirled the wine in her glass, tilting her head to the side. 'The fact that your company provides renewable energy to townships. The charity work. That video of you—'

'Autumn.'

'I was going to say presenting the cheque to the CF Institute,' she said dryly. 'Also, the donation to the non-profit caring for orphaned CF kids. How you spent the day with them.' The pause before her next words lasted only seconds. 'Though being the Bakery Boyfriend must have been what swayed her.'

She grinned. He wanted to scowl back, but of course he didn't. Instead, he smiled, and wished he could capture the moment to return to later. The little bubble of warmth floating in his chest because of her would no doubt pop soon, and he wanted to protect it for as long as he could.

He'd done the same thing in their relationship, when he'd started realising he couldn't have a future with Autumn. But he'd known then, just as he did now, that he was living on borrowed time. Seconds later, his time ran out.

'You don't have to be afraid,' she told him, settling the glass down. 'You know how to take care of a child.'

'I've never taken care of a baby.' The word came out hoarsely, and he cleared his throat. 'I don't know how to.'

'You'll learn.'

She said it so simply he wanted to believe her.

'How do you know?'

'When you interact with them enough, you're forced to. I'm speaking, of course, as someone who was coerced into taking care of my mother's friends' kids. Clearly, I'm an expert.' Her voice softened. 'Your baby is too small for you to mess up anyway,' she said gently. 'You just have to keep the kid alive.'

'What if I can't?' The words sprang from his tongue; his hands curled into fists. 'What if I can't keep him alive, Autumn? What then?'

CHAPTER FIVE

'WHAT?' AUTUMN ASKED, her voice shaky. 'Why would you think that?'

He took the glass from her hand, brought it to his lips, but set it down again before he could drink it. His knuckles were turning white as he gripped the counter instead, and then he lowered his arms. Deliberately, she thought.

'I didn't mean it,' he said after a long pause. 'But that's why you're here.' He offered her a forced smile. 'So I don't say stupid things like that again.'

'That's what I'm here for?'

'For moral support,' he confirmed.

'And part of providing moral support is making sure you don't say anything as concerning as you just did?'

'It's not concerning. It was…a joke.'

'A joke,' she repeated, staring at him.

He gave a curt nod, and she wondered if he really expected her to believe him. He didn't say anything else, which told her he did.

Hunter's entire demeanour had been concerning since she'd arrived. But this? This was the worst. And she knew it had something to do with his sister. What, how, she wasn't sure, but her gut told her that it did. Her gut was usually right when it came to Hunter.

He'd told her about his sister pretty early on. There hadn't been much detail in the information he'd provided though. Autumn only knew his sister had been sick with cystic fibrosis and had passed away at the age of ten.

Whenever she'd build up the courage to ask about it, he'd clam up and change the subject. Much as he was doing now—and maybe *that* was how she knew this had something to do with Janie.

It would make sense if he was afraid about his son being ill. She'd been snarky about it in her thoughts the day before—and now felt bad for it—but she knew how much carrying the cystic fibrosis gene weighed on him.

Before deciding to end their relationship, they'd had what felt like millions of conversations about it. He'd told her he didn't want children because there'd be a chance they might get sick, however small. He'd refused genetic counselling; he couldn't put them through what he'd been through, he'd told her. He hadn't wanted it—even the possibility of it—to hang over his kid's head as it had his.

'What about adoption?' she'd asked then.

'No.'

Her heart had broken. 'Just like that?'

'No,' he said, softer this time. 'I... I shouldn't have children. I won't be a good father.'

'Why would you say that?'

'It's true.' The look on his face had made her doubt it. 'I don't want to have a family.'

That had been their last conversation before ending things.

'Hunter,' she started, lifting a hand to her aching heart, 'I hope this isn't because you think you'll be a bad father.'

He lifted a shoulder.

'You won't be,' she assured him. She nearly reached out, grasped his hand. Praised herself when she didn't. 'But I can't help keep you from saying something concerning. I'd have to stop you from speaking entirely.'

His lips curved, then he sobered. 'Thank you for being here.'

She was about to say, 'It's a pleasure', but stopped herself. Felt an unreasonable pride for doing so, same as when she'd praised herself—also unreasonably—for not taking his hand.

It was just that... Those were things she would do to try and be perfect. The perfect supporter in this case. But she didn't want to touch him and feel the heat that touching him always brought. And being there for him *wasn't* a pleasure; no, it was torture.

They were small things, but they felt significant somehow. Selfish, but significant.

She left it at that, unable to make sense of it, though silence had fallen on them. The longer it extended, the harder the little men dancing in that space between her heart and stomach danced. The wilder they danced.

'Okay.' She bit her lip. 'Now *I'm* nervous.'

His eyes swept over her face, amusement taking some of the strain away. 'You don't have to be.'

She made a non-committal sound.

'You don't,' he insisted. 'Grace is going to look at you and know…' He trailed off.

'That we have a weird relationship?' she teased through the lump in her throat.

He didn't smile.

'No,' he said after a moment. 'She'll know I have support. She won't worry as much.'

'I doubt that.'

'Your support will help me be a decent parent.'

'That's a lot of pressure to put on a weird relationship,' she said lightly, though the lump was growing.

His eyes lifted to hers. 'Maybe. But I don't think she'll deny that you make me a better person.'

Her fingers tightened on the stem of her glass; her head went light. No, it was her heart. Filling with helium, floating up into her head, screwing with her thoughts. She forced herself to think of all the reasons why she couldn't allow herself to fall for his charm.

He had a child. There was no future for them. He didn't want a future with *her*.

It worked. Remembering all of it popped her heart, caused the broken, deflated pieces to fall back into her chest. Very deliberately, she brought the glass to her lips, took a deep sip.

'I know this isn't an ideal situation for either of us,' he said quietly. 'Least of all for you. I…appreciate you.'

She nodded. Searched her mind desperately for something to change the subject with.

'Did you warn her I'd be here?'

'Yes,' Hunter said. 'I told her I'd have a close friend with me.'

'Did you tell her it was me?' she asked. 'No, wait—did you say it like that?'

'No and yes.' He paused. 'I'm not sure what the second refers to.'

'Did you call me a "close" friend?'

She lifted her hands in air quotes, and lowered them both to her glass.

'You don't think we're close?'

'It's not about that. It's about you describing your ex-girlfriend as a close friend to the mother of your child.'

He shrugged. 'It's true.'

Warmth sank into her bones. A desperate, inappropriate warmth that had no business being in her body at all.

'Ten more minutes,' she said, for lack of anything else.

'Yeah.'

It was all either of them said for the longest time. Her mind teased her, told her to talk, though it provided nothing good to say. Only illogical things. Things unsuitable to the tension of the anticipation of the baby and his mother's arrival.

As if to taunt her further, it offered her the memory of how Hunter had looked at her when she'd arrived. Up to this moment, she'd been able to ignore it. Or not ignore it, since that seemed impossible, but to manage it.

She hadn't burst into flames when she'd met Hunter's eyes and seen the fire there. In fact, she'd *joked*. She'd pretended not to see how good he looked in his shirt and jeans. Hadn't commented on his smell when she'd forgotten to stop inhaling as she'd passed him. Automatically, unexpectedly, it had made her knees go weak. It smelled like nothing else in the world. It smelled like *Hunter*.

Her face started to warm, and, heaven help her, so did other parts of her body. She wanted to reach for her glass of wine, but it was empty. Considering Grace would be there any minute, she'd need her wits about her. Autumn couldn't pour herself another glass, regardless of how strong the temptation was.

She'd have to resist it just as she had to resist her attraction to him. She would put it aside. She'd done it with her emotional feelings for him; she could do it with her physical feelings, too. So she'd focus on…how annoyingly grumpy he was instead.

In defiance, her mind reminded her how attracted she was to that grumpiness. A combination of reticence and shyness struggling with the assertiveness he needed as a CEO of a company worth billions. The grumpiness made her want to strangle him and coddle him and—

She almost threw her hands up in frustration. Maybe she should jump him and get it over with. Maybe that would finally sate the heat. But she knew there was no sating this…this *need*. She'd spent two satisfactory years proving that.

'Are you okay?' Hunter asked, his eyes on her face.

It burned, and she turned, embarrassed. Logically, she knew he couldn't see into her head. He couldn't know she was thinking about pulling him into the bedroom when the mother of his child—*and his child*—were minutes away.

'Autumn?'

'I'm fine,' she said brightly, turning back. 'Sorry.' She pressed her hands to her cheeks. 'I think I drank the wine too quickly.'

He studied her, his lips parting as if he wanted to say

something, but the bell rang and distracted him. *Thank you*, she told the universe, even as her stomach rolled with nerves. She nodded at him, and he went to open the door as she smoothed down the front of her dress.

Seconds later, she grabbed the wine bottle and her wine glass and put them on the counter behind a wall separating part of the kitchen from the rest of it. She didn't want Grace to see she'd been drinking. The last thing she wanted was for Grace to realise how comfortable she was at Hunter's place. It would create an insider versus outsider impression Autumn wanted to avoid.

Although, to be honest, Autumn wasn't entirely sure which side she fell on.

Taking a deep breath, she rested a hand on her stomach as though somehow it would help still the dancing men there. It didn't. In fact, it didn't even encourage the air she'd breathed in to move to where the fluttering was.

She closed her eyes, cursed silently. Then she straightened her shoulders and moved back to the main part of the kitchen.

Hunter and Grace were already in the living room, front door closed. On the floor was a car seat that had, for the moment, no sound coming from it. Embarrassed that she'd taken so long to steady herself, she moved forward, her eyes stuck on Grace.

She was beautiful. Shorter than Autumn, her hair in a long, straight ponytail that fell to the middle of her back. Her features were dark; though they were tight now. Unhappy. When Grace saw Autumn, her spine straightened. Autumn understood. She wasn't feeling particularly at ease herself.

'Hi,' Autumn said, moving forward and offering a hand. 'I'm Autumn Bishop.'

'Grace Tatum,' the woman said, taking Autumn's hand. The grip was hot, a little sweaty, and Grace grimaced.

Autumn shook her head slightly, as if to say, *Never mind.* Grace's face eased somewhat.

'It's nice to meet you,' Grace continued, before dropping her hand. 'I'm sorry…these are the circumstances.'

'Oh,' Autumn said with a frown. 'You don't have to be.'

Grace's eyes slipped to Hunter's, then back to Autumn. 'You're not upset?'

'About what?'

Grace's brow knitted. 'Did Hunter tell you why I'm here? Or who I am?'

'Of course I did.' Hunter spoke for the first time. 'I wouldn't have asked her to join me if I hadn't been honest.'

Autumn sent Hunter a look, hoping it conveyed her message: *Calm down.* Grace wasn't questioning his integrity, which was what Hunter's defensive reaction implied. She was…curious. Uncertain. Hunter angled his head, as if understanding. She almost sighed out loud.

This is why you shouldn't have called me a close friend.

'I know who you are, Grace,' Autumn said. 'But I think you're under the wrong impression about who I am.' Her mouth curved, even as her stomach tightened in anxiety. 'Hunter and I are friends. *Only* friends.'

All the muscles in Hunter's body tightened. 'I told you that,' he said again.

Autumn gave him another look, but a strong desire for Grace to know he hadn't been lying about his and Autumn's relationship spurred his words. For reasons he'd rather not question, he wanted Autumn to know, too.

'I know,' Grace said softly. 'But I didn't know whether I should believe you. People aren't always honest about these things.'

'I am,' Hunter said firmly.

Autumn shook her head, as if she'd given up on him. 'It's true,' she said, 'he is. He's also a tad defensive, as you can tell.'

Grace smiled, her grip on the straps of the handbag she wore across her body tightening, then loosening.

'We're really only friends though,' Autumn said again. Again, Hunter felt something loop in his stomach. Why did her insistence about the nature of their relationship bother him so much? 'And if you're not comfortable with me being here, I'll leave.'

Hunter fought to keep the panic he felt from appearing on his face. Or taking a hold of his tongue. His expression remained blanked, hopefully. He kept quiet.

'Oh, no, that's not necessary,' Grace said. 'I…wish I had support.' Her eyes lowered to the car seat. Hunter hadn't been able to look down yet.

'You don't have anyone?' Autumn asked.

'None who were willing to help me with this,' Grace said with a faint smile. 'Hell of a thing to figure out when visiting those people got me into this situation.'

There was an awkward pause.

'You don't have any family?' Autumn asked softly.

Grace's face tightened. She stood a little taller. 'My parents died when I was younger. I have no siblings, and no extended family that would help.' Her eyes met Autumn's. 'Satisfied?'

'Of course,' Autumn said with a shake of her head. 'I didn't mean to imply… I'm sorry.'

Grace deflated. 'No,' she said after a beat. 'I'm sorry. I shouldn't have reacted like that.' She took a breath. 'It's just that… This has been harder than I expected. I thought I could—' She broke off. Another beat passed before she straightened her shoulders. 'I was starting my second year of articles when I found out I was pregnant. I worked for as long as I could, and I got maternity leave, but it's unpaid, and my savings have run out.'

'I can help,' Hunter said. His voice sounded harsh in his ears.

'No, thank you,' Grace said primly. 'It would only be a

temporary fix anyway. I have to finish my articles before I can start working, and I've had an offer at a law firm here.' Her hands tightened on the strap of her bag again. 'If I want to provide for Eli—and I do—I need to do this. The sooner, the better.' She hesitated. 'I want to do it now, before he grows up to realise being irresponsible got me here. I'm trying to counteract the irresponsible with the responsible.' Grace looked at him and winced. 'Sorry.'

He shrugged. He agreed with her assessment.

'Look, I know what you're thinking. What kind of mother would—'

'We're not,' Autumn interrupted.

Grace's expression softened. 'Thank you.' She ran a hand down her ponytail, before bringing the hair to rest over her shoulder. 'I want my son to believe I did everything I could to give him a good life. If it means being away from him for three months, then so be it. I'll do whatever I have to to give him his best life.'

'And you trust me to take care of him?' Hunter asked, unable to resist.

It had been a question that had plagued him since even before Autumn had brought it up. Since Grace had asked him to take care of Eli, in fact. He'd seen Janie's face in Eli's, and his mind had been inundated with memories and emotions. The question—though not the reasons for it—had been the only clear thing.

'In all honesty?' Grace asked. 'Yes. I know how that makes me look. But…but if I want to teach Eli to judge people fairly, then I can't mummy-shame mothers. Even if that mother is me.' She paused. 'My instincts tell me I can trust you. I've done a fair amount of research about you—I've watched videos and seen pictures—and you seem like a decent person. So do you,' Grace added, addressing Autumn. Autumn simply nodded.

Grace turned her attention back to Hunter.

'The little I can remember about our night together

makes me think it's okay to trust you. Besides, he's your son, too, and you know me just as well as I know you. If I want you to trust me, I figure that has to go both ways.'

'Then there's something you should know,' Hunter forced himself to say. He felt Autumn shift closer to him. It helped him speak, despite the swelling that suddenly seemed to surround his vocal cords. 'There's a chance Eli might be sick.'

Grace's expression went blank.

CHAPTER SIX

THE MEN IN Autumn's stomach were still there. Their dancing had turned into something less wild now, more choreographed, their steps hammering in sync against her chest bone at the tension in the room. She took another step closer to Hunter.

'I'm a carrier of the cystic fibrosis gene.' Hunter's voice sounded detached. Autumn supposed it was the only way he could get himself through it. 'My... My sister had the disease.'

'Had?'

Autumn felt the muscles in Hunter's body coil. 'She passed away.'

'What?' Grace's face was stricken. 'Are you telling me my son could *die*?'

'No,' Autumn answered when Hunter didn't say anything. 'No,' she said again for good measure. 'Hunter's only a carrier of the gene.'

'What the hell does that mean?'

'For Eli to be sick,' Autumn continued after a quick glance at Hunter's face told her he wouldn't be replying, 'you have to be a carrier, too. Are you?'

'Of cystic fibrosis?' Grace shook her head. 'I don't know. My parents weren't sick. I... I don't know if there are other family members who have it.' She sucked in her lip. 'I should ask. I should—'

'Grace,' Autumn interrupted the spiral. 'You know that you're not sick, right?' she asked. Grace nodded. 'So even if you are a carrier, Eli only has a twenty-five per cent chance of having this disease.'

'But...but what if he *is* sick?' Grace's eyes widened; her voice dropped. 'What if I didn't notice?'

'This isn't your fault,' Autumn said firmly. She took a breath. 'It's not either of your faults.' She waited a beat. 'It might not even be something we have to worry about. We should make sure of that first.'

'How?' Grace asked.

It seemed that Hunter had lost his voice. Autumn almost sighed.

'Babies aren't automatically tested for CF here when they're born, but we can request a test. We'll do that as soon as possible. We'll make an appointment.'

'My flight to Johannesburg is in three hours,' Grace whispered. 'I don't have the money to change it. I start work *tomorrow morning*,' she added more urgently.

Autumn glanced over at Hunter again, but he was still staring straight ahead, as if to escape the conversation.

'We can do this without you.' Autumn deliberately softened her voice. 'We'll keep in touch every step of the way. Trust, right?' she said, when Grace didn't reply.

Grace nodded slowly. 'Okay.' Her chest heaved. 'I can't do everything by myself.' That part was muttered. 'This is what we have to do. Co-parent. Share the responsibilities. Yeah?'

She gave a brave smile. When Hunter didn't say anything, Autumn nudged him. He blinked, rapidly, his gaze meeting Grace's.

'Of course.' He cleared his throat. 'We'll figure this out.'

'Okay.' Her gaze lowered to the car seat, then up to Hunter. 'Would you like to meet your son?'

Hunter nodded.

He'd watched a sci-fi movie once, where the lead character had been sucked into a different dimension. She walked and walked, but the dimension was nothingness. She refused to give up. She walked until her feet bled. Until she was dying of exertion and dehydration; still, she walked. And eventually, when she felt she couldn't go on, she found a door that had led home.

Seeing Eli for the first time was strangely like that.

Hunter felt as if he were in a different dimension. The insides of his body felt as though they were inflating, growing and growing, and soon his skin wouldn't be able to contain them. The air in his lungs seemed like too much, and perhaps that was what was causing his insides to inflate.

But Hunter kept looking at the little boy in Grace's arms.

Everything he'd been worried about faded to the background. Back to earth, he thought distractedly, while he was walking in this different dimension. As he took in Eli's features—the dark mass of hair, the small, puckered mouth—and saw his sister in them, he knew nothing would ever matter as much as this.

He'd felt the same way about Janie, he thought, blinking, mortified that tears heated his eyes.

Despite the overwhelming swell of emotion, he knew he would walk and walk and walk until his feet bled and he was dying if it meant walking to Eli. Thinking about everything he'd been through in his life, perhaps he already had.

'Hi,' Grace said softly. She shifted Eli in her arms so that he was facing Hunter. So that he was watching Hunter with the brown eyes that came from his family. 'Say hi to your dad, Eli.'

The baby didn't make a sound, just kept watching Hunter. Hunter couldn't resist his smile. The kid was already like him, realising talking wasn't as important as observing. Warmth sparked in his chest.

'Do you want to hold him?'

Hunter automatically took a step back before he felt a hand on his shoulder. He looked to his side, saw Autumn standing there. The hesitancy melted away.

'Yes. Please,' he said. 'How do I...?'

'Just support his neck like this.'

Grace showed him, speaking in soothing tones, though he didn't know whether that was for his benefit or Eli's. She seemed to have recovered from her earlier shock, or maybe he was witnessing her resilience when it came to parenting their son. Sensing the latter was true, Hunter's respect for her grew.

He thought no more of it when his son was successfully transferred to his arms.

Eli was so small. That was Hunter's first thought. He felt like a lumbering giant holding the little guy. He was sure he looked it, too. But it didn't matter that much to him. As long as Eli was safe and comfortable, Hunter didn't care whether he looked like a novice or a fool.

His second thought was that Eli was perfect. He didn't count Eli's fingers or toes; didn't know if he was sick or not. But he was perfect. And for the rest of his life, Hunter would make sure his son knew it.

His third thought...

He'd already turned to Autumn before he'd fully realised it. He lowered his forearm, where Eli's body was resting, showing him to Autumn.

'Did you see him?'

Her cheeks lifted in a small smile. 'I did. I do.'

'He's perfect.'

The smile widened. 'He is.'

'Do you want to hold him?' He turned to Grace, belatedly realising he shouldn't simply make those kinds of decisions. 'Can she?'

'Of course,' Grace said, lifting a hand.

Hunter looked back at Autumn. 'Do you?'

Autumn's eyes flicked from Grace to him. She pursed her lips, then relaxed them, and smiled at him again. 'I'd love to.'

He handed Eli over to her, imitating what Grace had done. Autumn accepted Eli easily, shifting as soon as she had a hold on him to get one more comfortably. Hunter stepped back, watching. Smiling. She already looked a million times more comfortable than he had, he was sure. She moved gently, back and forth, lifting a hand and taking Eli's hand with her thumb and index finger.

'It's very nice to meet you, Eli,' she said softly, still moving. 'My name is Autumn. I'm your dad's friend.' She shook Eli's hand. Hunter's heart swelled. 'I suppose that makes me your aunt. Not a real one,' she clarified, 'one of those weird ones who call themselves aunts but have no real relation.'

She looked at Grace. 'He's beautiful. Congratulations.'

Graced smiled. For the first time, it was completely genuine. 'Thank you.'

'You, too, Daddy,' Autumn said, looking at him now, too. 'Good work.'

Hunter didn't know how to feel. He supposed meeting Eli had something to do with it. He was overwhelmed. Emotions he hadn't felt in years had exploded inside him. A fierce protectiveness. A willingness to sacrifice anything to make Eli's life easier. He hadn't felt either of those things since Janie's death. Remembering them had a peculiar effect on his heart.

Except…

That wasn't entirely true, and perhaps that was what had put him off. He'd felt those same feelings with Autumn. They were somehow different at the same time, but just as fierce. And as terrifying.

It took seeing her hold his son to realise he'd been scared when he'd realised what she wanted from their relationship. They were completely normal things to want: spending a life together, having a family. Hell, *he* wanted them—with her. But he hadn't been able to risk it. Because risking it meant the possibility of…of losing it, too.

He wouldn't be able to handle that. Not again.

'Can I explain his schedule to you?' Grace asked.

Hunter blinked. Slowly nodded.

'I've written it all down, but basically...'

She told him about Eli's feeding and sleep schedule, explaining it with the book she'd written it down in. Hunter listened attentively, relieved to have something other than his thoughts to focus on.

'You can call me any time of the day or night,' Grace said at the end of it. 'I'll answer when I can, and get in touch as soon as possible after if I can't.'

'Okay.'

'If you need anything—'

'I'll call,' Hunter told her. 'I'll have my lawyer get in touch about child support. We can discuss custody once you're settled back here.'

Grace stared at him. 'I don't—'

'Let me know if anything concerns you,' Hunter said, as if Grace hadn't interrupted. 'Now, do you have a way to get to the airport?'

She was exhausted. More than ever before. Grace had left shortly after she and Hunter had discussed Eli's schedule. Autumn had suggested she and Hunter give Grace a private moment to say goodbye, and things had been disturbingly tense as they'd waited outside on the patio. After Grace had left, Autumn had watched Hunter try to feed Eli.

Eli had started crying almost immediately after his mother had closed the door. Hunter had given Autumn a panicked look, and, calmly, she reminded Hunter of Grace's parting instructions—a bottle, then sleep. She made the bottle while Hunter tried to calm Eli, but his efforts were futile. The baby only cried louder, in those ragged, hoarse sobs only babies possessed.

She silently asked the universe why it had done this. Hunter needed a baby that barely cried; one that wouldn't scare him away from parenting his kid. But the universe refused to take responsibility, gesturing wildly in her personified state at the awkward way Hunter was holding his son. He was clearly uncomfortable with Eli, the ease he'd shown when he'd first held the boy disappearing now that Grace was gone.

She finished the bottle quickly, then offered it to Hunter. He shook his head, taking it from her hand and setting it on the table before handing Eli to her. She accepted without a complaint, though her insides wanted her to. Loudly. Vehemently. Just as the emotions she was still processing demanded.

Because they made her feel as though she'd been ploughed over by an avalanche, she didn't. She could only imagine what he was going through. So she'd give him the benefit of the doubt for now.

And ignore your own feelings in the process.

She did exactly that. Though her heart begged her to take heed of the carnage this experience had left in its wake, she fed Eli. Burped him. Put him to sleep. She ignored Hunter's piercing gaze as he watched it all—to judge himself with later, she knew. When she finally set down Eli in the brand-new crib she found in Hunter's spare room, her body was aching from the strain.

'Are you okay?' he asked eventually.

'I should be asking you that,' she said, as her heart screamed.

'This was…intense.'

'Yes.'

'So you're not okay.'

She didn't answer. The silence stretched.

'I'm sorry,' he said.

She shook her head. 'Don't… You have nothing to apologise for.'

'I couldn't even feed my son.'

'You didn't try,' she said sharply. Released a breath. 'Hold on. I need a moment.'

He gave it to her.

She closed her eyes. Struggled to gain control of her emotions. The truth was, she wished she hadn't agreed to be there that evening. What she'd witnessed had twisted her gut. It had been touching and beautiful. It had obviously impacted Hunter.

It had taken all of her strength not to sink down to the floor and sob.

Seeing Hunter—*her* Hunter—holding a baby, looking at the child as if he were the most important thing in Hunter's life had broken her. Because she couldn't help but think of how it would have been to see Hunter look at *their* child like that. If only he'd been open to taking a chance with her.

She opened her eyes again when she heard Hunter closing the windows and doors. He joined her on the couch when he saw her watching him, sitting at the opposite end. They spent another while in silence.

'You're going to have to try,' she said eventually. 'Even when things are hard.'

'I know.'

'That's not enough. You have to do, too.'

'I know.'

The anger in his tone put her back up.

'No,' she said. Whatever had been holding her back before had disappeared. '*You* asked for help. How is it fair that you're angry at me simply because you don't like what I have to say?'

'I'm not angry at you,' he snapped.

'Really? You seem pretty angry.'

'I am, but not at you. Or about what you've said.' He paused. 'I'm angry at myself.'

'Why?'

'Because I'm acting exactly like my father did.'

CHAPTER SEVEN

'TELL ME.'

It was a simple question; he heard it as a command. He wasn't sure what authority Autumn had over him. Didn't know why he felt he needed to obey her. Still, he did.

'He didn't help to take care of Janie,' he said. He didn't want to tiptoe around it any longer. But it felt strange speaking plainly. 'When she was sick.'

'Okay,' Autumn said after a moment. 'What does that have to do with the way you're treating Eli now?'

'I'm… I'm not taking care of him.' Couldn't she see it? 'I'm not doing what I should be doing.'

'You say that as if you don't have a choice in the matter.'

His reply died on his lips before he could utter it. It took a long time for him to ask, 'But what if I don't do it right?'

'Do you think Janie would have cared whether your father did it *right*?' she asked. 'Or would it have been more important to her that he tried?'

He had no reply for that, so he nodded, accepting the slight accusation in her tone. He had those accusations, too, of himself. Could see that he was conveniently leaning in to the excuse of his father for the moment. Wasn't sure how he knew it—or why he saw it so clearly—but he was excusing his behaviour when he shouldn't be.

A part of him continued to do it. It reminded him of how the meeting had been harder than he'd expected. Telling Grace that their child might be sick had been harder than expected. Hearing the utter terror in her voice had transported him back to each doctor's appointment he'd accompanied his mother to.

He'd been much too young to accompany her and listen to such news, he'd realised later. He'd also realised that she'd needed the support, even if it had come from her barely eleven—then thirteen, then sixteen-year-old son. Because even at that age Hunter had heard the fear in his mother's voice as she'd asked the doctor questions about Janie's condition. He'd go stand beside her, take her hand and squeeze. Then he'd go back to Janie and try to distract her.

The memories had paralysed him. When Grace had left and Eli had started crying, there had been a moment when he'd wanted to run away. He'd seen his father in that, and had, for the first time, sympathised with the man. Had Calvin Lee been terrified, too? Had he felt too overwhelmed to do anything about his child's needs?

It was a complicated thing to empathise with his father. On the one hand, he could understand his father's actions. On the other, they'd contributed to his. The memories that had Hunter feeling terrified and overwhelmed might not have been a factor had his father stepped up. It had spurred him to step up, long enough to try to comfort Eli.

But it hadn't worked. Holding Eli's shaking body in his arms had crushed something inside him. He'd desperately grasped at his father's behaviour as a crutch then.

He no longer could now. Because of Autumn.

He was in this situation because of Autumn.

'None of this would have happened if we hadn't broken up,' he said quietly, anger pulsing in his body, in his veins.

'You're…you're blaming this on our break-up?'

His sanity intervened, keeping him from replying.

'You can't blame me for your actions.'

'What about *your* actions?' he demanded.

Apparently, his sanity had fled to greener pastures.

'What?'

'You suspected I didn't want to have a family long before you brought it up, didn't you?'

'What does that have to do with this?'

'We shouldn't have stayed together as long as we did.'

Her eyes widened. The bright lights in his living room

allowed him to see every emotion in them. Guilt pierced his body; he plastered the holes closed with anger.

'Why did you stay, Autumn? If we'd ended things sooner, I wouldn't have been as broken. I wouldn't have fallen as deep and—'

'You're saying it's my fault for not walking away sooner?' Her voice was small, but firm.

'I... I wouldn't have done this if—'

'No,' she said in the same tone. She stood, too, and gave him a look that had every guilty hole in his body open and bleeding. 'I won't let you malign a relationship I, for some silly reason, still hold cherished memories of. I'm going to leave.'

Panic opened his mouth before sanity could.

'What about Eli?'

'He has his more than capable father to take care of him.'

'I *can't.*'

'You have an entire book with instructions.' She paused. Continued more quietly. 'I'm not going to stay here when you're emotional and overwhelmed and lashing out at me because you don't know how to deal with it.'

He was embarrassed at his words, his anger, now that the emotion had passed. Added to it was how embarrassed he was that she knew him so well.

She stood, grabbing her handbag. As she put it on her shoulder, she studied him.

'You're going to be fine.'

He didn't reply.

'You're going to be okay,' Autumn said again, walking to the door. 'I know it doesn't seem like that right now, but you will be.'

She met his eyes, her brown eyes blazing with emotion that had his heart quickening.

'She's lovely, by the way. Grace. So is your son.' She turned, opened the door. 'You have a beautiful family,' she called over her shoulder.

Then she was gone.

He stood before he realised it; paused when he did. He wanted to go after her. Felt compelled to, if he was being honest, though he didn't know what he'd say to her. Trusting that instinct, he walked to the door, then belatedly turned and grabbed the baby monitor. The guilt was somewhat tamed when he saw Eli sleeping soundly. His grip tightened on the device as he opened the door. When he got to the driveway, he stopped.

Since it was evening, the outdoor lighting had already gone on automatically. It gave him the perfect view of Autumn, sitting in her car, her hands braced at ten and twelve on the steering wheel. From where he stood, he could see the white of her knuckles. Her head was hanging, so it took her wiping at her nose with the back of her wrist for him to realise she was crying.

He walked forward slowly, as if approaching a wounded animal. Her head shot up, making him pause as if *he* were the animal, caught in the headlights. But that terrible expression on her face made him think he'd been right in his initial assessment.

She was the wounded one.

He'd wounded her.

Tears fell steadily from her eyes, though they stared unblinkingly at him. Her face showed none of the quiet capability she'd displayed when she'd told him she was leaving. Whatever was there was raw and painful. He felt it as if it were his own emotion.

He moved without truly noticing it. Soon he was opening her car door, placing the monitor on the passenger seat. He reached under her seat then, adjusted it back, and unclicked her seat belt. Bracing a knee on the frame of the door, he pulled her into his arms, getting their bodies as comfortable as he could.

She was stiff at first, and he worried that he might have crossed a boundary. The thought had barely gone through his head before her arms circled his neck and a ragged breath—a sob—escaped from her lips.

And then the words, 'Why wasn't I enough for you, Hunter?'

His arms tightened around her. He could do nothing else as her body shook against his. Each shake sent a stake through his heart. Each stake convinced him he'd been selfish to put her through this. Blaming her for his actions? For his love for her? For his broken heart after their break-up?

He should be blaming himself for staying. For realising as he'd fallen for her that he couldn't give her what she wanted. For ignoring his own experiences for so long that it had taken falling in love and wanting a future to make him realise he couldn't risk having it. Losing it.

He didn't see how a romantic relationship with her would end differently. But a friendship? He wouldn't lose her if she was his friend. He'd been sure of that a week after their break-up. After his one-night stand. He'd felt as if he'd reached some kind of rock bottom then. He'd been under the water again; Autumn, his only way to the surface.

Because of it, he hadn't been surprised when he'd found himself driving to the bakery under the guise of ordering cupcakes for a colleague's birthday.

She'd called him out immediately.

'Really?' she asked dryly. 'There isn't any other place in the actual city of Cape Town for you to get cupcakes from? You had to drive almost an hour to get them from your ex-girlfriend's bakery?'

He winced. It had been the first time he'd realised she was his *ex*-girlfriend.

'They're for Ted,' he replied after a moment. 'He won't accept cupcakes from anyone else.'

She narrowed her eyes. 'You're playing dirty.' She sighed. 'Of course I'll make Ted's birthday cupcakes. It's in two weeks, right?'

'Right.'

There was a beat. 'You know you could have just called this order in.'

'I know.'

Her expression softened. 'I'm glad you didn't. It's nice to see you're still in one piece.'

He'd stayed for a cup of coffee, invited her to a movie that weekend. By the time he'd picked up the cupcakes, their relationship had turned into something new. They'd called it friendship, but it hadn't felt as simple as friendship. It had felt deeper, considering all they'd shared. Though neither of them would ever admit it. At least, they wouldn't have before now.

He shifted when she leaned back. She avoided his gaze as she reached into her handbag, pulling out tissues and dealing with the remnants of the tears. When she finally looked at him, there was no wetness on her face.

But her face was red, podgy; her eyes swollen, as were her nose and lips. It quickened his breath. Made him wonder at her beauty, even in that moment.

'I'm sorry,' she said.

'You don't have to apologise.' He shifted, so he could see her better. 'I should be the one saying sorry.'

'No, I—'

'Why don't you think you were enough for me?' he interrupted.

Her face turned a deeper shade of red and she sniffled. 'Do you really blame me for Eli?'

'No,' he said. 'That wasn't fair.'

'Feelings aren't fair.'

'Good point.' He tried to gather his thoughts. 'There's a part of me that feels that way. But I know it's illogical.'

'It is,' she said quietly. She met his gaze, her face flushing again. 'I tried. I asked about genetic testing. I suggested adoption. I… I tried to make this work.'

'I couldn't give you what you wanted.'

'*You* have it now though.'

Her logic was sound. 'The problem wasn't with you.'

'Hard to believe that considering the current situation.' She looked down at her hands.

He released a shaky breath. 'The current situation is… This is because of my actions. I was wrong to blame you. It was my mistake. Fully.'

Her fingers traced the lines on her palms. He watched the movement. Willed it to hypnotise him. Perhaps then he'd forget she hadn't replied. She hadn't accepted his apology either. The only thing he thought could make it right was to absolve her of the responsibility.

'You don't have to go through this with me. I'm sorry I asked for help.'

She lifted a shoulder. 'We're friends.' Her voice cracked.

'No.' He lifted a hand, cupped her cheek. 'We pretend to be friends. For the sake of the people around us. For the sake of ourselves, too.' His thumb brushed across her skin. 'But we're not friends, Autumn.'

'Okay,' she whispered raggedly. 'What do you call this?'

He laughed, though not out of humour. 'I don't know.' He sobered. 'I honestly don't know.'

Seconds passed.

'Maybe it's better if I'm not a part of this,' she said.

His hand dropped, but she caught it, pulling it into her lap. Her thumbs traced the lines of his palm now.

'Look what it's done to this friendship—or whatever this is—already.'

Pressure built in his chest.

'I felt so stupid in there today,' she continued, 'talking about what *we* were going to do when I have no part in this.'

'You do,' he said, compelled by only heaven knew what. 'You're my…my person.'

Amusement touched her face. 'Is that what I am?'

His lips curved. 'Unless you have another description.'

She leaned back against the seat, her gaze not leaving

his face. 'I don't.' She let out a shaky breath. 'We should have left it at exes.'

His heart ached. 'Okay.'

'It would have been easier.'

'I know.'

'I mean, you'd still be in this situation,' she continued. 'But I would be traipsing in the fields of my estate, thinking about the good old days when you and I were together.'

'You're right,' he said a beat later. 'You don't have to do this.'

She gave him a shrewd look. 'Obviously I wouldn't be traipsing in any field. I'd be missing my person.' Her mouth offered him a half-smile. 'Like it or not, that's what you are.'

'I like it,' he said quietly. He pulled his hand from her grip, taking one of hers in return and bringing it to his lips. 'I'm lucky to have you.'

She lifted her free hand, brushed it over his hair before letting it rest on his shoulder. 'You are.'

He smiled, and it was a long while before he reached for the baby monitor and pulled back. He pressed a kiss to her forehead, standing clear of the car.

'You're free to pull out of this whenever you want to. Whenever you need to,' he added.

She nodded, adjusted her seat and clicked her seat belt back into place. She started the car.

'Thank you.'

'Thank *you*.'

He slammed the door closed and watched as she drove away. When his feet eventually moved, they took him back to the house. Back to his responsibilities.

His guilt followed him.

CHAPTER EIGHT

AUTUMN HATED THAT Hunter had seen her cry. She should have waited until she was at home to let go of her control. At the very least, she should have waited until she was *driving* home. But no, she'd cried in his driveway. Naturally, he'd caught her. And she'd allowed him to comfort her. Confessed her private feelings of inadequacy to him.

Lovely.

She wished she were stronger when it came to him. Or anyone she loved, she realised when she thought of it. Suddenly, doing what he wanted or expected—what her sister, mother, or father wanted or expected—felt like weakness. Which was why she was considering his offer.

You're free to pull out of this whenever you want to. Whenever you need to.

She suspected she needed to. For her own mental health. To move on without him, too. It was time.

That Saturday, she was still trying to come to terms with it. Or force herself into actually doing it. But a five-year-old girl made sure Autumn didn't have time to dwell on it.

A screech brought her to the bakery kitchen. At first, the only thing Autumn could see was the box of the three-tiered cake lying on the floor. Moments later, a woman rushed through the kitchen doors behind Autumn, gasping when she saw the cake. In quick movements, she pulled a small blonde-haired girl to her side, making Autumn notice her for the first time. Her brain filled in the rest.

'Autumn,' Mandy said, dragging her eyes from the floor to Autumn. 'I turned my back for a second. I needed—' She broke off with a moan.

Autumn turned to the mother.

'I thought she was in the bathroom.' The woman's fingers dug into her daughter's shoulders, pulling the girl back against her. 'She's only five.'

Autumn was tempted to ask the mother how old *she* was since she was responsible for the girl. And really, how did she *think* her daughter was in the bathroom?

She gave herself a moment to suppress the thoughts, then to figure out what the hell she was going to do. Exhaling shakily, she met the mother's eyes.

'It's okay. You can finish your meal.'

Visibly relieved, the woman nodded. 'Thank you so much.' Before she left the kitchen, she said, 'I am sorry.'

Autumn nodded, not bothering to reply verbally when she wasn't sure what she'd say. She waited a few seconds after the woman left, then looked at Mandy.

'We have to check the damage.'

'Do we?' Mandy asked in a thin, hopeful voice.

Autumn gave her an indulgent smile, despite the nerves pulsing in her stomach. She squatted so she could straighten the box, Mandy immediately lowering to help. A shifting sound came from inside that had them exchanging a worried look. Together, they set the box on the counter. In careful, quiet movements, they unwrapped the cake.

The tiers had separated, which Autumn had expected considering the impact. But the cake had fallen on its decorated side, destroying the perfect arrangement of flowers they'd toiled over. Some of the fondant had been spoiled, too, particularly between the tiers, but, all things considered, the damage was minimal. It would have been a lot worse if the cake hadn't been packed.

Autumn released a breath. 'Okay, this isn't the end of the world. We'll just reassemble the tiers, fix up the moulds between them. We can check to see if we have some other flowers—' She broke off. 'Why are you looking at me like that?'

'Because you said "we".'

'Yes. You and me.'

'It's my niece's first birthday, remember?' Mandy winced apologetically. 'I'm taking those cupcakes—' she pointed to another box on the counter '—and I have to help set up. But I can call and tell them—'

'No, you go. That isn't something you should miss. Now?' she asked. Mandy nodded. 'Okay, you'll leave now. But I can do this by myself.' That was for her benefit as much as Mandy's. 'Besides, everyone else is here. Wait staff, kitchen staff. Everything will be fine.'

As she said it, one of her waiters burst into the kitchen.

'One of my tables is asking for a manager. His eggs were too soft, and then, not soft enough.'

Autumn opened her mouth, but Mandy waved a hand. 'I'll take care of it.'

Mandy and the waiter left, and Autumn tried to figure out her plan. When panic threatened, she told herself she could do this. This part of her work was the one sphere where she *had* done it. Repeatedly. Successfully. The uncertainty that was her constant companion in life shrank back in the kitchen, though there were moments, like now, where it beat at the doors.

She would not let it in.

The damage could have been worse, she thought again. The entire cake could have been smashed and lying in pieces on the floor. This she could fix, though she had only three hours to do so before delivery. It wouldn't look exactly like the one her client, an old school friend who'd insisted Taste of Autumn make her wedding cake, had ordered, but it wouldn't be terrible.

She wanted to call and warn Mel about the latest development, but she knew she couldn't. She didn't want Mel to worry on her wedding day, especially since there'd still be a Taste of Autumn cake there. But she would deliver the thing herself, explain the situation, and make some kind of restitution. Pleased with the plan, she got to work. She'd just started making the icing when Mandy opened the door.

'Leaving?'

'Yeah.' Mandy's face contorted. 'Are you sure you don't want me to stay and help? I can be late—'

'No,' Autumn interrupted, sifting icing sugar into the butter she had creamed. 'You will not be late. Everything will be fine.'

'Okay, but I'm glad Hunter's here.' Mandy's voice dropped. 'Though he looks a bit the worse for wear. And he has a *baby*.'

Autumn whipped around, spreading icing sugar all over the floor. 'What?'

Mandy gave her an amused look before she moved and Hunter walked into the kitchen. Mandy was right; he did look bad. There were dark circles under his eyes, his hair was a mess, and, though not creased, his clothes looked untidy. Autumn's stomach flipped nevertheless, her heart joining in.

'You've had an interesting morning,' Hunter said, his quiet voice steadying her for alarming reasons.

'A hellish morning,' she corrected. 'What are you, um, doing here?'

'Helping.'

'You brought Eli?'

'We're a package deal.'

Autumn absorbed that piece of information. Then her eyes moved to Mandy. 'You called him?'

'No, and clearly you didn't either.' Mandy grinned. 'He must be a gift from the universe.'

Hunter's lips curved into a half-smile. 'I'll keep an eye on things out here.'

They were both gone before Autumn could fully process the conversation. She shook her head, and went back to making the icing. When it was done, she turned her attention to the cake. She removed all the damaged parts and reassembled the three tiers. Then she filled a piping bag and played with different star tips as she tried to fix the spoiled fondant moulds between the tiers.

When she was satisfied, she took a step back. It wasn't noticeably different from the original design—she hoped— and would have to do considering the time constraints. Next she focused on the cascading flowers that had run from the top layer of the cake to the bottom. Half of the flowers were missing since they'd been made of gum paste and had cracked or broken during the fall.

She searched the kitchen for replacements, but could only find three. Sighing, she used some leftover fondant and flattened and folded, adding layer to layer, making small flowers and bigger ones, before setting them aside. When she thought she had enough, she checked the time.

She'd been busy for over an hour. Felt it in the stiffness of her upper body. Figuring she could take a quick break while the fondant settled from her manipulation, she popped out of the kitchen. Her eyes moved over the small bakery café. When nothing jumped out at her, she turned to Hunter.

'You're doing a good job.'

'Are you checking on me?'

'No,' she said with a small smile, 'I'm taking a break.' Her eyes lowered to the pram Hunter was rocking back and forth. 'He's sleeping?'

'Has been since I put him in the car to come here.' Hunter rolled his shoulders. 'It's the only thing that puts him to sleep.'

'Did you ask Grace about it?'

'No.'

She waited for more. Nothing came.

Not your business, Autumn, she warned herself. Found herself speaking anyway.

'Why not?'

'He's off his schedule.'

She forced herself not to react. 'So you didn't want to ask because…'

'She might ask about the schedule.'

Now she stopped herself from rolling her eyes. With a little sigh, she asked, 'Have you eaten yet?'

'No.'

'A grilled cheese and bacon sandwich?' It was his usual order. 'I can throw in a smoothie?'

'Just the sandwich. Wouldn't mind a soft drink. Something with caffeine.'

'Coming right up.'

She gave the order to the kitchen, took out two soft drinks and settled opposite Hunter at one of the free tables in the bakery. He was still rocking the pram.

'I'm sure it'll be fine if you stop doing that.' She nodded her head in the pram's direction.

'How do you know?' he asked.

'Surely you've tried?'

He shook his head. 'I don't want to. What if he wakes up?'

She stared at him. 'You put him back to sleep?'

'Another car ride?' He shook his head again. 'I'm tired of driving.'

'So you came here?' she asked. 'An hour's drive from your house?'

He blushed. For the life of her, she couldn't figure out why.

A part of her wanted to offer her help. He looked so tired, and his arm must have been going lame. But she didn't. She didn't know what kept her from it—or asking about how things were going with Eli—but a small flicker of pride sparked inside her because of it. Then, shame.

'Thank you,' she said. 'You didn't have to step in.'

'I got to distract myself from how tired I am by glower-ing at a man who couldn't decide how he wanted his eggs.' Hunter shrugged. 'I should be thanking you.'

She laughed uneasily, her mind telling her not to fall into the trap of asking him why he was tired. But the traitorous organ abdicated before it could warn her against the memories.

When Hunter had visited over the weekends, she'd spend her Saturdays at the café and he'd join her. Usually, he'd do his own work, but on occasion he'd settle in the kitchen, content with just watching her.

She'd grown used to it during their relationship, especially in the kitchen. It didn't matter if it was at her place or his; at the bakery or her parents' house. He didn't seem to care that there were better things to do. He would simply sit and watch her go through the motions of doing something.

It had been unnerving at first.

She'd thought perhaps he was waiting for her to do something wrong. It had made her clumsy. After she'd had to toss out ingredients for a recipe she knew like the back of her hand, she'd told herself to get it together. She wanted people to see her, didn't she? To value her? That meant people had to watch her.

It still made her anxious. And the anxiety angered her. She was tired of worrying about what other people would see when they looked at her. She didn't want to anticipate the failures they'd see in her in case she had to defend them. She wanted to stop comparing herself and finding herself lacking. She'd done it with her sister. In a weak, disgraceful moment, she'd done it with Grace.

Her face burned at the memory of it. How, in a vulnerable moment in his driveway, she'd revealed it to Hunter.

'What's wrong?' he asked her.

'Nothing.' She breathed a sigh of relief when they were interrupted by their food. When the waiter left, she said,

'I'm assuming the universe didn't really send you here to help today.'

He looked amused. 'No.'

'Why are you here, then?'

The blush returned, though now she could see the tension around his eyes, his lips. He didn't answer her, and they ate their meal in a terse silence. Hunter kept rocking Eli's pram, with his foot while he ate and then again afterwards with his hand.

'The store's closing in half an hour,' she told him when they were done. 'It'll probably take me another hour to finish up here and then I'll have to deliver the cake.'

She was about to tell him he should go but another thought popped into her mind.

'Oh.'

'What?' Hunter asked.

She looked at him. 'I forgot I have to take this cake to the venue.'

'But you said—'

'No, I mean I'm going to have to see people. I can't go looking like this.' She gestured down to the black pants and top she wore beneath the apron she'd forgotten to take off. 'I'll get there the same time the guests will, probably.'

'I don't see a problem.'

'Of course you don't,' she said, amused despite herself. 'But seriously, I went to high school with the bride. Her in-laws only agreed to hire me because I'm a Bishop.' The eye-roll she gave was less humoured. 'I'm going as an heiress, not an entrepreneur.'

'You have time to change, don't you?'

'Yeah, but I have to close up and—'

'I'll do it.'

'Are you sure?' she asked. 'You have Eli.'

Hunter looked over at the sleeping baby. Automatically, Autumn did, too. She hadn't realised she'd been avoiding looking at him until that moment. Her subconscious must have known what those puckered lips, sucking on a non-existent dummy, would do to her.

'He still seems okay.'

'Hunter…' Her voice had softened. 'You don't have to do this.'

'Let me help. Please.'

It sounded as if he was begging, and it hit her in the gut. She stood up, then surprised herself by kissing his cheek. 'Thank you.'

She returned to the kitchen, refusing to think about what had just happened. Instead, she focused on the cake. True to her prediction, it took an hour to finish. She stood back, examining the end product. She thought she might have pulled it off. The comments her staff made as they trailed in and out of the kitchen, going through the end-of-day routine, seemed to support that thought.

But the real test was when she called Hunter to see it. He had no decorating experience, and yet felt the need to comment on her work whenever he could. Usually, it annoyed her. Today, she needed it.

'So?' she asked when he stood staring at it. Eli had woken up, and Hunter was giving him a bottle as he examined the cake. She ignored the adorable scene, kept her eyes on Hunter's face. 'Is it good enough?'

'No.'

Her face fell. 'No?'

'Not good enough, no.' He turned to face her. The air around them changed as she took in his expression. 'Just good. Perfect, in fact.'

Her heart exploded in her chest. They stood, staring at one another for only heaven knew how long. Soon, Autumn felt herself leaning towards him, compelled by the stirring in his eyes; the answer in her belly. She thought about how, if she rose to her toes, she would be able to touch her lips to his and maybe that stirring would stop…

Eli pulled his head away from his bottle and let out a hoarse cry.

'It's okay,' she said, though Hunter hadn't apologised. 'I need to take a shower and change anyway.' She looked at the baby, face red from the tears. 'Are you going to be okay to lock up?'

Hunter rocked Eli, trying to comfort him. It didn't work.

'How about I just stay here and watch things, and wait until you can lock up?'

She nodded. 'I'll be quick.'

CHAPTER NINE

IT WAS THE least he could do considering all she'd done for him.

That was what he thought as he walked around the bakery, trying to get Eli to calm down. He had a terrible feeling that he was doing something wrong with his son. It was the only explanation he could come up with. Their interactions consisted mostly of feeding and changing nappies—a hell of a thing to have to learn based on Internet searches—and driving.

If it had come in any form of a routine, Hunter would have called it a win. It didn't come close to the schedule Grace had given him either. The fact that there *was* a schedule at all seemed to confirm he was doing something wrong. Combined with what today was, being unable to take care of his son had churned his stomach. And he'd found himself driving an hour to Autumn's bakery because he'd needed to.

Realising Eli wouldn't stop crying anyway, Hunter carried the cake Autumn had boxed before she'd left to his car, leaving Eli in the cooler shop. He returned quickly, his baby's throaty sobs tearing up his heart. He pushed the pram outside, locked up the bakery, and got Eli settled before driving the short distance to Autumn's house.

He drove slowly, as much for the cake's benefit as Eli's. The sobs turned into quiet moans, as they had for the past three days. Hunter parked in the shade, but left the car on so the air-conditioner could keep the cake cool. He took out Eli's car seat, knowing Eli would need to be changed, and knocked on Autumn's door. When there was no answer, he rang the doorbell. Eventually, he tested the door and found it open.

'Autumn?' he called, not wanting her to get a fright. 'It's Hunter. I'm downstairs. I locked up the bakery and brought the cake. I just need to change Eli.'

'Thank you!' she answered. 'I'll be down in a second.'

The blow-dryer went on, and he realised what had prevented her from hearing him. She was diffusing her curls, he thought, remembering the countless times he'd watched her do it. Almost as many times as he'd watched her in the kitchen.

It had always been one of his favourite activities to watch her work. She had a skill in the kitchen that was worth watching. An ease, a grace that made that skill seem second nature, as if it was a reflex she'd crafted over the years, like walking or driving.

When they'd still been together, he'd watched her unashamedly. Now that they were broken up, he did it on the sly, refusing to be robbed of the simple pleasure.

The disappointment that he hadn't been able to do it today faded the moment he saw Autumn at the top of the staircase. He'd finished changing Eli—at least he'd proved adequate at that—moments before, and was waiting for her. A strong wave of emotion settled over him. Primitive and too embarrassing for him ever to contemplate out loud.

He felt as if he'd been transported into a teenage coming-of-age movie. His mouth was dry as Autumn descended, his pulse throbbing heavily in his ears; in other parts of his body. Exactly like a teenage boy seeing his prom date for the first time.

Except Autumn wasn't his. Not in the way he wanted. She'd acquiesced to being his person, but he didn't think she knew the extent of it. Of how desperately he wanted to be *her* person. But he couldn't give her what she wanted. And, if he was being honest with himself, he didn't deserve to.

'What?' she asked when she reached him. She lifted a hand to her hair, pushing a stray curl into the mass of them at the back of her head. 'Do I not look appropriate for a wedding?'

He blinked. Realised he'd been staring. He swallowed. 'You look perfect.'

As he said the words, his eyes dipped over her again.

She wore a blue dress with thin straps and a V neckline, cinched at her waist. The skirt part was made from two pieces of material crossed over each other, reminding him of the wrap dresses she liked to wear. This design created a V at the front, too, revealing a solid portion of firm legs. He imagined the material could be nudged open, providing access to her thighs...

'Oh,' she said hoarsely.

The colour on her cheeks deepened so much he almost didn't notice she wore blush. The rest of her make-up was done perfectly. Her eyes looked more prominent, her lips fuller. Along with the gold earrings dangling from her ears, she looked...breathtaking.

She cleared her throat. 'Thank you.'

He nodded, though he couldn't take his eyes from her face. 'I have the car running outside with the cake.'

She smelled fresh, soft, like the field of flowers outside her house.

'Thank you.'

He nodded again, and forgot all attempts at acting normal.

He was standing so close he could see the triangle of freckles beneath her left eye. She hated it; had once complained that Summer had got an even spread of them and she'd got whatever had been left. But he thought it made her unique. Her uniqueness made her beautiful, and that beauty burned in his stomach.

He took a deliberate step back and tightened his hold on Eli, who had quietened and was staring at Autumn, too.

'Eli thinks you look good, too.'

Her eyes lowered to Eli, then softened, though Hunter didn't miss the caution there.

'May I?' she asked, opening her arms.

'Of course.'

He handed Eli over and she looked down at the baby. The lips he'd wanted to kiss seconds ago curved into a smile. Hunter shook his arms out—not because they ached from the effort of carrying his son, but because they'd wanted to pull her closer. Mould her to his body, so he could feel her softness. Explore how much of his body still belonged to her.

'He's quiet,' Hunter said then, distracted by it. Thankfully.

'Yeah,' Autumn cooed, holding Eli's hand. 'I think he likes me.'

Hunter didn't respond.

'Is that a problem?' Autumn asked softly.

'No,' he replied immediately. 'No, it's not.' He shoved away the unwelcome doubts; ignored the voice that said *I told you so.* 'Where do you need to take the cake to?'

She told him, though hesitantly, as if she was afraid of his response.

He gritted his teeth. 'I'll drive you.'

'Oh, you don't have to do that.'

'The cake's already in my car. You'll need help loading and unloading it.' He took a breath. 'And this is the quietest Eli's been outside a car since Grace left. He likes you. I want to give him as long as I can with someone he likes.'

'Hunter.'

He didn't know what she saw on his face as she said his name. Whatever it was had her nodding.

'Can you grab that?'

She pointed to her handbag and coat on a stand next to the door. He took them. As soon as they'd strapped Eli into the car, they were driving.

The start of the trip was quiet enough for Hunter to

take stock of his body. He felt as if he'd spent the day working out, and he hadn't even done anything significant. He didn't dare do the same for his mind. Instead, he tried to distract it.

'You make wedding cakes every weekend now, don't you?'

'More or less.'

'*More?* How do you do *more*?' he asked, navigating the decline of the mountain leading into Cape Town carefully, mindful of the baby and the cake. 'It's exhausting.'

She laughed. 'Maybe you're just exhausted.'

She was sitting in the back of the car, next to Eli. The cake was in front with him. He didn't dare look into the mirror to check her expression. He was afraid of what he'd see.

'We have timelines,' she continued after a pause. 'Everything happens according to a plan made well in advance.'

'You also have the café.'

'I'm running a business. You do it. You know.'

'Maybe I don't remember as well since I've been on leave with Eli.' He looked in the mirror then. Laughed at the look she gave him. 'Fine. It's a fair point.'

'We're both entrepreneurs,' she said. 'We have people depending on us. Not only those who work for us, but those who depend on the work we produce.'

'Except I have a second-in-command to lean on.'

'I have Mandy and my team.' The words were all he got for the next couple of kilometres. 'My father agrees with you. He wants me to give Mandy more responsibility. Or hire someone else to deal with the day-to-day running of the café.'

Surprise rippled over him at the statement. Autumn rarely spoke about her family. In fact, he'd first assumed they were estranged. She'd told him that her father had had an affair a while back, and it had caused some familial distance. He'd accepted that…until she'd introduced him to her parents and sister and he hadn't noticed the distance. At least not with Autumn and any of the members of her family.

He had noticed her fatigue after though.

'You spoke to your father about this?'

'He came around a couple of weeks ago. To check on his investment,' she added dryly.

'That's what he told you?'

'Not in so many words.'

'Why would you say that, then?'

'It's true.'

He didn't have to look at her to know she was shrugging. 'Why couldn't he be checking on his daughter?'

'Same thing.'

'No,' he said quietly. 'It's not.' He paused. 'I have a father who isn't interested in me or anything I do. He never comes around.'

'He didn't invest in your company.'

'Your father has enough money not to care about what you do with your business.' He let it sit. 'It does sound like he cares about you though.'

He'd always believed it. Saw it in the way her father interacted with her. His pride, his presence, both of which he'd never got from his own father. The former not ever, even when he'd taken Calvin's place with Janie's care; the latter not since his parents' divorce.

He wondered why Autumn had never been able to see it. Or why she told him she and her family weren't close when they still had dinners and she still attended parties and planned anniversaries—

'Autumn,' he said with a frown. 'Didn't you drive to Wilderness last weekend for your parents' anniversary?'

'Yes.'

'So you only got back…' He trailed off with a headshake. 'You should have chased me away.'

'When you came to my door in the middle of the night distraught?' she asked lightly. 'I don't think so.'

'You must have been exhausted.'

'I am. I was, I mean.'

He looked into the mirror, then dragged his eyes back to the road. 'You are.' He paused. 'You haven't been sleeping.'

'I've been sleeping,' she said defensively. She sighed. 'Not well.'

Is it because of what you said to me? That you think you weren't enough for me?

She hadn't answered him when he'd asked; he doubted she wanted to speak about it now. Especially when mentioning her father had reminded him of her relationship with her family.

But something told him what she'd said had something to do with that.

'You know…' He clenched a jaw when the words stuck. Deliberately relaxed it. 'I didn't have a child with someone else because I didn't want one with you. You know that, right?'

CHAPTER TEN

AUTUMN SUCKED IN her breath, just as she had when they'd been at her house. The question felt as intimate as her fantasy of him drawing her close, lining his body with hers. Close enough for her to remember what she was missing; what she'd never have.

His expression then had been intense, a combination of want and self-denial. It was intense now, too, based on what she could see in the mirror. But there was an emotion there that twisted her insides.

'You're not doing anyone any favours by feeling guilty,' Autumn said quietly, ignoring his actual question.

'It's hard not to,' he said, fingers tight on the steering wheel. 'I feel like I…' He hesitated. 'I feel like I cheated on you. Or betrayed you, at the very least.'

Me, too.

She pushed the words away. Knew she couldn't answer his question about whether she knew he hadn't wanted a child with someone else. She was apparently still working through it. It annoyed her that he was poking at a fresh injury, one that had had no time to heal.

'I won't try and change your mind about that,' she said slowly. 'One, because I can't tell you how to feel. Two, because it's unfair of you to expect me to.' She swallowed down the lump in her throat. 'Three? You need to focus on the present, Hunter. On the future. For the sake of your son.' She looked at the little boy who'd fallen asleep in his car seat, then out of the window. 'Guilt is a useless emotion.'

As was hurt, she thought, determined not to let the fingers of it fist around her heart.

Instead, her own fingers curled where her hand rested

on her knee. Stopping them, she spread them over the skin there instead, almost sighing when they automatically tightened and dug into her flesh. It was pointless trying to stop them. Probably just as pointless as the anger that had coated the hurt and caused the reaction.

To be fair, her anger wasn't entirely directed at Hunter. She was mostly angry at herself. Because the weakness she'd accused herself of having by being vulnerable was there, fluttering through her body. Her reluctance to accept her father's interest as genuine, ricocheting in her chest. Most of all, her inability to accept that Hunter's decisions didn't reflect on her taunted her. Reminded her of all the times she'd thought of her parents' actions in the same way.

Did their focus on turning Summer into the Bishop heir mean they didn't see Autumn as worthy? Had their urging her into the kitchen been an opportunity to get her out of their way? Did they bring her out to mingle at their parties to placate her?

Why am I treated differently? What am I doing wrong?

Those questions were there every time her parents would talk to her about Summer. Before the affair, it had been because Summer hadn't been open about her life. After, because Summer had distanced herself.

Autumn had been so frustrated that she'd once told her mother Summer didn't need their concern.

'Of course she does.' Lynette Bishop had tutted. 'She's not like you.'

In that, Autumn had identified the real problem.

You're not like her.

She'd carried that with her long before her mother had said the words. Long enough that it had formed her into a person who tried to please everyone she met. Because she might not have been Summer, but she could be better. She'd taken what Summer hadn't done—opened up to people, engaged with them, been interested in them—

and incorporated it into her own personality. She'd seen what people needed and given it to them.

She'd become more popular almost immediately. With her parents' friends and acquaintances, who'd *oohed* and *aahed* over their charming daughter. With her teachers, who'd seen a hard-working girl, and her peers, who'd seen her money. All the while, she'd been aware of the pretence. Of the shifting and the changing. But it hadn't mattered, because people had preferred *her*.

Not the people she cared about most though.

The anger had been there long before now. She couldn't deny some of it had been aimed at Summer. Her sister didn't deserve it. It wasn't Summer's fault that Autumn compared herself to Summer and found herself lacking. Or that their parents did.

But she'd let it keep her from seeing Summer's pain. After their father's affair, Summer had withdrawn from the family. Autumn hadn't had the same reaction. She hadn't been as hurt, more affronted for her mother's sake than anything else. Since her mother had worked through it, Autumn had moved on. She'd known Summer hadn't—hadn't understood why either—but she'd done nothing about it.

She should have pushed Summer to tell her why. To help her understand. But no, Autumn had only discovered the truth at her parents' anniversary weekend. She could do nothing about what her sister had gone through now.

That was the cost of comparison, she thought suddenly. It put her at the centre of every experience, even if it was only to highlight her mistakes, her faults. But it blinded her to other people's experiences. That blindness kept her from acting. In this case, it had kept her from reaching out to her sister. What else had it kept her from doing?

Before Autumn could stew about it, Hunter spoke.

'I didn't mean to upset you.'

'You didn't,' she answered automatically. She bit the

inside of her cheek. 'Well, it's not completely you. I'm upset at myself.'

'Why?'

How could she phrase this? Her tendency to compare herself wasn't something she waved around, least of all to the people she cared about. What would they think about the mess that was her self-esteem?

She settled for describing the situation with her sister, leaving comparisons and her guilt out of it.

'Summer knew about my father's affair long before we did.'

She explained what had happened, including the events of her parents' anniversary where everything had come to light. She felt some of the pressure ease from her chest as the words spilled from her lips. He listened quietly, not interrupting once, not even for clarity. Not that she'd expected him to. Hunter had a singular talent for listening. No, for making her feel heard. For someone who felt as if she'd been shouting into the void her entire life, the experience was heady.

You're my person.

He was hers, too.

'You know it wasn't your fault,' Hunter said as he turned onto the road that would take them to the wedding venue. It was a long gravel path. Hunter drove slowly.

'You would say that.'

'Why?'

'Because you're my...friend.'

His cheek lifted in a smile. 'You hesitated.'

'No.'

The cheek lifted higher. 'Regardless,' he said after a moment, 'you couldn't have done anything about it. You didn't know.'

'I knew she was upset,' Autumn pointed out.

She looked out of the window again, at the fields that

stretched out on either side of the gravel road. There was a herd of cows in the distance. Five goats ate grass closer to them, giving them blank stares as they drove by.

'If I'd pushed her into telling me,' Autumn continued, 'she wouldn't have gone through it alone.'

'I see.'

She looked at him. 'What does that mean?'

He lifted a shoulder. 'Exactly what I said.'

'But *what* do you see, Hunter?'

'Well,' he said. 'Didn't you ask her why she couldn't move on?'

'Not in so many words.'

'But you checked on her.'

She nodded, though she didn't think he saw it.

'You encouraged her to make up with your parents?'

'Yes.' There was barely a beat before she added, 'But that was before I knew why she couldn't.'

'Because she didn't tell you.'

'Stop trying to make me feel better.'

He laughed. 'I'm trying to make you see the truth. Your sister chose not to tell you. She had the opportunity to.' His voice softened, all traces of amusement fading. 'You can't blame yourself for that, Autumn.'

'I can,' she muttered. 'I do.'

He laughed again, kindly, and pulled into a parking space close to the venue entrance.

'One question,' he asked as she unclicked her safety belt and peered into the car seat to check on Eli. As soon as the car had stopped, his eyes had popped open. She felt a wave of sympathy for Hunter's predicament.

'What is it?'

'Have you told her about this?' He waited as she pulled Eli out of the car seat. 'About him?'

She opened her mouth, but his expression told her he didn't expect an answer. He already knew what it was.

* * *

All things considered, the Thompsons responded well to the mess-up with the cake.

The bridal couple were still taking their photos, so perhaps that was a premature evaluation. But based on the reaction of the groom's parents, Autumn's friend's in-laws, the couple wouldn't care too much. Not if they were similar to the Thompsons in any way.

They were the kind of people who enjoyed dropping names. Hunter knew this because within the first ten minutes after being introduced, they'd mentioned the caterers, who were from a five-star hotel; Mel's dress designer, who was from a well-known international design house; the specialised wine for the day, which was produced by an in-demand local vintner; and, of course, the cake.

Having Autumn Bishop, heiress and owner of a wildly popular bakery, make the cake had softened the blow. Having her deliver it personally, where all the guests could see her, could mitigate any mistake. Having *#BakeryBoyfriend* deliver said cake with Autumn, he was stunned to learn, earned them an invitation to the wedding. Even with a baby.

'Oh, Mr and Mrs Thompson, we couldn't,' Autumn said with a polite smile. 'We couldn't impose.'

'Oh, you're not imposing.' Mrs Thompson waved a hand. 'There's more than enough space.'

She gestured to the venue, which was currently only half filled with guests. Since the bride and groom hadn't arrived yet, this seemed about right. Hunter assumed she wasn't pointing out attendance though. No, she was showing them the vast amount of space that would allow them to join the wedding as guests.

He supposed in some circles, this would be impressive. The round tables that filled the area, leaving enough room for a forest of trees—or so it looked like—to line each of the walls. Expensive chandeliers hung from the roof, over a dance floor that had been raised from the ground with insignia embossed into wood. He assumed it was the couple's initials, but considering the way Mrs Thompson was beaming, he wouldn't be surprised if she told him it was hers.

'It's lovely, but we can't.' Autumn spoke firmly, though there was a lyricism to the words that made Hunter wonder if she was truly rejecting them. 'We have the baby.'

Mrs Thompson peered at Eli, who was being traitorously quiet in Autumn's arms. 'Is it yours?'

'He,' Autumn said deliberately, 'is not.' There was a slight beat before she continued. 'I think we'll wait for Mel and Ed outside.'

'Well,' Mr Thompson said when his wife looked at him in panic, 'at least have a drink on us?'

'Of course,' Autumn said smoothly. 'Do you honestly think we wouldn't take advantage of that gorgeous bar?'

The compliment seemed to soothe any ruffled feathers, and soon he and Autumn were walking to the outdoor bar.

'Good work,' he said softly, manoeuvring Eli's pram as he followed her.

She angled her head back, offered him a smile. 'Thank you. It's a gift.'

He chuckled. Though he knew she was teasing, she was right. Autumn had a gift. It wasn't charm as much as a deep understanding of how people wanted to be treated. How they needed to be treated. He supposed there was a certain kind of charm in that, not that he'd ever be able to understand it. He understood it in Autumn though. She cared about people. Whether it was her ex-boyfriend-turned-friend or her sister, she would rather hurt herself than the people she loved.

Cared about, he corrected instantly. She didn't love him. That part of their lives was over. It would do neither of them any good to think otherwise.

When they reached the bar outside, Hunter saw Autumn hadn't merely been charming the Thompsons. The bar was genuinely beautiful. It looked as if it had been carved out of porcelain; white, glossy, with intricate patterns that looked as if it belonged in a museum. It seemed like a waste to have it at a wedding.

'Did you know this was here?' Hunter asked, standing next to Autumn.

'Yeah.'

She turned to him. She was directly under him, forcing her to look up and him to look down. Exactly as they'd need to if they wanted to kiss.

Fortunately, Eli kept that from happening.

Fortunately.

'I've been here before.' Was it just him, or did her voice sound breathy? 'It's one of those places rich people like having their events at.'

'Are you talking about yourself?' he asked, his eyes disobediently dipping to her lips. 'Or the people in your circle?'

'My parents' circle,' she said.

When he dragged his gaze up, he saw that hers was on his mouth. Her lips parted, and it took all his strength not to dip his head and taste her. As if she'd realised the danger, her head snapped up, and she shifted away, pulling Eli closer to her body before turning to the barperson.

He didn't think she'd known that the woman had been there, more that it had been blind hope to escape whatever web of attraction they were in. But she ordered herself a juice, and gestured for him to make his own order. He stuck with water.

'You could use something stronger, I'm sure,' she commented as the barwoman readied their drinks.

'So could you.'

'Yes, but Eli.'

The simple reason had his entire chest quaking with emotion. 'You still could,' he said determinedly. 'Eli means *I* can't drink. Plus, I'm driving.'

'Yet he's falling asleep in *my* arms.'

She gave him a catlike smile that told him she wouldn't entertain the conversation further. Which was good. He didn't want to thank her for helping his son sleep when it felt like verbalising his failure. He knew how exhausted Eli must be. The brief moments of sleep Eli had managed in the car couldn't have been enough. Disrupting his routine must have had a hell of an effect, too.

So it made no sense then that Hunter was thinking about leaning forward and teaching her what that smile would bring her.

Relief pacified some of the ache in his body when the bartender handed him their drinks. He took both of them gladly. It gave him something to do with his hands. The distraction of it gave his mind something else to focus on.

And yet, when she turned, his eyes dipped to the curve of her shoulders, the slope of her back, her butt, her legs. He swallowed.

'He's asleep,' she said softly. 'I think it means we can put him in the pram.'

'He usually wakes up,' he protested, but she was already lowering Eli into the pram, strapping him in. Hunter held his breath, waiting for the inevitable screech. It didn't come.

Of course.

'Come on,' she said so brightly he didn't have an opportunity to be upset about it. 'I want to show you something.'

'What?' he managed to ask, handing her the drinks when she gestured for them. Then she was walking beyond the boundary of the patio outside the venue, ignoring his question, and he had no choice but to follow her with the pram.

This is not a good idea, a voice inside his head scolded. It was the voice that had kept him out of trouble in school when he'd been tempted to use his fists to let out his frustrations about what had been happening at home. His anger at the injustice of losing the little girl he loved more than anything else. Anger he'd neatly aimed at his father.

Surprised by the thought, he tried to shake it off. The point was that that voice had kept him out of trouble. It had encouraged him to keep his head in the books. To expel his energy by exercising in the safety of his backyard.

It was a good, old friend. A trusted friend. Not one he should ignore because another, more tempting voice was cheering him forward.

He ignored it.

The two of them walked together wordlessly, the only sound the rattling of the pram against the narrow gravel path. Thick trees lined it; more stood tall in the distance. Because of the silence, the further down the path they walked, the clearer he could hear the trickle of water. It was louder before long, and she offered him a delighted smile as they turned a corner.

'Ta-da!' she said, opening her arms.

He smiled before he saw what she was showing him. When he saw, his lips stilled. It was a waterfall, which he'd gathered from the sound. But he hadn't expected it to be this beautiful.

The water gushed out of cracks in a mountain-like rock formation, with greenery bursting through random parts of the rocks. It flowed into a large body of water, then trailed further down into a narrower part that disappeared between the trees. The water was clear enough for him to see brown pebbles and an occasional sliver of colour indicating fish.

'Why haven't I heard about this place before?' he asked, checking that Eli was still asleep before he lowered to his haunches and stuck his hand into the water.

It was cool, refreshing, alerting him to how heated he was. He was tempted to throw off his clothes and dip his entire body into it. But he could only imagine what having fewer clothes on would tempt him into doing.

'Do you know of all the beautiful places in Cape Town?' she asked, putting their drinks a short distance away before lowering herself beside him.

When he realised she was going to sit down on the grass, he pulled her up enough to stop the momentum of her action. He sat, legs stretched out in front of him, and pulled her over his lap. By the time she reacted, she was already sitting on him.

'Hunter,' she said, sounding scandalised. His lips twitched. 'What are you doing?'

'I didn't want you to stain your dress.'

'Staining your pants is better?'

'I don't have to speak to clients soon.'

'Oh.' The righteous indignation deflated out her body. 'Thank you, then.'

She sniffed.

He hid his grin. 'You're welcome.'

She shifted on his lap, getting comfortable, and he thanked the heavens he'd thought to put her across his thighs instead of on top of him. If she'd moved like that there...

He swallowed, trying hard to act like the grown man he was and not the teenage boy she made him feel like. As if in answer to that thought, his eyes dipped to the curves of her breasts, and his mouth began to water, as if he could taste—

'Hunter?'

His eyes lifted, and he blushed. He should just hide in the water while he still had his dignity.

Because hiding would be so dignified.

'You're still not answering me,' she said softly, amusement dancing in her voice.

'What did you say?'

'I asked whether this is comfortable for you.'

'No,' he said immediately. She gave a sparkling laugh that had his lips curving.

'It was your idea.'

'I regret it.'

She immediately stiffened. 'Do you? I can—'

'Relax,' he told her, resting a hand on her thigh. 'I was joking.'

She looked down at her thigh, at his hand, and turned her head to his. Her eyelashes fluttered.

'No, you weren't.'

He didn't know if the trickling water had made him feel romantic. Or her proximity. Or the fact that she was looking at him as if she didn't want to move. But he said, 'No, I wasn't.'

CHAPTER ELEVEN

TERRIBLE IDEA, AUTUMN. This is a terrible idea. You can't undo this once you do it. Stop. Save yourself.

Her brain was being very logical with these thoughts, these observations. Problem was, she didn't want logic. Not when Hunter was looking at her as if he were hungry and hadn't eaten in years. If she were the food, she supposed that scenario wasn't entirely untrue.

Well, he was about to feast now.

They closed the distance at the same time. Autumn's hands lifted and gripped his face; Hunter's arms circled her waist and pulled her closer to him. Then they were kissing. Deeply, desperately.

His lips were soft, familiar, and knew exactly how to move against her so that all the blood pooled to the pit of her stomach. He angled his head as his tongue swept into her mouth, and she groaned, then pushed even closer to him. She was dimly aware of her skin shooting out in goosebumps; her breasts tightening; the rest of her body aching.

She knew, too, that they were going too fast. Their mouths were fused so urgently. Their hands were moving recklessly now, too. Hers eagerly ran over the bumps of his shoulders, the muscles of his back. They gripped the material of his shirt when his mouth left hers and found her neck, kissing and suckling on that spot where her neck met her shoulder that he knew drove her crazy.

'Hunter,' she gasped, even as she tilted her neck, exposing the skin to him. 'Stop.'

He immediately did, rearing his head back. His eyes were dark, hungry, fierce, and it sent a pang of desire through her already over-stimulated body.

'This isn't a good idea.'

He swallowed. Nodded.

'We should do it again. Slower. So we can enjoy it more.'

His gaze flew to hers, his eyes crinkling, and he leaned forward. She laughed, pulling back.

'Standing.'

Seconds later they were both standing. They stepped away from the drinks they'd miraculously managed to avoid knocking over during their passion. Now they stood, centimetres away from one another, staring.

'You're having second thoughts,' he said softly.

She laughed as a ball of nerves dissolved in her stomach. 'Aren't you?'

'Yes.'

She lifted her eyebrows. 'Then why are you asking me this?'

'I won't take advantage of you.'

Her lips curved. 'What if I want you to take advantage of me?'

She closed the distance between them, placed her hands at the top of his shoulders, before sliding them down to his chest.

His hands closed over hers, keeping her from moving lower.

'You want me to take advantage of you?'

'Like this,' she clarified. 'Yes, I do.'

'Autumn, I don't want…' He paused, his brow furrowing with intensity. 'I don't want you to feel like you…'

She waited, but he didn't finish it.

'Hunter,' she said softly, 'we both know this can't go beyond this moment.'

The frowned deepened. She wondered how she could find it cute.

'But we have this moment,' she continued with a slight

shake of her head. 'I, for one, would like to use it more productively than—'

His lips on hers silenced her, and she smiled into his mouth, then moaned when his tongue touched hers again. He'd dropped his hands, allowing her to make better use of her own. She ran them over his shoulders, down the thick curves of his biceps, his forearms, before taking his hands that had fallen to his sides. Thinking they were going to waste there, she moved them both to her hips.

Immediately, his hands gripped her flesh, squeezing, kneading, before they slowly moved up to her waist. Her skin shot out in gooseflesh again, unsurprisingly. His mouth was doing sinful things to hers, nibbling and nipping and coaxing; his hands imprinting on her skin.

He pulled away from her then, though not enough for their embrace to lose intimacy. One hand lifted to her cheek, his thumb brushing over the skin there. His eyes moved over her face swiftly. Seconds later, they did so more deliberately. The first felt as if he were checking for something; the second, as if he were committing it to memory.

It changed the air. It had been static and frenzied, even when their kissing had grown slower; now it felt heavy with meaning. Emotion.

His gaze met hers. 'You're the most beautiful woman I've ever seen.'

She'd heard the compliment before. Hell, she'd heard the compliment from *him* before. But it had never felt this…charged. Or life-changing. Her heart tightened in her chest, as if, with those words, he'd reached inside and grasped it, holding it firm in his hands.

Heaven only knew why that had her reaching for him again.

She pressed her lips to his, gave him a hard kiss before she dropped her head to his chest. She felt his hesitation before his arms closed around her, drawing her against his body.

She missed it. The raw, sexy passion of kissing him and the soothing emotion of being in his arms. She missed how she felt like the only woman in the world when he touched her, and how, when they were like this, she truly believed he thought she was the most beautiful woman.

Most of all, she missed loving this man. She missed imagining a future with him.

In that future, she didn't have to try so hard. She didn't compare herself to others. Wasn't changing herself to be like others. She was enough for him. She was enough for herself.

But that future was a fantasy. Reality was that she did compare herself to others. She did everything she could to make them like her. It meant she hated a part of herself— *that* part of herself—since it was the cause of her feelings of inadequacy.

Reality was that she didn't have a future with Hunter. She'd tried to have one with him, tried so incredibly hard. But it didn't change that he didn't want her. Not enough to even consider a compromise for their future together. Or even a *conversation*. No, he shut down or gave her the thinnest answer.

She could see it now. She understood it. As clearly as she saw and understood that her own issues had been an obstacle to their future, too.

The fact that he hadn't wanted a family had spoken to her fears of not being good enough. Her mind had screamed he hadn't wanted a family with *her*; the rest of her had accepted it. Had used Eli's existence as proof of it. Except now, that didn't seem like an adequate explanation. Hunter had turned to *her* after discovering he had a son. He'd asked *her* for help. Why would he do that if he didn't believe her good enough?

But she was so used to blaming herself. Faulting herself.

She was tired of it.

Perhaps it was that fatigue that helped her see she'd left Hunter for reasons other than what she'd told herself. She'd wanted a family and he hadn't, yes, but she'd wanted him more. A part of her had known that even then. So maybe, beneath that, she'd simply recognised that, just like with her family, she would have always felt second best with him.

His fears would come first.

She couldn't fault him for it. His trauma was significant. He'd lost a sister, someone he'd cared for deeply. Someone he'd taken care of. His parents had fought all the time, then divorced. Even before that, his father had been emotionally absent. People didn't just get over things like that. They had to work through it. But he barely acknowledged it. He kept it all bottled up inside. It would cast a shadow over everything he did. Just like what had happened with Summer. Just like…

Just like what she was doing to herself.

She stepped out of his arms. The look he gave her in response was inscrutable. It told her he knew something had happened in her head. She wasn't sure if it was because she had it written on her face, or because he knew her so well. Or a combination of both, since if she did have something written on her face, he would be able to read it.

She scooped down and collected her juice, downing it. The sugar seared its way down her throat, sizzling as it settled in her stomach. She wished she had another one. She wished she could drown herself in the sweetness so that she could burn off all the emotion that suddenly felt as if it were written on her skin.

As she made her way back up the path, she didn't wait for Hunter to follow her. Nor did she check that he was, though she didn't have to. She could hear the pram behind her. Knew his big, sexy body was easily handling both the piece of equipment and the awkward incline of the path. Unlike hers, she thought, her heels dipping into the ground for the fourth time.

If he says anything about it, she stewed, when she heard him take a breath behind her. But he must have changed his mind because no words were spoken. When she heard the breathing again, she realised he'd simply caught up with her. Grunting, she pushed forward, only to have a low-hanging branch thwart her.

She'd missed it, her gaze being on the ground ahead of her, and she'd walked directly into it. She felt a scratch against her forehead, but the real problem came after, when she tried to move and the branch got caught in her hair. Her first reaction was to pull forward, which did nothing, though she did hear a crackle that told her she'd break her hair if she kept pulling.

'Stop,' Hunter said before she could still.

'I was going to,' she mumbled.

He made a non-committal sound and stepped in front of her, examining the situation. She kept her eyes down, but he was standing so close that she could only see the torso she'd run her hands over minutes before. She lifted her gaze to his throat, but that reminded her that she hadn't kissed it when she'd had the chance. She knew what would happen if she looked higher, if she saw his lips, or his cheeks, or his eyes, so she closed her own and waited for it to be over.

It only succeeded in sharpening her other senses. It reminded her that she'd forgotten to hold her breath. Now she was forced to inhale Hunter's scent mixed with the earthy smell of the trees. She switched to breathing through her mouth, but somewhere in her mind she knew she'd always remember that potent combination. Already knew she'd smell it in her dreams.

She nearly sobbed.

'It's done,' he said seconds later, smoothing down her hair.

She opened her eyes, but he hadn't moved. He was studying her again, though this time he hadn't managed to keep his expression unreadable. She knew exactly what she saw there: regret.

Heat flushed her face as Hunter stepped back. She mumbled a 'thank you' before walking past him, pressing her lips together when they started trembling.

No, she commanded herself. She would not cry. She would not think about the kisses. In fact, she would pretend they hadn't happened. If she did, she could pretend the rest of it hadn't happened either. She would happily be able to ignore that she'd allowed her insecurities to taint every relationship, every decision she'd made in her life. And that she wanted Hunter, still, but couldn't do a damn thing about him not wanting her.

When they reached the patio, she heard laughter. Three steps later, she saw the wedding party outside the venue, enjoying a drink.

'Autumn!' Mel said, spotting her. 'Ed's parents mentioned you were here somewhere! They said something about the cake?'

'Yes, though let me first say *wow*! You look stunning, Mel,' Autumn said, examining the sparkly dress, feeling her heart vibrate as she did. 'Your eyes must have spun back in your head, Ed.'

Ed pushed up his glasses with a grin. 'Pretty accurate description.' He looked lovingly at his new wife.

'So,' Autumn said with a small smile, not wanting to linger, 'there was an accident with your cake today.' She explained it as concisely as she could. 'It won't be exactly what you expected, but I still think it's special.'

'Well,' Mel said, exchanging a look with Ed, 'we've actually seen it. My mum sent me a photo as soon as it arrived.' She paused. 'We love it!'

'You do?' Autumn asked, relief bursting in her chest. 'Oh, I'm so glad.'

'You shouldn't have been worried,' Mel replied, squeezing Autumn's shoulder. 'We love all your designs. And this still has everything we wanted, but it's somehow better.' She shimmied her shoulders in excitement. 'We can't thank you enough.'

'I'm glad you like it,' Autumn said. 'Though I'll still offer you a free cake on your first anniversary for the trouble.'

Mel and Ed's eyes widened.

'Oh, you don't have to do that.'

'I know I don't *have* to,' Autumn said. 'I want to.'

'Thank you,' Mel said, blinking. She beamed up at Ed. 'And I thought this day couldn't get any better,' she told him dreamily.

Ed grinned. 'Thank you, Autumn. We appreciate it.'

'Don't mention it.'

'Can we entice you to stay?' Ed asked after a beat. 'My mum told me she invited you—' his eyes shifted to behind Autumn '—and your boyfriend.'

Autumn stepped to the side, startled that she'd forgotten about Hunter. More so by the fact that Ed had called Hunter her boyfriend.

'Um, sorry. This is Hunter,' she said, though she knew it wasn't necessary.

Before Hunter could say anything, Eli let out an ear-splitting scream.

'Oh,' Mel said. 'I didn't realise you had a baby.'

'I don't.' Autumn forced a smile before waving a hand at Hunter, who'd started to reach into the pram. 'You have to drive,' she told him, picking up Eli. She figured after how long he'd slept, he either needed food or a diaper change. Probably both. 'As you can see, we really can't stay. But thank you.'

'Oh, yes.' Mel's frown deepened. 'Thank *you*.'

'Again, I'm sorry for the inconvenience. I look forward to hearing from you next year about the cake.' She stepped off the patio into the car park. 'It was nice seeing you again.'

She did a general wave, then followed Hunter to the car.

Neither of them spoke while she busied herself with changing Eli on the back seat. It took some creativity, but she managed. Soon he was in his seat, his little mouth suckling on a bottle of formula Hunter had had the foresight to prepare, and Hunter pulled out onto the road without a word.

But Eli calming down was bad for her brain. It meant she no longer had anything to distract herself with. Almost immediately she thought about how she'd wished she could have given a different answer to the Thompsons. To Mel. She wanted Hunter to be hers.

She wanted a wedding of her own. Thought of all the times she'd planned it in her head. Long before she'd met Hunter, admittedly. She'd walk into a wedding venue and wish for her own. Those desires had become more real when they'd been together. When a wedding, marriage, had been a possibility. But it wasn't now, so why had she still felt that vibration in her chest when she'd looked at Mel's dress?

And why was she wishing she could have given a different answer about Eli, too? He wasn't hers. He would never be.

'Have you spoken with Grace?' she blurted out, desperate to get away from the hopelessness.

'Yes.'

'*Spoken* spoken,' she clarified. 'Not messaged. Or emailed.'

His silence was telling. She let out a breath.

'Hunter, you can't run away from the fact that you're struggling.'

'I'm not.'

She lifted her brow when their eyes met in the mirror. He sighed.

'I don't want her to think I can't do this,' he admitted in a tight voice.

'You *can* do it.'

'Really? He hasn't slept in my arms once the last three days. Or quietened there, for that matter.'

She heard him damning himself in those words. She heaved another breath.

'Okay,' she said, though she knew it was a bad idea. But then, what was another one in the grand scheme of things? 'Let's go to your house.'

'What?'

'You need to stop being scared of your son, Hunter. I'm going to show you how.'

CHAPTER TWELVE

'YOU'RE SCARED OF HIM,' Autumn said for what felt like the millionth time. He gritted his teeth for what felt like the millionth time, too.

'I'm not scared of him,' he said. 'It's new.'

'It's not new. You took care of your sister.'

'I was six when she was born. I did the bare minimum when she was a baby.'

He wasn't actually sure that was true. He couldn't remember doing anything for Janie when she was a baby, though there was a high likelihood that he had helped in some way. His childhood up until the moment she'd died had been helping to take care of Janie.

His heart expanded in his chest, testing the limits of its confines. Seconds later, it shrank back to its usual size. The feeling stayed—expanding, shrinking—making him ill.

He wasn't upset about it. He'd expected some sort of physical reaction long before that moment. In fact, he'd expected it after his mother had called that morning.

'Are you okay?' she'd asked without preamble.

'Good morning to you, too, Mum,' he'd said.

Since he hadn't been able to sleep, he'd already been up, driving around Cape Town, trying to get Eli to nap. At that moment, Eli had been. Thankfully. Hunter wasn't sure how he'd explain the crying baby to his mother. He hadn't got to that point in his head yet. Hadn't been sure how he'd explain his one-night-stand baby to his mother.

'I'm fine. Why?'

'What do you mean "why"?' Her voice had lowered, as if she didn't want anyone to know what she was saying. 'Today's...you know.'

It had taken him too long to realise what she was talking about. When he had, he'd closed his eyes with a little breath.

'I'm okay,' he'd said after a moment. 'Are you?'

'Fine.' His mother had cleared her throat. 'I have the day planned out. No second free.'

'No second to think.'

'Which is the point,' she'd reminded him. Her tone had softened. 'You sure you're fine?'

'I am.'

When he'd disconnected, he'd taken a moment to let the shame flood his body. Then he'd driven directly to Autumn's place. He'd needed the comfort. Was embarrassed by how much. Not that it beat the embarrassment he'd felt at the fact that he'd forgotten the anniversary of his sister's death. Thirteen years ago, he'd lost Janie. And he hadn't remembered.

He wasn't sure why he hadn't remembered. His mother was a big enough part of his life that he'd noticed her absence in the past few weeks. She'd gone to Greece this time; she needed to be anywhere other than Cape Town, where Janie had died. She'd followed the custom every anniversary for the last twelve years. The first anniversary, she had been home, and still married. It had been rough enough that she'd finally filed for divorce.

The following year, she'd gone on her first overseas trip. Hunter had stayed at home alone since it had been during his final school year, and he hadn't been able to miss any days because of final exams. Besides, he'd preferred home over staying with his father, who he hadn't seen since the divorce.

Janie's illness had changed his father so much that he didn't seem to care about his healthy child. Hunter understood that distance now. He was doing it with Eli. When he'd seen how much better Autumn was at taking care of his son, he'd stepped aside and let her do it.

Was that how his father had felt? Inadequate and helpless? Or had he just been selfish? Caring about his own feelings more than he had Janie's?

If Hunter couldn't take care of his son now, when he seemed healthy, what would happen if Eli was sick? Would he put even more distance between him and his son? Would he follow in his father's footsteps and detach himself from the family?

'Hunter.'

His head moved in the direction of the voice, but it took some time to realise who was calling him. He had to figure out where he was first.

'Sorry.' He closed his eyes.

'Hunter.' Her voice softened. He opened his eyes again. 'What's wrong?'

'Nothing's wrong.'

'Something's wrong,' she dismissed with confidence. 'You're quiet.'

'I'm always quiet.'

'True.' Her lips curved. 'But you have different kinds of quietness. There's the normal, broody kind. Then there's the "something's wrong" kind. You're doing the latter.'

He wanted to laugh, but was afraid it would reveal the hysteria brewing inside him. 'You know me too well.'

'My curse.'

A curse. Now he did laugh. Then walked outside because he didn't want laughter to turn into tears. Shame, guilt, confusion sat like bricks in his throat. Then there was the grief, holding those emotions together like cement.

A curse.

He currently felt cursed himself. As if he couldn't do anything right for his son. Or in his life at all, he thought, remembering that he'd left Autumn inside the house without any answers. The fact that she was there in any capacity proved that he was doing something wrong. She didn't deserve to be dragged into this.

Except…he needed her.

That felt like a curse, too. Needing her so deeply but being unable to be with her. Not in the way he wanted. But this was safer. It was safer to let her take care of Eli, too. He wouldn't hurt them this way. He wouldn't lose them this way.

'Hunter.'

The voice was urgent at his side, and he turned, wondering how long she'd been there. And what she'd seen.

'Hunter,' she said again, edging closer to him. Her hands lifted and her thumbs brushed his cheeks. Only then did he realise tears had been falling from his eyes.

Damn it.

He stepped away from her, took a ragged breath. He was embarrassed at the vulnerability of it. The tears were an outward display of the turmoil going on inside him. He couldn't hide the tears as he did the turmoil. He couldn't hide that he was broken and hurting and his emotions made no sense.

'I'm worried about you,' she said, twisting her hands together.

'You shouldn't be. I don't deserve it.'

'Of course you do,' she said dismissively.

Her passion nearly made him smile; the concern made him want to give her something. Anything.

'The test,' he said quietly. 'It's on Monday.'

'This coming Monday?' she asked. He nodded. 'Oh.' Paused. 'Do you want to talk about it?'

He took a long time to answer. Mostly because until he'd mentioned it, he hadn't realised the test had been weighing on his mind, too.

'I keep thinking about what happens if Eli is sick,' he said slowly.

'What happens?'

'Where to begin?' He gave a humourless laugh. 'He'll have a tough life. I wouldn't know how to raise him.'

'In terms of his practical needs?'

'No. No, that I'd be able to do.' He knew that much. 'I... I want to be a good father. I'm not sure I can be if I end up spending my life trying not to be like my father.'

'Why would you be like him?'

'I have that gene inside me. Just like the CF gene I carry.' He took a breath. 'If Eli's sick, maybe that would trigger something inside me. The "Terrible Father" gene.'

She took the revelation in her stride. 'Is that why you're scared to take care of Eli?'

'I'm not—' He broke off on a sigh. 'Maybe.'

'Right.' There was a long pause. 'Did I tell you part of why Summer divorced Wyatt was because she was afraid he would turn into my father?' She was looking out onto the pool, her arms folded. The stance was so casual she might have been at a party. 'Another big reveal from the anniversary weekend.'

'I'm...not following.'

'I'm getting there,' she replied patiently. 'She never told Wyatt about it. She couldn't. It would have meant telling him about my father's secret, and she was paralysed by keeping it. So she asked for a divorce.'

He waited now, sensing there was a point.

'She gave up on the thing that made her the happiest because of my father.'

'Are you talking about us?'

She looked at him, the curves of her cheeks flirting with her eyes though it wasn't a smile she gave him. 'Not directly. Although if you are keeping Eli at a distance because of your father, you've done that with me, too. Before we broke up,' she clarified. 'You pulled away, put distance between us. It was how I knew.' Her gaze dropped for a second. 'But what I meant is that she allowed my father's actions to influence her own. His mistakes became her mistakes. She almost lost the love of her life because of it. I'm not saying that's what's happening here,' she said quickly, and, though it was dark, he could tell she was blushing.

'I know.' He waited a beat. 'You're saying to be careful not to let my father's mistakes become my own because I'm fixated on avoiding them.'

'Yes.' She paused. 'You have the power to change your life, Hunter. You can be a good father if you want to be. You only need to be yourself.' She tightened her arms around herself. 'But you need to stop using him as an excuse.'

He didn't bother denying it. He knew it was true. Had realised it early on in this experience. He'd even had empathy for his father after he'd struggled to deal with Eli; he had even more now that Autumn had outlined his own actions. His habits, it seemed.

When Hunter felt overwhelmed, he put up barriers. They protected him against other people's opinions. Their expectations. But they also kept out the support he needed, causing him to be so overwhelmed he ended up crying without even realising it.

As he thought it, panic rose inside him. It tossed out the other emotions that had been building up in his throat as it took residence there. As it choked him. It made no sense to respond this way to something that hadn't been a surprise. He'd known what Autumn had told him to some extent. Facing it in its entirety now was burdensome, but he shouldn't have been reacting like this.

Until he remembered the barriers had first been erected when he'd stepped in to help take care of Janie.

He hadn't wanted his mother to know how scared he'd been that he'd do something wrong. He hadn't wanted his father to know how angry he'd been at being put in the position of a parent when he'd still been a child. The barriers *had* become a habit. Not only to protect himself, but to protect those around him.

Except they had kept him from identifying his own emotions. Had boxed them in rather than out. Perhaps not all his emotions, but one very specific emotion. It came in waves at unexpected times. Had him clinging to the only person who could calm him, to the point that he'd redefined their relationship so he wouldn't lose her.

Grief.

He'd pushed it so far down that he only dealt with it subconsciously. He'd refused a chance at a family with Autumn because of it. He was keeping his distance from Eli because of it, too. His relationship with his parents had likely also been affected by it. The lack of a relationship with his father seemed to prove that.

But he didn't have time to wonder which other actions in his life had been driven by the emotion. Panic had given way to grief, and, with the barriers gone, nothing could protect him from the onslaught. He stumbled to the table, lowering his body to a chair as the pain saturated his body. Bracing his elbows on his thighs, he dropped his head into his hands, and shut his eyes when heat arrived at them in wave after wave.

He heard the sound of Autumn dragging a chair next to his, then felt the warmth of her arm around him. The weight of her head hit his shoulder, and blindly he reached for her hand, not in the least surprised when he found it.

In silence they sat as he waited out the grief. He didn't bother wiping at the tears. They came randomly, whenever a memory of his sister would stroll into his head. Her laughter echoed in his memories; that one askew tooth she'd had flashing before his eyes. She'd been happier than any kid he'd known. He'd fought for that. His mom had, too.

'Why are we turning it into a game?' he'd complained one day when his mother had encouraged him to play with Janie during her airway clearance therapy.

'So that it's not something negative for her,' his mother had replied. Her eyes had rested on him, and she'd lowered herself until they were face to face. 'This is the only life she knows, Hunter. We can make that life happy for her. You and me.'

He'd do the same for Eli, he thought fiercely. If Eli was sick, Hunter would make sure his son led a happy life. The vow felt like fresh air when all he'd been inhaling was smog. He'd told Autumn he wouldn't know how to raise Eli if he was sick, but now Hunter knew. He'd always known. He'd just...shoved it behind the barrier. But Janie had shown him. Perhaps it was time he allowed her to show him more.

He took a breath. Immediately, Autumn straightened. She started to pull her hand away, but stilled when he resisted.

'I didn't mean for that to happen,' he said.

'I figured.' She paused. 'What did happen?'

'Today's... It's the anniversary today.'

He didn't have to elaborate; she understood. Her grip tightened. It comforted his aching heart.

'Is that why you came to the bakery?'

'I needed the distraction.' From Eli, too, he thought, then frowned. 'Where is Eli?'

'In the pram.'

She gestured with her head. The pram was a few metres away from them. He hadn't even noticed.

'Is he sleeping?'

'He was when I put him down.'

He shook his head. 'I don't know how you do it.'

'By being relaxed,' she said softly, squeezing his hand before she let go and went to check on Eli. 'I think he senses your discomfort around him. Your fear,' she explained. 'I suppose I could have made that clearer earlier.'

'Maybe.' He paused. 'I was scared when I helped with Janie, too.'

She studied his face. 'Why?'

'I thought she might...' He trailed off when the emotion rose again. 'She did,' he ended lamely.

Her eyes widened, then her expression became unreadable. 'You can't let that affect you here.' Her tone was clipped, as if he were a disobedient student and she the teacher.

'Excuse me?'

'It's the same thing as with your father.' With each word, her voice got cooler. Detached. 'You can't raise Eli if you expect him to die.'

He winced, but his spine straightened. 'I...don't.'

'Good,' she said. 'Now, we can try again with Eli in the morning. For now, we rest. It's been a long day.'

'The morning?'

'Do you mind me staying over?'

His brain melted, but somehow he shook his head.

'Good. I'll spend the night with him. You get a good night's sleep.'

He opened his mouth to refuse, so he wasn't sure how he found himself in his bedroom shortly after. Or how he got through a shower, stumbled into bed, and fell asleep.

She was completely disorientated when she woke up. The room was dark, vaguely familiar and cool. Her brain noted this idly as it adjusted to being awake. It took longer to realise she was awake in Hunter's house.

She shot up, looking around more alertly this time. It wasn't the baby's room. She was in one of Hunter's guest bedrooms. The dark blue curtains had been drawn and the air-conditioning had been put on at a respectable temperature. Her body ached, and with a small groan she remembered the discomfort from the night before.

Eli wasn't a fussy baby, at least not with her. But he was still a baby and he woke up every two to three hours for a feeding and a change. After the work day she'd had the day before, the disruptions weren't ideal. After the emotional afternoon and evening she'd had, the disruptions were perfect. She didn't have to think about Hunter crying, or about the realisations she'd had as she'd told him about Summer's mistakes.

Her body on the other hand...

Autumn tried to remember where she'd fallen asleep. It must have been the armchair in Eli's room. She'd dozed in it all night, hence the aching body. But if she'd fallen asleep there, it must have meant Hunter had brought her here. Which also meant she'd been sleeping for far too long. Sighing, she got up, showered, and put on her clothes from the day before.

The smell of bacon hit her as she walked into the kitchen. When she saw the coffee pot, she suddenly smelled that, too. She was already drinking a cup when Hunter walked through the front door with Eli.

She frowned. 'Was he being fussy again? Did you have to take him for a drive?'

'Good morning,' he said mildly. 'No. We went to get you something to wear.'

'Oh,' she said, setting her cup down on the table as Hunter took Eli out of the pram. She was surprised to see him awake...and not crying.

'He's been okay?' she asked, resisting the urge to walk to Eli and snuggle him. It was surprisingly difficult. She didn't like the feeling it stirred in her belly, or the realisation that it stirred any emotion in her at all.

'He's been better.' There was a pause. 'I'm trying to take your advice.'

'Good.'

He took something out of the pram, then extended a hand to offer her a packet. She took it, wondering why things had suddenly become awkward. Was it because of what had just happened inside her? Or were they both trying too hard to pretend the day before hadn't happened?

'Thank you for buying this,' she said, determined to act normally. She would even pretend her insides hadn't turned into mush because he'd thought to buy her clothes. 'I'm not sure this is appropriate for daywear.'

'I wanted you to be comfortable.' He settled Eli in a baby bouncer on the dining-room table and went to pour himself a cup of coffee. 'I thought that would work.'

He gestured to the dress she'd removed from the bag. It was a red and white button-down polka dot dress. She shook it out, draped it over her front.

'It looks like it'll fit,' he said.

She checked the label. 'It's my size, so it should.' She slanted him a look. 'You remembered.'

He angled his head, but didn't comment. The rest of the packet contained white sneakers, socks, some toiletries, underwear... Top and bottom.

'Thorough.'

He shrugged, though she thought she saw a faint glow on his face. 'You're my guest.'

'Hmm.' She threw the dress over her arm and picked up the bag with her free hand. 'I'll go change.'

She did so quickly, pleased to find that most of the items fitted. The underwear was a size too small, though she didn't know if she could blame that on Hunter being optimistic about seeing her or—

No.

Right. She wasn't supposed to be thinking about that. Hunter wouldn't be seeing her in the too small underwear. Optimism wasn't an option. It wasn't as though either of them was hopeful they'd be making out and seeing each other without clothes. She certainly wasn't. She wasn't remembering how his mouth had felt when it had nibbled her neck right at that—

No.

Oops.

She smoothed down the front of the dress, poked her hair so that the curls didn't look as wild, then left the bedroom. When she found Hunter and Eli missing, she immediately went to the patio, unsure of how to feel about the fact that she knew he was there. They'd shared many Sunday mornings when she was off work doing exactly this. She was off today, too, but they weren't together, and it felt different.

'Do I pass inspection?' she said, walking in.

She did a quick twirl for him, throwing out her hands. When she faced him again, she found both father and son smiling at her.

'Oh,' she said with a little laugh. Her tummy jumped at Hunter's smile, but she focused on Eli's instead. 'Has he smiled before?'

Hunter looked at Eli. 'Not that I've seen.'

She twirled again, got the same reaction—just from Eli this time—and told herself she wouldn't do it for a third.

'Well, now we know,' she said before sitting down in front of the plate she assumed Hunter had prepared for her. 'How…er…how did you manage to do this all this morning?'

'I was operating on a good night's sleep for the first time in a while.'

She studied him. Saw that he wasn't only referring to the nights since he'd had Eli. She nodded, picked up her knife and fork. Deliberately, she cut a piece of bacon and toast, but found him looking at her before she could put them in her mouth.

'What?' she said when he didn't speak. 'Do I look funny?'

'You look charming.'

She almost choked on the food she'd been chewing, but managed to swallow down the bite before she said, 'Charming? What am I? Your grandmother?'

He chuckled. 'I've never seen you in something like this.'

She focused on her plate again. 'And yet you bought it for me. Why?'

'I don't know. I thought it would suit you.'

'Because I'm so charming,' she said dryly.

He grinned. 'Yeah.'

She rolled her eyes good-naturedly. 'I'm not charming,' she told him. 'Just good at giving people what they want.'

She continued eating her meal in silence. When she was done, he said, 'That's exactly what I thought yesterday after seeing you with the Thompsons. You have a gift.'

She sat back with her cup of coffee, holding it with both hands. 'I wouldn't call it a gift.'

'I would. You care about people. Enough to give them what they want.'

'That's a strange way to describe being a people pleaser.'

She was so stunned by the words that for a full ten seconds, she blinked rapidly. His wide-eyed reaction didn't even trouble her.

'That's how you see yourself?' he asked eventually.

She chewed on the inside of her lip. 'I suppose.' Then, realising she didn't want to restrain herself, she continued. 'I mould to people's expectations, Hunter. It's not a gift. It's a reminder.'

'Of what?'

'How inauthentic I am? How no matter what I do, I'm never good enough?'

She hated the garbage spilling from her lips. Didn't make it any less true.

'Did I…did I make you think this?' he asked.

She sighed. 'It's not just you. It's everyone. No matter what I do, people don't…like me.' She cringed.

His expression was alarmed, then transitioned into thoughtful. His eyes didn't leave hers; it felt as if he saw through her. Uncomfortable, she avoided his gaze, studying his garden. There were high walls enclosing the property, not allowing for a view of the surroundings as her place did. But inside the walls was spectacular enough that she could forgive him.

Bright flowerbeds lined the walls, with tall trees in every corner. It made the pool in the middle of the area seem like an oasis. The water sparkled in its blueness, tempting anyone who looked at it to jump into its depths. There was a bench just beyond the pool, directly opposite where Autumn was sitting, with enough grass in front of the pool, before the patio, for kids to run and have fun.

Eli would be happy here, she thought. Her heart ached, just a little.

'Autumn.' When she turned, Hunter's expression was unreadable. 'Why can't you see yourself the way other people do?'

There was a moment before a lump travelled to her throat and her eyes burned. Before the emotions weighed down her composure and she had to fight off tears. In that moment, she thought about the question—and had no good answer to give. The realisation devastated her.

'I know,' she said into the silence that extended. Of course he wouldn't say anything that would give her an easy out. His talent for making her feel seen had its downside: he *saw* her. 'Or rather, I *think*, there's a...discrepancy between how I see myself and how other people might see me.'

She thought about the day before, when she'd realised she saw other people's actions as a reflection on herself. And how she'd gone through her entire life allowing it to affect her decisions. Her relationships.

'I'm working on it.'

'Are you?' he asked quietly. 'How?'

'What do you mean how?' she retorted. 'How are you planning on telling your mother about Eli? I'm assuming you haven't.'

It was the first thing she'd thought of, but she regretted it as soon as she saw his expression.

'No, I haven't,' Hunter replied. 'It's not the right time.'

She blinked, then closed her eyes when she realised. 'I'm sorry. That was unnecessary.'

'But relevant.' His gaze was steady on her. 'I'd like to

tell her in person. After the test results come back so that I can have that answer for her.'

She silently groaned.

That's what you get for acting like a jerk.

'Can you tell me how you're working on it now?'

'Okay.' There was a beat. 'I...don't know.'

'Then let me make a suggestion.' It wasn't a question, but she nodded. 'When people show you how much they care about you, believe them.'

Those words echoed in her head as she excused herself to do the dishes. He'd protested, but had seemingly understood she'd needed the space when she'd insisted. She carried their plates and mugs to the kitchen, forgoing the dishwasher and washing the dishes manually.

It was soothing, the act of it. Made her feel useful, which distracted her from the way Hunter's advice had unsettled her.

Ha! a voice in her head said. A spokesman, she assumed, for the feelings she was trying to ignore. She tried to reason with it, though she was well aware of what that said about her mental stability. *You're messy*, she told it, hoping it would carry the message to the rest of her emotions. *Confusing and complicated and so damn messy.*

Reasoning didn't work, so she was forced to think about how he'd told her to do the one thing she had trouble with. Her self-esteem kept her from seeing the true motivation behind people's actions. And since she saw people's actions as reflections on herself, how could she take his advice?

She wanted to. Understood it in a way she hadn't before that weekend. The only answer she could come up with was that she had to work on the way she saw herself. But that seemed like an impossible feat. So impossible, she spent most of her menial task worrying about it.

CHAPTER THIRTEEN

'AUTUMN.'

Her head whipped to Hunter. 'What?'

'We're here.'

She looked around and saw that they'd arrived at her house. After she'd finished the dishes, she'd asked him to drop her off at home. Her mind was a mess and she was afraid of how much he'd see if she stayed there. So she'd pretended not to see his disappointment. Tried not to notice the tension in his body the entire drive home.

Now she was ignoring her own disappointment at the unwelcome thought that had popped into her head with his announcement of their arrival.

I'm going to miss you and Eli.

She grabbed the plastic bag she had her things in, and opened the door. 'Thank—'

He was already at the opposite side of the car, strapping a sleeping Eli into the pram.

'What are you doing?'

'We need to talk.'

'No.'

'No?'

'No,' she confirmed. 'We already talked. Now we—*I*—need some time to recover.'

'Okay.'

But he wheeled the pram around, stopping on the pathway to her front door. With a frustrated sigh, she joined him.

'I need a break from this,' she blurted out when she stopped in front of him. 'This is hard, Hunter. Harder than I thought it was going to be.'

'I know. I'm sorry.'

'No,' she said again. 'I don't want you to apologise.'

'What *do* you want?'

'I want… I don't know, Hunter. A bunch of things I can't have.'

'Me, too,' he admitted softly.

'Like what?'

'I see you with Eli and I… I wish it had been you.' His voice was as steady as ever, which annoyed her, considering he'd sent off an earthquake in her mind.

'This,' she said through tight lips. 'This is why it's so hard.'

'Autumn,' he said, taking a step closer. 'You've already helped me more than you can know. You're…perfect to me.'

'I'm not.'

He took her hand. 'How, then, do you make me feel like I'm capable of doing more than I think I can? You believe I can raise Eli and be a good father. It makes me feel like…' He trailed off and looked at their hands. 'I'll be holding onto that feeling for a long time. But you don't deserve to go through this. You deserve more.'

She didn't try to hide the tears burning in her eyes.

'Why?' she asked hoarsely. 'Why do I deserve more?'

'I just told you.' He paused. 'You steady me.'

'What does that matter when you don't want me?'

'What?' His voice was rough. 'Of course I want you.'

'You had me.' She shrugged. 'But your past was more important than your present. Or your future.'

'That's not fair.'

'No,' she agreed. 'But it is true.'

There was a long, drawn-out silence before he cupped her face.

'I'm sorry,' he whispered, leaning forward, kissing her forehead. 'It's not you.'

She couldn't believe him, but when he moved back, she lifted her hands and gripped his face.

'A goodbye?' she asked impulsively. Desperately.

His gaze dipped to the lips she'd wet with her tongue. It slid to behind her to check on Eli, then it heated and he nodded.

When their lips met, fireworks shot to the sky.

She resisted the urge to take and take so she could fill the part of her she knew would be empty once he left. She ignored the greed to make more memories, too. Hot ones, sweet ones, a combination. She ignored it all and focused only on the moment. On his mouth moving against hers.

As it always did, his kiss awoke parts of her body reserved only for him. The thrill of it started low in her belly, spreading out. Spreading down. She wanted to invite him into her house, to entertain her body now that it was awake. But she knew they shouldn't. So she settled for the warmth spiralling out in her abdomen. For the way her heart *pitter-pattered* in her chest.

She opened her mouth to his tongue, inviting it to plunder and claim. It did neither. It teased and it offered. It tangled with hers, gifting her memories with its sweetness, its gentleness anyway. Her breath was swept away with it; with the thought of that precious gift. Her body was swept away with the skimming of his fingers over her neck, her shoulders, the sides of her breasts.

She gasped when skimming became gripping. When his hands dug into the flesh of her backside and brought her against the hardness of his body. Her breath was already gone, but that took away any remnants there might have been. And feeling him against her, understanding the immensity of what she'd lost, caused her to pull back and pant for air.

'Inside. Now.'

The words had barely been said before he left her embrace and pushed the pram to her front door. Then he was back in front of her, lifting her up and finding her mouth again. She could stay like this for ever, she thought, his steps sending vibrations through her hyperaware body. Their mouths could be fused for all eternity. She would gladly sacrifice convenience for the sake of it. If it meant she could always feel this full, this light, this vibrant, she would sacrifice any convenience.

He fumbled with the doorknob, and she realised it was locked. Wrenching her mouth from his, she told him, 'Back pocket.'

He smiled and she kissed him again, because, damn it, that smile was sexy and confident and he was the hottest man she'd ever kissed. His hands slid into her back pocket, lingering, kneading, then he drew out the key and fumbled with the lock this time. But when the door swung open, he didn't move.

She moaned into his mouth, encouraging him, before she realised he'd stopped kissing her back.

'Hunter, what—?'

She stopped when his eyes shifted to behind her. Though she had no idea what she would see, she squeezed her thighs, gesturing that he put her down. He did, and she shifted so that she was in front of him when she turned, determined to cover the part of his body that hadn't yet got the memo that they'd been interrupted.

'Summer,' she said when she finally got her senses back. She was relieved it was her sister. It could have been worse. 'I didn't know you were back from the lodge.' She put her weight on her right leg. 'I…er…didn't see your car.'

'Wyatt dropped me off on his way into town,' Summer replied, coolly amused. 'I thought I'd spend some time with my sister, but clearly that was—' her eyes shifted to Hunter; the amusement deepened '—presumptuous.'

'Nonsense,' Autumn said, voice strangled. 'Hunter was just leaving.'

She turned and gave him an apologetic look. His expression was unreadable.

'Thank you,' he said. 'For everything.'

She clenched her hands to keep from reaching out to him. 'You're welcome.'

'I guess I'll see you…around.'

'Yes,' she said weakly.

'It was nice seeing you again, Summer,' Hunter said, politely.

'Same here.'

He nodded at Autumn before dragging the pram away and heading back to his car. She gave a small wave when he was done strapping Eli in, and worried when she felt as if she were waving off a part of herself. She was still staring long after he'd driven away, even when Summer came to stand beside her and put an arm around her shoulders.

'Was that a baby with Hunter?'

Autumn gave a hoarse laugh. 'Would you believe that you imagined it?' She leaned her head on Summer's shoulder, letting herself take the comfort her sister was offering.

'What happened?' Summer asked after a moment.

'A lot,' Autumn admitted. She straightened. 'If I'm going to tell you, let's go inside. I'd rather die of mortification inside my home than outside it.'

Summer laughed, and they went inside. Her sister headed directly to the kitchen. Autumn followed slowly, sliding onto the kitchen stool and plopping her head into her hands. She watched as Summer made them both a cup of tea, and would have been amused at the irony of it if humour hadn't been the last thing she was willing to feel.

Less than two weeks earlier, Autumn had done the same thing for Summer. Making her a cup of tea after Summer had seen her ex-husband, Wyatt, for the first time in two years. Tea solved a multitude of sins. It had been their philosophy long before they were old enough to indulge in it. She felt a surge of gratitude for her sister and their relationship, but guilt followed closely. She'd been jealous of Summer her entire life and her sister hadn't deserved it. Because of it—because of her own selfish feelings—Autumn hadn't been there for her sister when Summer had needed her.

Autumn sank her head down so that her chin rested on the kitchen table.

When Summer turned around, she laughed sympathetically.

'Oh, no, is it that bad?'

'Yes,' Autumn mock sobbed as she rested her forehead on the counter now, making the words come out muffled. 'Everything is too complicated and I can't—'

'Wind,' Summer interrupted, using the nickname she'd given Autumn when they'd been children. An ode to the season she'd been named after and the fact that Summer believed her to be a whirlwind of goodness. Autumn almost laughed. 'I can't hear what you're saying.'

She forced her head up. 'Sorry. I was saying that everything is complicated and I'm *tired.*'

Now Summer's laugh sounded sparkling. 'You sound exactly like I did at the lodge. In fact,' she said, picking up the two mugs and handing Autumn hers, 'after I told Wyatt I loved him, I also said I was tired.'

Autumn regarded her sister sullenly. 'And now you're well rested and it's all sunshine and roses.'

'I wouldn't say well rested...' Summer's eyes twinkled, and she ducked when Autumn threw a dishcloth at her. 'I'm sorry, I'm sorry.' She laughed. 'I couldn't resist!'

'Try harder.'

Summer straightened her face, then sobered for real. 'Okay.' She leaned over the counter, sipped from her tea. 'Tell me what's happening.'

'No.'

Summer tilted her head. 'I'm sorry?'

'I can't tell you what's happening until I apologise.'

She set her cup down, took Summer's out of her hands before threading their fingers together.

'I'm so sorry about what you went through, Sun,' she

said, using the nickname she'd given Summer in response to the one Summer had given her. 'I'm sorry I didn't see what it really was and push you to tell me more.' Her throat got tighter and tighter as she spoke, so her last words were said in a thin voice. 'I should have seen it. I should have suspected it. I was—'

'Wind,' Summer interrupted. 'You don't have to apologise. You didn't do this to me.'

'I didn't see it either.'

'Because I hid it. That was the entire point.'

'But I should have—'

'Why?'

'I'm your sister. Your twin sister.'

'Fraternal twins.'

'As if that makes a difference.'

Summer angled her head in acceptance. 'Doesn't change that you didn't do anything wrong.'

'I should have known.'

'Why do you keep saying that?' Summer asked. 'How should you have known? Why should you have known?'

'I told you—'

'That's not it though. Sisters don't know everything about one another.' She dipped her head. 'Have you told me everything about you, Wind? I think not. Or I wouldn't have opened the door to you and your ex-boyfriend making out. Hot and heavy, I might add.'

Her cheeks flushed. 'These are...recent occurrences.'

'Are they?' Summer's voice was dry.

Autumn sighed. 'If I were a better sister, I would have known.'

'Ah, so that's it.' Summer picked up her tea. 'Missing this makes you feel inadequate.'

She blinked. 'How did you know?'

'I'm your sister,' Summer said, sticking out her tongue. 'Honestly though? I've seen you try, all your life. But no one expects you to be perfect.'

'Mum and Dad do,' Autumn said softly, the words slipping from her lips.

'What?'

She swallowed, tracing a finger along the outline of the mug. 'I've spent a good portion of my life trying to be perfect so they would notice me.'

'I... *What?*'

She lifted her shoulders.

'Autumn, I had no idea.'

'Why would you? It's what I've always done.'

'But why didn't I—?' She broke off. 'Okay, first off, this feels like we've done a role reversal. I'm wondering why I haven't seen any of this and you're telling me it's okay that I didn't.' She shook her head. 'Second. Wind, why do you think they don't see you? They love you.'

'Of course they love me. They just prefer you.'

'Why do you say that?'

'You were the one who was groomed to take over from Dad. They always asked about you. Everyone preferred you.'

There was a shocked silence. Summer shook her head.

'Dad groomed me because I had more of an aptitude for the business.' Summer tilted her head. 'Though he probably regrets that now.'

'Because you didn't end up there?'

'No,' Summer said with a small frown. 'Because you've got a successful business and you did it without much help.'

'He gave me the start-up cash,' she pointed out.

'He doesn't care about money,' Summer said with a wave of her hand. 'He cares about skills. Abilities. Look at how he groomed Wyatt. Wyatt had nothing but skill and ability. Money isn't a factor for Dad.'

Autumn wondered what it meant that Hunter had said the same thing.

'I think Dad had a very narrow idea of who you were,'

Summer said contemplatively. 'He saw your talent in the kitchen and thought you'd only be good at that. I'm sure he expected your bakery to be a small operation, not the juggernaut it currently is.'

'Wait—did you just say Dad saw my talent in the kitchen?'

'Yeah. Mum and Dad. Why else do you think they kept asking you to create things for their parties? They wanted to show you off.'

'But—'

'And if you're talking about Mum asking about me, it's because she was worried about me. Trust me,' she added with a shake of her head, 'parents don't talk about their easy children as much as they do their harder ones.'

She squeezed Autumn's hand.

'Then you said everyone prefers me?' There was a pause. 'Please don't tell me you're talking about Timothy Rogers again?'

Autumn wanted to shake her head, but she ended up nodding instead. Summer rolled her eyes. 'He was an immature jerk for asking you to the dance. Probably still is. Now, what else do I need to poke holes into so you'll believe you're a formidable woman?' she asked with a wicked smile.

Autumn tried to smile back, but her sister's claims had her head spinning and nothing she wanted to do with her face seemed to be happening.

It was strange to hear Summer's account of her life. Strange—though that didn't feel like the right description—how Autumn had used the same experiences Summer had positively recounted as negative reflections on her character. She'd had a fear and fed it so often with examples she'd framed with blinders on that it had grown and taken over her life. Her relationships. Her views of family.

A clear example of it was her bakery. She'd been so disappointed that she hadn't been chosen to run Bishop

Enterprises that she didn't see the support her father had given her with the bakery. She hadn't even allowed herself to see that things had turned out exactly the way they should have. She had her dream job. The bursts of creativity she had while designing her pastries or a wedding cake fed her soul. Running the café fed her mind. And she was damn good at them both.

Seeing that, saying it, even in her mind, loosened a knot in her stomach. Her hand lifted to it, acknowledging it. That knot had been there as long as she could remember. Would it change anything now that it was gone?

'I'm sorry you had to deal with all this alone,' Summer said quietly. 'I know what it's like. It sucks,' she added without skipping a beat.

Autumn laughed. 'Well, we are twins. I suppose that means we'll share the same experiences.' She hissed out a breath. 'You don't have to apologise. This isn't your fault.'

'Ditto.'

'You know,' Autumn said after a moment, 'I used to feel so invisible around you.'

Summer's cheek lifted in a half-smile. 'Funny. I used to feel that way about you.'

'You did?'

'Not to the extent that I'd try to get Mum and Dad's attention,' Summer clarified. 'But I remember thinking, not that long ago, actually, how much better you would have dealt with it if you'd been the one to find out about the affair. If Dad had asked you to keep it a secret.'

'I would have done the same thing you did.'

'That's not true.' Summer shook her head. 'You know how to deal with things instinctively. You don't struggle. You just…do.'

She saw the truth in that. Linked it to what Hunter had said about giving people what they wanted. Before, she'd seen it as a flaw, but maybe it was a strength.

'Why didn't you tell me?' Autumn asked.

'Because *I* don't know how to deal with things instinctively,' Summer said with a smirk. 'I struggle.'

'How did you think you were dealing with it?'

'Poorly. I knew that. I wanted to tell you, but I suppose…' Summer sighed. 'I was trapped by my own fears. It meant I needed to trust someone and I wasn't sure I could after what happened with Dad.'

'But that's in the past now, right?' Autumn prompted. 'Because you know you can trust me.'

'I didn't even know you were struggling,' Summer replied softly. 'I should have.'

'The point was that you didn't.'

Summer smiled. 'I'm getting there. I'll get there.'

Autumn reached out and squeezed her hand. 'Me, too.'

She felt better now that Summer knew everything. Not having to hide it any more took some of the pressure off. She was glad they were on the same page about what had happened to Summer, too.

She shook her head. 'We were idiots for keeping this from each other.'

'Yeah.'

'But we're okay?'

'Of course.'

'And you and Wyatt are…'

Summer's face turned dreamy. 'Great. It's nice to talk with someone you love.'

'I know.'

'With Hunter?'

'With you,' she said dryly.

'Oh.' Autumn smiled when Summer's expression turned disappointed. 'Well. I'm here whenever you want to talk.'

'Thank you.'

They drank their tea in silence. When Autumn finished hers, Summer let out an impatient breath.

'I'm here if you want to talk about Hunter, Wind.'

'I don't.'

'You're just going to let me wonder about that kiss—
and that *baby*—without getting details?'

She studied her sister's face, and decided she'd kept se-
crets for far too long. 'It's his baby. He's a father.'

'What?'

Pleased with the reaction, Autumn began to tell her
sister the story.

CHAPTER FOURTEEN

IT HAD BEEN three hours since Hunter had dropped Autumn off and experienced the kind of embarrassment he actively tried to avoid. But that wasn't the reason he was still thinking about it.

He could still taste and feel her. It was probably good that they hadn't been able to make love. He could only imagine how his body would have betrayed him then. How the memories would have killed him. But at least he was thinking about something other than Eli's cystic fibrosis test the next day.

It was happening the next morning, ten o'clock, and his stomach was churning from the worry. If his son was sick, he knew what kind of life Eli would have. The growth problems, the stomach issues, the respiratory symptoms, the daily therapy. Depending on how sick he got and how quickly, he'd be in and out of hospital. They'd have to be extra careful in public areas because he'd be more susceptible to germs. He'd never have a life like a normal kid, and Hunter would have to watch his child suffer in the same way that Janie had. And his length of life might be just as short...

He closed his eyes against the pain.

Opened them when the doorbell rang.

He wasn't expecting any visitors. The only person who would arrive at his house unexpectedly—his mother—was in Greece. He swung open the door, distracted by his thoughts, and blinked.

'Autumn?' he asked, shock tightening his throat. 'What are you doing here?'

Her eyes went from his head down to his toes. He resisted the urge to shuffle his weight. He was wearing an old T-shirt, track pants and no shoes. He'd changed as soon as he got home, figuring he'd spend the day walking Eli up and down the house and wanted to be comfortable. Since it was his normal work-from-home outfit, she'd seen him in it countless times before. So why did he feel naked now?

'You can change, right?'

'Yeah. Wait. What's happening?'

She walked past him, giving him a whiff of her perfume. He shut the door before the wind could take it away, desperate—slightly ashamed—to have something of her.

'I'm here to distract you.'

'What? Why?'

'I was being selfish earlier,' she said, avoiding his eyes. 'I shouldn't have left. I said I'd help and then I got into my own head—'

'Autumn,' he interrupted. 'You don't have to do this if it's hard for you.'

She stepped forward and cupped his face. 'I know.' She stayed there long enough for the heat to scar his face, then stepped back. Took another step back, too, as if the first hadn't taken her far enough away. 'You've dealt with losing Janie alone for far too long. Your mother leaves every year and your father's never really been here. With Eli...' She shook her head. 'You don't have to be alone with Eli.'

He opened his mouth, but nothing came out. He hoped she saw his answer, his thanks, on his face. The way she blushed, bit her lip and looked down at her boots made him think she did.

She looked cute, he noticed, though it was the wrong time to. She wore ankle boots and a white summer dress. A denim jacket hung over her handbag at her side. He wanted to throw her over his shoulder and take her to his bedroom.

'I don't know what to say,' he rasped. From emotion and desire.

'You don't have to say anything.' She looked around. 'Where's Eli?'

'Sleeping in his room.'

Her eyebrows rose. 'Without you having to drive some-where first?'

'Yeah.' He ran a hand over his head. 'I think he's as ex-hausted as I am. Now that I'm not freaking him out, he's probably feeling it.'

'Or maybe you're finding your rhythm as a father.'

He angled his head, accepting her comment though he didn't believe it. It had been five days, four of which had gone poorly. He'd need every one of the days before Grace got back to find his rhythm, and then he'd need a new rhythm.

An unexpected panic fluttered in his chest.

'How are you going to distract me?' he asked, to dis-tract himself.

'It's a surprise.' She threw her jacket and handbag on the couch. 'We have to wait until Eli wakes up, so if you want to do some work or catch a nap yourself, feel free.'

'I don't think I'd be able to sleep.'

'So do something you haven't been able to in the past week,' she suggested.

'Like what?'

She shrugged, went into the kitchen and began opening his cupboards. He had no idea what she was looking for, but when she looked at him, she quirked a brow.

'You can't think of one thing?'

'Gym,' he said, flushing. 'I'll go to the gym.'

She waved a hand and continued her search, and he moved to his home gym. His muscles ached by the time he was done. Probably not his best idea considering he didn't know what Autumn had planned for the night, but he had no choice. It allowed him an escape from his thoughts. An added bonus was that it helped him not to go into the kitchen and try to get Autumn to help distract him. Heaven knew where that would lead. He did, too, and he *liked* it.

Yeah, the gym was better.

When he walked into the kitchen after his shower, he

got a waft of sweet warmth that immediately made his mouth water. His eyes widened when he saw the batch of cookies on the table, before they settled on Eli, who was gurgling contentedly in his bouncer. There was a clank beneath the counter and then Autumn was standing, setting a brand-new batch on a cooling rack.

'Oh, hey,' she said, smiling sweetly. 'I didn't hear you come in.'

He grunted, annoyed at what her smile did to him.

'I hope you don't mind that I kept busy,' she continued, as if he hadn't been grumpy with her, gesturing to the cookies. 'Two batches of chocolate chip and peanut butter cookies. I know they're your favourite.'

'Where did you find the ingredients?'

'The shop. You didn't have anything,' she said indignantly, 'and Eli was still fast asleep, so I ran out.' She brushed a curl from her face. 'He hasn't been awake for that long, but I have fed and changed him already. I also packed a bag. He's good to go. Are you?'

His gaze had been following the curl she'd brushed away, which had joined the rest in a wild halo of hair around her face.

'Am I okay?' he asked, feeling a little jittery.

She tilted her head in question. He dipped his own, gesturing to his clothes. Her eyes sparkled.

'You're fine. We're not doing anything that requires a certain dress code.'

'You never know.'

'You do know. I just told you.'

'You said that the last time, too,' he replied darkly.

Her laugh was light and happy. 'Are you still mad about that? It was a social media challenge, Hunter. No one cared about your T-shirt and shorts.'

'If I'd known you were going to film me, I would have put more thought into the outfit.'

'But you didn't, and look how well it turned out!' she exclaimed. 'I promise there'll be no filming tonight.'

He narrowed his eyes.

'And you're dressed perfectly appropriately for what we're doing.'

'Which is?'

'Nah uh, you're going to have to wait and see.' She came around the counter, her eyes fluttering over his jeans and shirt. 'You look nice,' she said, sincerely.

'So do you.'

She smiled. 'Look at us. Two nice-looking people going out for the evening.'

His mouth half curved. 'Let's go before you say something stupider.'

Or before *he* responded in a stupid way. Like kissing her.

She took her keys from the counter, then walked back into the kitchen and checked that the oven was off. As she did, he stole a warm cookie, savouring the delicious heat of it. He finished that one, put a second in his mouth before retrieving Eli's pram and putting the go bag in it. He finished eating and took Eli out of the bouncer.

Autumn was watching them when he turned, and she offered him a small smile. Then she covered the cookies with a net he had no idea whether he'd owned or she'd bought. She was leading him to his car not long after since Eli's car seat was already in it, a cookie in her own hand.

He didn't recognise the route she drove. But he took advantage of the moment and Eli's quiet gurgles to close his eyes. He wouldn't sleep, but his mind was too tired to think. For the remainder of the trip he was able to rest, only opening his eyes when the car stopped.

'Here we are.'

'Mini golf?'

'Putt-putt,' she corrected.

He just looked at her.

She wrinkled her nose. 'You're not thrilled with this?'

'I'm…surprised.'

'Why?'

'I don't know. I thought you'd do something less…' He trailed off, unsure of what he wanted to say.

'Well, it's no more, no less,' she said after a moment. 'It is what it is.'

He smiled. 'That made no sense.'

'No,' she agreed with a sniff. 'But it's too late to take it back. Come on.'

They got out of the car, and she gestured in front of her. 'Welcome to paradise, my lord.'

He laughed softly, though he agreed with her assessment. The mini golf course had been built on a beachside promenade that stretched between Mouille Point and Sea Point in Cape Town along the Atlantic Seaboard. There were children screeching in the park nearby, and couples already playing on the large course. People jogged and walked along the beachside paving; others sat on the benches on the lawn, enjoying the view.

The sounds all mixed with the waves crashing against the side of the promenade, flowing over and crashing against rocks that stood out in the ocean. The sun was beginning to lower in the sky. It added oranges and yellows to the blue, and with the wind gently blowing, it did feel like paradise.

'Thank you, milady,' he replied, turning towards her. She quirked her eyebrow, asking if it would suffice for the evening's entertainment. He nodded.

'Then let's go get some tickets.'

The game went by faster than he expected. It could have been because he was dividing his attention between Eli and watching Autumn. She was much more interesting than trying to earn points, though he tried, urged on by his competitive nature. But as soon as his turn was over, he'd pay attention to her again.

He liked that she was talking too much. It meant that she was nervous, or trying to distract him. Or both. It pleased him immensely. She chatted about the bakery and how they'd had to decline requests for wedding cakes because they were stretched so thin.

'I know I have to hire more people,' she said, bending over her putter. The wind swept past them, lifting the skirt of her dress slightly. He purposefully averted his gaze. 'But that feels like a task that'll keep me from doing more.'

'It will for a while.' He watched her ball slide past the hole. 'You're busy. Successful. You need more support. Doing it now will help sustain your business long-term.'

'You sound like my father.'

He stiffened, remembering how their conversation had gone the day before. 'He knows business.'

'He does.' She considered her ball thoughtfully. 'So do you. It's probably time I listened.'

He blinked. 'Yeah,' he said slowly, wondering how far he could push it. 'In fact, you're probably in a good position to think about expansion.'

'As in, expanding the bakery itself?'

'As in, expanding the brand,' he replied, relaxing as amusement spread through him. 'Different branches. Or having the wedding cakes be a separate business to the everyday of the bakery and café. Different staff, and you can oversee them all. That kind of thing.'

She didn't reply, and they continued their game. He won, though he was fairly certain it was because she was distracted. Since it distracted her from noticing him watching her, too, he didn't mind.

He couldn't help himself. His mind, his heart were demanding he memorise every inch of her face. They were afraid the chances to do so would be ending soon, though he had no evidence to prove that. He only had a feeling in his gut. A growing, pulsing feeling that felt very much like the panic he'd experienced earlier when he'd thought about Grace returning.

So he'd remember how she tilted her head from side to

side as she considered the ball. When she didn't, he knew she was thinking about what he'd said. He noted how she'd suck in her lip when she was waiting for him to finish his turn. How the wind blew her curls around her face; how she brushed at them without a second thought. And the smile on her face whenever she checked on Eli. Protective and content. As if Eli were hers.

As if he were *theirs*.

Hunter had meant it when he'd told her that: he did wish he'd conceived Eli with her. Seeing her take care of Eli—of him, too—though it had only been the last two days, had awoken that fierce need inside him. It almost overshadowed his fears; but thinking that immediately caused them to flare again. They pointed out that his genetic code hadn't changed. That his reluctance to have a broken family was still there.

The possibility of losing her was there, too. Then again, that seemed to follow him around regardless of the nature of their relationship. What else could that feeling in his gut be? He was dreading the moment they were no longer in each other's lives. It seemed inevitable. Now he realised it always had been.

Nausea rolled in his stomach as he thought about it. He didn't want to not have access to her beauty, her quirks. She drew his attention. Hell, she drew everyone's attention. He saw the way people looked at her. Something deep and primal would beat inside him every time he noticed their interest. Unashamedly, he'd look at them until they saw him watching, enjoying it a little too much when they scurried off in embarrassment.

As he thought of it, his heart twisted on itself. Begged him to make the aching stop. To leave her behind before she could leave him.

The thought paralysed him for a full minute. Even when his body had started moving again after they'd got drinks and food from a nearby vendor, his mind felt frozen.

'What's wrong?' she asked. She'd finished her hot dog already, and was now holding Eli, patting him on the back since he'd started to get fussy.

'Nothing.'

'Hunter.'

He finished his hot dog. Took a long sip from his soft drink.

'Tomorrow.'

It was all he said.

'Do you want to postpone it?' she asked tentatively. 'Maybe a bit longer after the anniversary—'

'No,' he cut her off. 'The sooner we know, the better.'

'Of course,' she murmured. Silence stretched, then she said, 'What was the worst part of Janie's illness?'

He stared at her as his mind went from frozen to gushing water. He got up, threw the empty can in the bin. Sat back down and threaded his fingers together.

Those days seemed like such a long time ago. A different life. A different version of himself. He'd been so scared of Janie dying. He'd done everything in his power to keep her alive. And then she'd died anyway.

The same thing could happen to Eli.

'Thinking she'd get better.'

She lowered to the bench slowly, still patting Eli's back as she rocked back and forth.

'I'm sorry.'

'You were right,' he said, eyes on the sky and its rainbow of colours. 'I can't let go of what happened to Janie. It'll always be something I carry with me.'

'No one's asking you to let go of it,' she replied, surprise clear in her tone. '*I* wasn't.' Her hand stilled on Eli's back, then the patting continued. 'The past is important to who we are. I just don't believe it should be more important than who we can be. Or what we can have.'

He didn't reply. She exhaled.

'I see now how hypocritical this was of me,' she said. 'I expected you to want to work through your past when I didn't want to work through mine. Not let go of,' she clarified, 'but…acknowledge, at least. The best-case scenario is to work through it, I guess.'

'What was I supposed to acknowledge?' he demanded quietly as his stomach burned. 'That my sister's illness made me afraid of having children in case they got sick? That my parents' fighting made me worry that that would happen in my relationships, too?' His throat was tightening now. 'I did that. I told you that.'

'Yet I only found out yesterday that her illness and your father's response to it made you afraid you'd be a bad father. Or that there's a part of you that blames yourself for her death.'

He blinked. She continued more gently.

'You said the worst part of taking care of Janie was hoping she'd get better. Last night you said you were scared of her dying.' She tightened her hold on Eli. 'I think you believe you could have done something to make her better.' Her voice softened. 'Or to keep her from dying.'

She was right. That was the fear rattling around inside him. The fear he couldn't identify.

'And we never fought, Hunter,' she added. He thought she might be wanting to distract him from that bombshell. 'If we argued, we resolved it quickly enough for you not to worry we'd end up broken.'

'But we did,' he said automatically.

'Because there was one thing we couldn't resolve. This.'

'You don't understand.'

'Exactly. That's my point.' Eli gave a little whine, as if sensing the tension. Autumn stood again. 'I did the same thing,' she told him. 'I never told you I felt as though I had to please people. My entire life I felt second best to Summer and it changed everything about me. *I* changed everything about me so I could feel like I was enough.'

He didn't understand how she could ever doubt that. And felt guilty that he hadn't seen as much of it as he should have.

'You are, Autumn. You're more than enough.'

Her lips curved. 'I'm trying to believe that. I can see that I should, anyway.' She paused. 'When we broke up, I didn't see it or believe it. I thought you thought I wasn't good enough to have a family with. He—' she nudged her shoulder forward, gesturing to Eli '—felt like proof of that.'

She continued before he could say anything.

'I also didn't see until recently that part of why I left was because I knew I'd always come second after your past, Hunter. You're not willing to move on.'

Surprise hit him square in the chest. 'I made you feel second best?' He shook his head. 'Because my sister died?'

'That's not what I said.'

'But you think it's a choice,' he ground out. 'That carrying this pain, this guilt is—'

He broke off when it all became too much. When he finally acknowledged the guilt. When his eyes burned, and his throat sharpened. He didn't like it. It felt too much like the vulnerability of the night before, and they were in public now. He couldn't cry in front of strangers.

'I know it's not a choice,' Autumn said, moving forward and shielding him against most people who were looking. 'Our break-up was because of my issues, too. Clearly. I was so focused on how inadequate I felt and the anger I had at my family for making me feel that way—' She broke off with a little breath. 'It hid the real issue, which is that I have low self-esteem.'

There was a pause, as if she couldn't believe she'd said it. Then her eyes met his.

'Maybe your anger at your father—and worrying about your genes and repeating your parents' relationship—is doing the same thing.'

'The guilt?'

She smiled at him sadly. 'I can't answer that for you, Hunter. But you don't have to figure it out now.' She looked down at Eli, then moved to pick up his bag. 'Come on, let's go. Your son is tired.'

CHAPTER FIFTEEN

HER CONVERSATION WITH Summer had reminded her how important it was to have support. She'd immediately thought about Hunter, and how his mother wasn't home and how Grace wasn't nearby. She knew he wouldn't ask Ted to come over and keep him company. She also knew that spending time alone with Eli would only remind him of what was coming the next day so she'd driven to Hunter's place.

She didn't need her mental voice to tell her it wasn't her responsibility to distract him. But she wanted to offer him support. She was his friend and that was what friends did. A lie, that voice had said, and she'd accepted it as such. She preferred not to think of the motivations for it.

Her plan had been putt-putt and dinner. It hadn't included the cup of coffee she was currently making them. Nor had it involved a conversation where she bore her soul and got nothing but turmoil in return. A part of her ached at that, though she wasn't sure what it had expected. A miraculous realisation of just how stuck he was in the past? And how selfish did it make her that that answer was yes?

'You know,' she said, because talking was better than thinking, 'that expansion plan is interesting. I bet I could ask my father for advice. It would likely bridge some of the gap.'

She walked over to the couch, handed him the coffee. When she reached down to the biscuits she had placed there earlier, she saw a significant portion of them already missing. She hid her amusement.

'That's a surprise.'

'I know,' she replied. 'But if I want to move away

from the anger, I need to acknowledge my mistakes.' She winced. 'That wasn't a dig at you.'

'I didn't think it was.'

She smiled. He smiled back.

And for the longest moment, it felt as if nothing had gone wrong between them.

'Do you think your father knows about this distance?' he asked, sipping from his coffee. The action looked deliberate.

'I don't know,' she admitted. 'Based on the conversation I had with Summer, I don't think so. None of them knew how I felt.'

'Neither did I.'

In that, she knew he was telling her there were things about her he hadn't known either.

'That was deliberate,' she answered. 'I didn't want you to know I felt inadequate. Partly because I didn't want you to notice it, and see all the flaws that feeling that way made me so familiar with. And partly because it in itself felt like a flaw. A weakness.'

'You felt like this throughout our relationship?'

She nodded. 'For most of my life.'

'How didn't I see it?' he asked accusingly; he wasn't accusing her though. Then he blinked and met her eyes. 'Have I been *that* focused on my own stuff?'

She didn't know how to reply. Another consequence of a lifetime of people pleasing was a desire not to hurt their feelings. But her silence told him what he wanted to know anyway, and he slid into his own thoughts, not drinking his coffee, not eating the biscuits.

She knew what he was feeling. She'd felt that way the night before, seeing him cry. The realisation that their relationship hadn't been as good as they'd thought before its end was jarring. The fact that the other person had been hurting and they hadn't seen it, painful.

It made her want to distract him again. But the idea she

had to do so was bad. Terrible. It would probably make him angry again. She took a moment to consider whether it was worth the risk. Her eyes swept his face—his tight, miserable expression.

Screw it.

She got up, got his phone off the counter. She searched for the relevant song on the Internet, connected to his speakers, and pressed Play. When it started, he looked up.

At least it was soft enough that she wouldn't wake Eli.

'What are you doing?'

'Teaching you how to do this properly,' she said lightly. 'It's been bothering me for ever.'

'You didn't seem to have a problem when you put it on the Internet.'

'No, I didn't,' she agreed. 'But that's because part of your appeal was how poorly you danced.'

A deep rumble sounded from his chest. With delight, she realised he'd growled at her. *An actual growl.* Fortunately, she wasn't stupid enough to let him see her amusement. Though she was tempted.

'Stand up,' she commanded him.

'No.'

'Fine,' she said, and began to do the ridiculous social media dance he hated right in his line of view.

He watched her without expression, even as she did the moves wildly, more ridiculously. When that didn't even make him smile, she began to improvise, adding in sounds and moves that grew more terrible as she went along. He didn't respond at all, and she narrowed her eyes, stopping.

'You don't find me entertaining?' she asked, offended.

'I do. Just not now.'

She didn't believe it. She was always, without fail, able to cheer him up. Even if for a moment. She blamed her next actions—her next terrible, *terrible* actions—on the unexpectedness of being unable to amuse him.

'Okay.' She kicked off her shoes, pulled off her socks. 'I guess I'm going to have to play dirty.'

'What are you doing?'

'What do you think I'm doing?' she asked irritably, throwing off her jacket. 'I'm distracting you.'

'You're…'

His voice faded when she pulled her dress over her head. His eyes widened, and his entire face contorted in surprise—then desire. She didn't bother taking off her underwear. It wasn't necessary, and she was pretty sure it would get her into more trouble than she was bargaining for if she did.

'Your pool is probably at the exact right temperature now, isn't it?' she asked nonchalantly, dragging open the glass doors that led out onto the patio and yard. She grabbed the baby monitor off the table, hoping Eli wouldn't wake up soon. 'I bet it is. Do you mind if I go for a swim?'

She directed the question over her shoulder. He was still sitting. Still staring. She almost laughed, grateful for her choice in underwear that evening. The red colour did wonderful things to her skin, and the lace accentuated the curves of the body she'd learnt to love.

He finally noticed her looking at him, and his Adam's apple bobbed as he shook his head.

She kept her smirk for when she turned around, placing the baby monitor onto the grass before diving into the pool. The water was a shock of cool at first, and her body braced against it before she relaxed and surfaced. When she did, she realised it was pleasant, as she'd predicted.

She kicked her legs, pushing a hand against her curls to get them out of her face. She would regret wetting them so late in the evening later, when she got into bed and realised the thickness of them had retained most of the water. It was worth it though, she thought, remembering the look on Hunter's face as she'd stripped.

There was a splash and the water rippled. She stopped thinking about it.

He surfaced metres away from her. Close enough for her to see desire still simmering on his face; far enough that he couldn't do anything about it.

Yet.

'No,' she told him shakily. She cleared her throat. 'I mean, we're not going to make out in this pool.'

He smiled. 'I know.'

'You do?'

'Yes,' he replied solemnly. 'It would only lead to me making love to you on the ground next to the pool.' She gaped at him. 'If you're lucky, I'll take you to my bedroom.'

'I was going to offer to stay over tonight,' she said once she'd found her voice again. 'Now I'm thinking that might not be a good idea.'

His face sobered. 'Nothing will happen if you don't want it to.'

If you don't want it to.

He was putting this decision in her hands. She'd literally jumped on him earlier that day, and he was forcing her to make this decision. Which was probably why he'd done it, she thought, and almost smiled.

'I don't,' she said softly. 'It wouldn't be a good idea if we did.'

'You didn't think so earlier.'

'That was before I spoke with my sister.'

Summer had been sympathetic to her situation, but she'd warned Autumn to be honest about what she wanted—and what she could have. She wanted Hunter. She knew it. Was tired of lying to herself about it. But she also couldn't have him. Sleeping with him wouldn't make accepting that, facing it, any easier. So she wouldn't.

'Remind me to send her a thank-you note,' he said darkly.

'You should,' Autumn said with a laugh. 'Trust me, this is a path we shouldn't go down.' She swam closer to him, putting her hands on his shoulders. 'You know that, Hunter. It's easy to forget when we're like this. Alone in the dark. Under the night sky.' Her hands lifted to take his head. 'So we'll have to settle for this instead.'

'What's this?'

She plunged his head under the water before he could finish asking.

It was a while later that Eli's cries drew their attention. They'd worn themselves out playing in the pool like kids, and when they got Eli settled again, Hunter spread a blanket on the grass. She'd accepted a long-sleeved top from him, which was enough cover for her for the warm night. They lay under the stars, his head on her belly, her hands behind her head.

She was more relaxed than she'd been in a long time, regardless of the circumstances. Things seemed simpler in this moment, just as she'd told Hunter. So simple, she allowed herself to run her fingers through his hair.

'Hunter,' she said after what felt like for ever.

'Hmm?'

'Whatever happens tomorrow, you're going to be okay.'

He looked up at her. She brushed the hair from his forehead.

'Eli's going to be okay, too,' she added softly. 'Because he has you.'

'And you?'

She blinked against the heat that suddenly burnt in her eyes. 'And me.'

They'd fallen asleep on the grass. Some time during the evening, Eli's cries had woken them up. Hunter had waved Autumn off to bed, telling her he'd take care of Eli. It was a compulsion to do so, his mind and heart wanting to spend the last hours before the test with Eli in case it irrevocably changed their world.

He hadn't slept much after that, and the next morning he and Autumn got ready in silence. She wore the same clothes as the day before, and her hair was tied up this time. He missed the curls around her face, but he didn't say it. He didn't say much of anything until they reached the hospital. Even then.

He felt as if he were in a different world. Lights were brighter, people moved slower. The only thing that anchored him was Autumn, at his side. Then Eli, who he took and held and murmured to in comfort. He was comforting himself just as much as he was his son. More than, because the kid had no idea what was happening.

Hunter held Eli as they went through the testing. He'd been tempted to hand over the task to Autumn, but he remembered that his actions mattered. He wouldn't hand over his responsibilities to someone else, no matter how hard they were.

And this was hard.

First, they performed the sweat test so they could check the amount of chloride in Eli's sweat. Some kind of chemical was put on Eli's arm, before an electrical stimulation was applied to encourage his glands to produce sweat. He started crying immediately, and Hunter had to actively stop his fingers from clenching.

Autumn shifted closer. It helped soothe some of his tension, though he could feel hers. The next forty minutes were spent in the hell of waiting, of wishing they could take Eli's place. The kind of hell Hunter had experienced multiple times before with his sister.

And look how that ended.

He pushed away the unwelcome thought as they moved on to take blood samples. He'd asked that Eli be tested for the cystic fibrosis gene as well. He wanted Eli to have all the information when he grew up. Even hoped he'd be able to prepare Eli in a way his own parents hadn't done with him.

Eli screamed at that, too, and it was a relief when everything was over, though there was still a tense silence when they left the hospital building. It was punctuated only by throaty little moans Eli gave at sporadic intervals.

'That was…intense,' Autumn said when they got into the car. She sat in the back with Eli. It was almost routine now.

'Yes.'

'Are you okay?'

He shrugged, because in all honesty he didn't know. He called Grace on their way back to the house, speaking to her on Bluetooth and explaining how everything had gone. She'd asked him to call her right away, but he would have anyway. If the positions had been reversed, he would have wanted to know as soon as possible.

When they pulled into his driveway, they sat in silence for a moment, neither of them moving. Eli had fallen asleep, exhausted by the trauma of the day.

'I know you have to get back to the bakery,' Hunter started.

'I don't.'

'You don't?'

'I've taken the day off.' There was a short pause. 'Is it too late to get something to eat?'

More relief poured into his body as he gave a small laugh.

They agreed on takeaway Thai so they wouldn't have to drive again. Eli woke as they took him out of the car, and Hunter fed and changed him before settling him in his bouncer. He fussed, but apart from that, the rest of the day was remarkably easy.

By early afternoon, Eli had quietened enough that Autumn took him outside. When they saw how much he seemed to like it, Hunter spread out the blanket they'd fallen asleep on the night before again. He brought Eli's things closer, before going inside and getting himself and Autumn something to drink. Then he watched her.

She played with Eli effortlessly, as if she'd been made to do it, though he was too small to do anything but watch and occasionally gurgle and smile. He loved her excited squeal whenever that smile came. Loved when she told him the object of all her games was to elicit that smile. She eagerly offered to feed Eli, and his heart melted watching her do so.

He'd known long before then that he was still in love with her. He'd made excuses, told himself it wasn't relevant. But he didn't bother with that now. Now, he let the love touch the deep and damaged parts of his soul.

And was afraid of how much it healed them.

CHAPTER SIXTEEN

AUTUMN GOT THE call two days later at three in the afternoon.

'He's not sick,' Hunter said when she answered, forgoing the hello.

She put her hand to her mouth to prevent a sob from escaping. She was standing in front of the counter, visible to her entire bakery, and the small noise she made caught the attention of a few clients.

'Hold on,' she told Hunter.

She went into the kitchen to tell Mandy she was taking a break, ignoring the look of concern she got in return. She'd explain later, she thought, keeping her head down and walking out of the bakery. She only stopped when she was at her house. As she sat on the recliner at the patio, she let out a breath of relief. Hunter was still on the phone, waiting.

'I'm so glad to hear that,' she said shakily, not bothering to hide her emotion. 'You must be so relieved.'

'I am.' There was a pause. 'I really am.'

His voice cracked at the end. Autumn thought her heart did, too. She took an unsteady breath, then another, and another, until finally she couldn't fight the tears.

'Are you crying?' he asked.

'No.' She sniffled. 'Why would you think that?'

'No reason.'

She could hear the smile in his voice.

'Does this mean he doesn't carry the gene either?'

'We'll only get the results of that next week.'

'That's enough for now.'

'It is.' He waited a beat. 'Can you make a celebratory dinner?'

'I…'

She trailed off as logic caught up with her. Now that the testing was over, she had no real reason to go. She'd stopped lying to herself, which meant facing that they didn't have a friendship. They were clinging to each other because their relationship was special, but being Hunter's 'person' would only bring her heartache. She should wean herself off.

'I don't think that's a good idea,' she said with a constricted throat.

'Okay.'

The single word was ominous, and held more emotion than anything Hunter could have said.

'It's not... We shouldn't...' She let out a harsh breath. 'I'd have to leave now, Hunter,' she said lamely, settling for her professional responsibilities when the personal ones to herself didn't seem to be working. 'I can't leave closing up to Mandy again.'

'I understand.'

She closed her eyes. 'Do you?'

He didn't say anything.

'Hunter... I'm as relieved as you are about Eli not being sick.'

Which bothered her. She'd grown too attached to the baby. She wanted to say it was like those times when she'd been younger and pretended to be a mummy to whatever she could find. But she knew it was more than that. The emotion in her heart was too bright, too big to blame a game of pretence. Even more concerning was that she'd spent all of three days with Eli. Barely that. What would happen if she invested more time?

'I can't abandon my responsibilities,' she finished softly.

'We'll see you some other time, then.'

'Hunter—'

'I wanted you to know he wasn't sick,' Hunter interrupted. 'I didn't call to put you in a difficult position.' He paused. 'I didn't want you to worry.'

'I appreciate that. I really do.' Despite all of her logic about why she shouldn't get involved, the fact of it had her saying, 'Screw it. I'll be there.'

'What?'

'I'm coming to celebrate, Hunter.'

She wasn't sure how she knew he was grinning, but it had her grinning, too. And ignoring how, deep down, she knew she was making a mistake.

That one night of celebration morphed into something else altogether. Making that concession had led to making a million more. Autumn could blame no one but herself. She wanted to spend time with Eli and Hunter. Found herself drawn into the allure of their makeshift family. And all the while she knew she would pay the price for compromising on protecting herself.

She didn't think of that as she spent weekends at Hunter's, playing with Eli. Enjoying how he was growing; how he'd begun to trust them. After a month, she and Hunter had settled into their own routine. Autumn had found herself giving more responsibility to Mandy at work, and had finally hired additional staff to assist with the bakery's demands. She spent all her free time with Hunter and Eli.

Hunter had relaxed since Eli's test results had come back negative, more so when the blood test had confirmed Eli wasn't a carrier of cystic fibrosis either. He'd taken the relief of that news and channelled it into getting to know his son. He changed nappies and heated milk like a pro, though her favourite thing was listening to him speak to Eli about his work. As if the little boy could understand and help his father with the problem of renewable energy.

Since she made fun of Hunter because of it, Autumn would never admit that sometimes she wondered if Eli did understand. When his big brown eyes were so intent on what Hunter was saying. Or when he occasionally 'talked back' in the form of burps or gurgles. Hunter clearly enjoyed it when his son did those things, and was as attentive and intuitive a father as Autumn had always known he would be.

If she'd spent any time thinking about it, she could have anticipated how witnessing Hunter's transformation into a parent would make her feelings for him grow. But she was too distracted by playing house. Even as she began to see it, to feel it, she resisted it. Resisted how sexy, how enthralling she found watching him take care of Eli was.

She ignored the danger, too. Autumn knew it long before Summer warned her.

'Wind, why are you doing this to yourself?'

'I'm not doing anything,' she said defensively. 'I'm... being a good friend.'

Summer snorted, sticking a fork into the cupcake she'd ordered at the bakery. Summer had told Autumn she ate a cupcake with a fork to keep from staining her fingers. Autumn had retaliated that it was a mark of a psychopath.

'Is that what you're lying to yourself with?' Summer asked. 'You're not his friend, Autumn. *You* told me that. And now you're co-parenting Eli?' Summer frowned, shook her head. 'What happens when Eli's mother gets back? When there's no reason for you to spend all your time around Hunter?'

Autumn didn't reply, though she met her sister's gaze. Summer's voice softened.

'What do you think is going to happen when he realises you're still in love with him?'

'I'm not—'

Summer silenced her with a quirked eyebrow.

'Okay, fine.' Autumn said, with a little huff. 'I know what I'm doing.'

Summer looked at her sceptically. Autumn was forced to agree. Because she really, really didn't know what she was doing. The last time she had, she'd told Hunter she needed space. Hours later, she'd been at his house.

A part of her was waiting for him to choose her. She knew she was waiting in vain. It was the same thing that had happened towards the end of their relationship. She'd waited and waited, her insides shrivelling up more and more as she'd realised he wouldn't choose her.

But they'd both changed, the waiting part of her offered. She could sense it in herself. She'd left some of the anger behind. Felt more of it fade as she allowed herself to acknowledge her gifts. As she set tentative boundaries for herself with people. Hunter had left his obsession with becoming like his father behind, too. He was also facing his grief, she thought, remembering the times he'd compared taking care of Eli to his experience with Janie.

It happened almost naturally, and they were almost always good memories. He didn't freeze at the mention of her name, though his stories usually ended with him getting a sad, distant look on his face. She would, without fail, lean over and brush a kiss over his cheek, then grab Eli's little arms and pretend he was speaking to his father. Hunter would laugh, and play with Eli, exactly as she'd intended. She wanted to draw him back to the present. To remind him he had something, someone to help with the pain.

Perhaps those changes in them had been the cause of her waiting. But the fact that she knew the outcome wouldn't change told her that she was fooling herself. More importantly, it had an annoying voice in her head asking if she had really changed when she was in the same position with the same man.

It asked the question as the weeks passed and she spent her free time with the Lee men. When her heart swelled to a million times its normal size every time she saw Hunter. As a rush of love and protectiveness flooded her whenever she saw Eli. And when seeing them together had her body going heavy with an emotion she had no words for, but instinctively knew was dangerous.

And then it happened.

The decline into coolness was gradual. Slow. At first, she'd thought nothing of the cancelled plans. She'd missed Eli and Hunter, but the bakery had been busy, so she had been, too. Something clicked in Autumn's head when he cancelled again though. And again, and again. When she hadn't seen them in a week, she knew.

She began preparing herself for what was coming.

It had happened without him realising it. One moment he'd been living his life, taking care of his son, enjoying the company of his person. The next he'd realised he was part of a family.

And he *loved* it.

The fear had happened as unexpectedly. Grace had mentioned on their daily video calls that she'd be seeing Eli in less than six weeks. *Six weeks.* His mind had taken the words and enshrined them; there had been nothing and no one that could distract him from it. Grace would be back soon. The life he'd settled into with his son and his person—his family—would soon be over.

All of it had shaken him so much he'd begun cancelling his plans with Autumn. First, he'd claimed he had the flu. Then, he'd stopped giving excuses at all. He didn't want to lie to her when he was bracing for what he knew was inevitable.

Loss.

It didn't matter that caring for his son had eased the burden of grief he still carried around about Janie. The helplessness he'd had no idea had contributed to his grief—his guilt—had faded because he *could* help Eli. He didn't claim to understand it, but being able to do things for Eli somehow made up for what he hadn't been able to do for Janie.

Perhaps it was that Eli could live the life Janie hadn't

been able to. And Hunter could be there for Eli in the way he'd always wanted to with Janie.

It felt…powerful.

But what did that matter if he was about to lose his son?

The fear built and built, until he could see no way around it. It was as if the barriers he'd fought to tear down were back and closing in on him. Unsurprisingly, the feeling had him driving to Autumn's bakery. He got there around seven, an hour after the store closed. The light was still on when he arrived, and he tapped against the glass when he tried the door and found it locked.

Autumn looked up from behind the counter. There was a pause before she walked over and opened the door.

'Where's Eli?'

'My mum.' He felt a wave of shame and guilt for not telling her. 'She came back on Tuesday.'

She searched his face, then nodded.

'I need ten minutes. We can talk after. Wait at the bench.'

She closed the door again. After a brief hesitation, Hunter went to the bench she was talking about. It was a few metres from the store, and afforded whoever sat there the stunning view Autumn had all to herself when she went home.

The two of them would often share meals at the bench when they'd been dating. If Hunter came over for the weekend, he'd work while she was in the kitchen and they'd take lunch there. Or he'd sit there for a moment of quiet, and she'd bring him coffee as they watched the blue sky, enjoying the barely perceptible buzz from the city.

Tonight, the sky was turning from light to dark blue. A pink hue courted the clouds, merging with the orange of the sun. In a few minutes, those colours would turn into a navy darkness, a stunning backdrop to the stars that would twinkle inside it. Hunter wondered what was wrong with him that he thought it romantic.

Ten minutes later, she showed up at the bench. She didn't sit. He rose, faced her. She didn't speak. Just shoved her hands into the knitted jersey she'd thrown over her unofficial uniform of all black.

'How did you know I wanted to talk?' he asked, hedging his way into a conversation he had no idea how to start.

'Easy. We haven't spoken in over two weeks. It's your usual MO.'

He frowned. 'No.'

She rolled her eyes. 'You're right. You didn't do the same thing after I broached the topic of marriage when we were dating. We saw each other every weekend, every week for two years, and then you stop coming around, calling, answering phone calls.' She added with a detached tone, 'For two weeks.' She shrugged. 'This is almost identical.'

'It's not the same.'

'Right.'

The word dripped with sarcasm. It put a rod in his spine. Poured petrol over an anger he hadn't known was there.

'Okay. You're right. But I was dealing with things.'

Her expression remained stony. An illogical part of him lit a match, held it over the petrol.

'You're not going to ask me what?'

Her lips pursed. It was the only sign that she'd heard him.

'Autumn,' he said through clenched teeth. 'I'm trying here.'

'No,' she said. 'You're not. You're here because you need me.'

He opened his mouth. Closed it. Frowned.

She gave a mocking little laugh and turned on her heel. She was almost back on the path to the bakery when he found his voice again.

'That's it?' he called, his legs pushing him forward. 'You tell me I need you but you *walk away* from me?'

She'd stopped walking, but she only turned when he said that. Her expression was still carefully blank, but her eyes were fiery with emotion. He took a perverse satisfaction in that.

'Yes.'

She turned again, took another step forward.

The match dropped and a fire ignited.

'I knew I'd lose you some day, too.'

She stopped again.

'I thought you were different.'

She turned, her eyes ice.

'You're blaming this on me.' It was a statement. She tilted her head. 'I shouldn't be surprised. You still don't want to face the real issue, do you?'

'This again?'

'Why did you come here tonight?' she asked. 'Was it because you realised we were playing at being a family and you wanted your pretend wife to fulfil your—' her lips curved mockingly '—physical needs?'

'Don't,' he growled.

'So that's going too far?' Her voice had lost its edge now. It sounded curiously empty. 'You were fine with accusing me of being the one to walk away. Not to forget how you're ignoring that I would have given anything for us to stay together. In fact, I contorted myself in so many ways to be who you needed that I gave you *everything*.'

He opened his mouth but she ploughed on.

'So what do you need this time, Hunter?' She took a step forward. 'What did you come here for?'

'I don't want to lose you,' he blurted out, the surprise of her words creating a compulsion inside him to be as honest. With himself, too.

'You came here because you don't want to lose me?' she repeated.

It was close enough to the truth. He nodded.

'Why would you think you'd lose me?'

'It always happens.' Each word exposed more of himself. He didn't like it. He couldn't stop it. 'When Grace returns, everything will change. I'll lose you, and I'll lose Eli. I'll lose the family we had. We'll end up broken and I can't—'

He broke off when it felt as though there were no more air in his lungs. As if a snake had curled around them, and had gone in for the kill. When he fought it off and regained his breath, he looked at her and choked out his next words.

'I don't want to lose another person I love.'

CHAPTER SEVENTEEN

THIS MAN. THIS infuriating, complicated, *broken* man. How could she be angry with him when he said that? When he told her he was afraid to lose her? When he all but admitted he loved her?

Half of her had already crumbled into itself, falling at his feet and promising to do whatever he wanted. The other half was still angry with him. Furious, actually, because he'd ignored her for two weeks and now he needed her.

She listened to the angry half, because the other half was the old Autumn and she'd vowed not to regress when she'd been preparing for this conversation. The angry half apparently had control over her legs, and they propelled her into moving again. She was certain she would fall apart from the tension between the two halves soon. From the tension between wanting him, but also wanting more than she would ever get from him.

She deserved more.

It was a significant realisation. But the new Autumn accepted that she deserved what she wanted. She no longer believed she had to mould herself into someone else to receive her parents' love. Or to have a future with Hunter. She'd earned that by being there for them, helping them, supporting them. Like when she'd been there for her parents after the affair and they'd wanted to be a family again. Like when Hunter had come to her after finding out he was a father.

All of those actions had come from her. Because she'd wanted to do them. Because she was a good person, damn it, and good people deserved to feel wanted. They deserved to have people in their lives who treated them as if they were enough.

She loved Hunter, but she knew, even after his admissions, that he wasn't one of those people. She knew it *because* of those admissions.

So perhaps he had lost her.

'Did you hear what I said?' he asked, following behind her.

Without answering, she switched direction. She'd been going back to her store, but she'd already locked up and put the alarm on. Her house keys were in her pocket, and her handbag was safe in the bakery until the next morning. Besides, she needed home. The home she'd built. The place she'd created for herself. She'd mourn losing the men she loved there.

She'd mourn the time she'd lost by trying to be someone else there, too.

'Autumn. Autumn, damn it!'

She stopped when he jogged in front of her, blocking her path. When she tried to pass him on the left, he merely shifted his body. She didn't bother trying to go to his right.

'Get out of my way.'

'Did you hear what I said?'

'I did.'

'You don't have anything to say to me?'

She considered it. 'Yes, I do. I'm proud of you.'

A short silence followed. It told her he was surprised. 'Why?'

'This is your real issue.'

Another silence. 'Did you know?'

'Only when you said it,' she replied honestly. 'But it makes sense.'

'How?'

'No,' she said with a shake of her head. 'I can't figure this out for you.'

He exhaled. 'You're right.' There was a pause. 'I guess the thing with Grace is pretty clear.' She didn't answer.

Thought it best that he work it out for himself. 'I'm scared I'm going to lose Eli when she gets back.'

'Haven't you spoken about custody yet?'

'We said we'd do it when she gets back.'

She moved her tongue against her inner cheek. 'You could broach the subject now. It would help you feel better.'

He didn't reply.

'Look,' she said impatiently, though it was at herself because, despite her resolution, she was helping him. 'A woman who reaches out to the father of her child so she can pursue a career that'll allow for a better future for her son doesn't sound like someone who's going to run off with your kid.'

'I'll bring it up the next time we talk,' he answered after a pause. 'But what if—?'

'Hunter,' she interrupted. 'Are we done?'

She felt his gaze on her. 'I *have* lost you, haven't I?'

'That's what happens when you're careless with things.'

'I wasn't careless,' he said. 'I was *careful*. You mean so much to me and I didn't want my baggage to ruin that. Us.'

'So you didn't fight for our relationship,' she said slowly as the realisations just about fell on top of her. 'You didn't try to work through your baggage because you were afraid to lose me even if you did.'

'I pushed you away because I thought it would be easier. A choice.'

'Why did you come back?'

'It wasn't easier. I…needed you. And as friends—'

'There was less of a chance you'd lose me,' she finished. 'A bonus was that you didn't have to face your past to keep me.'

'Yes.'

She studied him in the silence that followed. Though she couldn't see the features of his face perfectly, she knew them like the back of her hand. As if she'd carved them herself. As if she'd created them.

She'd spent so much time studying that face. When they were dating, she'd just look at him sometimes. She'd enjoy how handsome he was. She'd enjoy his broody quietness that somehow elevated the lines of his face into something so striking it stole her breath.

Almost as clearly, she knew his emotions. His admission had cost him. He wasn't used to the vulnerability. He was worried about Grace returning. About the family they'd created. He was scared of losing it. Of losing Eli. Of losing her. After losing Janie, the fear was overwhelming. Eli had forced him to face the grief that he'd been running from for years. He felt raw from it, as if it were still fresh.

She wished she could do something to make him feel better. But that would mean assuring him he hadn't lost her, or them. If she did that, she'd be putting herself second. She couldn't tell Hunter to face his issues if she didn't face hers. And she didn't only want to face them; she wanted to work through them. So she couldn't revert back to old habits. She had to put herself first.

She would give him a chance to help her do so.

'You're an incredible father, Hunter,' she said slowly. 'Better than even I thought you could be, and I knew you had it in you.'

His ragged breath told her how much that meant to him. She couldn't let him enjoy it.

'I loved seeing that. I loved being there with you and Eli. I loved our little family.' She waited the briefest moment. 'It was always going to be temporary though. Eli isn't my child. You and I are just friends. We were pretending.'

'What if we weren't?'

'Do you really mean that?' she asked seriously, ignoring the hope. 'You're willing to take that chance?'

He stepped forward, as if he meant to assure her of it, but she shook her head. She wasn't sure he could see it until he stopped.

'I don't want you to say yes because you're afraid of losing me. I want you to say yes because you've realised being with me is more important than that fear.'

She put a hand on his chest, memorising the broad strength of the muscles beneath her fingers. She felt him trembling as she moved her hand from left to right. As she settled it over his heart.

'I love you,' she whispered to him, looking up. 'I know you know that. I also know you love me, too. But…do you love me enough?'

'I—I do love you.'

'That isn't what I asked.' She paused. 'I need you to tell me you won't let your fears control your actions. I'm not saying they won't influence them. And I don't expect you to toss them aside and forget they were there. But you can't relegate me into the role of a friend because you're scared of losing me. You can't opt out of taking care of your son because you're afraid you won't be a good enough parent. I need you to try. To choose me, and our family.'

'You make it sound so easy.'

Her fingers curled into a fist at his chest. 'This is the second time I'm asking you to choose me, Hunter.' She steeled herself. 'I won't ask you again.'

'I can't just let go of the fears,' he rasped, his hand covering hers.

'So you keep saying.' She stepped away from him, folded her arms when her hand wanted to reach for the warmth of his again. 'But I've seen you do it for Eli. You didn't shy away from him during the testing even though I know you were scared.'

'I…'

His voice trailed off, his confusion clear. She would have been more sympathetic, more patient if she didn't feel her throat tightening. If she couldn't feel herself beginning to pay for her honesty. For her bluntness.

So she pushed.

'Can you choose me, Hunter?'

'Can you get over what I did?'

'I already have,' she said, immediately understanding what he was asking. Understanding that he was lashing out, too. Diverting. 'I was hurt, but Eli... How can I blame you for Eli?'

She almost laughed at the ridiculousness of it.

'You wouldn't let me say it before, but I'm sorry. I didn't do it because I didn't believe you were good enough.'

'I know.'

And she did. For once, she believed him. He'd helped her to see that.

Oh, the irony of it.

'I want to choose you,' he whispered.

'I know.'

'What if—?'

He never finished the question. She soon realised he wouldn't. He was too afraid of the what ifs.

If he couldn't choose her now, after she'd bared her soul and asked him to, he never would. It was time to let go.

'It's okay,' she said carefully. 'You don't have to do this any more.' She took another deep breath. 'You can focus on being a good father to Eli. Don't worry about me.'

She walked past him, only pausing because he'd reached for her hand and gently pulled her back.

'Please...don't do this. I can't lose you.'

'You can't choose me either.'

She pulled her hand from his and walked to her house, opening her door and shutting it again without looking back. She made sure the door was locked, then pressed her back against it. The sobs came then. Wracking her body as she slid down to the ground.

CHAPTER EIGHTEEN

ALL THINGS CONSIDERED, Hunter's mother had taken the news that she was a grandmother in her stride. As he'd told Autumn, it had helped that he'd gone in with the information that Eli wasn't sick. Abby Lee had been visibly relieved at that piece of news. She'd been less impressed at the news that Autumn wasn't Eli's mother.

'I still can't believe it,' Abby said, settling on the couch with a cup of tea a few days after Hunter and Autumn had had their big conversation. Fight. Whatever.

He grunted.

'She was the first person you told,' his mother continued as if he hadn't responded so rudely, 'and she's the only person besides me who knows.'

'I would have told you first if you hadn't been—' he hesitated '—out of the country.'

Abby studied him. 'You mean, if it hadn't been the anniversary of Janie's death,' she corrected softly. 'But let's be honest, boy, you always would have told Autumn first.' She paused. 'She should have been the mother of your child.'

'Mother.'

Abby gave him a sharp look. 'I see right through you, Hunter. You're devastated by whatever happened between you and Autumn last week.'

He shook his head, but didn't correct her.

'Is it because you're a father to someone else's child?'

'No.'

The simple answer had a ripple of complicated emotions going off in his chest. It didn't cause it though. The emotions had already been poised, waiting to be set off from the moment Autumn had asked him to choose her.

The moment he'd opened his mouth and lost his voice. His ability to be courageous.

'Well, if she could swallow that...' Abby's gaze was still sharp, though her voice softened. 'What happened?'

He was tempted to confess everything. He wouldn't have to carry the weight of it by himself then. After all, now that he didn't have Autumn to share his life with, he'd have to find someone else to confide in.

The thought sent off another ripple in his chest, though this time it was of pain. He clamped his lips shut and shifted forward on the couch, setting his own coffee on the table. Randomly, he wished for biscuits. It was another hole Autumn had left in his life. She'd made sure his house had been full of treats in the weeks they'd spent together.

Damn it, he missed her.

'It has something to do with Janie, doesn't it?' Abby asked suddenly. She was watching him, her eyes searching his face in that intense way mothers had.

He frowned. 'I don't... No.'

'You're lying.'

'Yes,' he said after a moment. 'I lost her.'

'We lost her,' Abby said softly. 'I sometimes wonder what she'd be like now.'

'Stubborn.'

'Breaking hearts.'

They grinned at one another. It lasted longer than Hunter thought it would, and when it was over, it didn't feel as heavy as he'd expected. The consequence of sharing, he thought. Of ignoring barriers.

He considered it a moment longer, then said, 'I'm scared, Mum. I'm... I'm always scared.'

'About what?'

He told her. About his fears of turning into his father. Of being a bad father. Of having a family. He told her about how guilty he felt because of Janie. How afraid he was that he'd lose more people he loved. About his fears for when Grace got back.

He told her about how he'd lost Autumn because of those fears. He'd missed her pain, too obsessed with his own. How it was a pattern since he'd put his own feelings first when he'd found out about Eli, too. How he needed her, but had been paralysed when she'd asked him to choose her.

The words spilled out as if he'd been put under a spell. It didn't help that his mother sat patiently, listening without disruption. Her expression was unreadable, her posture relaxed.

There was a long silence when he was done, and nerves exploded in his chest, his mind racing with the possibilities of what she might be thinking.

'Have you been carrying this since Janie's death?'

'Probably before. It wasn't the most important thing then.'

Abby let out a breath. 'I have a lot of things to say about this. I'll say only a few of them now because they're important, and then we'll move on.' She set her tea down. 'You shouldn't have had to take as much responsibility for your sister as you did.'

'Mum—'

'No,' she interrupted him. 'Let me say this. I was overwhelmed and things with your father...' She exhaled. 'I'm sorry, Hunter. Janie wasn't your responsibility. And you were my responsibility just as much as she was. You shouldn't have had to go through this alone.'

'It's okay,' he mumbled, embarrassed that she felt the need to apologise. And yet...it helped.

'Right. Now that we have that out the way.' She smiled bravely. 'You protect yourself because that's what you saw your father do. It isn't a criticism,' she added. 'You had to because we didn't.'

'I don't blame you.'

'I know.' The smile was genuine this time. 'But you don't have to protect yourself for the rest of your life.'

'You don't know that.'

'I do,' Abby disagreed. 'Your fears don't control you, my boy. If they did, you would have run far away from Eli and the responsibility of raising a child.'

'I ran away from Autumn.'

'Probably because you had the option to,' his mother said contemplatively. 'You didn't have a choice with Eli. He depended on you. He forced you to face those fears.'

'So, what, I have to force Autumn into depending on me before I can face my fears with her?'

'If she told you she loved you, I think she already does.'

And he'd let her down.

'You're stronger than you think, Hunter. This doesn't have to define you. It doesn't have to keep you from having what you want.' She picked up her mug. 'I suppose you have to figure out what it is that you want, and how badly you want it. If that's Autumn, and you love her—' she gave him a look that told him they both knew it was, and he did '—your fear of losing her shouldn't be the cause of you losing her.'

She kissed him on the forehead and disappeared into Eli's room. Hunter silently thanked her for giving him the space. He stared at his mug, ignoring the coffee inside, trying to figure out how he felt.

The conversation he'd had with Autumn had left his mind in a shambles. His heart, too. Before he'd spiralled into the pit of his fears, he'd thought he'd been making progress. He'd started facing his grief more openly. He'd fully embraced being a father, and his experience in the first few weeks of being one—understanding his own father's reaction to an extent—had even had him thinking about reaching out to Calvin.

Even the family he, Autumn and Eli had formed hadn't

scared him that much, he realised now. The fears of brokenness had faded.

When Grace had spoken to him about coming back though, his instinctive reaction had burned up that progress and sent him back to the man he'd been before Eli had arrived. That had been the man who'd driven to Autumn on Friday night. A man desperate for his anchor. Whose needs and fears were more important than anything and anyone else.

It had even been that man who'd told his mother of his fears, Hunter thought. Because as he worked through it, he realised that some of those fears no longer applied. About turning into his father, about having a broken family. Some of them he was facing, like his guilt about Janie and what would happen when Grace got back.

He'd always been scared about being a bad father, but that, he thought, remembering his mother's response to his confession, might just come with the territory of being a parent. As for his fears about losing the people he loved…
Well, as his mother had said, they were the reason he'd lost Autumn.

She'd had every right to ask him to choose her. To walk away when he didn't. Though it was of no benefit to him, he was proud of her for doing so. He'd once asked her how she planned on working on her issues. She hadn't had an answer for him then. She'd more than made up for it now, strong woman that she was.

He was so in love with her. And he'd be with her now, if he'd followed her example and faced his issues.

But what if he did now?

The idea that he didn't have to be constrained by his fears seemed too good to be true. Which told him he was scared. Again. Despite the encouragement his heart was giving him.

The night he'd spoken with Autumn, he'd heard the encouragement. He hadn't been able to do anything then because he'd been too overwhelmed, panicked by the idea of losing her. But he heard it now, and he wanted to pay heed to it.

He would have to adjust, of course. He'd have to learn how to move without the weight of his fears around his ankles. To navigate the world with his new freedom. He wanted his freedom to take him to Autumn. He wanted...

He wanted to choose her.

His legs were carrying him to Eli's room before he'd realised it.

'Mum, Eli and I are going to see Autumn.'

Abby smiled brightly at him, bobbing Eli up and down. 'Okay.'

'I'll be back before lunchtime.'

'Bring Autumn with you, dear. I'd love to see her again.'

'I'm going to try damn hard to.'

'Language,' she sing-songed, but smiled approvingly.

Eli smiled approvingly, too.

Hunter grinned.

CHAPTER NINETEEN

'AUTUMN!'

Mandy burst into the kitchen with enough force that Autumn's hand shifted and plopped frosting all over the cake she'd been decorating.

'What is it? What's wrong?' Autumn glanced over in alarm.

'Er…nothing.'

'Nothing? You burst into the kitchen like a maniac because nothing's wrong?'

'I came here because there's…' Mandy's eyes were disturbingly bright. 'You should come inside.'

'I'm not going inside if there's nothing wrong,' Autumn said irritably, turning back to the cake and trying to fix the frosting. 'I'm going to stay back here where I don't have to talk with anyone.'

It had been her strategy since she and Hunter had spoken. Keep busy, avoid people. Ignore the hole in her heart because she'd left a piece of it with him as she'd walked away. Mandy constantly hovered around her, having been privy to a brief overview of what had happened. Autumn appreciated the concern, though she wasn't able to show it yet. Only her annoyance.

'Well, there's a really cute guest here to see you.'

Autumn paused. 'To see me?' She let out a breath. 'Mandy, please don't tell me you've brought another blind date to the bakery. I told you, I'm not interested in—'

'Autumn,' Mandy snapped. 'Just come out here.'

Sighing deeply, Autumn put down the offset spatula, turning.

'This better be good,' she said as she passed Mandy and walked through the door.

As soon as she entered the bakery, music began to play. She recognised the song. It was the one everyone had done the social media challenge to a couple of years ago. The one she'd tricked Hunter into dancing to. The one she'd tried to cheer him up with before Eli's test.

She tried to shake the memories off, knowing he was simply at the forefront of her mind. It was probably a co-incidence. Or the music had likely been playing all along and she'd missed it because she'd been concentrating on the cake.

Then she saw him.

She wasn't sure how she'd missed Hunter at all. He was standing in the middle of her bakery, ignoring the grins he was getting from her patrons. And he was dancing. Doing the moves as clumsily as she had when she'd been trying to cheer him up the night before Eli's test. Though it wasn't because he was trying to; rather, because he had a baby in his arms.

Her heart immediately turned into a puddle as she watched Hunter try and get Eli to do the moves with his limp little arms. Her eyes shifted over the room, where people watched gleefully, their eyes as bright as Mandy's had been. Then Autumn was looking at Hunter again, wondering why he was there. Trying to push down against the hope that had surged inside her at seeing him.

When the song ended, along with his terrible dancing, her customers clapped and cheered. She clapped, too, though her hands stilled when he walked towards her.

'Do you have a moment to talk to *#BakeryBoyfriend*?' Hunter asked softly, his voice breathless. 'Before you answer, consider that I come with *#BakeryBaby*.'

'How could I resist Bakery Baby?' she asked, amused. She held out her hands, quirking her brow in question. Hunter handed Eli over, and something settled in Autumn's heart as she held his comforting weight.

'I'm taking five, Mandy,' Autumn called behind her.

She followed Hunter outside, grateful for the warm day that prevented her from having to shield Eli from the wind. They walked until they were obscured by one of the trees close to the bakery, offering them privacy.

'Cheap shot,' she said, holding Eli tight against her. He rewarded her with a gurgle.

'I know.'

'Which is why you did it. The dance and bringing Eli with you.'

'Yes.'

'Why?'

'I would take any cheap shot if it got me points with you.'

'Why do you need points?'

'So you'd accept my apology.'

'What are you apologising for?'

He lifted a hand over his head, his expression wry. 'I guess I didn't earn any points then.'

'I didn't say that.' She kept her expression carefully blank. 'What are you apologising for? Why are you here?'

He took a long time to answer. Autumn used the time to cuddle Eli. She'd missed him, and she had no idea when he'd grown to be such a part of her. He wasn't even her kid. But she loved him, and her eyes burned at the idea that he'd grow up and she'd have no reason to be in his life.

Her heart burned that he'd grow up, and she wouldn't get the opportunity to see Hunter be his dad.

'You love him,' Hunter said after a moment. She blinked, and was relieved when she didn't feel the wetness she was certain was there fall down her cheeks.

'He's a baby,' she said, avoiding the question.

'Do you love all babies?'

'I...like all babies.'

Hunter gave her a patient look. It annoyed her. 'But you don't love them all.'

'No.'

'You love him, though.'

Her arms tightened around Eli. Lying felt as if she was betraying him. 'Yes, I do.'

Hunter's cheeks lifted, then he grew sober. 'I'm sorry for a lot of things when it comes to you, Autumn.' He paused, as if considering where to start. 'Mostly, I'm sorry for not telling you I choose you.'

'You don't have to apologise if that's how you feel,' she said softly, not meeting his eyes. A gasp passed her lips when he took her chin, lifted it.

'It's not how I feel. I wanted to choose you. I was just... I was scared.'

More air shuddered through her lips.

'Why are you here?' she asked hoarsely.

'I'm here to choose you.' His hand shifted to her cheek, caressing the skin there. 'I thought you were the most important thing in my life before you helped me see I was putting my fears ahead of you.'

His hand dropped and he squeezed his eyes shut. Opened them again. 'Something shut down inside me when I lost Janie. It didn't start again until I met you. I... I didn't know how to live with it. It was this...overwhelming love that made me want the things that had turned it off in the first place.' His voice lowered. 'The deeper I fell for you, the more I wanted those things, and the stronger the fears became. They were like a noise in my head getting louder and louder, and I couldn't hear you when you asked me to choose you that first time.'

'And now?' she whispered.

'Now... Now I see the noise kept me from hearing myself, too. I want you,' he said simply. 'I want the chance to listen to you now because I didn't before. I want to tell you you're the most amazing person and make you believe me. I want to see you face your issues and tell you how proud I am as you do.' A slow smile crossed his lips. 'I'm proud of you for knowing you're worth more than I was willing to offer you on Friday.'

He brushed a hand over Eli's head.

'I want you to be a family with me and Eli. We can figure out the rest as we go along.' He paused, and she saw the nerves on his face. 'If you can forgive me.'

She snuggled into Eli, then held him out and let Hunter take him.

'Are you saying this because you need me for something?'

'Yes.' There was barely a beat before he said, 'I need you because I love you.'

The lump in her throat that had been growing with his every word burst, showering warm emotion into her body.

'What about your fears?'

'I'm working on it,' he said dryly, and she remembered when she'd said the same words to him. Her lips curved. 'That's what I meant when I said we'd figure out the rest,' he continued. 'I have to work through them. But I know what my priorities are.' He pressed a kiss to Eli's head, his eyes heating when they met hers. 'You and Eli will always come first.'

She recognised his growth in those words. In the very fact that he was there. She didn't blame him for needing the time to figure it out, though she could have done without the heartbreak. But then, the heartbreak was necessary. Everything on this path had been necessary so they could be standing there in front of one another.

Her journey had been triggered when she'd found out the truth about Summer's experience. Realising what her issues had cost her with her sister had planted the seed. She had always been bound to face her anger and low self-esteem after that. Everything that had happened with Hunter, including walking away from him, had simply sped things up.

It had also been the growth of that seed.

As their gazes held, she felt as if it were finally blooming.

'I don't regret what we've been through, Hunter,' she said eventually. 'You shouldn't regret it either.' She waited a beat. 'Your fears have made you the man you are. If it wasn't for everything with your father, you wouldn't be as caring or as determined.' She hesitated only briefly before saying, 'If it wasn't for Janie, you wouldn't try to help people as much as you do. Or be strong for the people you love. Or try to protect them. Or love them so much you're afraid of losing them.'

His eyes flickered with emotion, but his gaze was steady.

'Does this mean you're accepting my apology?'

'You know I do.' Her heart shuddered, but she added, 'I love you, too.'

'I don't deserve you,' he whispered, putting his free arm around her. 'But I'm going to make sure you know our family is the most important thing. You'll never feel second best again.'

Autumn looked up, smiled. 'Damn right.'

She pushed up on her toes, her heart overflowing with love. But before she could reach Hunter's lips, Eli began to cry.

Their eyes met over his head, and they grinned.

EPILOGUE

Two years later

'It's NOT so much that I wanted a holiday,' Autumn said casually, talking to the two-and-a-half-year-old straddling her stomach. 'It's that I deserved one, you know?'

Eli nodded solemnly. 'Holl-day,' he offered, reaching for something on the blanket Autumn was lying on. He handed it to her.

'Is this for me?' Autumn said, looking down at the marshmallow.

Eli nodded again.

'You're sharing?'

'Share.'

He took the marshmallow from her, and stuffed it into his mouth. Autumn laughed. Heard the deep rumbling of a laugh come from behind her.

'Dada.'

Eli clapped his hands as Hunter scooped him up.

'Yeah, buddy,' Hunter said soothingly. 'It's Dada.'

'Don't be impressed by that handclap,' Autumn said. 'He did the same thing when I ate a chip. It's his new thing.'

Hunter chuckled. 'I'm always impressed by what he does.'

'Helping him set realistic expectations for when he's an adult,' she said, pushing up onto her forearms. She pretended to steal Eli's nose, and he squealed with delight, clapping.

'Okay,' she said, wrinkling her nose. 'That's pretty cute.'

'So are you.'

Hunter stole a kiss, and after a moment, Autumn heard him offer to take Eli into the field. She lay back down as they went off. Hunter's deep voice vibrated, and Eli's cheerful laughter filled the air.

Autumn could have never imagined her life would change so much in two years. That she could be so content with it when once upon a time she hadn't even been happy with herself. Her thumb automatically stretched to her ring finger, where the ring Hunter had given her a year before sat solidly.

'Are you sure?' she'd asked breathlessly when he'd got down on his knee in the middle the flower field he and Eli were currently running in.

'I've never been surer of anything in my life.'

'I don't expect this of you.'

'I know.'

'We're already a family,' she'd said softly. 'I don't need—'

'Autumn,' he'd interrupted. 'What part of "I want to marry you" didn't you understand? It was a statement, followed by a question. A simple yes or no will do.'

'Hang on,' she'd said with a frown. 'I need to make sure you're okay with this. Because I don't need it. And neither do you.'

'But I do,' he'd said, his expression softening. 'I do need it. I want to call you my wife and make that commitment to you. I want everyone to know that I choose you.'

Her eyes had filled, and she'd said yes, and now they were planning a wedding. She was marrying the father of her baby. It might not have been her biological child, but Eli was as much her baby as he was Grace's. She couldn't believe there was a time she'd doubted it. Even Grace had freely concurred when Eli had called Autumn 'Mama'. Autumn had blinked in surprise, but Grace had said, 'Yes, that's your mama. And I'm your—'

'Mama!' Eli had shouted, and they'd all laughed.

Grace had become part of their family in the last two

years, too. She was funny and smart, and loved Eli more than anything else. Autumn could have never anticipated she'd be such good friends with the woman her fiancé had conceived a child with. But that fact seemed so arbitrary, so irrelevant to the nature of their relationship. Hunter, too, had overcome his reservations about losing his son once he'd started speaking to Grace about it. They'd figured out the co-parenting thing wonderfully, and Eli was thriving because of it.

'Mama.'

Autumn opened her eyes to see the toddler's face a breath away. She laughed. 'Hey, baby.'

'Fowers fo' Mama.'

'You brought me flowers?' She sat up, melting when Eli handed her a bunch of uneven flowers from the field. 'Thank you, baby. Mama loves it.'

'Don't take all the credit,' Hunter said, grinning. 'I helped.'

Eli looked unconvincingly at his father, before waddling over to the marshmallows and eating another.

'Gosh, he's so big,' Autumn said, watching Eli. 'One of these days he's going to be able to say words.' She turned to Hunter. 'Actual sentences, I mean.'

'I know.' Hunter's eyes flitted to Eli, then rested on Autumn's. 'We should start talking about the next one.'

Her breath caught. 'What?'

'We should explore our options.'

'I thought… What about…? But—'

'Autumn,' he interrupted with a small smile. 'You're malfunctioning.'

She clamped her lips shut on what would have been more incoherency.

She hadn't brought up having another child because she thought she knew how he felt about it. Eli's existence and health hadn't changed Hunter's previous concerns. There was a chance their child could be sick. And if they weren't sick, there was a chance they could be a carrier. Hunter wanted to avoid both those possibilities.

Though she had answers to his concerns, like letting herself be tested for the CF gene, genetic counselling or adoption, she was also content with their family. So perhaps she hadn't brought it up because it wasn't that important any more. She was already a mother. She was weeks away from being a wife. She had the family she'd always wanted.

'I don't need to have another child.'

He pulled her closer and she easily went to him, resting between his legs. 'What if I do?'

'I think you'd have to explain why. Is it because you really want one? Or because you think I want one? Or—'

'Is this going to be like the proposal again?' There was a faint whine in his voice. Autumn smiled.

'Not if you use your words and explain.'

'Okay.' There was a long pause. 'I can't tell you I want another child because I'm not scared any more. We'd have to do testing and depending on those results, we might have to talk about something else.' He paused. 'But I want Eli to have what I had with Janie.'

'He could get that through Grace. It doesn't have to be us.'

'Then I guess I want to experience seeing Eli with a sibling to look out for.'

'You could get that with Grace, too.'

'I want it with you.' His voice softened. 'I suppose all of this is selfish, then. You've proved to me that families don't have to be broken. You've helped me move out of the shadow of my fear that I'd be a bad father.' He kissed her head. 'I want to do this with you again.'

Her heart melted, but she turned to face him. 'As long as none of this is because of me.'

Hunter cupped her face. 'It's all me, baby. I want this. If you do.'

She studied him. 'I do.' He kissed her, and she shook her head when they parted, embarrassed by the heat at her eyes. 'It's disgusting how much I love you.'

'Good thing you're going to be my wife.'

'Good thing you're going to be my husband.' They kissed again. 'What a perfect life,' she whispered, and smiled.

* * * * *

HIS TEXAS RUNAWAY

STELLA BAGWELL

To my beloved paint horse, Little Giant Sequoia,
who paced the fence until his daughter
was safely born.

Chapter One

Roslyn DuBose switched on the headlights and peered at the navigation map illuminated on the dashboard of her car. Wickenburg, Arizona, was less than three miles away. Surely she could hang on until she reached the small desert town. Pulling off to the side of a dark, lonely highway, even for a short rest, wasn't a safe option. Not for her, or her unborn baby.

Gripping the steering wheel, she blinked and hoped the cobwebs in front of her weary eyes would go away. For the past two days she'd driven over a thousand miles and fatigue was beginning to overtake her. Tonight she had no choice but to settle in for a rest. Hopefully when her father read the note she'd left for him back in Fort Worth, he'd understand and not intervene. But Martin DuBose wasn't an understanding or forgiving man. Sooner or later, he'd come after her.

Determined, Roslyn drove onward, toward the lights

dotting the dark horizon. Until the two-lane highway seemed to be coming at her in undulating waves.

God help her, she was going to faint!

The horrifying thought was zipping through her brain at the same time she spotted a brick building with a wide graveled parking area.

Wheeling the car to a halt beneath the dim glow of a security light, she turned off the engine and reached for a water bottle resting in the cup holder next to her seat.

Damn. It was empty. When had she downed the last of the water? Winslow? Flagstaff?

Resting her head against the seat, she splayed a hand upon the large mound where her waist used to be and felt the child moving against the bottom of her rib cage.

Hang on, little darlin'. In a minute I'll feel better. Then I'll find us a nice meal and a soft bed.

Another kick landed somewhere in the region of her bellybutton and if Roslyn hadn't been so exhausted she would've smiled at the notion of the baby reading her thoughts. For now, she was barely able to muster enough energy to peer beyond the windshield at the sign hanging over the door of the building.

Hollister Animal Clinic.

She'd parked in front of a veterinary clinic that appeared to be closed for the night. At least no one was around to accuse her of loitering, she thought, as she leaned her forehead against the steering wheel.

Just a minute or two more of rest, she promised herself, and then she'd move on.

On a normal day, Chandler Hollister tried to close his veterinarian business at six in the evening. But his days were rarely normal. On most evenings, he went far past seven or even eight at night, performing last-minute surgeries or dealing with emergencies that couldn't wait until morning. Such was the case tonight.

The last three hours he'd spent driving to a ranch in a remote corner of Yavapai County, then riding horseback to a rugged arroyo to doctor one cow who'd had difficulty calving. Being the only vet in the area made his job challenging, but he wouldn't change it for anything.

Now, as he drove the last half mile to Hollister Animal Clinic, he glanced at the digital clock on the truck dashboard. "Eight fifteen. Not too bad considering I've been up since four thirty this morning. I might actually get home to Three Rivers before ten tonight."

In the seat across from him, Chandler's young assistant let out a weary groan. "You might be feeling like a stud colt, but I'm dead beat. And we still have the horses to unload and put to bed for the night."

Chuckling, Chandler nudged the brim of his gray Stetson back off his forehead. "Trey, you're thirty years old. Six years younger than me. You should have energy to spare."

Trey grunted. "I'm not used to working sixteen hours a day, six days a week, like you are."

"You should be getting used to it," Chandler said wryly. "You've done it for the past two years."

"Yeah, and what am I getting for it? Besides a paycheck and a continual state of exhaustion?"

Chandler grinned. "Fulfillment, Trey. You can go home tonight knowing that cow and her little baby are going to be fine."

"They won't be fine if she and the baby can't climb out of the arroyo. If it rains—"

Chandler's laugh interrupted his words. "Rain? Are you kidding? There's no danger of seeing a drop of it for weeks. Besides, if it did start raining, old Amos would winch the pair out to higher ground."

"You're right. That old man is just like you, he'd try to help a sidewinder if he thought it was sick."

"Sometimes snakes need doctoring, too," Chandler replied.

The familiar sight of the clinic came into view and Trey promptly scooted to the edge of his seat. "Hey, Doc, a car is parked in front of the building. Sure doesn't look like it belongs to any of the girls, either."

Chandler flipped on the turn signal and steered the truck into the clinic's parking area. As he peered at the light-colored car parked at an angle to the building, he decided Trey's assessment was right. There wasn't a chance the unfamiliar vehicle belonged to any one of his staff.

"No," Chandler agreed. "That's a Jaguar. A fairly new one, at that."

Trey whistled under his breath. "Must be Mrs. Whitley with one of her Siamese cats. She's wealthy enough to drive a Jag. But how would the woman know you'd be back here tonight?"

"I doubt Mrs. Whitley would splurge on a luxury car. She's as miserly as her late husband used to be. But she'd win the trophy for showing up after hours." He drove on past the building and parked the truck and trailer near a maze of sheds and holding pens. "Take the horses on to the barn. I'll check out the car."

Trey opened the door and jumped to the ground. "Guess you're going to open up and take care of that damn cat."

"If need be. Or if you'd rather, I'll take care of the horses and you can deal with the cat," Chandler offered with a baiting grin.

"Oh, hell no. I've had enough scratches and bites for this month."

"Trey, it's only the second day of April."

"That's my point, Doc."

Chuckling, Chandler left Trey to deal with the horses and walked down a short slope to where the car was parked near the entrance of the clinic. The lights were off, and the tinted windows were up, making it difficult to see whether anyone was inside.

He rapped his knuckles on the driver's door and called out, "Hey, anyone in there?"

Long seconds passed without any response and Chandler was about to decide the car was empty when the window slid down a few inches and he found himself peering into a woman's wide, wary eyes.

"The clinic is closed for the night," Chandler told her. "Do you have an emergency?"

"Emergency?"

"An emergency with an animal," Chandler patiently explained. "Do you have a pet with you in the car?"

The eyes that had been warily studying him blinked and then the window lowered to reveal a very young woman. "Uh…no. No animal. I, uh, just stopped for a minute—to rest."

Frowning, he stepped closer. "Excuse me, miss, but you don't sound well. Do you need to get out and—"

Finishing the question would've been pointless as she suddenly flopped face-forward onto the steering wheel.

Recognizing she'd fainted, Chandler jerked on the door handle, only to discover it was locked. Without hesitation, he reached through the open window and released the latch.

Once the door swung wide, he leaned in and touched her shoulder. When she failed to respond, he felt for a pulse at the base of her neck. The faint, rapid thump wasn't ideal, but at least her heart was beating.

Carefully, he eased her head away from the wheel and touched a hand to her face. Beneath his palm, the soft skin felt clammy.

He was trying to decide whether to call an ambulance or carry her into the clinic, when she suddenly began to rouse.

"Ooh." She groaned and looked up at him. "Where... am I?"

"You're in Wickenburg. You're in your car," he calmly informed her. "Have you been ill?"

While Chandler waited for her to answer, his gaze dropped to the very pregnant belly touching the bottom of the steering wheel. Oh, damn. If she was a mare, he'd predict she wasn't far away from foaling.

Her brow furrowed with confusion. "No. I haven't been sick. I've been driving for a long time. If I could just trouble you for a drink of water—that's all I need."

He eased her shoulder back against the seat. "Don't try to move," he ordered. "I'll be right back."

Chandler hurriedly unlocked the heavy glass door on the front of the building and returned to the car. By then, she was sitting up straight and wiping a hand over her face.

"Let me help you into the clinic," he said. "Or if you think the baby is coming, I'll drive you to the hospital."

The hand on her face instantly fell to her belly. "Oh, I don't need a hospital. The baby isn't coming." She looked up at him. "I—I'm sorry to bother you. I got swimmy-headed and thought I'd better rest before I drove on. I can make it now."

Her face was as pale as the moon rising over the distant hill behind him. She wasn't in any shape to drive ten feet, much less a mile and a half, he decided.

He extended his hand out to her and ordered, "I'm not so sure. Take my hand and squeeze it."

She frowned. "Why?"

"Don't worry. I'm a doctor. My name is Chandler Hollister and I own this veterinary clinic where you've parked."

"Oh. You're an animal doctor."

He couldn't help grinning. "I've been known to doctor a few humans from time to time. After all, we're mostly two-legged animals."

"Uh… I suppose." She hesitated a moment, then finally placed her hand in his. "Nice to meet you, Dr. Hollister. I'm Roslyn DuBose."

Her fingers managed to fold around his, but he likened the touch to the gentle closing of a butterfly's wings. "Is that the most you can squeeze, Roslyn?"

"I'm sorry," she murmured. "I'm rather tired."

He didn't wait for her to say more. He leaned in closer and ordered, "Put your arms around my neck."

"Listen, Doctor, if this is another of your tests, I'm—"

"It's not a test. Put your arms around my neck. I'm going to carry you into the clinic."

"Oh, but I can walk," she protested. "Just give me a hand."

"You can walk later. Right now, do as I say."

To his relief, she followed his orders and he lifted her out of the car and into his arms.

As he started toward the clinic with her, Trey came jogging up to them.

"What the hell, Doc? She's not a cat!"

"Far from it," he told his assistant. "Go down to my office and make sure the couch is cleaned off. This young lady needs a few minutes of rest."

"Right. I got it."

At the entrance, the tall, lanky blond held the door open long enough for Chandler to step inside with his armload, then he sped down the hallway ahead of them.

By the time Chandler reached his private office, Trey had cleared the couch of clutter and propped a pillow at one end.

"Is she about to have the baby?" Trey asked as he stood to one side, watching anxiously as Chandler placed his latest patient on the couch. "Should I call the ambulance?"

Chandler carefully positioned the pillow beneath her head. "No. And no. Not yet, anyway," he told Trey. "Right now, I need a bottle of water from the fridge."

Trey fetched him the water, then Chandler squatted down at her side, quickly twisted off the lid and tilted the bottle to her lips.

"Drink, Ms. DuBose," he prompted. "It will help revive you."

She wrapped a hand around the bottle and drank thirstily. Once she had her fill, she said, "I'm so sorry about this. I don't want to be a bother to either of you."

"Don't worry." Chandler tried to reassure her with a gentle smile. "We're used to putting in overtime."

She leaned her head back against the pillow and drew in a long breath. "This is all my fault. I've been driving all day and haven't taken a break since I passed through Flagstaff."

"You're trying to get to your destination tonight?" Chandler's gaze roamed her face. He was an expert at gauging an animal's accurate age, especially horses. But humans were a different matter. Especially women. If he had to guess Ms. DuBose's age, the best he could narrow it down to was somewhere between twenty and twenty-five.

She had warm brown eyes that reminded him of toffee candy. Light brown hair fringed her forehead and waved gently to the tops of her shoulders. At the moment, her dusky pink lips were parted just enough to show the edges of very white teeth. Altogether, she was very lovely.

"I was only trying to reach Wickenburg tonight," she answered. "I, uh, planned to stay a couple of days here before I traveled on to… California."

She seemed hesitant about adding the last bit of information, but that was understandable, Chandler thought. He and Trey were total strangers to her.

"Good idea. You obviously need to rest." He walked over to a row of cabinets and pulled a blood-pressure cuff from a drawer, then plucked a stethoscope from the pocket of a lab coat hanging from a hall tree. "Let me see how you're ticking and then you might try to eat something."

She pointed to the blood-pressure cuff. "That's the kind you use on people. I must really be disoriented. I thought you said this was an animal clinic."

"Don't worry, miss," Trey said. "Sometimes folks that bring in their animals keel over themselves. Doc takes care of them, too."

Her expression skeptical, she said, "Oh. I guess it's my good fortune I stopped here."

"More like Trey's good fortune," Chandler said, as he once again squatted next to the couch and reached for Roslyn's arm. "He likes rescuing damsels in distress."

Trey's face reddened. "Oh, Doc, that's not so and you know it."

Chandler wrapped the cuff around her slender arm and pumped it tight. She remained quiet as he noted the numbers, but he could feel her gaze wandering over his face. He figured he looked like hell to her and smelled even worse. Long before daylight this morning he'd been called out on an emergency and hadn't taken time to shave. Since then he'd waded through cow and horse manure, tromped through pigpens and bloodied his jeans and shirt while castrating several colts.

From the looks of Roslyn DuBose, he figured she was accustomed to seeing men in suits and ties and wing-tips that never touched anything dirtier than a concrete sidewalk.

"Do I have a blood pressure, Dr. Hollister?" she asked with dry amusement.

Her soft voice pulled his attention back to her face. How would she look without the dark smudges of fatigue beneath her eyes and the tension at the corners of her mouth? Something or someone was definitely making her anxious.

"You do. Although it's still a little low. The water should help that. Drink all you can." He hung the stethoscope around his neck and started to rise, but at the last moment changed his mind. "Would you like for me to listen to the baby? Just to make sure he or she isn't in distress?"

"Oh, yes. I'd be very grateful.

He positioned the stethoscope back in his ears and placed the round metal diaphragm against her belly. After listening intently at several different spots, he gave her a thumbs-up sign.

"Sounds like a healthy girl. Is that what it is?"

She shook her head. "I don't know. I wanted to find out the gender the old-fashioned way. But I've been calling it a boy. Do you really think it's a girl?"

"Well, my brothers say I'm an expert at predicting a foal's gender. But that doesn't mean you should go out and buy everything in pink."

He walked back over to the cabinet to put away the

blood-pressure cuff and stethoscope. "Trey, did you see anything in the fridge to eat? The girls usually leave their lunch leftovers."

Trey said, "I think there's a piece of fried chicken and one of those cartons of yogurt. That's all."

"That's enough." He glanced over his shoulder to see the woman had relaxed enough to close her eyes. Chandler motioned for Trey to follow him out of the room.

Out in the hallway, the two men made their way to a stockroom, where medical supplies were stored on shelves and in refrigerators.

As Chandler rummaged through one of the refrigerators for the food, Trey asked in a hushed voice, "What do you think about her?"

"She's going to be okay. As far as I can tell, she's suffering from dehydration and exhaustion."

"No. I don't mean medically. I mean, what is she doing here? In Wickenburg?"

Chandler shot him a droll look. "I wouldn't know that any more than you. From what she says, she's on her way to California. Frankly, it's not our business."

Trey lifted his straw hat from his head, then plopped it back down as though the action would help him think. "Well, she sure is pretty."

"Yeah, she sure is."

"Wonder where her husband is. The guy must be an idiot for letting her get on the road in that condition."

"I'm not sure she has a husband."

Trey eyes widened. "What makes you think that, Doc? Did you ask her?"

"No. I didn't ask her. It's just an assumption. She isn't wearing a ring."

"Maybe that's because her hands are swollen and the

ring is too tight. My sister's hands stayed puffy when she was pregnant."

"Trey, you're watching too much TV. You're getting the idea you're a PI in a cowboy hat."

"Oh, shoot, I'm just trying to figure her out," Trey reasoned. "We don't ever get anyone like her here at the clinic."

Chandler placed the piece of chicken on a paper plate, then found a plastic spoon to go with the carton of yogurt. "I wouldn't start setting my sights on her, Trey. She'll be gone in a couple of days."

Trey snorted. "Hell, I'm not going to be guilty of setting my sights on any woman. I can barely take care of myself. But she's easy on the eyes. And I sorta feel bad for her. She seems kinda lost, don't you think?"

Chandler let out a long breath. In the twelve years since he'd opened the clinic, Trey was the best assistant he'd ever had. But sometimes the man's incessant chatter had Chandler longing for a piece of duct tape. However, this was one time Trey was voicing Chandler's exact thoughts.

"She'll be okay, Trey," Chandler reiterated. "And if you're finished with the horses, you can go on home. I can handle this. There's no need for you to keep hanging around."

Trey looked at him with surprise and then he grinned and winked. "I got it, Doc. You'd rather be alone with the lady. No problem. I'm out of here. Pronto. Like right now."

Chandler hardly needed to be alone with Roslyn Du-Bose. Not in the way Trey was suggesting. But he did need time to make sure she was capable of leaving the clinic under her own power. "I'll see you in the morning. At six. Remember? We have to be over to the Johnson ranch to geld his colts."

"Six. Yeah, I'll be here." He screwed his hat down tighter on his head and started out the door. "You can tell me all about Ms. DuBose then."

Roslyn pushed herself to a sitting position on the couch and glanced curiously around Dr. Hollister's office. The room was nothing like her OB's plush office and definitely nothing close to the luxurious suites that made up her father's corporate law firm back in Fort Worth.

Rectangular in shape, this office had a bare concrete floor and walls of whitewashed cinderblock. A large metal desk with a leather executive chair took up most of the left-hand side of the space. Two wooden chairs sat at odd angles in front of the desk that was used for consultations, she supposed. Although, the seats were presently filled with an odd assortment of clothing and leather riding tack. To the right of her, metal cabinets and shelves were loaded with boxes of medications and other medical supplies, while straight in front of her the wall was covered with an endless number of photographs, all involving animals. Most of the images were of horses, taken either in the winners' circle at the racetrack, or in an arena next to a trophy-presentation table. Along with the horses, there were pics of dogs, cats, raccoons and opossums.

The man clearly had an affinity for animals, she decided. And he had no need to surround himself with a lavish work area. The fact impressed her, almost as much as the gentleness of his hands and the kindness she'd found in his eyes.

She was still thinking about him when he suddenly walked through the door carrying a plate of food. As he moved toward her, she found her gaze riveted to his striking image.

He was at least an inch or two over six feet, and his

shoulders were so broad they stretched the denim fabric
of his Western shirt to the limit. As her eyes followed the
line of pearl snaps down to a square, silver belt buckle,
she noted that his lean waist was a huge contrast to the
breadth of his shoulders. Long, muscular legs strained
against the work-worn denim.

Lifting her gaze, she studied his rugged features,
which were made up of a square chin, and a jaw, covered with dark, rusty stubble. Beneath the gray cowboy
hat, his hair was dark enough to call black and lay in thick
waves until it reached the back of his collar. His eyes
were vivid blue, like the sky after a hard rain, and framed
by thick black lashes. The effect of his gaze was discon-
certing, but then, so was everything else about the man.

"I found something for you to snack on," he said, offering her the plate. "Eat what you can. It'll help revive you."

"Thanks. I am rather hungry." She picked up the
chicken leg and a paper napkin from the plate and began
to eat. Halfway through, she paused to glance at him. "As
soon as I eat, I'll be ready to leave. I don't want to keep
you any longer than I already have."

He relaxed against the corner of the couch and crossed
his boots out in front of him. The hems of his jeans were
ragged and stained green with manure, while the pant
legs were covered with dust and splotched with something dark, like blood. She didn't have to wonder if he
was a hardworking man. It was evident from the burnt
brown skin of his face, his calloused hands and dirty
clothes. Even though Fort Worth was known as "Cow-
town," and she'd seen plenty of men wearing boots and
Stetsons walking the sidewalks, she'd never been close
up to a man like him. His masculinity roared at her like
a lion warning her to beware.

He said, "Don't worry about it. This is normal hours for me."

She took a deep breath and tried to concentrate on the chicken. "Have you had this clinic very long?"

"Twelve years," he replied. "It's my second home."

"Where's your first home? In town?" The questions came out of her before she could stop them. But thankfully, he didn't seem to mind.

"No. I live about twenty-five minutes from here. On Three Rivers Ranch."

"You have a ranch?"

"Partly. It's owned and operated by the Hollister family. My brother Blake is the general manager, but my mom has the final say-so over everything."

She shook her head. "Sorry. I'm being nosy."

"Not really." He gestured toward the mound of baby covering most of her lap. "When are you due?"

"About four weeks. That's why I'm…making this trip now, before there's a chance I might go into labor."

"I'm not an OB, but I'd say there's a chance you might go into labor sooner than that."

Her cheeks burned with hot color. "I just look that way because I'm— I've gained a little extra weight these past couple of weeks."

"No. I don't mean you look big. It's just the way you're carrying. But like I said, I'm not an OB."

No. But he'd probably seen plenty of pregnant animals, she thought. Oh, God, what was she doing here in this Arizona town, without one friend or acquaintance within a thousand-mile radius? Had she lost her mind?

No, you've not lost your mind, Roslyn. You've finally found it. Along with the guts to be your own person, live your own life, deal with your own mistakes.

"I should be fine until I get to California," she said, wishing she felt as positive as she sounded.

"You have relatives there?"

She didn't know a single person in California. She'd chosen that state because it was as far west as she could get from Texas. Also, her late mother, who'd originally lived in Redding, had left Roslyn a small house and piece of property there.

"No. I, uh, own a place in Redding."

"That's where you intend to settle?"

The chicken leg eaten, she put down the plate and he handed her the carton of yogurt. It was topped with blueberries, one of her favorite flavors.

"That's my plan. I've never been there before, but I've heard the town is pretty." Oh, Lord, why had she told him that? Now he was probably thinking she was completely irresponsible and chasing after pipe dreams. But this man's view of her wasn't important. Once she walked out of this clinic, she'd never see him again.

"Uh, I guess you're wondering why I'm traveling alone. Without a man."

"The question did cross my mind," he admitted.

Her gaze fell to his left hand. There was no wedding band on his finger. But given the man's occupation, he might choose not to wear one. He could be going home to a woman tonight. One that would be waiting for him with a smile on her face and love in her heart. Or was that sort of fairy-tale life even real? She wondered bitterly.

Dipping the spoon into the yogurt, she said, "I'm not married. And don't plan to be—at least, not anytime soon. The baby's father turned out to be a first-class jerk. So he's out of the picture. Completely."

He stroked a thumb and forefinger over his chin as

he regarded her thoughtfully. "That's...unfortunate. The baby needs a daddy. There isn't any chance—"

"No!" she blurted before he could finish. "Shortly after he learned I was pregnant, he signed away all his paternal rights to the child. Since then, he's already moved on and married someone else."

"Is that the way you wanted it? Surely making him pay child support—"

Shaking her head, she said, "I don't need or want his money. Not that he actually had any money of his own, anyway. Besides, it's more important to me to have him totally out of my child's life."

"I'm sorry it didn't work out for you."

The empathy in his blue eyes was more than her frazzled emotions could bear and she purposely dropped her gaze to the yogurt. "Well, better now than later."

She began eating the yogurt, but it took effort to get each bite past her tight throat. She needed to get out of here, she thought—away from his perceptive gaze and unsettling presence.

After a long stretch of silence, he asked, "Have you already made reservations for a room in town?"

Focusing on the yogurt, she scooped out the last bite. "Uh, no. With it being early spring before vacationers hit the highways, I was hoping there would be plenty of vacancies."

"I'm sure there will be. But I..."

When he failed to go on, she looked up. "What? Is there some place in town I shouldn't stay?"

A faint smile tilted the corners of his lips. "No. That wasn't what I was about to say. I was thinking it would be far better if you'd come home with me."

Chapter Two

Chandler watched her eyes grow wide, her jaw drop. No doubt she was thinking he was some sort of pervert with a fetish for pregnant women. And he could hardly blame her.

It wasn't like him at all to invite a woman, a stranger at that, to spend the night at his family home. In fact, he'd never done such a thing. Sure, he'd taken home plenty of strays to nurture. But none of those strays had been the two-legged kind with pretty brown eyes and a shy smile.

"Home—with you?" she asked, her voice little more than a squeak.

"I'm speaking as a doctor, Roslyn. You've just suffered a fainting spell. I'd feel better if you weren't alone," he reasoned.

Her head began to swing back and forth. "I don't want to sound ungrateful, Mr. Hollister, but I don't know the first thing about you."

Lifting his hat from his head, he thrust a hand through his hair, then levered the hat back in place. His body was crying for food and a bed. But he was a long way off from either.

"Then I'll tell you a few things. The Hollister family has lived in Yavapai County for more than a hundred and seventy years and have owned and operated Three Rivers Ranch for just as long. My younger brother Joseph is a deputy sheriff for the same county and my sister, Vivian, is a park ranger over at Lake Pleasant State Park. Holt, another younger brother, has the reputation of being one of the best horse trainers in the southwest. And our mother, Maureen, is tougher than all her kids put together."

"Earlier, you mentioned your older brother, Blake. The ranch manager. I assumed he was the only sibling you had."

The surprise in her voice suggested she wasn't from a large family. He wanted to ask her if that was the case, but decided now was hardly the time.

"The Hollisters are a big family and we're all very close. I failed to mention I have another younger sister besides Vivian. Camille is living in the southern part of the state on one of our other ranches, Red Bluff. As for Three Rivers, Blake and his wife and three children live there, along with me, Holt and Mom. Vivian and her daughter used to live there, too, but she married recently and moved up to Camp Verde. So you see, there will be plenty of chaperones around the place."

"It sounds like you have a reputable family," she said after a moment. "And it's very hospitable of you to offer, but I'd feel like an intruder. A room in town will be perfectly fine."

"Not if you start feeling ill and need help. Trust me,

we have plenty of spare rooms in the ranch house. Along with a cook and a housekeeper. You won't be an intrusion. Far from it. Mom loves company. We all do."

She didn't reply and Chandler could see she was softening to the idea.

"I'm a stranger to you," she argued, but with far less enthusiasm. "For all you know I could be dishonest. A con woman or some evil person out to steal you blind."

Long years of working with the public had taught Chandler all about people. Sometimes it wasn't easy to see a person's true character. Other times all it took was a look into their eyes. He'd spotted plenty of emotions in Roslyn's brown eyes, but none of them had been close to sinister.

"You're not a con woman. You're alone and driving cross country, when you really should be home with your feet up," he added pointedly.

She winced at his last remark and Chandler decided then and there that she was most likely running from someone. If it wasn't the baby's father, then it had to be someone who'd been putting pressure on her. He hated to think a lovely girl like her had reached such a point in her life. Moreover, if he was smart, he wouldn't get involved with her, even for one or two nights. But Trey had hit the mark when he'd said that Roslyn seemed "kinda lost." And Chandler was a sucker for any animal or person who needed to find their way back home.

"Okay," she said, relenting. "I can see you're a gentleman. And it would be nice to really rest for a night."

Chandler was more than pleased at her answer. He was downright joyous. It was a reaction that had the sensible side of him silently cursing. What the hell was he thinking? He didn't have time to concern himself with the welfare of a pregnant runaway.

Still, Chandler couldn't keep a grin off his face. "Great. I'll get busy locking up the clinic and then we'll head on out to Three Rivers. While I take care of things you might want to visit the ladies' room. It's a long, bumpy ride to the ranch."

"Thank you. I appreciate your thoughtfulness."

He rose from the couch and offered her his hand. "Let me help you down the hall. I want to make sure you're steady on your feet before I leave you on your own."

She laughed. "If you're this attentive to your animal patients, you must have a whopping business."

The sound of her laughter was genuine and sweet, and eased some of the fatigue from Chandler's weary body. "Let's just say I can't remember a day when my schedule wasn't booked solid."

With her little hand wrapped around his, he helped her from the couch and purposely kept a steadying hold on her elbow.

"Are you dizzy?" he asked. "Do your legs feel sturdy enough to support you?"

"Oh, yes. I'm feeling much stronger now. I can make it on my own."

In spite of her insistence, he held on to her until they reached the door to the restroom. "Take your time," he told her. "And when you're finished, just wait for me up front in the waiting area."

Fifteen minutes later, Roslyn was sitting in the passenger seat of Chandler's truck. Her overnight case, filled with everything she needed for a night's stay, was sitting behind her, on the back seat.

"Sorry about having to leave your car, Roslyn, but part of the road to Three Rivers is rather rough. I promise it will be safe parked behind the clinic. There are security cameras all around the property and I've never had anything vandalized or stolen. Besides, I really don't think you're up to driving another twenty or so minutes."

Sighing, she rested her head on the back of the seat, while thinking how nice it felt to have this big, strong man handling everything for her. Even if it was just for this short evening.

"I'm not worried about my car. It's covered with tons of insurance. Besides, once I get to where I'm going I plan to trade it in for something more practical."

Roslyn had never wanted the Jaguar to begin with, but Martin, her father, had always insisted she had to drive a luxury car, not some cheap, middle-of-the-road compact. Otherwise, everyone would get the idea that the law offices of DuBose, Walker and Finley were going broke.

The idea had her silently snorting. If her father never earned another penny in his life, he'd still have an obscene amount of money stashed away in several banks. At the age of seventy he was still driven by his work, still obsessed with adding more power behind his name and seeing his fortune grow. But all the wealth or notoriety of Martin DuBose hadn't been able to buy his wife's health or to keep her from dying. Maybe someday he would realize that, she thought sadly. Perhaps one day he might regret the time he could've been spending with his wife and daughter, instead of in a courtroom.

Chandler said, "Everyone on Three Rivers has to be practical and drive a truck. After a while the rough road would shake a car to pieces."

"Is your home that remote?" she asked.

"We have a few neighbors, but there are miles in between all of us."

"I've always lived in the city." She peered out at what little she could see from the path of the headlights. Now and then they passed groups of mesquite trees, or a ragged patch of prickly pear. Otherwise the countryside appeared open and bare. "I do wish it was daylight so I could see everything. This is the first time I've been in Arizona."

"What do you think so far?"

"It's beautiful. And rugged. And wild."

He tossed a grin in her direction. "You left out hot. It gets as hot as hell here."

"Well, Fort Worth isn't exactly cool in the summer months." She'd not meant to come out with that, but what the heck. It didn't matter if Chandler knew where she was from. He wasn't going to broadcast the information.

"I noticed the Texas plates on your car. I've been trying to figure out what part of the state you might be from. I know it's so big that it's referred to in regions. North, south, east and west. I know some folks from South Texas, but they don't sound like you."

"That's right. I was born and raised in North Texas."

"But now you've left. Any regrets?"

"There will be places and people I'll miss," she confessed. "But no. No regrets."

"The Hollister family has been rooted here for so long I can't imagine living anywhere else."

"Your sisters must feel differently about that," she said thoughtfully.

"Well, love changes some people. Vivian is happy to live on the reservation with her husband. Now Camille is just the opposite. She's avoiding Three Rivers and Wickenburg because of a lost love. Or so she thinks."

A lost love. After Erich gave her an engagement ring and vowed his undying devotion, Roslyn had discovered he'd had been seeing other women. And with that shocking discovery, she'd believed she'd lost the one love of her life. But soon afterward, she'd realized she'd not lost anything. Rather, she'd escaped making a giant mistake with a man who knew nothing about real love.

"Men think with their heads. Not their hearts," she murmured more to herself than to him.

"Not always."

That brought her head around, and as she studied his profile, which was illuminated by the dash panel lights, she wondered if he'd ever trusted his heart to a woman and had it broken. She couldn't imagine him grieving over a broken romance. She could, however, imagine him having passionate sex without promises or strings attached.

"Are you married, Dr. Hollister?"

His short laugh was an answer in itself. "No. I barely have time to eat, much less see after a wife and kids."

For some inexplicable reason, his response saddened her. It shouldn't matter to her that this man was completely devoted to his career. "Well, it's good that you know your limitations."

"Hmm. I didn't know I had limitations. I just thought I was a busy man."

She forced herself to smile. "Sorry. You'll have to overlook me. I'm rather tired and things aren't coming out of my mouth exactly right."

"Well, just a few more miles and we'll be at Three Rivers. You can put up your feet and eat some of Reeva's good cooking."

Three Rivers. Each time he spoke the name it was like he was speaking of a place close to heaven. And for this one night that was exactly what she needed.

Fifteen minutes later, Chandler helped Roslyn into the house. After depositing her in a comfortable chair in the den, he went looking for his mother.

"Mom! Are you in here?" he called as he entered the large kitchen located at the back of the house.

Reeva, a tall slender woman in her early seventies with a long salt-and-pepper braid, was standing at the sink. She looked over her shoulder at him and frowned.

"You're filthy and I'm shutting down the kitchen."

"Tell me something I don't know. Like where is Mom."

"She's down at the foaling barn with Holt. Better not go down there. You know that they'll put you to work and you don't look like you can stand on your feet much longer."

After working on Three Rivers for too many years to count, Reeva was crusty and cranky and very astute.

"Well, I'm going to have to call her up here because I've brought company home with me. And I'm not sure where to put her."

Reeva turned away from the sink to level a speculative glare at him. "Company? 'Her'? Have you brought a mama dog home with you?"

"No. This is a girl. A pregnant girl."

"Oh, Lord."

At that moment, the back door of the kitchen opened and Maureen Hollister entered the room. She was dressed in her usual work attire, which consisted of jeans, a long-sleeved shirt and cowboy boots. Her chestnut hair was slightly threaded with silver and pulled into a ponytail at the back of her head. At sixty-three, she was ageless and beautiful. She was also the glue that held the Hollister family together.

"Mom, thank God, you're here." He crossed the room and latched on to her arm. "You have to come with me. There's someone in the den waiting to meet you."

As he pulled her out of the kitchen, Maureen shot him a comical look. "Son, please tell me you're joking. I can't deal with company tonight! We've been branding calves all day and then one of Holt's mares, Tootsie, finally decided to give birth. And you know how he feels about that mare—you'd think his own child was being born. And—"

As they headed down a long hallway toward the den, Chandler pulled his mother to a halt. "Mom, I know it's late. And I know you don't need anything else to deal with tonight. But this girl—I just couldn't leave her there at the clinic. She needs rest and a woman's touch right now."

Her expression softened. "Oh, Chandler. Don't tell me you've brought home another stray."

Rather than trying to explain, Chandler gave his mother a tired smile. "Just come to the den with me."

When they entered the long room, Roslyn was sitting in an armchair with her back to them. But as soon as she heard their footsteps on the parquet floor, she rose to face them.

"Oh, my!" Maureen gasped. "You're a woman!"

"What were you expecting, Mom?" Chandler asked wryly.

She slanted Chandler a reproving look. "A dog with pups. Or a pregnant cat. Or a mother raccoon with her kits."

Leaving her son's side, Maureen rushed over to Roslyn and reached for her hands. "Hello. I'm Maureen Hollister," she said, introducing herself. "And you are?"

She smiled tentatively at his mother, "I'm Roslyn Du-Bose," she said, then cast Chandler a hopeless look. "And I'm sorry to interrupt your evening like this. I tried to tell your son that I'd be an intrusion, but he insisted on bringing me out here."

"Roslyn has been driving for long hours and she had a

little fainting spell," Chandler explained. "I thought she needed a quiet rest where someone would be around if she experienced another light-headed spell."

Roslyn continued to look apologetic and Chandler wondered if she was unaccustomed to asking people for help. Or maybe she simply felt awkward because she was among strangers. Either way, Chandler wanted her to trust him and his family. She needed to understand she was safe here.

She glanced at Maureen. "I could've gone to a motel, Mrs. Hollister, believe me."

Maureen immediately wrapped a supportive arm around Roslyn's shoulders. "Oh, honey, I'm so glad that you didn't. You're not in any condition to be staying by yourself. And company is always welcome here at Three Rivers. Did you bring a bag with you?"

Before Roslyn could answer, Chandler said, "I left it at the stairwell. I'll carry it upstairs. Which room?"

"The one across from Vivian's old room should be fine. I believe Jazelle freshened it up only a few days ago."

Maureen urged Roslyn forward and Chandler followed them out of the room and into another hallway that intersected with a wide staircase.

"Where's Blake and Katherine and the kids?" Chandler asked his mother as he picked up Roslyn's case and proceeded to climb the steps behind the two women.

"You never know what time it is, Chandler. It's late. They've retired for the night," Maureen answered. Then she explained to Roslyn, "My oldest son and his family stay on the third floor. They don't want the twins crying to disturb the rest of us."

"Hah! That's just an excuse to get away from all the noise we make down here," Chandler said jokingly, then tossed another question at his mother. "If it's so late, what's Reeva still doing in the kitchen?"

"Tessa and Joe and Little Joe came over for dinner, so Reeva made several extra dishes. I couldn't help her with the cleaning up because Holt called me down to the foaling barn." She glanced over at their houseguest. "Just a regular night on the ranch, Roslyn. Around here, you never know what's going to happen next."

On the second floor, they walked halfway down a wide passageway to a partially open door and entered a bedroom decorated in reds and browns and furnished with a queen-size bed and a large chest made of knotty pine.

Chandler said, "If the room looks masculine, Roslyn, that's because this used to be Holt's room. He moved downstairs a few years ago."

"During foaling season Holt is called out at all hours of the night," Maureen explained. "And as our resident vet, Chandler usually has to go with him."

"But even when it's not foaling season, Holt is coming home at all hours of the night," Chandler added with a sly chuckle.

Maureen let out a good-natured groan. "Chandler, our guest doesn't want to hear about the playboy of the family."

"No," he agreed. "She needs for us to get out of here and let her rest." He placed Roslyn's bag on the end of the bed.

His mother gestured toward a door in the far left corner of the room. "There's a private bath there with a shower. You should find plenty of towels and things. And if you get chilled in the night you'll find extra blankets in the closet. Now with that settled, are you hungry?"

"Thank you. I'm fine. Dr. Hollister gave me a chicken leg and a carton of yogurt."

Maureen rolled her eyes. "First of all, he's not Dr. Hollister around here. You'd better call him Chandler, or Doc, or Bones, or something like that, so we'll know who you mean. And secondly, a chicken leg and a bit of yogurt does not qualify as a meal. Especially when you're eating for a little one, too. I'll bring you some of the leftovers from dinner."

Chandler gave Roslyn a wink. "You probably ought to listen to her. She's had six of us."

"I'm not an expert on carrying babies, but by the time Camille was born, I felt darn close to it," Maureen said with a chuckle, then reached for Chandler's arm. "Come on. Let's leave Roslyn alone so she can get comfortable and ready for bed.

She tugged Chandler out the door and didn't let loose of his arm until they'd reached the landing at the bottom of the stairs.

Deliberately lowering her voice, she said, "Okay. What's going on? You've brought home plenty of things over the years, Chandler, but never anything like this!"

He glanced up the stairs just to make sure Roslyn hadn't followed and could hear them discussing her. "Well, it's pretty simple, Mom. When Trey and I returned to the clinic tonight, Roslyn's car was parked near the front of the building. Seems she'd gotten dizzy and pulled off the highway. I found her sitting inside the vehicle. She was a bit disoriented and while I was trying to question her, she fainted. As best as I could tell from dehydration and exhaustion."

"But where is she from? Who is she? Anyone you know?"

He shook his head. "She's from Fort Worth and apparently driving herself to California."

"The poor little thing," Maureen murmured with empathy. "No one was with her? Where's her husband?"

He grimaced. "She doesn't have one. And from what she tells me, she isn't going to have one. I think the baby's father turned out to be…uh, not the good guy she thought him to be."

"Oh. That's just awful."

"Well, I apologize for springing a guest on you this way, Mom, but I hated to think of her at a motel."

She released the grip on his arm and gently patted his shoulder. "No need for an apology, son. This is your home, too. Besides, you did the right thing. Roslyn might not even have the extra money for a motel room."

The two of them moved away from the landing and started toward the kitchen. As they walked together, Chandler said, "Wrong, Mom. Roslyn appears to be wealthy. She's driving a Jaguar and did you notice her clothing? I'm sure the pieces will have fancy labels inside."

"Hmm. I didn't notice her clothing," she admitted. "Did you ask her why she's traveling west?"

"No. It's none of my business. But from everything she's said, she's not going back to Texas. I'm guessing she's trying to get away from something or someone. Kinda like our Camille. In any case, I didn't think it would hurt to help her out for a night."

"Or two?" Maureen suggested slyly. "For the baby's sake."

Chandler glanced skeptically at his mother. "I don't believe she'll stick around for a second night. Unless you can persuade her—for the baby's sake."

Maureen gave him a clever smile. "All right, son. I'll give it a try."

He leaned over and pecked a kiss at the end of her eyebrow. "Thanks, Mom."

She didn't respond and by the time they reached the end of the hallway, Chandler was shocked to see a tear trickling down her cheek. Maureen Hollister never cried or rarely showed an emotional crack in her tough, ranchwoman armor.

Before she could shoulder her way through the swinging doors leading into the kitchen, he caught her by the arm. "Mom, I see a tear in your eye! What in the world is wrong?"

She blinked. "Nothing is wrong. I was just thinking." Smiling wanly, she cupped her hand against the side of his face. "Have I ever told you just how much you remind me of Joel?"

A tight knot of grief twisted in the middle of Chandler's chest. "Oh, Mom, don't compare me to Dad. It isn't fair. I could never be the man that he was."

"Not exactly. But you are like him in so many ways. And that's a comfort to me, Chandler. Always remember that," she said gently, then her mood instantly brightened and, smiling, she urged him through the swinging doors. "Let's see what Reeva has left for you in the warming drawer. You might have to share it with your little Texas stray."

She was a stray all right, Chandler thought. But she didn't belong to him. Like any other stray he'd picked up in the past, he could afford to offer her food and a temporary home. But he wasn't about to risk offering her a piece of his heart.

Chapter Three

By the time Maureen returned with a tray of food Roslyn had taken a quick shower and dressed in a pair of yellow cotton pajamas and matching robe.

"If you'd like to prop yourself up in bed and eat that's fine," Maureen told her. "You won't hurt the spread if you spill anything."

"That's okay," Roslyn told her. "I'll just sit here in the armchair. It's very comfortable."

She settled herself in the soft green chair and allowed Maureen to place the tray on her lap. On it, there was a plate filled with braised beef ribs, a small bowl of *charro* beans, two flour tortillas and a dish of apple-crumb cobbler. Just looking at the food caused her half-empty stomach to growl with need.

"I thought I wasn't hungry. But looking at this makes me feel like I'm starved," Roslyn admitted. "Thank you for bringing it up, Mrs. Hollister. I, uh, never expected you to wait on me like this."

"I'm Maureen to you. And it was no problem bringing the meal to you. I hope you like it. Reeva is a wonderful cook. We've had her in the family for years." She took a seat on the foot of the bed. "You don't mind if I stay while you eat, do you?"

"Why no. It's nice to have company," Roslyn admitted. "For the past two days I've pretty much been talking to myself. Traveling alone gets a little lonesome."

Maureen smiled with understanding, and not for the first time since she'd met Chandler's mother, Roslyn was totally awed by the woman. Not only was she beautiful and strong, but she was also warm and genuine.

"I know what you mean. I drive up to Prescott fairly often. Which is not that far, but it's much nicer when someone makes the trip with me. Chandler tells me you're from Fort Worth."

Roslyn nodded as she swallowed a piece of the tender beef. "I was born in Fort Worth and have lived there all my twenty-five years."

"Twenty-five. Oh, dear, at your age, I'd been married for four years. Blake was about two years old then and I was pregnant with Chandler. That's been a long time ago."

Roslyn's mother, Geneva, had been thirty years old before she'd married Martin. Two years later, she'd given birth to her one and only child, Roslyn. She'd been a fragile woman who'd never had the strength to show any sort of independence. All of her life, she'd stood in Martin's shadow and lived only to please him. Roslyn couldn't imagine this woman knuckling under to anyone.

"That's hard to imagine," Roslyn admitted. "You look so young."

"You're too kind." Chuckling, she glanced down at

herself. "I'm not exactly looking my best. I did have on a dress for dinner, but then duty called at the foaling barn."

"Do you have lots of horses and cows on the ranch?" Roslyn asked curiously.

Maureen nodded. "Holt can tell you the exact number of horses. Probably somewhere between a hundred and fifty to a hundred and seventy-five head. Blake keeps count of the cows. They number in the thousands. That's counting the ones down at Red Bluff and on our grazing land near Prescott."

"Oh, it sounds like Three Rivers Ranch is a large business."

"Very large," Maureen said. "It takes a lot of hands to keep everything going. Along with me and Blake and Holt and Chandler."

Roslyn tore off a piece of the tortilla and dipped it into the spicy beans. She'd never tasted anything quite so delicious. Or maybe going twelve hours without eating had left her so famished a piece of burnt toast would have been tasty.

"And your husband?" Roslyn asked. "What part does he do on the ranch?"

Maureen cleared her throat. "Joel died a few years ago—from a horse incident. Before that, my husband was the general manager of the ranch. After Joel died, Blake took over the position. Believe me, at that time my oldest son didn't want to step into his father's boots and I couldn't blame him. It's a heavy responsibility. But as the oldest and most qualified, he had to...well, become the head of the ranch so to speak."

Roslyn wasn't expecting to hear anything like this from Chandler's mother and the fact that this family hadn't gone without their share of heartache made her feel a kinship with this woman.

"I'm so sorry, Maureen. I shouldn't have asked. I just assumed that—"

Roslyn waved a dismissive hand to halt her words of apology. "Don't be sorry. Dear God, I've been a blessed woman. I was given many wonderful years with Joel and I have six beautiful children to show for it. So tell me about you. Do you have family back in Fort Worth?"

Roslyn couldn't see that holding back the truth from this woman would do any good. She'd be leaving here in the morning. Even if Maureen decided to take it upon herself to call Martin DuBose, something Roslyn sincerely doubted the woman would do, there was no way her father could get here that quickly. Unless he chartered a plane.

"I have a father and a paternal aunt. My mother died five years ago of leukemia."

Maureen shook her head. "Twenty years old is too young to lose your mother. But we don't have a choice in those matters, do we?"

The gentle, understanding expression on Maureen's face made Roslyn want to lay her head on the woman's shoulder and weep until she could weep no more.

"No," Roslyn said, her voice thick with emotion. "And it was very hard seeing her go through years of treatments and suffering. But I...really miss her. Especially now with the baby coming. And my father—he's very condemning about my choice not to marry the baby's father. You see, he's from an older generation. And the DuBose name is important to him in the social circles of Fort Worth and Dallas. I've pretty much become an embarrassment to him. But... I can't let that bother me anymore. My only concern is my baby. And making sure it has a nice, loving home."

"And that is exactly what you should be concerned about," Maureen said firmly. "When is your baby due?"

"In four weeks. I told Chandler that's why I was traveling now. I need to get to where I'm going before the baby is born."

Maureen left her seat on the bed and came to stand in front of Roslyn. "I don't want to sound bossy, or have you thinking I'm trying to tell you what to do. I'm sure you've already heard plenty of that from your father. But as a mother, I feel like I should advise you that you shouldn't put too much stock in your due date. Babies, especially first ones, can be unpredictable. You really need to be settled now. With someone around to help you in case you do go into labor."

Not for anything did she want Maureen to see how alone and anxious she'd been feeling about the future. Yes, she had plenty of money for housing and living expenses, she had plenty of medical insurance to cover her and the baby's hospital care. Yet none of that could make up for having a loving man at her side.

"You're right, Maureen. And I was hoping to get away from Fort Worth last month so I would have more time. But Dad always seemed to be watching my every move. Finally, three days ago, he flew up to Wyoming on business, so I managed to make my getaway."

"You didn't want him to know you were leaving?"

Roslyn grimaced as she stirred a spoon through the beans. "No. There would've been an ugly scene. He would've done everything in his power to stop me. You see, he wants me to think I'm incapable of taking care of myself or my baby. He wants me to stay dependent on him."

"So he can more or less control your life," Maureen said sagely. "Some parents have a hard time letting go."

Roslyn could've told Chandler's mother that her father had more issues than just letting go of his child. He'd controlled every aspect of his wife's life. Even after Geneva's death, he'd gone against her wishes to be buried next to her parents in California. Instead, he'd thought it more fitting to do it his way with a lavish funeral and burial in Fort Worth. But Maureen didn't need to know about the DuBose family problems. It was bad enough to admit she'd had to resort to running away in order to escape the man.

Sighing, she looked up at Chandler's mother. "Forgive me, Maureen. I shouldn't be telling you any of this. And it…sounds so petty. Except…it isn't."

Maureen laid a comforting hand on Roslyn's shoulder. "I'm glad you can talk to me. Just remember that family problems don't get solved in a day. Tomorrow things will look brighter, I promise. Right now just concentrate on finishing your meal and I'll pick up the tray in a few minutes."

She gave her shoulder another pat, then started out of the room. When she reached the door, Roslyn called to her.

"Maureen, thank you, again. And please thank Chandler for me. He was very kind to help me the way he did."

Maureen gave her a wink. "He may not look it, but Chandler's a big softie. I'll give him your thanks."

She gently closed the door behind her and Roslyn, lost in thought, lowered her fork and looked around her.

Three Rivers Ranch house was not like anything she'd expected. Instead of a Spanish-style hacienda, it was a three-story wood frame. The inside had a rustic feel, while at the same time being warm and comfortable.

Judging by her surroundings, Roslyn could see the Hollisters didn't lack for money. Yet if she'd met Chandler or Maureen on the street, she would've never guessed they were wealthy. Unlike her father, who never failed to flaunt his riches.

Stop it, Roslyn. Quit thinking about your father. Quit blaming or judging him for being rich. His need for wealth and high regard from others are his own problems. Not yours. You're out of it now.

But was she really? Roslyn questioned the grim voice going off in her head. True, these past two days she'd been on the road, she'd been out from under his thumb. But would she ever be able to move past the emotional prison he'd kept her and her mother in for all those years? She had to think so. She had to believe that somewhere, someday, she would meet a man who would love her just for being her and together they'd make a home filled with warmth and happiness.

The next morning, as soon as Chandler arrived at work, he expected Trey to start badgering him with questions about Roslyn. But it wasn't until after they'd dealt with the colts on the Johnson ranch and were driving back to the clinic that Trey finally brought up the subject.

"So what happened with your visitor last night?" Trey asked. "Did you finally get her sent on her way?"

Roslyn hadn't been *his* visitor, but correcting Trey on that point would be useless. "I guess you could put it that way. I took her home to the ranch."

Trey shifted slightly in the seat and gawked at him. "The hell you say!"

Chandler very nearly laughed. "That's right. In her condition she was in no shape to be left alone at a hotel. I thought it best to let Mom take over."

"Oh. Guess that was a surprise for Maureen."

"Mom is always ready for anything." Chandler glanced

at his watch. He'd left Three Rivers at five this morning. More than four hours had passed since he'd operated on the five colts for Mr. Johnson and headed back to Wickenburg. By now he figured Roslyn was champing at the bit to get on the road again. In fact, he wouldn't be surprised to learn she'd already caught a ride into town with one of the hands and drove off in that sleek little Jaguar she considered impractical.

"Is she planning to stay around Wickenburg?" Trey asked.

Chandler couldn't foresee that happening, even if a part of him wanted it to. Which didn't make one iota of sense. She was far too young for him, not to mention pregnant with another man's child. Even if he was in the market for romance, he didn't need to set his sights on a woman like Roslyn. Still, it would be nice if she stayed around until the baby was born. Just so he'd know the two of them were okay.

"No. She says she's headed for California. She has property there."

"Well, she sure is a—"

"Pretty little thing," Chandler said, finishing for him.

Trey shot him an annoyed look. "Now how did you know I was going to say that?"

"Because you said it last night and you tend to repeat yourself."

"Well, I wasn't wrong about that, was I? I mean, I'm not a man who goes around looking at pregnant women, but she was nice. Kinda soft and sweet. You know what I mean?"

Chandler hadn't thought about the softness or sweetness of a woman for a long time. It was something he tried not to think about. Sure, in his younger years he'd done the dating merry-go-round. He'd even had a couple of relationships he'd believed would turn into something more serious. But with both of those women, his job and the ranch had gotten in the way. Since then he'd decided to keep his mind on his work and away from romance.

"Yeah, Trey. I know what you mean." He glanced over at the tall, raw-boned man, who usually had an affable smile on his face. "Just why haven't you gotten yourself a wife, anyway? You ought to have a wife and three kids already."

Trey looked at him and sputtered, "Wife and kids! Hell, you're six years older than me and you don't have a family. Why are you picking on me? Just think about it, Doc. If I had a wife she probably wouldn't like it if I got the urge to go to the Fandango on a Friday night. She probably wouldn't like me going on any night. And that might cause big problems."

Chandler chuckled. "Yeah, big problems."

At the intersection of Highways 60 and 83, Chandler made a left. After two more miles the clinic came into view. As soon as he turned into the parking area and drove past the building, he glanced to the spot where he'd parked Roslyn's car last night.

"Well, what do you know, it's still there," he murmured more to himself than to Trey.

"What's still there? What are you talking about?"

He braked the truck to a halt beneath a pair of Joshua trees and killed the motor. "Roslyn's car. It's still there. I thought she'd be gone by now. I guess Mom must have done some fast talking."

Trey winked at him. "Whose idea was that? Yours or your mom's?"

Chandler shook his head. "I don't have time for your nonsense. This place is running over with horse vans and cattle trailers. Go see what's going on at the barns. If it's anything you or Jimmy can't handle, tell them they'll have to wait their turn."

"Got it, Doc."

Trey hurried away in the direction of the barn and Chandler headed to the clinic. As he walked, he pulled out his cell phone and checked his messages. Near the top was a new one from his mother.

Roslyn is staying one more night.

He slipped the phone back into his pocket and as he entered the back door of the clinic, he very nearly collided with Cybil. The tall, middle-aged woman with a mass of frizzy blond curls had worked as his main assistant with the small animal patients for the past five years. Chandler relied on her to keep things moving smoothly and somehow she managed to do it.

"Good thing there's a smile on your face, Doc. The waiting room is jammed this morning and Mr. Fields is already grumbling about missing his morning coffee at Conchita's."

Mr. Fields was in his eighties and believed his age gave him the right to talk as loudly and sharply as he wanted, no matter where he happened to be or whom he was addressing. "Don't tell me that dog of his has swallowed another piece of plastic."

Chandler started walking down the hallway to his office and Cybil made a U-turn to follow him.

"No. It's his cat this time," she answered. "A facial cyst. I've put her and Mr. Fields in examining room two."

In his office, Chandler pulled on a lab coat and hung a stethoscope around his neck. "What's in room one?"

"A dog with a nose full of prickly pear spines. And room three is a rooster. Something is wrong with his eye."

"While I deal with the cat, sedate the dog," he ordered, then glanced questioningly at Cybil. "And a rooster, you say? It's not a fighting cock, is it? If it is, I'll have to report it to law officials."

"No worries there. It's a pet."

"That's a relief. I don't have time to spend my morning talking with a Yavapai deputy. Even if the deputy turned out to be my brother Joe."

Grabbing a pen from his desk, Chandler crammed it into the pocket on his lab coat and motioned for Cybil to follow him down the hallway.

As the two of them strode rapidly toward the examining rooms, Cybil said, "What's the deal with the fancy car, Doc? Surely you're not planning to drive it back and forth to the ranch."

He should have realized the staff had spotted Roslyn's car parked behind the building and immediately begun to speculate.

"Not mine. It belongs to a visitor—at the ranch," he said, deciding that was the easiest way to explain things. Besides, he could count on Trey to eventually spread the gossip about a young pregnant woman fainting in the parking lot.

Later that afternoon, at the ranch house, Roslyn sat in an armchair watching Katherine and Blake's twins, Andrew and Abagail, toddle precariously between the couch and a nearby love seat.

"The twins only took their first steps a couple of days ago. Now they both think they have walking mastered," Katherine said with a laugh. "Nick, our older son, didn't walk until he was a year old. So I wasn't expecting these two to start racing around at nine months."

Roslyn said, "I've been reading about the different

stages of a baby's life and what to expect about teething and walking and that sort of thing. But I guess nothing is cut and dried."

Katherine chuckled again. "Don't count on anything being normal."

The babies weren't identical, but they did resemble each other. Both were dressed in yellow rompers and shoes with soles solid enough for walking. They each had dark curly hair, gray-blue eyes and dimples in their chins. It was obvious that Katherine adored them and from what she'd already told Roslyn, their father, Blake, thought the world revolved around the babies.

As Roslyn watched them play, she couldn't help but think how different things would've been if Erich, her ex-fiancé, hadn't turned out to be a philandering, money-grubbing creep. By now, the two of them would have been married and instead of preparing to give birth alone, she'd have a husband by her side. But given the revelation of the man's true nature, she was very lucky not to have him in her life. In fact, she thanked God that she'd discovered the real Erich before their elaborate wedding plans had taken place.

Shaking away those grim thoughts, she smiled at the twins. At the moment the babies didn't want to stray very far from their mother, but Roslyn figured that would soon change. "Your babies are beautiful, Katherine. I wish mine was here already."

"Don't worry. He or she will be here soon enough. Then you'll be wondering if you'll ever sit down for more than five minutes at a time." The amused expression on the woman's face turned empathetic. "I suppose you'll be starting to work after the baby comes. I imagine some of your friends have already warned you that's the hardest part of being a mother. I'm a secretary three days a week for a school superintendent in Wickenburg and I love my job. But leaving the babies is still tough. Thankfully, Jazelle takes care of them while I'm at work. She's wonderful with them and I don't have to worry."

"Oh, I thought Jazelle was the housekeeper."

"Jazelle is the housekeeper, along with assistant cook, maid, errand runner, nanny and everything in between."

If Roslyn had chosen to stay in Fort Worth, her father would've hired the most expensive nanny he could find for his grandchild. And it wouldn't stop there. He'd eventually be telling Roslyn how to dress the child, where it should go to school, what friends it should have, and the sort of career and education it would need to be successful. The control would never end. Just as it hadn't ended with Roslyn, until three days ago, when she'd packed everything she could into the Jaguar and driven away from the DuBose palatial home.

"I'm hoping that when the time comes I can find a trustworthy nanny. But I won't be going to work until the baby is a few months old. To be honest, I've not decided what I want to do in the way of a job." As soon as she finished speaking, her cheeks grew hot with embarrassment. "Oh, Lord, that makes me sound like a ditzy schoolgirl."

"No. You don't sound ditzy. More like you don't have everything quite planned out yet. But I'm sure you'll get there," Katherine gently replied.

Roslyn sighed. "To be honest, Katherine, I've never had the opportunity to have a job. My father would never allow it."

Katherine frowned. "I've never heard of such. But I guess he had his reasons."

Roslyn refrained from rolling her eyes. "I did graduate from college with a degree in business, but that was more or less to pacify my father. He thought his one and only child should have a college education. He just never intended to let me use it. A wealthy man doesn't need the women in his family to help make a living. That's his mind-set."

Katherine shook her head. "Strange that we've both had difficult fathers. Except mine was on the opposite end of the spectrum from yours. He was an alcoholic and by the time I reached high school I had to find odd jobs to help the family stay afloat. My mom pretty much made all the household income. But Dad died a few years ago. And now that I look back on it, the work and the scraping by made me a stronger person. I only wish that Dad could've seen the twins. He would've adored them."

This woman was wishing her difficult father was still in her life, while Roslyn was wishing she'd never see hers again. The realization made her feel small and spoiled and ungrateful, yet on the other hand, she had to believe she'd made the right decision to leave her father's house. For herself and for her baby.

"I'm thinking your father probably can see the babies," Roslyn said softly.

Katherine nodded. "I'm thinking so, too. And back to your father not wanting you to hold down a job—doesn't he realize there are plenty of other reasons for a woman to work, other than making money? For instance, my mother-in-law, Maureen. Blake has repeatedly told her that the ranch can afford to put on another hand to take her place. But she'd never agree to such a thing. And frankly, I'm glad she feels that way. Working keeps her young and gives her a purpose."

Early this morning, when Roslyn had come downstairs for breakfast, most everyone had already eaten and they were all hustling and bustling to get to their jobs. She'd

not seen Chandler anywhere and then she'd overheard
Reeva telling Maureen that he'd left the house at five and
she'd sent a sack of breakfast tacos with him.

*I barely have time to eat, much less see after a wife
and kids.*

Last night, when Roslyn had asked Chandler whether
he was married, she'd hoped his response had been exag-
gerated. She'd even wondered if he might even be using
his job as an excuse to remain a bachelor. But she was
beginning to see he'd been telling the truth. His veterinary practice consumed his time.

Thoughts about the man were still drifting through
her mind, when Andrew toddled in her direction. Roslyn held out her arms to encourage the baby to come to
her, but his attention was instantly distracted by a tiny
object on the floor. The baby plopped on his rear and
reached for the fuzzy piece, but before he could poke
it into his mouth, Katherine left the couch and grabbed
her son's fist.

"Andy, that's nasty," Katherine told the baby. "Let
Mommy have it."

The toddler allowed his mother to pull the object from
his grip, then immediately regretted handing it over. He
puckered up and began to whimper as his mother dropped
the ball of hair and lint into a small trash basket.

"Sorry about that, Kat," Jazelle said as she entered the
den carrying a tray loaded with an insulated coffeepot
and two cups. "It's probably a wad of horse hair. I swept
this room earlier, but Holt came traipsing through here
a while ago wearing his chaps."

"Don't worry about it, Jazelle," Katherine told her. "If
there's one tiny speck on the floor, the babies will find it."

The housekeeper set the tray on a nearby wall table

to keep it out of the twin's reach. "I made decaffeinated coffee so you could have a cup, too, Roslyn."

Roslyn gave her a grateful smile. "Thank you, Jazelle. All of you here on the ranch have been so thoughtful and caring that you're making me feel like a princess. Honestly, I'm all over my fainting spell. In fact, I should have left today. But your mother insisted I stay another night."

"Of course you need to stay another night," Jazelle told her. "Kat and I don't get many female visitors out here. And Reeva loves it when she has someone new to cook for."

Jazelle poured the coffee, adding cream to Roslyn's before she handed the cups to her and Katherine, then disappeared from the den. Once she was gone, Roslyn rose from the chair and, carrying her cup with her, began to amble around the long room.

The wooden parquet floor possessed a warm brown patina and was dotted here and there with cowhide rugs. The tongue-and-groove walls were painted a sandy beige and covered with enlarged photos depicting various scenes of ranch life. At one end was a huge rock fireplace with a wide hearth. Presently the screen was closed, but Roslyn could easily imagine a huge crackling fire and the family gathered around, relaxing on the leather furniture that was scarred and softened from years of use.

"This house has so much character," Roslyn commented. "Nothing seems to be new and I love that about it."

"After more than a hundred and seventy years, a house develops a life of its own, I suppose. This one certainly has its own personality. The first time I ever saw this place I was only a young girl. And even then, I was awed by the rooms. The way it all looked and felt and smelled. Nothing much has changed since then, except the people who live and work here have all aged. And then, of course, Mr. Hollister—Joel—is gone. Losing him is still hard for the family to take."

Stepping onto the fireplace hearth, Roslyn picked up a photo from the mantel and gazed thoughtfully at the group of men circled around a branding fire. She could easily recognize Chandler standing by his brothers Blake and Holt, whom she'd met this morning. Along with them was a younger, dark-haired man, she guessed to be their brother Joseph. Another, older man was squatted on the heels of his boots as he held a branding iron to the low flames. He very much resembled Chandler.

"I'm guessing the man holding the branding iron in this photo is Mr. Hollister," Roslyn remarked. "Chandler looks like him."

"You're right. That's Joel. What I remember about him was his kindness, like Chandler. And like Holt, he was a big teaser." Katherine left the couch and joined Roslyn on the hearth. "I don't expect Chandler or Maureen mentioned any details to you about Joel's death. It's not something any of them want to talk about."

"Last night Maureen told me her husband had died from a horse incident," Roslyn replied.

"Well, that's basically the way the sheriff's department ruled it. Death by accident. But none of Maureen's children believe that's what actually happened to Joel. There are too many reasons to debunk the accident ruling. They all think someone killed Joel, then staged the horse dragging to make it look like an accident."

A chill rushed over Roslyn as she carefully placed the photo back on the mantel. "Are you saying the family believes someone actually murdered Mr. Hollister?"

Katherine nodded. "They've slowly been finding a few

clues. But so far there's still too many missing pieces to convince law officials to reopen the case."

"What about Maureen? Does she believe her husband was murdered?"

Katherine shook her head. "We used to think she believed it. In fact, she was in complete favor of Joe and his brothers searching for the truth. But these past several months, she seems to have had a change of heart about the matter. She tells us she wants to quit dwelling on it and put the whole matter behind her."

"You're frowning, Katherine. And I guess I don't understand why. Wouldn't putting it all behind her be a good thing for Maureen? I mean, it's such an ugly, depressing idea."

"I agree. It is ugly. But Maureen has always wanted to know the truth of what happened to her husband. Something has happened to cause a change in her."

"How awful for her," Roslyn murmured ruefully. "And here I've been feeling sorry for myself because my father wants to tie a ball and chain around my ankle. All I can say is that Maureen must be an extraordinarily strong woman to have gone through so much sorrow and still come out smiling."

"She's definitely an iron lady," Katherine agreed.

Roslyn would've liked to ask her lovely new friend more questions about the Hollister family, but at that moment both twins began to fuss. As Katherine went to tend to her babies, Roslyn gazed once again at the photo.

When she'd lost her mother, it had torn out her heart. She'd felt as though she'd lost everything. She hated to think what Mr. Hollister's death had done to Chandler. Last night he'd seemed so kind and genuine. Even now she could recall the way the corners of his lips had tilted with amusement and the way his blue eyes had sparkled like sunlight on water. Being near him had made her feel good and protected and deep-down warm. The feeling was like nothing she'd experienced before and if she was being totally honest, she was still here on Three Rivers Ranch because she wanted to see the man again.

Chapter Four

After the chaotic schedule of the morning and early afternoon, Chandler hadn't expected to make it home by dinnertime, but somehow the large animal patients had tapered off and he and Cybil had managed to clear out the last of the small animal cases by regular closing hour.

Now as he jammed the tails of a white shirt into his blue jeans and brushed back his damp black hair, he almost didn't notice the exhaustion that was seeping into his bones. After all, how could he think about being tired when he was going to see Roslyn again?

He'd reached the bottom of the stairs and was heading toward the den when he heard a male wolf whistle behind him.

Glancing over his shoulder, he watched his brother striding purposefully toward him. With thick, rusty brown hair and an inch or two less than Chandler's six foot two, Holt was lean and as tough as a boot. He also attracted women like flies to honey.

"You look dapper tonight," Holt stated with a clever grin. "You even combed your hair. Guess you're wanting to make an impression on our little houseguest, huh?"

Chandler let out a good-natured groan. "Don't go there, Holt. The woman is pregnant. Or did you fail to notice?"

Holt's grin grew wider. "I noticed. What's the deal with her, anyway?"

Chandler looked at him with wry disbelief. "Don't tell me you haven't already asked Mom."

Holt put on his innocent face. "No. There are some things a guy doesn't want to discuss with his mother."

Chandler barked out a short laugh. "Sure, Holt. Since when did you turn into a sensitive guy?"

With the entrance of the den fast approaching, Holt grabbed him by the arm to stop him. "Oh, c'mon, Chandler, level with me. What's she doing here, really?"

Annoyed that Holt was using up time Chandler could be spending with Roslyn, he said, "She needed a bit of help, that's all. Don't worry. She's not out to steal us blind."

"That thought never entered my mind. But there are other ways a woman can cause a man trouble."

"You ought to know."

"Damn it, Chandler! I'm serious."

With a placating grin, Chandler placed a hand on Holt's shoulder and urged him forward. "Thanks for your concern, little brother. I realize I'm not as experienced as you when it comes to women, but I think I can manage to keep myself safe."

"Okay. Be flip. But one of these days you're going to get that big ol' soft heart of yours broken."

Holt's prediction pulled a chuckle from Chandler. He wasn't in one place long enough for a woman to get any kind of hold on him. "And one of these days all the women in Yavapai County are going to discover that you don't have a heart."

Holt shot him a pained look. "Ouch. After being insulted like that I'm going to need a double shot of bourbon before dinner."

"Just be sure you don't get into the expensive whiskey Mom saves for Sam," Chandler warned. "She'll have a fit."

Holt chuckled craftily. "You got that wrong. Sam would be the one to have a fit."

The two men entered the den and Chandler instantly spotted Roslyn sitting on the couch with Maureen. She was wearing a pale yellow dress with a sash that tied in a small bow beneath her breasts. The soft fabric draped over her belly, emphasizing the fact that she was in the latter part of her pregnancy. Part of her shiny hair was pinned to the crown of her head, while a few tendrils fell against the back of her neck. She looked utterly feminine and completely charming, and as he moved deeper into the room, he found he couldn't tear his gaze away from her.

"Chandler! This is a pleasant surprise!" Maureen exclaimed as she spotted him working his way to the couch.

He bent to kiss his mother's cheek. "Good evening, Mom. For once we managed to close the clinic before eight o'clock at night."

"I'm happy to hear it. And you've arrived just in time." Maureen stood and gestured for Chandler to take the cushion she'd just vacated. "You can keep Roslyn company while I go to the kitchen and check on Reeva."

Since when did Reeva need checking on? Chandler came close to asking his mother the question, but at the last moment decided there was no need to look a gift horse in the mouth.

"My pleasure," Chandler said. "That is, if Roslyn doesn't mind sharing the couch with me."

As Maureen moved away, Roslyn smiled up at him. The warm expression melted something deep in the middle of his chest. The feeling caused Holt's prophecy to whisper through Chandler's head, but he promptly shook it away. When it came to matters of the heart, Holt was clueless.

"Hello, Chandler," she said. "I'd love for you to join me."

He eased down beside her and crossed his ankles out in front of him. "Has Jazelle passed around any drinks yet?" he asked, then before Roslyn could answer, he spotted the housekeeper. "There she comes now. I hope she remembered you can't have anything with alcohol."

Roslyn laughed softly. "You do sound like a doctor, Doc."

Her happy mood was uplifting and he figured he would burst if he didn't smile back at her. "There's something about mothers-to-be that brings out my protective nature," he explained. Then he asked, "You have rosy cheeks tonight—are you feeling stronger?"

"I'm feeling wonderful. Everyone here at the ranch has been so kind. And they won't allow me to lift a finger. Much more of this and I'll get to thinking I'm a princess instead of pregnant."

"Everyone treated Katherine like a princess, too, while she was carrying the twins. And for good reason. She suffered with nausea during the first trimester."

"I think Katherine could still use a little extra pampering. She's been chasing the twins around all afternoon."

Chandler glanced around the room. "I don't see her or Blake. They must have gone out tonight?"

"Your brother and sister-in-law are upstairs putting the twins to bed," Jazelle said, answering his question. "They should be down shortly."

Jazelle lowered the tray in front of them and Chandler pointed to a long-stemmed glass half-full of dark wine. "Is that for me?"

"Just for you, Doc. And the pink glass with ice is for Roslyn. Reeva mixed up ginger ale, cherry syrup and lime juice. It's one of her specialties."

"Sounds yummy. Thank you, Jazelle," Roslyn told her.

Chandler handed the glass with the special concoction to Roslyn and Jazelle moved on to Holt, who'd sunk into an armchair across from them.

"Your bourbon and Coke, Holt," Jazelle told him. "The best stuff."

Holt gave her an appreciative grin. "I think we'll keep you around, Jazelle."

"Thanks, Holt. It's good to know my job is secure," she said drily.

Holt laughed and Jazelle went on her way.

Chandler glanced over to see Roslyn had been taking in the playful exchange between Holt and the housekeeper. "Have you met my brothers yet?" Chandler asked her.

"I met them both early this morning at breakfast. Holt was telling me about one of his mares foaling a colt last night. And I didn't know that the word *colt* specifically meant the baby was male. He explained to me that the females are fillies and the males are colts. And then Blake explained the difference between heifers and steers."

"Our lessons for the day," Holt said with a grin. "And

no, we were both nice. We didn't call Roslyn a greenhorn."

Chandler looked at her and wondered what she'd been thinking today about his home and his family. Probably that everything here on Three Rivers seemed big and rowdy and a little too coarse for her taste. Yet the sparkle in her brown eyes seemed to imply she was enjoying herself.

What difference does any of that make, Chandler? The woman is here on a momentary basis. And once she leaves here you'll never hear or see her again. Just keep that in mind before you let those brown eyes make you a little gaga.

Chandler sipped his wine and tried to shake away the chiding whispers in his head. "Fort Worth is known for being horse and cattle country. I'm surprised you don't know anything about ranching," Chandler told her.

"My father is a corporate lawyer," she explained. "And we've always lived in the city. On occasion, I see cowboys around town, but that's about as close as I've ever gotten to a cow or horse. Dad has handled a few cases in the past for wealthy ranchers, but I never met them."

"All the more reason you should hang around Three Rivers for a while," Holt suggested with a grin. "You can learn plenty about ranch life around here."

She appeared to be searching for a reply when Holt's phone made a chirping noise.

Frowning, he pulled the phone from his shirt pocket. "Excuse me, you two. This message might be important."

While Holt scanned the text, Chandler turned his attention back to Roslyn. "Did you venture outside today and look around the place?"

She nodded. "I went as far as the front porch and the back patio. It's all very beautiful, Chandler. And from the front porch, you can see for miles. It's very different from where I lived. We didn't have a front porch for sitting and the only thing you can see when you're standing there are houses around us. Don't get me wrong. They're all lavish homes with perfect lawns, but it's not like seeing the rugged mountains and stretches of desert."

Chandler wondered what she thought about the stark contrast between Three Rivers and her home back in Fort Worth. Obviously, she'd lived a privileged life, but he also got the feeling that she'd been missing something very important. Otherwise, she would still be there instead of heading to somewhere she'd never seen in California.

"The ranch looks more isolated than it actually is. Joseph and his wife and baby live only a few miles from here on the Bar X Ranch. I wish they were coming to dinner tonight. You would've enjoyed meeting them. Tessa is twenty-seven now, I think. Only a couple of years older than you, so I'm sure you'd find things in common to talk about."

"Katherine mentioned to me that Tessa is originally from a ranching family in Nevada. And how she traveled down here to Arizona on her own," she replied. "So I guess in a way we do have something in common."

"Well, I'd say you're both young, adventurous women." With an emphasis on the *young* part, Chandler thought. Roslyn was eleven years younger than him. Some folks would think that many years would create a giant chasm between a man and a woman. Yet strangely, he didn't feel the gap.

Across from them, Holt slipped the phone back into his pocket and bolted back the last of his drink. "Excuse me, you two. I have to go to the foaling barn."

"Do you need me?" Chandler asked.

Shaking his head, Holt rose from the chair. "Thanks,

brother, but I think I can handle this. Tell Mom I should be back in time to eat. And save a seat next to Roslyn for me," he added with a wink.

"She wants to enjoy her dinner, brother, not listen to your nonsense." Chandler grinned, then shooed him onward. "Let me know if you need me at the barn."

Holt left the den by way of the French doors that opened on to the back patio. Once he was out of sight, Roslyn said, "From what Jazelle and Katherine told me, Holt is crazy about horses."

"And women. And in that order. The horses come first with Holt and then the women."

"Hmm. You two men do seem to love your animals," she said, an impish smile softening her words.

"It's a cowboy thing," he jokingly explained. "Did you leave a pet back in Fort Worth?"

Her expression abruptly sobered. "I've never had a pet of any kind. Dad always said they were nasty and he didn't want them around the house."

With each little revelation she made about her life back in Texas, Chandler was patching together a picture of her father and it wasn't exactly a pretty one. "What about your mom? She didn't like animals, either?"

She sighed. "Mom died five years ago. She liked animals, but she was the sort that always went by Dad's rules. No matter how unduly strict they were. I had friends who had cats and dogs, though, and one had a rabbit named Moe. He was especially sweet."

Like Chandler, she'd lost a parent, too. But unlike him and his siblings, they'd been left with a parent who made sure each of her children felt loved and happy. In that way, he'd been blessed.

"I'm sorry about your mother," he said gently. "Were you two close?"

Her eyelids lowered as she took a sip from her glass, but not before Chandler had spotted a flash of pain in her eyes. "She was…very special. She was everything to me."

The tiny break he heard in her voice was like a punch to his gut. His father had been his hero. Losing him had jerked something out of Chandler that he couldn't define or explain. How did a man explain a hole that refused to heal?

"Did she have an accident?" Chandler asked.

"No, she suffered through a long battle with leukemia. After she died, the house didn't seem like a home anymore. Not that it ever was a home like—" she gestured around the room "—you Hollisters have."

"Thank you. But I don't want you to be misguided by what you've seen last night and today. Things aren't always rosy around here. We have our problems—like all families do."

"Everyone has problems." She gave him a wan smile. "But I have the feeling that you Hollisters deal with your problems together."

And she didn't have that togetherness. Was that what she was trying to tell him? That, except for a rigid father, she was all alone?

Well, hell, Chandler. The answer to that is pretty obvious, isn't it? She's alone and intent on traveling to any place she thinks she can make herself a happier place to live.

The monologue going off in his head was too sad to ponder and he joked in an effort to lighten the moment. "Yes, put that way I guess we do. But the disagreements can get loud at times."

She chuckled. "I'm willing to bet as kids that you and your brothers got into some pretty rowdy scuffles."

"Well, Blake was never a hothead and Joseph was the

baby of us boys, so those two were rarely in on the fisti-cuffs. But Holt and I would go at it. When that happened Dad would usually let us fight to the finish. But Mom was a different matter. She'd break us apart and send us to our rooms to let us stew over our behavior." He glanced up just in time to see Maureen entering the room. "Speak-ing of Mom, here she comes. Let's hope she's going to tell us dinner is ready. I'm so hungry I could gnaw on a piece of raw macaroni."

Laughing, Roslyn laid a hand on his forearm. "I wouldn't advise that, Chandler. You might choke."

He tried not to notice that she was touching him. After all, it was just casual contact that meant nothing. And yet the warmth of her hand sent an unexpected spurt of pleasure through him.

"Dinner is ready," Maureen called out.

Chandler rose from the couch, then offered his hand down to Roslyn. "Let's go eat, shall we?"

Roslyn took his hand and once he'd gently pulled her to her feet, she didn't hesitate to wrap her arm through his. The gesture reminded him that he was more than an overworked veterinarian. He was a man who'd gone a very long time without the company of a woman.

"I'm looking forward to every bite," she assured him. Then, using her free hand, she patted the top of her belly. "And I'm sure Baby is, too. Years from now, I'll be sure and tell him that he once had dinner on a real Arizona ranch."

And years from now Chandler would still remember this beautiful pregnant stranger, who'd stopped on his doorstep long enough to carve a little niche in his heart.

Later that evening, after everyone retired to the den for coffee and dessert, Chandler and Blake were discussing vaccination schedules when Maureen crossed the room and clamped a hold on Chandler's arm.

She said, "Sorry to interrupt you two, but I need to speak with you, Chandler. Alone, in my office."

Blake waggled his eyebrows in a teasing manner. "Better watch out, brother," he warned. "Mom's sounding like a school principal."

He winked at his brother. "If you hear me yelling, better come to my rescue, Blake,"

"Oh, bull," Maureen scolded the two men. "I don't have my dander up. At least, not tonight. I just want Chandler's ear for a few minutes."

"Sure, Mom. Lead the way."

He followed his mother out of the den and down the wide hallway to a study that used to serve as his father's office. After Joel's death, Maureen had taken over the chore of balancing the books for the ranch house, along with the bunkhouse expenditures. As for the bulk of the paperwork associated with the business end of the ranch, Blake and his secretary handled that monumental task in his office, which was located down at the ranch yard.

"I'm sorry to pull you away from your brother," Maureen said as the two of them entered the office. "I realize you two don't get enough time with each other. So I'll try to keep this short."

Most of the space inside the long, narrow room was taken up with a large mahogany desk with an executive chair, two heavy wooden chairs, a set of filing cabinets and shelves jammed with an array of books and folders. While his father had been alive, the room had always held the scents of leather and strong coffee. But now that his mother had taken over the space, that had changed to a mixture of lemon furniture polish and juniper.

She switched on a banker's lamp on the desk, then

looked at him pointedly. "Just how much do you care about Roslyn DuBose?"

The blunt question had Chandler staring at her in disbelief and he tried not to stutter. "What are you talking about?"

"I'm talking about our houseguest. I want to know what you think about her."

For his mother's sake, he bit back the curse word on the end of his tongue. "Great balls of fire, Mom! I only met her last night."

"Yes. And you brought her home with you."

"Because she needed help," he reasoned.

"There are plenty of people around Wickenburg who need help. You don't bring any of them home with you."

Chandler thought he'd quit blushing years ago. Leave it to his mother to bring a shade of red to his face.

"All right, Mom, I get your point. But when I first discovered Roslyn in her car, the situation was a bit urgent. All in all, I didn't want her going off on her own and having another fainting spell."

Her sigh was a sound of impatience. "I'm hardly chiding you about this, son. I'm trying to gauge your feelings about her, that's all."

Why was his mother persisting about *his* feelings? Where Roslyn was concerned he didn't have any. Except for caring about her general well-being.

Liar. Liar. You've enjoyed every second you've spent in Roslyn's company. All day today, she's occupied your thoughts. You've been dreading her leaving and wondering how you're going to forget her once she's gone.

The reproachful voice in his head made him want to groan out loud. "Look, Mom, Roslyn is fine now—at least, physically. And you heard her say during dinner that she plans to leave in the morning. So she'll be out of your hair soon."

The grimace on Maureen's face said he'd clearly disappointed her. "Chandler, I ought to give you a swift kick in the ass."

His eyebrows shot up. "Why? What have I done?"

"You're assuming that I want Roslyn to leave."

Chandler made an openhanded gesture. "Don't you?"

She frowned at him. "Absolutely not. The girl needs us. In so many ways."

Chandler's mind began to spin. "Oh, now, Mom, I don't know exactly what you have on your mind, but Roslyn isn't your responsibility, or mine."

She eased a hip onto the corner of her desk and pierced him with a thoughtful gaze. "You're right. She isn't. At her age and single, she isn't anybody's responsibility. But I thought…well, we have plenty of extra room. And Reeva throws out enough food to feed three or four more people. It wouldn't hurt to ask her to stay on with us for a while—at least, until she has the baby."

Stay until she gave birth? But that would be days, weeks even, Chandler thought. By then she would be starting to feel like family. By then, the tender, protective feeling he got whenever he was near her might turn into something more serious. Something that could wind up being very painful.

"Mom, she's a stranger. We don't know her. Not really. Maybe this is what she had planned all along. Maybe she'd heard about the Hollisters and deliberately parked at the clinic last night just as a way to get her foot in the door."

Her expression suddenly sheepish, Maureen nodded. "God forgive me, but those same concerns crossed my mind. That why—this morning I did some checking up. Or let's just say I had someone do some checking for me."

Chandler was surprised. Normally his mother was far too trusting. "You didn't call her father directly, did you?"

"No. Nothing like that. I just wanted to make sure that Martin DuBose existed and that Roslyn's story was true."

Just thinking that Roslyn might not be truthful made Chandler feel like a heel. "And?"

"Everything she's told us checked out. And from what my source told me, the old man is known as a real cold codger."

It was a relief to hear Roslyn had been honest with them, yet it was sad, too. She didn't deserve that kind of father.

He said, "Well, obviously she isn't lacking money. I believe right now she's trying to get over the mistake she made with the baby's father. And she's longing for a place to call home. That's what I'm thinking."

"A home is exactly what she needs for herself and the baby—whenever it arrives." Her expression rueful, she asked, "Did you know her mother died?"

"Yes. She told me." Chandler shook his head. "And I can see, when she mentions her father—there's a look on her face that is so full of anguish and resentment I know it can't be an act."

Maureen smiled gently. "There's a look on your face, too, whenever you're near her."

Chandler let out a short laugh to cover his awkwardness. "Mom, you're all wrong. Sure, she's pretty. And I like her—a lot. But that's all. For Pete's sake, she's going to have a baby."

"That fact only makes her more precious."

"And she's years young for me. Besides, I'm already

hooked up with the clinic and the ranch. No. Don't be matchmaking for me. It won't work."

She let out a long sigh. "Okay, Chandler. No matchmaking. All I ask is that you take Roslyn aside and convince her that she needs to stay here on the ranch. At least, until after the baby arrives and she gets back on her feet."

Why in hell was his mother doing this to him? Didn't he have enough on his plate to deal with? Hadn't she stopped to notice that he was stretched to the breaking point?

Thrusting a hand through his hair, he tried to tamp down his frustration. "Me? Why me? She thinks you're wonderful. You're a mother figure to her—she'll listen to you."

Maureen shook her head. "You're the one who first found her and took care of her. You're the one she trusted enough to allow you to bring her out here to the ranch. You're the one she feels connected to."

Maybe his mother could see all of that, but Chandler sure couldn't. Hardly thirty minutes had passed since Roslyn had announced at the dinner table that she'd be leaving tomorrow. That didn't sound like the woman felt a connection to him or the ranch.

But maybe she was leaving because no one had asked her to stay. The thought rambled through his head as he began to move aimlessly around the room.

"I didn't realize this was going to put such a strain on you, son," she said cunningly. "Perhaps it would be better if I get Holt to speak with her. He knows exactly what to say to a woman."

He paused to stare at her. "Like hell! Holt doesn't know how to talk to a woman like Roslyn!"

"What do you mean, *like* Roslyn?" she asked sagely.

"She's young and pretty. Holt knows all about those kind of women. And every other kind, I might add."

Chandler wondered how it was that his mother always knew exactly which buttons to push to make her children comply with her wishes.

"Is it really that important to you that Roslyn stay? I mean, you have more than you can deal with as it is."

Shrugging, she said, "Well, with Camille living down at Red Bluff and Vivian and Hannah gone to the reservation, I'm feeling a little lost for my daughters and granddaughter. It would be nice to have Roslyn and the baby around. And maybe, in turn, we can help her get things righted in her heart."

There was no way he could argue that point. Especially when the whole family had been concerned about the gradual change taking place with their mother. A change that had nothing to do with her daughters and granddaughter moving out. No, they all believed it had something to do with Joel's death and uncovering the truth.

If Roslyn and the coming baby would be a pleasant distraction for his mother, even if only for a few weeks, then he was all for it. And perhaps in the long run, a stay here would help Roslyn, too.

"All right, Mom. I'll talk with her. But I'm sure not going to make any promises. I think she has going west on her mind."

"Then you need to convince her that Arizona is west enough," Maureen said brightly, then straightened to her feet. "Come on. I've already had Jazelle light a fire out on the back patio. You can take Roslyn out there to have your private talk."

"Mom, I've already warned you about matchmaking. I don't need a fire to get the point across to Roslyn."

Taking Chandler by the arm once again, Maureen urged him out of the office. "Good grief, son, you have matchmaking on the brain. This has nothing to do with that. I just want Roslyn to feel warm and relaxed when you bring up the question about her staying."

His mother was maneuvering him. That much was obvious. And normally Chandler would've already dug in his heels. But this wasn't Maureen's usual behavior. She never stuck her nose in any of her children's personal business, unless they asked for her help or guidance. And in the end, what would it hurt to comply with her wishes? After all, he was a grown man. His mother could just do so much leading.

Chapter Five

The flames in the fire pit sent flickering fingers of orange and yellow light across the patio and lit Chandler's features with a golden hue. Roslyn had no idea why he'd invited her out here. Especially when she figured he had to be weary from the long workday he'd put in. No doubt the comfortable furniture in the den would be more relaxing to him. Whatever his reason for this outdoor excursion, she was glad he'd made the suggestion.

The fire warmed the cool desert air and when she gazed beyond the patio toward the ranch yard, she could see the clear night sky was stamped with thousands of stars. It was a beautiful night and her last night here. She wanted to savor every moment of it before she said goodbye to the ranch and the friends she'd made here.

"Are you warm enough?" he asked. "I can stoke the fire if you're feeling chilled."

"I'm perfect," she assured him. "The fire feels great."

He was sitting next to her on the wide rock ledge that

surrounded the fire pit—close enough for her to reach over and touch him. If she was inclined to do such a thing. And, oh, yes, she was feeling very inclined. All through dinner, she'd thought about touching him in ways that had caught her completely off guard.

After learning of Erich's unfaithfulness, she'd felt so angry and betrayed that she'd been certain it would take years before she'd ever feel any sort of desire for a man. She'd believed it would take an emotional earthquake before she'd be able to trust any man. Yet, from the moment she'd met Chandler, she'd felt an instant connection. A belief that she could put her trust in him. It was crazy.

"I have a confession to make, Roslyn. I brought you out here to the patio for a reason."

His remark cut into her tumultuous thoughts and she looked at him with blank surprise. "A reason? Oh. You must have wanted to get me out of the den so that Maureen could have a private word with the rest of the family."

He shook his head. "No. She and I already had private words in her office. And...well, to be frank, we were discussing you."

Jolted, she turned her knees so that she was facing him head-on. "What about me? Did she—?" Her mouth was suddenly so dry she couldn't swallow. "Has she contacted my father?"

He frowned. "Mom wouldn't do anything like that. None of us would. Not unless you asked us to."

Relief pushed a long breath from her lungs. "I'm sorry. It's just that... I can't deal with him. Not now. Maybe never."

"You sound very bitter, Roslyn."

"I'm sorry," she said again. "I'm sure you and your family think I'm an ungrateful brat. But believe me,

Chandler, I didn't leave Fort Worth on an impulsive whim. Ever since Mother died, I've wanted to leave. There was nothing there left for me. Not emotionally, or in any other way."

"That was five years ago," he stated. "Something must have kept you there."

She shrugged. "Hope, I suppose. I kept hoping that with Mother gone, Dad might actually need me around to fill the void. That didn't happen. He has his work. But then Erich started showing interest in me and we started dating. After that, things got much better."

"Your father approved of the union?"

Her laugh was short and dry. "Erich was from an old, respectable family, who'd been friends with my parents for many years. When we eventually got engaged Dad was thrilled. In his eyes we were the perfect match. And for the first time I could ever remember, he actually acted as though he was proud of me."

"What happened when your engagement ended?" he asked.

She sighed. "Dad went from being proud to blaming me for the whole breakup. According to him, if I'd made myself more desirable, Erich would've never turned to other women."

His blue eyes made a slow survey of her face and Roslyn wondered what he was thinking. That she was a real mess? That her father had probably been right about her inability to hold on to her fiancé? Oh, Lord, it was all so embarrassing.

"That was a terrible thing to say to you, Roslyn. You needed his support, not recriminations."

"Well, I didn't expect anything more from him. But that's enough about my problems. You brought me out here to talk and I'm rambling." She gave him the cheeriest smile she could muster. "So what did you need to speak with me about?"

He didn't immediately answer and she got the impression he was uncomfortable. The idea bothered her greatly. Last night, when he'd walked up to her car window, she'd found a friend. She didn't want that to change.

"Your plans for leaving tomorrow," he said finally. "Mom wants you to stay put. Here on the ranch—with us."

This was the last thing she'd expected to come out of his mouth and she stared at him in disbelief.

A half grin cocked up one corner of his lips. "Does that surprise you?"

"No. It stuns me." Without a shred of warning, tears filled her eyes and when she spoke again, her voice was a choked whisper. "Maureen is too kind for her own good."

"Mom's always had a big heart. But she's not a pushover. She doesn't offer an invitation like this unless she really means it."

Rising to her feet, she walked aimlessly to the edge of the patio and stared out at the night sky. Only minutes ago, she'd been thinking how Three Rivers was so beautiful and peaceful. She felt protected and wanted here, something she'd not felt since her mother died. To spend more time with this family would be a dream come true. On the other hand, she wasn't at all sure it would be wise. Especially when she looked at Chandler. He made her feel things she shouldn't be feeling. And think about things that had nothing to do with the plans she'd made for her and her baby's future.

Glancing over her shoulder, she saw that he was watching her and waiting patiently for a response. She drew in a deep breath and let it out. "I honestly don't know what to say, Chandler. This is all so sudden and unexpected."

He left the fire pit and came to stand next to her. Roslyn tried not to notice the alluring male scent emanating from his clothes and the way his muscular body towered over hers. Everything about the man reminded her that she was a woman. One with an empty hole in her heart.

"I'm sure you weren't thinking about staying on here," he said. "But—"

"It's not a good idea, Chandler," she interrupted, while purposely keeping her gaze on the sky. "Your mother is a very busy woman. As are the rest of you. I'd only be a nuisance."

"You're hardly a child that needs to be watched over," he countered. "Aren't you really worried that you'll be bored out of your mind staying out here?"

His question took her by surprise and she swung her gaze to his skeptical face. "Bored? Are you joking? Compared to the DuBose home this place is as busy as the Dallas-Fort Worth airport terminal. Something always seems to be going on."

"Yes, but it's not like the city, where you can go shopping or find all kinds of entertainment to keep you occupied."

"That sort of thing gets old quick. Is that what you think my life consisted of back in Fort Worth? Shopping and entertainment?"

His smile was sheepish. "The thought might've crossed my mind. What did you do with your time back in Texas?"

"Well, like I told Katherine, Dad would never allow me or Mother to work. But I still managed to make myself useful by helping plan charity events for children's causes, doing volunteer work at the girls club and tutoring a few high-school students with their math. That sort of thing."

"All of those are commendable tasks," he said. "But

you're at the age where…well, you could've been building a career for yourself. Or maybe you never wanted one."

She grimaced. "I never thought too much about it, Chandler. To go against Dad would've made my mother very unhappy. And with her being so ill, the issue of my future didn't seem very important. After she died, I finished getting my college degree in business. But it was mostly just to have a piece of paper to show I wasn't a complete dunce."

"I don't believe anyone would want to label you a dunce," he said wryly. "And congratulations on the degree. I hope one day you'll decide to use it."

She looked away from him and swallowed hard. "Yes, from now on my life is going to be different. I might have lost my father, but I've gained my freedom. You can't imagine what that feels like."

His hand was suddenly lying upon her shoulder and the warmth from it spread all the way down her arm and into the tips of her fingers. "You know, staying here for a while, until the baby comes, will give you time to adjust to all these changes you're going through. And we'll all be around to help—if you need us."

Us? Did that mean him, too? The mere idea that he cared about her well-being made her feel more special than she'd ever felt in her life. Even more than the moment when Erich had slipped a diamond engagement ring on her finger. How could that be?

"Do you—? Would you mind if I stay?" she asked haltingly.

A wry smile twisted his lips. "Why would I? Both of my sisters are living away now and Mom needs a stand-in daughter to nurture. Whatever makes her happy makes the rest of the family happy."

So he wanted her around for his mother's sake, she

thought. Well, that was certainly better than not wanting her around at all.

"Put that way, I can hardly refuse," she said. "But I'll tell you true, Chandler, it's hard for me to believe that you and your family want to take on a burden like me. I'm overwhelmed by your generosity. Really, I am."

The hand on her shoulder lifted and he grazed the knuckles gently against her cheek. "I don't want to hear you say you're a burden. Ever again. Hear me?"

"If you say so."

"I do. Say so." He curled his arm around her shoulder and urged her toward the French doors leading into the den. "Come on, let's go back in and tell Mom you're going to stay. She'll be very happy."

Walking along beside him with his arm curled protectively around her, she almost felt as if she belonged here. "You know what, Chandler? It makes me very happy, too."

During the next week Roslyn drove her car from the clinic to the ranch and moved all her things into the upstairs bedroom she'd been using since the first night she'd arrived on the ranch. Maureen had offered her a larger room with a sitting area, but Roslyn had assured the woman she didn't want to change. The coziness of the smaller room appealed to her. She particularly loved the rustic pine furniture and the padded window seat, where she could sit and watch the busy comings and goings of the cowboys down at the ranch yard.

In the meantime, Katherine had managed to get Roslyn an appointment with the OB, who'd delivered her and Blake's twins nine months ago. Yesterday she'd kindly accompanied Roslyn into Wickenburg to meet with the doctor, and after a thorough exam, he'd pronounced both her and the baby healthy. According to him, she should plan on going into labor in another four weeks. Give or take a few days.

Which meant Roslyn had a month, maybe more, to live on the ranch before she'd need to pack up and head on to California. And during that time, she intended to enjoy every second spent with the Hollister family.

Now, as she sat on the front porch of the ranch house, she was on her cell phone, trying to convey to her best friend back in Fort Worth exactly why she was somewhere in Arizona, soaking up the spring sunshine and doing her best to put her father and Erich Parker far behind her.

"You can't imagine how good it is to hear your voice, Roslyn. It's been a week and a half or more since you left and I haven't heard a peep from you until this very moment. I'll be honest, I almost contacted your father, just to see if he knew where you were."

Roslyn groaned with frustration. "Oh, Nikki! I specifically asked you not to say a word to him and you promised!"

"I said *almost*. I didn't. But look, Ros, I had a right to be worried. We've been friends since...well, our kindergarten days together. And I'm not one bit happy about you leaving. If you'd wanted to get out of your father's house that badly, you could've moved in with me. Or gotten an apartment somewhere in the city. Or even moved to Dallas. God knows your father would never go over there looking for you. He sees that city as the devil's playground."

Roslyn pinched the bridge of her nose. She'd been dreading making this call to her old friend, because she knew beforehand that the other woman was going to put up an argument. Still, Nikki had been her closest friend since they were small girls. Roslyn couldn't just dismiss her from her life.

"Well, you needn't worry any longer," Roslyn told her.

"I'm in a beautiful place with a very nice family. And I intend to stay here until a couple of weeks or so after the baby is born."

"Exactly where are you? And who are these people? Can you trust them?"

"I'm in Arizona—in the desert. And as to the people I'm living with, they're a well-known and respected family. I wouldn't be here if I couldn't trust them," she answered evasively.

"That's not telling me much," Nikki grumbled. "And I've been trying to call you for days! Don't you have cell service there?"

Roslyn grimaced. "As soon as I left Fort Worth I turned off my old phone and didn't make any calls or texts. I didn't want my father to be able to track my route."

Yesterday, when she and Katherine had been in Wickenburg, she'd purchased a new phone with a different number, so she wouldn't have to worry about her father tracing her through connecting tower pings. Nor was she ready to tell Nikki her exact location. Her friend was well-meaning and would never intentionally go against Roslyn's wishes, but she often spoke without thinking. If she let Roslyn's whereabouts slip to mutual friends, the information would eventually make it to her father.

"I thought all of Arizona was desert," Nikki said.

Roslyn smiled. "Geography never was your best subject."

Her friend chuckled. "Funny, isn't it? I barely know where to find Texas on the map and I end up working for a travel agency. Good thing all I have to do is make reservations."

"It's a very good thing," Roslyn joked, then asked, "So how are things going with you? Still dating Randy?"

There was a long, pregnant pause before her friend

finally answered. "No. He decided to enter the marines. He'll be leaving for California in a few weeks."

"And he didn't ask you to go along with him?"

Nikki sighed and Roslyn could picture the other woman frowning and absently twining her long red hair around her finger. "He did. But I told him no."

Roslyn gasped. "But why, Nikki? You're crazy about the guy? Why let him slip away?"

Another sigh sounded in Roslyn's ear. "I don't want to leave Mom. Not in her present state of mind."

"My dear friend, it's not your fault that your father decided to divorce your mother and go live on the east coast with another woman."

Nikki was silent for another long moment and then she said, "No. But if I left Mom, too, I'm not quite sure she could handle being totally alone. Maybe later when she's had time to adjust to the loss."

Later would probably be too late for Nikki to make the life she'd wanted with Randy, but Roslyn was in no position to give her friend that sort of grim advice. Not when she'd already had a broken engagement and an unexpected pregnancy with a man who'd turned out to be a liar and a cheat.

After visiting with Nikki a few more minutes, she ended the call and was about to walk back into the house, when she noticed a truck like Chandler's coming up the long driveway. Pausing, she watched the dusty vehicle stop near the front gate and the busy doctor climb to the ground.

This past week, she'd scarcely seen the man. Once in the early morning, he'd been exiting the house by way of the kitchen. On that occasion he'd paused long enough to tell her good-morning and that he had to hurry to the clinic to deal with an emergency. Then one night she'd gone to the kitchen for a glass of milk and found him eating his supper, while going through a stack of medical records. He'd looked very tired and though he'd invited her to take a seat and join him, she'd not wanted to hang around and make a nuisance of herself.

But today was different. Today he looked full of energy as he trotted up the wide steps.

"Well, hello, Roslyn," he said with a broad smile. "How's the little mother-to-be?"

Blushing, she smiled at him and tried to ignore the way her heart was dancing a silly little jig in the middle of her chest. "I'm fine, thank you. You're home very early, aren't you? There's still a few hours of daylight left," she commented.

He chuckled. "There'd better be. My receptionist crossed out this late afternoon so I could get away from the clinic. There are times I have to work for the ranch and this is one of them. Blake wants me to check on two different herds of cattle. Some of the hands have reported a few of the cows having pink eye."

"Are you talking about the same sort of pink eye that humans have?" she asked.

"No. It's different. Bovine pink eye isn't contagious to humans. But if left untreated in cattle it can easily spread through the whole herd." His gaze traveled up and down the length of her. "Say, you're wearing jeans. And boots, too! Nice!"

Her cheeks turned a deeper pink at his compliment. "Thank you. I got them yesterday when Katherine and I went to town." She smoothed a hand over the loose blue gingham shirt covering her baby bump. "I thought the jeans would be practical for wearing here on the ranch. And she talked me into the boots to go with them."

"Boots are a necessary footwear on a ranch," he said

with a grin, then slanted her a thoughtful look. "Are you busy right now?"

She laughed softly. "Busy? What would I be doing? Each time I offer to sweep or pick up, or help in the kitchen, I'm told to sit down. I'm beginning to feel like a sitting hen."

His grin turned sly. "Then how would you like to go with me? The road out to the grazing range is fairly smooth and you won't have to get out of the truck unless you want to."

She had to stop herself from jumping up and down with excitement. "Oh, I would love to go. I've only walked down to the ranch yard twice since I've been here and that's as much of the ranch that I've had a chance to see."

"Then it's about time you saw more of it. Can you be ready to go in five minutes?"

"Sure."

"Then meet me in the kitchen. The truck we'll be taking is parked out back."

"I'll be right there," she promised.

After a quick trip to the ladies' room and grabbing a light jacket from the closet, Roslyn hurried down to the kitchen, where she found Reeva loading Chandler down with a thermos of coffee and a plastic bag filled with homemade cookies.

"We're not going on a picnic, Reeva," Chandler told her. "Seeing a cow with pink eye doesn't exactly give a man an appetite."

"I'm not worried about you, Chandler. This is mainly for Roslyn. She's eating for two, you know. And this is her last month, the time when the baby is putting on weight. She needs plenty of calories. And I made the coffee decaffeinated just for her."

Chandler shared a knowing smile with Roslyn as he

ushered her out the back door. "I'm sure you've guessed by now that Reeva mothers all of us."

"It's pretty obvious," Roslyn agreed. "Maureen told me that Reeva has a grown daughter and one grandchild in California, but that she rarely sees them."

"That's right. Her daughter, Liz, is one of those people who wants everyone to believe she was born at the top of the social circle. It embarrasses her that Reeva works as a cook. In fact, Reeva says her daughter tells her friends that her mother works as a secretary."

"How sad. Sounds like this Liz has misguided priorities," Roslyn replied. "Especially when Reeva is such a wonderful person. I honestly don't know where she finds all her energy. She never quits working. But then, neither do you."

With a hand on her elbow he helped her down a set of short rock steps, and kept the steadying hold on her arm as they walked to a white truck with the 3R brand painted on the door.

"I wouldn't know what to do with myself if I wasn't busy," he said.

"How about take a nap?" she suggested impishly.

He laughed and she laughed with him and for the first time since Roslyn had left her home in Texas, she felt the heaviness in her heart lift and fly away with the warm desert breeze. It felt so wonderful to be with this man, she thought. His company made her almost forget that she would soon be a single mother and that the man who'd proposed to love her had not really loved her at all.

"You're very funny at times, Roslyn," he said, as he helped her into the work truck. "I like that. As for the nap, I wouldn't know how to do that, either."

He shut the door, then went to the back of the truck and let out a loud whistle. She turned just in time to see him lowering the tailgate and two yellow short-haired dogs leaping into the truck bed. After he'd closed the gate, he joined her in the cab.

"I've seen several dogs around the barns. Some were this color and others were spotted with longer hair. Are they all pets? Or working dogs?"

"I guess you could call them both. But mostly they're working dogs. This pair that's going with us today are Black Mouth Curs and very good at rounding up cattle. I don't expect I'll need them to work today, but they like to go with me. They're very sweet and social, so you can pet them if you'd like. They won't take off your hand. The spotted dogs you've seen around the ranch yard are Australian shepherds. I raise and train them to work cattle, also. That is, when I have the time."

He opened the console between the seats and dropped the thermos and cookies into the storage space. "I'll put these in here so they won't end up rolling under our feet. You can get them out whenever you'd like."

"I honestly don't want to ruin my appetite," she told him. "Reeva is cooking something special. Polish sausage and macaroni and cheese."

Laughing, he glanced in her direction. "That's not special. That's plain ol' comfort food."

She chuckled. "Maybe that's why I love it."

He started the truck and reversed out of the small parking area behind the house. As they drove past the ranch yard, she noticed a group of mounted cowboys, riding away from the ranch.

"Where are they going? To round up cattle?"

"Not at this time of day. They're probably going to ride fence line to make sure there are no posts or wires down. It's a never-ending job."

"Can't they do that job in a vehicle?"

"A few cross fences can be checked from a vehicle. Most of the ranges, however, are too rough for vehicles to travel over. And Mom has always kept Dad's policy of not using ATVs or helicopters on the ranch."

"Why? Just to keep with the older tradition of doing everything on horseback?"

"Well, the Hollisters are all about tradition. But the main reason is that loud machinery puts undue stress on the cattle and can even cause them to be injured. Ninety-five percent of the time, a cowboy can ride his horse quietly into a herd and the cattle will remain still and calm. Try doing that with an ATV and they'll stampede in every direction."

"Oh, I wasn't aware of that." She looked at him and smiled. "I guess you can tell I'm very ignorant about ranching."

"Would you like to learn?"

"I would like to learn," she answered, then added, "This will probably sound silly to you, but before I came here to Three Rivers, I never really got acquainted with being outdoors and I've discovered that I like it. There's something soothing about being surrounded by nature. It's given me a different perspective about life."

"I think that's very true."

He shoved the floor shift into a higher gear, but still maintained a slow pace. The narrow road they were traveling was dirt and wound randomly through clumps of blooming sage and tall saguaros. She'd never seen such wild and rugged countryside, yet its enchanting beauty couldn't draw her attention completely away from Chandler.

Beneath his gray Stetson, his black hair gleamed like a crow's wing, while his blue eyes were as striking as the azure sky. The Western shirt hugging his shoulders and torso was fashioned of khaki material and looked as if it had been tailor-made to fit his muscular build. His presence was so big and masculine it seemed to fill up the entire cab of the truck.

"Do you think you might look for an outdoor job once you get settled in Redding?" he asked.

Reining in her wandering thoughts, she focused on his question—one that had been plaguing her ever since she'd learned she was going to be raising a child without the help of its father.

"I haven't thought that far ahead yet. The main reason I was going to Redding was because Dad doesn't know anything about the property I own. So he wouldn't know to look for me there. The place was one secret my mother kept from him. Because she knew he'd find a way to take the place away from her, or me."

"I see."

Did he really? She doubted it. Because it was hard for anyone to understand that kind of behavior.

"Well, I feel confident they'll be some sort of job there for me," she said as cheerfully as she could. "One thing for sure, I'm not trained to do any sort of outdoor job. My college degree is in business. Dad picked out the subject. He thought that was more fitting for a woman."

He glanced in her direction. "What would you have chosen for yourself, Roslyn?"

She pondered his question for a moment and realized how cocooned her life had been until she'd started dating Erich. And even then, she probably wouldn't have gotten engaged if it hadn't been for her father pushing the issue.

"I don't know. That's awful to admit, isn't it?" She turned slightly toward him. "It's hard to explain, Chandler, but when you grow up with someone else choosing everything for you, then your imagination and dreams never really have a chance to flourish. Each time I tried to plan something on my own, it was always interrupted or changed. I realize now just how spineless a person I've been. For years I did everything my father's way. And then when Erich came along I did everything his way."

"And now?" he asked.

Straightening her shoulders, she said, "Now I'm going to follow my own convictions. I'm going to think for myself and my baby."

"I'm glad to hear that, Roslyn."

Wondering if he was making fun of her, she glanced at his rugged profile. Yet there was no amusement to be found on his face and the fact filled her with simple joy. More than anything, she wanted this man to see her as smart and strong and capable.

"You know, Chandler, it's almost staggering to think there's a whole new world out there and I can do and be what I want. I'm not sure what that is yet. Except that I want to be the best mother I can possibly be. And the love I give to my child won't come with chains."

He reached over and gave her hand an encouraging squeeze and Roslyn was swamped with the urge to wrap her fingers around his and never let go.

"I think you're going to be a very good mother, Roslyn. And whatever else you want to be."

His words caused her throat to grow thick with emotion. "You're a morale booster, Chandler."

Thank goodness he hadn't seemed to notice the husky note in her voice. If he ever figured out just how attracted she was to him, he'd probably run for the hills and stay there until she left Three Rivers.

Chuckling, he joked, "You need to come to the clinic and meet my staff. They all call me a tyrant. An exaggeration, in my opinion. Since I don't ask them to do any more than I do during a fourteen-hour workday."

He was teasing, but she seriously wondered why he didn't cut down his work hours.

He'd said he didn't have time for a family of his own. Yet every time she laid eyes on the man she felt certain he'd been born to love a woman, to nurture a brood of children.

Chandler Hollister doesn't want a family, Roslyn. When are you going to get that through your head? The man is thirty-six years old. There's a reason he's chosen to remain a bachelor for so long. And don't go getting the idea that you could be the woman to change him.

Blocking out the cynical voice in her head, she placed a hand on the side of her belly. The subtle movement beneath her fingers reassured her. It also reminded her that the baby would soon be born. Her entire focus would change to being a mother and providing a safe and loving home for her child. There wouldn't be room in her thoughts for a man. Especially a man who had no romantic interest in her at all. And yet, he continued to live in her mind like a sweet, recurring dream.

"You've gone quiet, Roslyn. Are you okay?"

"I'm perfect."

As long as I'm with you.

She didn't know where that thought had come from, but she had a sneaky suspicion it had come straight from her heart.

Chapter Six

Chandler drove for another three miles before he finally stopped the truck next to a wide, shallow creek lined with willows and salt cedar. Off to their left, about a hundred yards away, a herd of black cattle grazed at tufts of grass growing among the chaparral.

"Would you like to walk with me part of the way to see the cattle?" he asked. "Or would you rather remain here in the truck? The engine is diesel, so it's perfectly safe to leave it idling with the air-conditioner going."

"I'm not that much of a softy." She patted the top of her stomach. "I realize this big tummy makes me look off balance, but I'm pretty sure-footed. I'd like to walk with you."

He grinned. "Great. Just stay put and I'll help you down from the truck."

After he'd carefully helped her to the ground, he opened the tailgate and the two dogs leaped out. Roslyn expected them to take off barking and chasing the cattle, but instead they remained obediently at Chandler's side.

"I'm impressed. The dogs aren't running wild. You must be a good trainer," she told him.

He chuckled. "These two are no-nonsense. But a few others get it in their head that it's more fun to play. The key is patience."

"I'm trying to store up all my patience, so I'll have plenty when the baby arrives."

"Better store more for its teenage years. Mom said she couldn't have made it through those years without Dad to keep us corralled."

But her child wouldn't have a dad. Unless she found a man that she loved with all her heart. Some generous-hearted man who wouldn't mind being a father to another man's child.

After a moment passed and she didn't reply, he said, "I'm sorry, Roslyn. I wasn't thinking—about the dad part. But I have a feeling that you're going to have a husband long before that baby gets to be a teenager."

Only if I met someone like you.

And her chances of meeting and marrying a man like Chandler were about the same as finding the end of a rainbow. That kind of stuff only happened in fairy tales. Not in Roslyn's life.

"I wouldn't count on it. But that's years away. Anything can happen." She looked at him and forced a bright smile on her face. "Right?"

He didn't smile back. Instead, he studied her for a long thoughtful moment before he finally murmured, "Sure. Anything can happen."

They walked on toward the herd of gazing cattle and Roslyn purposely turned her attention to their surroundings. The sunshine was hot on her face and the breeze carried the scents of sage and wildflowers. Small birds fluttered around the Joshua trees, while in the far distance, a copse of pines dotted the slopes of a mountain. Roslyn had never been in a wilderness like this before, with nothing around her but rugged land, cattle and wildlife.

The awed appreciation she was feeling must have shown on her face, because he suddenly asked, "I realize I'm repeating myself, but are you okay, Roslyn? You look a bit dazed."

She cast him a quick, reassuring smile. "Sorry, Chandler. I guess I've been staring with my mouth open, haven't I? This land is so beautiful. Everything about it intrigues me. I could probably ask you a thousand questions."

A faint smile tilted his lips. "A thousand questions, huh? Well, ask away. I might be able to answer a few."

"Well, for starters, I'm curious about how many herds of cattle there are on Three Rivers?"

"I can't give you an exact number. The count changes. But it usually ranges around twenty separate herds." He gestured toward the cattle. "This one is number eleven. And the next one we need to look at is number twelve. 'Course, that's not all the cattle we own. We have about three or four more thousand head on our grazing land up by Prescott. And a thousand or so down at Red Bluff. What's the next question?"

"The water. I noticed a creek runs through this little valley. Does it supply enough water during the dry seasons for the cattle to drink?"

"No. This is one of three creeks on the ranch. This one and another a couple of miles from here dry up completely. The other keeps a bit of water in certain places. But we have deep water wells with pumps and other irrigation methods to handle the ranch's needs."

She digested that information, then said, "So there actually are three rivers on the ranch. I figured the ranch's name was just something someone made up."

He shook his head. "My great-great-great-grandfather named the ranch for the three small rivers that converge on our property."

"Gosh, that many 'greats' meant he came to this land a long time ago," she said. "I can't imagine how wild and uninhabited this area must've been back then."

"The first Hollisters came here in 1845. At that time, Edmond and Helena were newlyweds. She was very young—sixteen, I think. He was about ten years older. Mom has a couple of old tintypes of them on their wedding day. I'll show them to you sometime."

"I'd like that," she said, while thinking how very rooted Chandler must feel. He knew why the older generations of Hollisters had come here, why they had stayed and why they would always remain on this spot of ground. How would it feel to have that sort of solid foundation beneath her feet? She could only wonder. She knew very little about her ancestors and those she knew about had been scattered.

"Since there are still Hollisters here on the ranch, I'm assuming Edmond and Helena had children."

"Two boys and a girl," he replied. "My brother Joseph is named after their first son. The girl died as a child from dysentery."

"How sad. I'm sure in those days a medical doctor would've been a long distance away."

"Yes. And medicine wasn't always that helpful."

By now the cattle were less than twenty yards away. Some had lifted their heads and were curiously watching their approach.

Chandler placed a hand on Roslyn's shoulder to stop her forward progress. "This is as close as I want you to get, Roslyn. The cattle are gentle, but sometimes the new mothers can be overly protective. If one charged and hurt you or the baby, I'd never forgive myself." He pointed to their right, where a pair of Joshua trees grew close together. "You might stand over there in the shade. If anything runs in your direction get behind the trees."

"Don't worry. I will."

He walked on into the herd of cattle and Roslyn made her way over to the Joshua trees. From there, she watched as he moved from one calf to the next, searching for signs of scours. Oddly enough, the animals seemed to trust him and several times he managed to get his hands on the calves for a closer examination.

After about ten minutes, she saw him draw a cell phone from his shirt pocket and make a call. Once he'd ended the conversation, he walked over to where she was waiting. He didn't appear overly concerned, but she was learning he was a cool, laid-back type of guy. She'd heard Holt say Chandler was more like their late father than any of the brothers. Perhaps he got his easygoing manner from Joel, along with his striking looks.

"Did some of the cows have pink eye?" she asked.

"A few. I've made a call for some of the hands to bring a trailer out here. I want the calves and their mothers hauled back to the barns at the ranch yard. The cows need to be treated with medications. The calves look okay, but for obvious reasons they need to stay with their mothers."

"Will the cows eyes get well?" she asked.

He nodded. "Yes. Thankfully, the hands spotted the problem early. Blake will appoint two or three men to care for them for the next few days. Don't worry. They'll be fine."

"So what do we do now? Go look at the next herd?"

"Not yet." He wrapped his hand around her arm.

"We'll have to wait here until the cowboys arrive so I can show them which calves need to be loaded. I'm sorry, Roslyn. Looks like it's going to be a long while before we head back to the ranch."

"Don't apologize," she told him. "I'm enjoying every minute of this."

His blue eyes swept over her face and Roslyn got the faint impression he was glad she'd come along. "Okay. Let's walk down to the creek and sit in the shade. Or would you rather wait in the truck?"

"I'm all for the creek," she told him happily. "Just lead the way."

Chandler didn't know what had possessed him to invite Roslyn to join him on this working trek. This wasn't any place for a pregnant woman, who wasn't used to the outdoors. Moreover, spending time with her wasn't really a wise thing to do. For the most part, he didn't want her getting the wrong idea about his motives. She might get to thinking he was in the market for romance, or even worse, for a ready-made family.

But she was just so damn pretty and being with her made him feel young and full of energy. He supposed his brothers, especially Holt, would consider him crazy for being attracted to a pregnant woman. After all, Chandler could easily find himself a date, if he wanted one. There were plenty of women around who were more than willing to go out with him. Some had even gone so far as to call and invite him for a night on the town. But none of those women came close to piquing his interest. And he especially didn't want to waste what little spare time he had being bored by a female whose favorite subject was herself.

Beneath the shade of a gnarled mesquite tree, Chan-

dler sat on a fallen log and allowed his gaze to follow
Roslyn's graceful movements as she walked along the
creek bank. A pair of butterflies hovering near a branch
of blooming salt cedar had presently caught her attention
and as he studied her from afar, he decided that being a
city girl hadn't stopped her from taking to life here on
Three Rivers. It was a fact that surprised him greatly.
Although, a part of him wondered if the novelty would
soon wear off. The same way it had quickly worn off with
Vivian's ex-husband. The ink had hardly dried on his
sister's marriage license before Garth had grown bored
with living twenty miles from town. A small town at that.

Years had passed before Vivian had finally put their
divorce behind her and found the love of her life in Sawyer Whitehorse. His sister was incredibly happy now,
but Chandler hadn't forgotten the heartache she'd gone
through before she'd met Sawyer. And he sure as hell
didn't want to take a chance on the same thing happening to him. And yet there were times he felt very lonely.
Times he wished for a woman who would love him and
whom he could love in return. A woman he could build
a life with and grow old with.

"You're welcome to come share my seat," he called to
Roslyn. "You're probably getting tired."

She turned from the water's edge and walked over to
where he was sitting. "I'm not really tired, but if it will
make you feel better I'll sit," she said.

She eased down next to him and Chandler was suddenly overcome with her nearness and the soft feelings
she evoked in him. She smelled of lily of the valley and
her skin held an inner glow, as if she'd been sprinkled
with stardust. The night at the clinic when she'd fainted,
he'd touched her face and wrapped his hand around her
tiny wrist. Beneath his fingertips, she'd felt as delicate

and smooth as the dewy petal of a flower. Days had passed since that night, yet he'd not forgotten how it had felt to touch her, to cradle her in his arms.

"It'll take a while for the men to get out here with the trailer and then a few more minutes to tag the right cow-calf pairs. If I take you back to the ranch in an exhausted condition, Mom and Reeva will skin my hide."

She laughed lightly and the sound made him smile along with her. It was good to hear her laugh. After all she'd apparently gone through with her father and the broken engagement, he figured she deserved to be happy. He wanted her to be happy.

"Don't worry. I won't cause you to get skinned," she said, then glanced wondrously around her. "There's so much here to look at and experience. I'm never going to forget this place. Thank you for bringing me with you today."

As he watched the wind play with the brown hair lying against her neck, he wondered what she would think if he scooted closer and nuzzled his nose against her cheek. How would she respond if he touched his lips to her lips?

He couldn't allow himself to wonder about such things, he scolded himself. Sure, she'd be here for the next few weeks, but after that she'd be saying goodbye. Kissing her would be all wrong. And yet the urge had been eating at him from the first moment she'd given him one of those sweet smiles.

"Thank you for joining me, Roslyn," he said, while wondering if his voice sounded as strained to her as it did to him. "Cows aren't as good company as you are."

Laughing softly, she turned to look at him and as soon as their gazes met, her laughter sobered. Something warm and smoky filtered into her brown eyes and all of a sudden Chandler was having trouble breathing.

"I—I'm glad to know I provide a bit more companionship than a cow," she murmured.

Before he realized what he was doing, his hand was sliding gently up and down her arm. Surprise flickered across her face, but to his relief she didn't pull away.

"You're very beautiful, Roslyn. I'm sure that's a tired old line you've heard over and over. But that's the way I see you."

She swallowed and he wondered if being near him was affecting her as much as touching her was rattling his senses.

"I'm not beautiful," she protested. "And other than Erich, I've not spent much time in a man's company."

"Why not? And don't tell me the guys back in Fort Worth treated you like a wallflower. I'd never believe it."

She looked out at the shallow water moving sluggishly over the rocky riverbed and Chandler could plainly see sadness etched upon her features. He didn't like seeing it. Didn't like the idea that she'd ever suffered a moment of sorrow.

"Oh, I was asked out often enough. But I usually turned down the offers. I spent most of my teenaged years at home with my mother. You see, all through my high school years she was very sick and I didn't want to leave her alone. Dad hired a private nurse to care for her. But that wasn't the same as having her daughter with her."

"What about your father? Surely he was with his wife."

Her grunt was a mocking sound. "Only when it suited him. And that wasn't often. Don't misunderstand me, Dad always provided lavishly for us. But not with his time or his affections. I guess that's why my mother and I clung to each other. I could see I was losing her and she was basically the only family I had. I realized every minute I spent with her would soon end. So I…"

Her last words trailed off on a hopeless note and he finished the sentence for her. "You neglected yourself in the process."

A faint frown on her face, she looked at him. "I wouldn't call it neglected. I just didn't do the things that my friends were doing at the time. Dances, ballgames, dates—I wasn't much interested. By the time I graduated high school, Mom had grown much worse. I didn't want to go to college, but she insisted. She wanted my life to be normal even though hers wasn't."

"That's because she loved you," he said softly.

She smiled at him, but Chandler was focused more on the bright tears in her eyes.

"How did you know I needed to hear that?" she asked softly.

"Maybe because being a vet isn't always easy. Or maybe because my dad died and I don't really know why. We may never know."

She turned slightly toward him and then her hand reached out and touched the side of his face. The tender contact caused his insides to melt like candy on his tongue.

"Chandler, I—I've never met anyone like you. You make me feel like I'm worth something. You make me feel wanted. And that means more to me than you'll ever know."

Her words should've set off alarm bells in his head. Instead, his heart gathered them up like a starving man at the dinner table.

Leaning toward her, his eyes delved into hers. "I've never met anyone like you, Roslyn. And I'm glad you stopped at the clinic. Glad our paths met that night."

"Really?"

Doubt put a waver in her voice, but Chandler's was

strong and steady as he answered. "Yes. Really. Otherwise, I'd never know what it was like to know you—to do this."

Her eyebrows lifted slightly. "This?"

All finished with thinking, Chandler cupped a hand against the back of her head and drew his face close to hers.

"Chandler, what are you…doing? Thinking…?"

As she whispered the question, her warm breath fanned his lips. The sensation was totally erotic and whetted his appetite to kiss her even more.

"I'm not thinking," he admitted, desire turning his voice gruff. "I'm hoping…that you want to kiss me as much as I want to kiss you."

"I do. Oh, yes, Chandler, I do."

Her response barely had time to register in his brain before she took the initiative and touched her lips to his.

Soft. Incredibly soft. Like the wisps of a cloud brushing against his face. She kissed each corner of his lips, then moved to a nearby dimple. Chandler exhaled a shaky breath, while his fingers tangled around her silky hair.

She whispered his name again and then her lips were back on his, open, fierce and hungry. Giving him exactly what he wanted and more.

Groaning with pleasure, Chandler's arms instantly wrapped around her shoulders and drew her upper body close to his. She moaned in response and, not caring about the consequences, he deepened the kiss until their surroundings faded to little more than flashes of sky and ground.

He hardly noticed the insistent buzzing in his shirt pocket and even when he did recognize the sound as his phone, he chose to ignore it.

But Roslyn didn't. She pulled back and sucked in a shaky breath. "You should probably answer that," she said, her gaze purposely avoiding his. "It might be an emergency."

Her raspy voice sounded as though she'd just woken from a deep sleep, making him wonder if she'd been just as lost in their kiss as he'd been.

Hell, Chandler, even if she had been turned on by you, that didn't mean anything. Except that she wasn't immune to physical pleasure. Don't be a fool and start thinking the kiss had been important to her. You've gone down that road before and it's a road to nowhere. Just remember that.

Shoving out a long breath, he did his best to ignore the jaded voice in his head. "Yeah. I'll see who it is," he muttered. "Could be the hands trying to locate which range we're on."

Roslyn rose from the log and while she ambled over to a shady portion at the water's edge, Chandler pulled the cell phone from his pocket. Seeing the call had originated from the clinic, he punched the call-back button and Cybil answered before the first ring ended. She immediately apologized for interrupting him, then hurriedly went on to explain a situation with two kittens suffering from coccidia.

Chandler patiently instructed, "Yes, if the test came back showing coccidia parasites they'll need to be dosed immediately. With the same medication we use for the swine and poultry. Just weigh each kitten carefully. If they're alert and willing to drink, don't bother with drips. The owner can take them back home. If they're weak and listless better hold them over and hydrate them. Ten days of medication and soft food. Got it?"

After Cybil had assured him she had all the instructions she needed, Chandler ended the call and walked over to stand next to Roslyn. She didn't bother to look at him. Instead she stared straight ahead as though she'd decided the two of them had connected enough for one day.

"Sorry for the interruption, Roslyn. My assistant back at the clinic is trying to deal with sick kittens without my help. Intestinal issues. Must be the day for such things," he said wryly.

"Must be," she quietly replied.

He touched a hand to her shoulder and she glanced up at him. As her brown eyes scanned his face, he could see they were shadowed with confusion and doubts. Damn it! He'd not meant to cause her any anguish or uncertainty. He'd simply wanted to be close to her. He still wanted it.

"I hope you're not sorry about that kiss, Roslyn. I don't want you to…regret what just happened with us."

A lost, lonely sigh slipped past her lips and Chandler desperately wanted to pull her into his arms. He wanted to reassure her that she could trust him to never hurt her. But could he really make her such a promise, when he had no idea what she might eventually ask from him?

"I don't regret it," she said quietly. "I'm just a little embarrassed because— Oh, I don't know why I—"

When she didn't continue, he gently squared her shoulders so that she was facing him. "I don't know why you'd be embarrassed, Roslyn. Because it was nice. Very nice."

She closed her eyes and swallowed and for a moment Chandler thought she was about to cry. And he didn't know what he'd do if a tear did roll down her cheek. Hate himself for the rest of his life, he supposed.

Her eyes opened and he could see a look of wonder swimming in the brown depths. "But I kissed you like… well, you're probably thinking I'm some sort of hussy or something. That it's no wonder I'm pregnant out of wedlock."

If she hadn't look so remorseful he would've laughed

out loud. "Roslyn, you're thinking is so off the mark it's funny. But I'm not going to laugh. Because I can see that you're serious and…oh, honey, you are so—" He cupped his hand to the side of her face and in that moment it felt as though his heart was about to burst with some strange, new emotion he'd never felt before. "You're precious, Roslyn. You could never be a hussy."

"So you say. But I'm not going to pretend, Chandler. When I'm with you I'm really not myself." She frowned. "I'm beginning to wonder if these last days of my pregnancy are doing something to my senses."

Smiling, he stroked the tip of his forefinger along the shell-pink color splashed across her cheekbone. "What's my excuse? I'm the one who instigated the whole thing."

"You're a man. You don't need a reason to kiss a woman. Do you?"

Her question caused the smile on his face to linger. "I always thought a reason was necessary. But in your case, just looking at you gives me a good enough reason."

Her nostrils flared as she drew in a deep breath and then she was pulling away and turning her back to him. "I'm eight months pregnant in case you haven't noticed."

"I've noticed. A lot." He stepped around to the front of her and laid a hand on the side of her belly. "You know, in my line of work I see pregnancy just about every day. Yes, I'm talking about animals now. But animal or human, it's a wondrous and beautiful thing. If you're thinking your thick waistline makes you any less desirable than the next woman, your thinking is all wrong."

Her eyes misted over and Chandler suddenly realized that she was far more to him than a pretty face with soft, kissable lips. But he could hardly admit the fact to himself, much less to her.

"Chandler, I'm only going to be here for a few weeks. I don't think it would be wise to let myself kiss you again."

Even though he understood that she was probably being practical and smart, her words left him flat. And somewhat surprised. Especially after the passionate way she'd responded to his kiss. But perhaps she was right about this last stage of her pregnancy affecting her senses. Under other circumstances she might not have been interested in kissing him in any form or fashion.

After all, she was eleven years younger. He probably came across as an old man to her. Not a guy she'd want to start a relationship with.

Relationship. Was that what he wanted with Roslyn? Something more than a few dates? Something that wouldn't end with a kiss on the cheek and a relieved goodbye?

The questions were bantering around in his brain when the movement of the baby rippled beneath his hand. The sensation waylaid his revolving thoughts and he looked at her with new appreciation.

"The baby must be taking dance lessons. Right now I think she's doing a tap number."

She smiled. "I'm beginning to think my child is going to be a dancer or some sort of athlete."

The night she'd fainted at the clinic and he'd listened to the baby's heartbeat, he'd been in doctor mode. Only the health of the child had been in his thoughts. But everything was different now. Roslyn was swiftly becoming a part of his life, along with the baby. He didn't know whether that was a good or bad thing. Either way, he couldn't seem to stop his feelings from escalating.

He smiled back at her. "Or a rancher, schoolteacher, doctor—anything he or she wants to be," he suggested.

She pressed a hand over his and the contact reminded

him that the baby had veered their conversation on a different path. With the ranch hands likely to arrive any moment, he wanted to get back to what had just happened between them.

"About the kiss, Roslyn. I think we were both enjoying it. And I don't think it would be unwise for me to kiss you again. Or for you to kiss me. If that's what we both wanted," he added slyly.

For a moment she looked ready to argue the point, but then her lips pressed together and created an impish dimple in her left cheek. "Chandler, I'm beginning to think your nickname should be Naughty Doc rather than just Doc."

In the time it took blink his eyes, she'd chosen to make light of the whole thing. Which was probably best for both of them, Chandler decided. He shouldn't want to make an issue over one little kiss. Trouble was for Chandler, it had been far more than just one little kiss.

He coughed up a chuckle and hoped it sounded authentic. Behind them, the rattle of a fast-approaching stock trailer signaled the arrival of the ranch hands.

"The cowboys are here," she said, stating the obvious.

"Yeah. I'd better get over to the herd."

"I'll wait here," she informed him. "I don't want to get in the way and be a nuisance."

A nuisance? Never, he thought, as he walked briskly out to join the men. But she was definitely a lovely temptation. One that he damn well needed to resist. Otherwise, when she left Three Rivers, she was liable to take his heart with her.

Chapter Seven

Two days later, Chandler showed up halfway through the evening meal. As he took a seat next to Roslyn, she noticed his damp black hair had been combed back from his face and the tails of a white shirt tucked haphazardly into his jeans. He looked even more fatigued than usual and Roslyn was suddenly overwhelmed with the urge to wrap her arms around him.

"Sorry, everyone, for being late," he apologized. "Things got hectic at the clinic."

Blake passed a platter of what was left of the fried chicken down the table to Chandler. "Things are *always* hectic at the clinic," Blake said with an edge of impatience. "I don't know when you're going to break down and hire more help. Specifically another vet to handle the patients you don't have time for."

Chandler forked two pieces of chicken onto his plate, then reached for a bowl of mashed potatoes. "I *specifi-*

cally don't want another vet," he replied to his brother's comment. "I might not like the way he does things. And I sure as hell don't want the clinic's reputation ruined by an outside quack."

"Wow, Chandler, who put a burr under your saddle?" Holt asked from his seat across the table.

Roslyn had been wondering the same thing. She'd never seen Chandler show this much frustration before.

"You two, leave your brother alone," Maureen said to Blake and Holt. "Can't you see he's stressed?"

Holt snickered. "Stressed. Chandler needs to try climbing on a bunch of two-year-olds and he'll learn what stress really is. That's after his ass hits the ground a few times."

Roslyn watched a muscle jump in Chandler's jaw, but he refrained from making a retort.

Down the table, Maureen glared at her younger son, while Blake shook his head. "Ease up, Holt. You know good and well that our brother puts in far too many hours working."

"I don't want anyone's sympathy." Chandler's voice was gruff, and his eyebrows pulled together in a scowl. "What I need is more help at the clinic. And not another vet," he said to Blake. "Cybil's sister had some sort of accident and hurt her back. The past few days she's been taking off to help care for her sister's kids."

Holt slapped a hand on the tabletop. "I got it, brother! Why don't you let Roslyn help you out? I'm sure she'd love dealing with the small animals."

"That's a wonderful idea, Holt," Maureen said, then directed an encouraging smile at Roslyn. "What do you say, Ros? Have you ever spent any time at an animal clinic?"

Roslyn wondered how the conversation had moved so

quickly to include her. "Um, no. I haven't," she answered Maureen. "Other than recuperating in Chandler's office the night I fainted. But I'd be willing to learn."

Judging from the glower on Chandler's face, he wanted miles and miles separating her from his animal clinic.

He slanted a rueful glance at her. "I don't think that would be wise, Roslyn. You'd have to be on your feet. And you'd have to avoid the cat litter. And—"

"Chandler, quit being a stuffed shirt," Maureen interrupted. "Roslyn is young and healthy. Lots of women work on their feet right up until they give birth. Why, when I was pregnant with you kids I was riding up until my seventh month and helping in the branding pen up until my due date. Roslyn is a woman who's going to have a baby. Not a piece of porcelain you have to keep safely on a shelf."

"Maureen is right," Roslyn told him. "I'm not a weakling. In fact, the exercise will be good for me. And helping out at the clinic would make me feel productive instead of like a sponge."

Unconvinced, he said, "You don't know the first thing about animals."

"Well, I can always fetch things for you and clean up," she argued. "That should help a little. And I can learn the rest as I go."

"Sounds good to me," Holt said with a grin, then asked shrewdly, "Or are you afraid the place will run over with guys wanting to get a look at your pretty assistant?"

"Blake, would you please stuff a chicken leg in Holt's mouth?" Maureen said. "Anything to shut him up."

Holt laughed. "Oh, Mom, you know I'm only teasing Chandler. He'd think I was sick if I didn't give him a hard time."

Maureen drained her wineglass, then reached for the

tall, dark bottle sitting near her elbow. Roslyn had never seen the woman refill her glass at dinner, but maybe the trip she'd made to Phoenix this morning had made the day extra taxing for her.

"Yes, you're always teasing, Holt. But instead of telling Chandler what he *ought* to be doing, why don't you tell us what you *have* been doing—with the horses. I had a long conversation today with the foreman of the Tumbleweed Ranch in Nevada. They're wanting twenty head of our mares and ten yearlings."

"Twenty head of mares?" Holt guffawed. "Over my dead body. They're the lifeblood of our remuda. And we've never sold a yearling off this ranch before. Each one has a chance to prove himself worthy of a lifetime home here on Three Rivers. Surely you set him straight on all of that, didn't you?"

From the corner of her eye, Roslyn noticed Chandler was carefully watching his mother's reaction.

"No. I told him we might be able to come up with half that number," Maureen quipped, then took another long sip of wine. "But I did explain that he'd need to talk with you and Blake before a deal could be made."

Holt's mouth dropped open and for a split second Roslyn thought the man was going to curse a blue streak in front of his mother and everyone else. But just as quickly, his jaw snapped shut and he directed a dark stare at Blake.

Blake slanted their mother an annoyed look, before turning his gaze back to his younger brother. "Don't worry, Holt. I'll give the foreman a call and explain to him that our number of broodmares is exactly where we want it to be. And the yearlings are off-limits."

After Blake's words trailed away, no one else made any kind of remark about the horses. And for the first time since Roslyn had come to the ranch, the atmosphere around the Hollister dinner table felt strained.

The remainder of the meal passed in silence and afterward, Roslyn chose to skip dessert in the den. Instead, she carried a cup of coffee to the front porch, where she could watch the last streaks of red-gold sunlight sink below a row of desert hills.

"Care if I join you?"

Roslyn glanced around to see Chandler stepping onto the porch and closing the door behind him.

"You're very welcome to join me," she told him. "It's a beautiful evening out here."

He walked over to where she stood resting a shoulder against one of the porch post.

"And as awkward as hell inside," he added wryly. "Sorry about all that at the dinner table, Roslyn. I hope you know it's nothing about you. Sometimes we get on each other's nerves."

She turned so that she was facing him. "From what I've gathered since I've been here, Holt is very particular about the horses. I got the impression he was more than a little vexed with your mother when she mentioned selling a few."

He let out a heavy sigh. "Long before Dad died, he appointed Holt manager of the horse division. And rightly so. He knows equines inside and out. And to tell you the truth, he can probably doctor them as good, or better than I can. He loves each and every baby he raises like his own child, and he only sells the ones that end up unable to handle the rigors of ranch work. Holt always has the final say so over the horses. That's why…it seemed a little peculiar to us brothers that Mom didn't set the Nevada rancher straight, right off. And for her to imply we might sell ten mares and five yearlings—it's worrisome, Roslyn. She's not herself."

Could be he was also thinking his mother had been amiss when she'd agreed with the suggestion of Roslyn working at the clinic. She hoped not. The idea of working with Chandler and his staff was very appealing. True, it would allow her to spend more time in his company, but it would also give her a real purpose until the baby arrived.

She said, "Maureen was gone to Phoenix for most of the day today—to a cattle-buyers meeting. I'm sure she's tired."

He frowned. "Hmm. She's gone to Phoenix several times in the past few months. I wasn't aware she was going again today."

"I heard her telling Reeva that she'd decided at the last minute to go." She darted a glance at him. "And now you're going to think I go around the house eavesdropping on conversations."

Smiling wanly, he touched a forefinger to the tip of her nose. "Your nose is too little to make you a busybody. But let's forget about Mom for now. We need to discuss this matter about you and the clinic. Let's go sit," he suggested.

With his hand against the small of her back, he guided her over to a wicker love seat padded with striped cushions. The touch of his hand was warm and instantly reminded her of the kiss they'd shared out on the range.

That kiss. She'd never experienced anything like it before. Even now, the memory of the embrace heated her cheeks and twisted knots in the pit of her stomach. Kissing Chandler had been like downing a shot of straight whiskey—wickedly hot and instantly intoxicating. These past couple of days, she'd been desperately trying to get the whole incident out of her mind. But rather than forgetting, her thoughts had been stuck on *that kiss*. And him.

"Look, Chandler, I'm sorry your mother and brother put you on the spot about me working at the clinic. If you're afraid I'll be in the way, I'll understand."

"I never said I thought you'd be in the way."

She shook her head. "You didn't have to. I could see misgivings on your face. But that's okay. You and your family have already done so much for me. You hardly need to give me a job."

He reached for her hand and she gladly allowed him to fold her fingers inside his big warm palm.

"My reservations have nothing to do with you getting underfoot. If that was the case I would've fired Trey a year ago. I'm more concerned about your health and the baby's."

"Well, if I start getting weary, I can always sit down and put up my feet. You see, I know the boss," she added impishly. "He won't mind."

His eyes twinkled. "I see—you're already expecting favoritism."

She chuckled. "Just a little."

"Well, you'd have to drive yourself back and forth to the clinic. Riding with me is out of the question. Some days I might be leaving at four thirty in the morning and not returning until midnight."

"That's no problem. If the ranch has an extra vehicle I can use, I know how to drive," she reasoned.

He squeezed her fingers. "Just the drive here and back might be tiring for you."

"Oh, Chandler, I'm not that fragile. Really. And it would make me feel good to be able to do something for you—to take some of the work off your shoulders."

As he studied her face, she couldn't help notice how

the last rays of sunlight were touching his face, illuminating the black whiskers that had emerged above his dark skin. Just thinking about touching her lips to his jaw and experiencing the raspy sensation against the tip of her tongue was enough to send a shiver down her spine.

"You mean that, don't you?"

Her gaze met his and she wondered if he could see the feelings that were billowing up inside of her, making her ache to touch him.

"I do," she said simply.

His eyes remained connected to hers for another long moment before he finally looked away. "I'm not sure it's the right thing to do. But I can see the whole thing is important to you."

"It's very important, Chandler. When I leave here with my baby I'm eventually going to have to find a job. I want to be able to tell an employer that I've worked for a few days in my life, at least. But more than that, I need to prove to myself that I can contribute."

"You've already told me that you did volunteer work back in Fort Worth. Obviously you can contribute to a cause."

"That's true," she admitted. "And my work there was appreciated. But it's not the same as punching a time clock."

Chandler laughed. "Thankfully my staff doesn't punch a time clock. Otherwise, I'd have to pay them for so much overtime, I'd go broke."

Roslyn chuckled along with him. "Well, Doc, you wouldn't have to worry about paying me anything. I'd be an intern."

His expression sobered and Roslyn's breath caught in her throat as his thumb gently stroked the back of her hand.

"No pay. No job."

"Oh, but—" She started to argue and then her eyes widened with sudden dawning. "Are you saying that you're going to give me a try at the clinic?"

He shrugged as a wry smile tilted one corner of his lips. "Against my better judgment. But the minute it becomes too much for you to handle, that's it."

With a little cry of delight, she flung her arms around his neck and smacked a kiss on his cheek. "Thank you, Chandler. Thank you!"

"You're very welcome," he murmured.

For a moment, his hand came up to mesh in her hair and while she savored the feel of his fingers against her scalp, she allowed her cheek to rest against his and her nostrils to breathe in the masculine scent of his hair and skin.

He was rough and rugged and all hard muscle. And she could have stayed like that forever, close to him, touching him. But the door to the house opened and she pulled back before anyone could spot the embrace.

"Well, I wondered where you two had gone."

Holt walked over and sank into a chair sitting at an angle to Chandler's side of the love seat. He was carrying a squatty glass partially filled with ice and a dark liquid that Roslyn assumed was whiskey and cola.

"I figured you were in the den with your feet up. Enjoying coffee and pie," Chandler said to him.

"It's too damn quiet in the den," he remarked. "It's like a tomb in there. And tonight I need something a heck of a lot stronger than coffee."

"Katherine never showed up with Andy and Abby, or Nick?" Chandler asked. "The twins would supply plenty of noise."

Holt shook his head. "According to Blake, Nick has

gone over to the reservation to stay the night with Hannah. And the twins are fussy from teething and Katherine is keeping them upstairs this evening so their crying won't get on everyone's nerves."

"Aww, I should go help her," Roslyn said. "She probably hasn't had a chance to eat dinner."

"Blake is helping her," Holt informed her. "Please don't leave me out here alone with only my hairy-legged brother for company. I've had a hell of a day. And you're a much prettier diversion than he is."

Chandler cocked an eyebrow at him. "What's been happening today? Been breaking colts?"

"Only this morning. The afternoon I spent with Joe. You know how he and Blake go out every week searching for clues. Well, Blake had a bunch of banking business to deal with today and couldn't go. So that left me to go with Joe—this time on horseback. I was beginning to think it was going to take an earthquake to get Joe headed back to the ranch. We were out there for hours."

Roslyn could see Chandler's interest was suddenly piqued. He leaned slightly toward his brother. "Find anything more than rock and sagebrush?"

Snorting, he answered, "Two sidewinders and a Gila monster. One of the sidewinders nearly got my hand. I was moving a rock and didn't see it."

"Nothing pertaining to Dad?" Chandler persisted.

Holt nodded. "That's why I came out here to talk to you. I didn't want to mention any of this in front of Mom. God knows she's not been herself here lately. And you know how she's gotten about Dad's death. She doesn't want us digging, or looking, or even talking about any of it."

Chandler's sigh was burdened with worry. "Yeah. I know. But that doesn't mean we have to stop searching for answers. That's our right. He was our father. If we ever do get enough to put a theory together, then we can tell her."

"That's the way Joe and Blake feel about it, too." He wiped a hand over his face, then dug into the front pocket of his jeans. "We found two things today. That's why Joe didn't want to quit. He was like a bloodhound that had picked up the scent of the trail."

He handed Chandler the two items. "Do those look familiar?"

Chandler leaned back in the love seat and closely examined the small objects in the palm of his hand. One was a triangle of tattered fabric, the other an intricately carved piece of silver shaped like the end of a leather belt.

Chandler's eyes widened perceptively. "Why, this is a piece of Dad's shirt! The blue-and-gray plaid he had on the day he died. And this belt tip—there's no doubt it was his! That's his initials on the back. Didn't Blake give that to him for a birthday gift?"

Holt nodded soberly. "We found them not far from water well number nine."

Shaking his head with disbelief, Chandler said, "But we've gone over and over that area. How did you happen to stumble across these?"

Holt took a long swig of his drink and as Roslyn's gaze bounced between the two men, it was very clear that this was a significant finding. Not that she knew any particulars about their father's death. Except that they'd found Joel dangling from beneath his horse. His boot had hung in the stirrup and he'd been lugged over the ground for a long distance.

"You remember the arroyo where we found Dad's spur rowel?" Holt asked.

Chandler nodded as he tested the weave of the fabric

between his thumb and forefinger. The colors were very faded and the edges jagged and frayed. Roslyn could only wonder what he was thinking and feeling. Even to this day, it hurt her deeply to look at her mother's clothing and personal items, which were still stored away in her bedroom. A room that, to Roslyn, seemed like a prison cell. For so many reasons.

"That was about two years ago." Chandler leveled a skeptical look at Holt. "Don't tell me these things were near it!"

"Not there. About a quarter mile north is a narrow gulch that runs for about two hundred yards. For some reason Joe got the hunch that we ought to look in it. He found the belt tip at the bottom of the wash. I found the piece of fabric hung on a juniper root about midway up the bank."

Chandler's head swung back and forth as though he was having trouble digesting Holt's news. "What does Joe think now?"

"We all thought that whatever happened with Dad initially took place in the first gulch by the water well, right?"

Chandler said, "It's a logical assumption since that's where his spur rowel was found. But these things you've found today puts a hole in that theory."

"After today, Joe seems to believe the fight, or ambush, or whatever the hell occurred, started in the gulch north of there. Afterward, Major Bob took off running in the direction of home. That would have most likely carried the horse, with Dad dragging from the stirrup, into the gulch where the spur rowel was dislodged."

The horrible image caused Roslyn to outwardly shiver and Chandler immediately wrapped his arm protectively around her shoulders. "You're getting cold, Roslyn. We should go in."

"No. I'm not cold. I'm just thinking—" She hesitated, unsure of how to convey her thoughts on the matter. "Well, it's none of my business, but from a woman's viewpoint, I can understand why Maureen wants to put Joel's death behind her. I'm sure each time the subject is brought up, a piece of her heart is torn out."

Holt said, "That's why she's not going to see these things. I'm going to let Joe keep them over at the Bar X. That way there won't be any chance of her stumbling across them."

Chandler nodded, then asked his brother, "Did you know Mom had gone to Phoenix today?"

"Not until Reeva told me and Joe before we left the ranch right after lunch. Why?"

"Because I think she's doing more than going to a cattleman's meeting."

Holt made a cynical grunt. "Hell, Chandler, of course she's doing more than that. You think she'd go to Phoenix without doing some shopping for her grandkids?"

Chandler cast a wry glance at Roslyn, then turned his attention back to Holt. "She probably is doing a bit of shopping. But I also think she might be seeing Uncle Gil."

"Who's Uncle Gil?" Roslyn asked, then, realizing how she sounded, quickly apologized. "Forgive me, you two. This is none of my business. In fact, I really should go inside and let you two discuss your family in private."

Chandler kept his arm firmly around her shoulders. "Sit still."

"Yeah, sit still, Roslyn," Holt added. "You're living here with us and that makes you close to being family."

"And we know you're not going to repeat any of this," Chandler added.

"Of course not. To tell you the truth, I've been all ears because I—I'm so fond of Maureen. She's been so good to me and she deserves to be happy. But tonight at dinner she seemed far from it."

Chandler's expression softened as he looked at Roslyn. "That's why I was harping on the trip to Phoenix. There's some connection there."

"You mentioned Uncle Gil," Holt prodded. "Why? Mom visits him from time to time when she goes to Phoenix. That's no secret."

Chandler explained to Roslyn. "Uncle Gil is our father's brother. He's worked for the city police department for many years. He's an investigator now."

"Oh." She thought about this for a moment. "Then you're thinking she's asked him to do some sort of investigating? About your father?"

"That's possible," Holt said.

Chandler shook his head. "No. I'm thinking she's seeing him—like in an emotionally dependent way."

Holt swore beneath his breath. Not at Chandler, but at the whole idea about their mother. "Have you gone daffy, brother? Mom was crazy about Dad. She worshipped the ground he walked on."

"That's exactly why I'm thinking this," Chandler told him. "She needs someone outside of us kids to lean on— to share her feelings with. Gil knows Mom well and he's like Dad in so many ways. Would it be that crazy for her to feel drawn to the man?"

Holt belted back the last of his drink. "Hell, Chandler, nothing surprises me anymore. I just wish Viv hadn't moved so far away. I miss her so much."

Chandler was about to make some sort of reply when the buzzing of a phone sounded.

Holt looked around. "Is that someone's phone going off?"

"It's yours," Chandler told him. "Mine is in the house on the charger."

Heaving out a weary breath, Holt pulled the phone from his jeans pocket. As soon as he glanced at the face, he rose to his feet. "You two enjoy the rest of your evening. I have to go to the horse barn."

"Need help?" Chandler asked.

"Thanks, brother. Not this time."

Holt didn't bother going back into the house to change clothes or return his whiskey glass. Instead he leaped off the end of the porch and took off in a long stride toward the horse barn.

Chandler watched his brother move off into the rapidly falling darkness. "Holt is overworked," he said. "But he's too stubborn to hire another horse trainer to help him with the load. He doesn't think anyone can handle the horses as well as he does."

"Seems like I've heard that his older brother suffers from the same sort of mind-set," Roslyn said shrewdly.

He cast her a sheepish look, then chuckled. "It's something that runs in our DNA, I guess. Blake had it, too. Until marrying Katherine finally convinced him to hire a secretary."

"I've not met Florence, but I've heard your mother speak highly of her," Roslyn told him. "How does Blake feel about having a secretary?"

"It took him a while to trust Florence with important matters. But he soon learned she's like a drill sergeant— no-nonsense. Now if he needs to be out of the office, he doesn't think twice about leaving her in charge. And he doesn't have to work after dinner to catch up on paperwork."

Roslyn gave him a coy smile. "Instead, he can spend time with his wife and children."

"Point well taken," he said. "But I already have six employees to help me run the clinic. Two work up front to deal with appointments and paperwork. Two more assist me in the treatment rooms and two more help me take care of the large animals outside the clinic."

The night Roslyn had fainted, she recalled meeting Trey, but other than him, she'd not seen any other staff members around the place. She'd guessed he might have two or three employees all together. "Wow! I had no idea. You must be an extremely good veterinarian."

He let out a short laugh. "I don't know about good. But I'm the *only* vet in the area. Otherwise, a person has to drive down toward Phoenix or as far north as Prescott to get an animal treated."

"Now I understand why you have such a heavy workload. And why your family thinks you should hire an associate."

The hand resting against her upper arm moved up and down ever so slightly against her bare skin. Roslyn instinctively wanted to scoot closer to his side and rest her head upon his strong shoulder. She wanted to tell him how much she adored every moment of his company. But would he even care to know her intimate thoughts?

His short laugh had nothing to do with being amused. "My family wants me to work less at the clinic and more here on the ranch. Which I understand. I'm a Hollister. I should be doing my fair share. But I don't want to be restricted to just working here on Three Rivers. Do you know how many suffering animals would go without medical care if I had never opened the clinic?"

"Many, I'm sure," she answered.

"Over the years, the count would be in the hundreds and hundreds. I wouldn't be happy about that."

"No. You wouldn't be happy," she agreed.

A stretch of silence passed and as the baby's movements pushed against her abdomen, she wondered what she was really doing here, living with a family she'd met only two weeks ago. Deluding herself? Dreaming that Chandler might grow some serious feelings toward her and the baby? She was being a fool.

He said, "Now you're sitting there wondering why I don't hire an associate."

"I don't have to wonder. I can see that you're like Holt in that manner. You want things done as you would do them. And I imagine that finding another veterinarian with your dedication would be hard to do."

Appreciation softened his features. "I think you do understand."

More than he'd ever guess, Roslyn thought, glumly. Yes, he was as particular about his animal clinic as Holt was about Three Rivers horseflesh. The two men were proud of their abilities and their reputations. And rightly so. But with Chandler, she got the impression there was another reason altogether why he liked going solo. Working fourteen hours a day gave him a good excuse not to get seriously involved with a woman. Not to tie himself to a marriage and children. Why he wanted to avoid that kind of commitment, she didn't know. Nor should she want to know. But God help her, she did.

"I try," she said wanly, then scooted to the edge of the seat with the intention of rising to her feet. "I think it's time I get back inside. Jazelle went home early, so Reeva might need some help in the kitchen."

Chandler's hand wrapped over her forearm. "Not yet. There's something I want to discuss with you."

Her heart began to tap out an anxious rhythm as she turned her head to look at him. Had he already decided he didn't want her at the clinic? Or did he want to talk about that torrid kiss they'd shared out on the range?

"Okay. About what?"

"Your father."

His blunt answer jolted her and sent her mind spinning with questions. Why should Martin DuBose concern him? Unless…oh, no! Surely he or someone else in the family hadn't gone back on their word and contacted him. If so, she'd have to run again. She'd have to leave Three Rivers Ranch and Chandler behind.

She wasn't ready for that. She wasn't sure she'd ever be ready to tell this man goodbye.

Chapter Eight

A cool chill ran through Roslyn and she wrapped her arms around herself in an attempt to ward off a shiver. "My father? What about him?"

His gaze scanned her face and Roslyn noticed how even in the waning twilight, his blue eyes were vivid and oh, so striking.

"About contacting him and letting him know where you are," he answered.

She tried not to gasp. Did Chandler honestly believe she ought to contact her father? If he did, it was because he didn't understand.

"No. I haven't gotten in touch with him by phone or mail or any other way," she stiffly. "And it will be a long time before I do."

Silence followed her sharp reply and then he finally said, "I was just thinking that, well, now that you've been here a while and had time to ponder about everything, that you might've had a change of heart."

She was so surprised by his comment that she twisted around on the seat in order to face him head-on. "Are you joking, Chandler? A change of heart? I'm sorry. I know he's my father and I shouldn't have ill feelings toward him, but I—" She shook her head. "I can't deal with him now. He'd be threatening to take my baby, my money, everything I have just to pressure me back under his wing."

"That's hard to believe. Why would he be that callous to his own daughter?"

She let out an unladylike snort. "Because he's a controlling man. Because my being pregnant and single, and now a runaway, has put a blight on his good name. He wants to try to smooth it all over. And having me home would make it appear that all was well within our family. What little is left of it," she added bitterly.

"That kind of thinking went out the door years ago," he argued.

She nodded ruefully. "My father is seventy now. Not that his age is an excuse. But he was raised in a different culture. Where women were expected to remain in the background."

"People can change. And a baby has a way of changing a person," Chandler gently suggested. "Could be that once your father gets a look at his grandchild his whole attitude will soften."

A pang of regret hit Roslyn's chest. "That would be wonderful, Chandler. But I don't much believe in fairy tales anymore. Do you?"

His hand slid up her arm and wrapped over the top of her shoulder. For a moment Roslyn thought he was going to pull her into his arms. Or, at least, that's what every fiber in her body was screaming for him to do. But instead, his fingers began to knead her flesh, which promptly sent rivulets of heat throughout her body.

"No. But you hiding yourself away from your parent isn't good, Roslyn. Not for you or your baby."

"Maybe it isn't," she admitted. "But I'm not ready to risk this freedom I have right now, Chandler."

He gave her a wan smile. "Well, talking about Dad's death a few minutes ago—it made me wish better things for you, Roslyn."

Her heart melting, she leaned forward and touched a hand to the side of his face. "It made me wish better things for both of us," she whispered.

A groan sounded deep in his throat and then his lips were suddenly brushing against her cheek and over her nose. Softly, gently, he continued on a downward path, purposely avoiding her lips. By the time he planted a tiny kiss in the middle of her chin, her breathing had turned into shallow little sups and her heart was beating with slow, anxious thuds.

She sighed as the scent of him filtered into her nostrils and filled her head with erotic desires that no pregnant woman should be feeling. But, oh, she *was* thinking and feeling. And she wanted more from him. So much more.

"I've been thinking about our kiss, Roslyn. A lot."

Our kiss. Yes, it had been a together thing, she thought, with one giving as much as the other. During those moments in his arms she'd never felt so connected to a man or so totally and wonderfully lost in his kiss.

"I would've never guessed it," she murmured.

His chuckle was low and sexy and caused his breath to warm her lips.

"Why? Because I haven't tried to repeat it?"

"Something like that."

"You said it be unwise to kiss me again. Remember?"

Her hands trembled as she placed them upon his chest.

The warmth beneath her palms made her want to push aside his shirt and explore the hard expanse of muscle.

"I remember. But I could've been...wrong."

"You were wrong." His lips lightly grazed hers. "Because something this good has to be right."

Wise or not, by now, Roslyn didn't care. She wanted him. In all the ways a woman could want a man.

With a tiny groan, she leaned into him and curled her arms around his neck. He reacted by fastening his lips over hers in a searching kiss.

Instantly, her senses were plunged into a vortex of pleasure so great that it rendered her helpless. All she could do was hang onto him and hope the kiss never ended.

Unfortunately, Chandler did finally break the contact between them, and as his head pulled away from hers, Roslyn was stunned and embarrassed to feel a mist of tears fill her eyes.

Not wanting him to guess how emotionally shaken the kiss had left her, she quickly rose from the seat and walked to the edge of the porch.

As she stood there, staring out at the night sky, she was forced to link her hands together to still their trembling. Yet nothing could stop the quiver that had started somewhere deep inside her and settled in the middle of her chest.

And she didn't need a doctor to diagnose the cause of her malady. She'd been struck by a massive dose of fear. She was falling for the wrong man. Again.

"Roslyn? Are you angry with me?"

She swallowed and hoped she could speak without sounding like she was choking. "No. Why should I be angry?"

"I'm not sure. Unless you're thinking I'm just being a flirt—playing with you."

Aren't you? She pushed the question off her tongue. Asking it would ruin everything. He'd have to admit that he didn't have serious intentions toward her and that would make it very awkward to work with him at the clinic. No, if she was going to leave Three Rivers with even a shred of pride, she needed to keep the question to herself. And her feelings under wrap.

"Don't worry, Chandler. I'm not thinking that you're getting serious. After all, it was just a little kiss. I'm sure you've had hundreds of them. The majority much nicer than mine." She stepped past him. "If you'll excuse me, I really need to go in now."

Before she was halfway to the door, his hand closed around her upper arm. Her mouth open, she whirled around to confront him, but he didn't give her time to get one word out.

He tugged her into the circle of his arms and plastered a long, searing kiss on her lips.

By the time he lifted his head, she could only stare in total bewilderment at the raw look of desire on his face.

"Even if I'd had a thousand kisses none of them would come close to being as nice as yours."

Too stunned to utter a word, she pulled out of his arms and hurried into the house.

By the middle of the next week, Roslyn felt as though she was a full-fledged employee at Hollister Animal Hospital and she was enjoying every minute she spent there. The four women and two men already on staff had welcomed her warmly and made her feel a part of their little group. She'd not expected that. In fact, she'd feared they would see her as a nuisance they had to endure because she was a friend of Chandler's.

A friend. Was that really the right description for the connection between her and Chandler? Not exactly, she thought, as she munched her way through the last of the lunch Reeva had packed for her. She and Chandler weren't lovers. They weren't even boyfriend and girlfriend. Well, maybe in her mind they were, but not in reality. And yet with each passing day, she recognized her feelings for him were growing deeper and stronger. And she was helpless to stop them.

"Well, I could sit out here for at least another hour and enjoy the sunshine, but I'd better get back inside. If I don't get those orders for meds in they probably won't be shipped today."

Roslyn glanced across the wooden picnic table at Loretta, a young redheaded woman who took care of most of the clinic's paperwork. She lived some twenty-five miles north in the tiny town of Congress. She was sweet and funny and single, and Chandler often referred to her as Miss Prospector because on the weekends she went digging in creek beds, searching for a stray gold nugget.

Roslyn enjoyed the woman's company and the two of them had fallen into the habit of sharing their lunch together in the little patch of fenced-in yard behind the clinic.

"I should probably go back in, too," Roslyn said as she gathered up the remains of her lunch. "Chandler was going to return a few phone calls while the rest of us had lunch. He's probably back to seeing patients."

Loretta shook her head. "He never got to the phone calls. A few minutes ago, he left word at the front office that he and Trey were leaving on an emergency call. I don't expect them back for a while. So put up your feet and rest a few more minutes."

Roslyn smiled at her. "If you insist."

"I do," she said cheerily, then headed back into the building.

With Loretta gone, Roslyn decided to use the quiet moment to call Nikki back in Fort Worth.

As soon as she told her friend that she was presently at work, on her lunch break, a loud gasp rattled Roslyn's ear.

"Work? Are you kidding me? Doing what?"

Roslyn chuckled at the shocked tone in Nikki's voice. "No kidding, Nikki. I'm working at an animal hospital. And you can't imagine how much I'm enjoying it."

"I can't imagine you at an animal hospital, period. Just exactly what are you doing there? Working as a receptionist or in bookkeeping?"

Roslyn glanced around the small fenced-in yard. From her shaded seat, she could see a portion of the barn and connecting pens. Jimmy, the other male assistant on staff, was presently tending to a cow. As of yet, Roslyn hadn't visited the barn area, but she hoped to. She wanted to learn as much about the large animals as she did the small ones.

"No. I work back in the treatment area. Right now I'm mostly cleaning up and fetching things like medicines and bandages and things like that. I've not actually helped to treat an animal yet, but Chandler said I will soon. He says I'm learning fast."

"So this isn't just a grooming-and-kenneling business," she stated.

Roslyn had to choke back a laugh. "No. There's a real doctor here—treating life-and-death situations. In fact, Chandler just finished up a cesarian section on a beagle hound. I got to watch the whole procedure so I'm hoping next time I might get to assist him."

"Oh, yuck, you watched something that gross? How could you?"

Yes, Nikki would find it gross. As much as Roslyn had always loved her dear friend, Nikki had never been an animal-loving, outdoors type of girl. She was the girly type who was always ready to go to the mall and get her nails done. Or spend the afternoon shopping for high heels.

"Because the dog was in great distress and would've died if Chandler hadn't performed the surgery. Now the mother and pups will all be fine."

"Uh, who is this Chandler person you keep mentioning?"

The center of her universe, Roslyn thought. To Nikki, she said, "He's the vet that owns the hospital. Actually, I'm living with his family. So that's how I wound up getting the job."

"Oh. So the vet is a man?"

Roslyn sipped milk from a small carton, but found the self-discipline to keep away from the zip-locked bag of homemade snickerdoodles.

"Yes. And he's a very good vet, I might add. He sees tons of patients. Mostly cats and dogs and horses and cows. But he also treats birds and reptiles. In fact, a parrot was here this morning. Poor thing had a case of mites."

Nikki's laugh was full of disbelief. "Roslyn, listen to you! I can't believe you're into this animal thing! And why have you started work at this point in your pregnancy? You're just a week or two away from having the baby."

"One of the women on staff needed extra time off for personal reasons, so I wanted to help out. As for the timing, I still have several more days until I reach my due date. And to tell you the truth, I feel much better moving around and doing things. Actually, I've never felt better in my life."

Or more alive, Roslyn could've added. This past week since she'd begun work at the clinic, her whole world had quickly started to change.

"Well, I'll admit you've never sounded this happy," Nikki said coyly. "Does that joyous ring in your voice have anything to do with your boss?"

"My boss? You mean Chandler?"

"Yes. The vet. Tell me more about him. Is he young? Good-looking?"

Roslyn groaned. "Don't even go there, Nikki. And before you start peppering me with more questions, I'll give you this much. He's young, but older than me. And yes, he's very good-looking."

"And single?"

"Determinedly so."

Nikki chuckled knowingly. "The challenging type, huh. But aren't they all?"

Roslyn closed her eyes and tried not think about a future beyond her time with Chandler and his family. She wanted to cherish each and every day while she was here. Not picture the loneliness that would follow her to California.

She sighed. "All relationships are challenging, Nikki. Some more than others. Anyway, I don't expect to run into a man who wants to hitch himself to a single mother."

"Don't kid yourself, Ros. You're everything a man would want."

Roslyn glanced down at her burgeoning waistline and laughed. "You should see me, Nikki. I look like a watermelon."

Nikki made a scoffing sound. "You're not going to look that way for much longer. In a couple of months you're going to have that fabulous figure of yours back."

If you're thinking your thick waistline makes you any less desirable than the next woman, your thinking is all wrong.

Chandler's gently spoken words whispered through her head. He'd sounded so sincere and when he'd laid his hand on her belly and felt the baby move, she'd thought there was something akin to love on his face. But a woman could imagine anything when she was looking at a man with her heart rather than her eyes, she thought dismally.

"Hah! Two months won't get me there. But thanks for the thought, anyway." A quick glance at her watch told her she'd been talking longer than planned. "My lunch time is up, Nikki. I need to get back to work."

Nikki let out a disappointed sigh. "Okay. I'll say goodbye, even though I still have tons of questions to ask you. Like when are you coming home? And have you talked to your dad?"

Home? She'd not known what being home really meant until she'd met Chandler and moved into the ranch house on Three Rivers. But she wasn't ready to share her feelings with Nikki.

"I'm never coming back to Fort Worth. Once I get settled permanently you can fly out to see me and the baby. In fact, the baby might need her auntie to change a few diapers."

Nikki's laugh was dubious. "I should warn you that I tried changing a diaper once on my cousin's first baby. It was disastrous for me and little Caleb. But for you, dear Ros, I'll take baby-care lessons before I come for a visit."

Laughing at that, Roslyn ended the call and quickly made her way back into the clinic.

After a hurried lunch at a little roadside café in Yarnell, Chandler called the clinic to let the receptionist know he'd be returning in the next thirty minutes.

"Let me drive this time," Trey suggested, as the two men approached the black truck sitting at the edge of the dusty parking lot. "You need the rest."

Chandler responded with a short, dry laugh. "Do I look like I'm getting feeble, or something?"

"Not even close. You've had a long morning, that's all."

Chandler couldn't argue that point. He'd left the ranch before daylight and hadn't stopped until a few minutes ago to wolf down a plate of tamales and beans.

Pulling the keys from his jeans pocket, he tossed them to Trey. "Have at it. Just make sure your foot doesn't get too heavy. You don't need another speeding ticket on your record."

"Oh, Doc, I haven't had a speeding ticket in at least, uh…at least three months," he said sheepishly.

Chandler grunted. "I'd hate to be your insurance agent."

"I don't know why," Trey retorted. "He's making a small fortune off me."

They climbed into the truck and as Trey gunned it onto the highway, Chandler gave up and scooted down in the seat.

"Wake me up five miles before we reach town," Chandler told him.

"Sure, Doc. You go right ahead and get you a nice nap. You deserve it."

Closing his eyes, Chandler tilted his hat over his face.

Yet as sleep-deprived as he was, his brain wouldn't shut down. How could it? If he wasn't working he was thinking about Roslyn and wondering why he'd ever been crazy enough to kiss her. Now he wanted more than her kisses. He wanted to make love to her. He wanted to be close to her in every way a man could be close to a woman. But even if she wanted the same thing, the timing was all wrong. She was about to have the baby. And afterward? He could only guess how she might feel about him when that time arrived.

The steady hum of the motor was suddenly drowned out by the loud burst of the radio.

Chandler sat straight up and screwed his hat back onto his head. "What are you doing?"

Trey jabbed a forefinger at the radio. "Sorry, Doc, I had to turn it up. That's one of my favorite songs."

Chandler's gaze went from his grinning face to the panel on the dashboard displaying the name of the song being played by the satellite station.

His jaw dropped as he looked at Trey. "Since when did you start listening to standards?"

A grimace wrinkled Trey's lean face. "And what, may I ask, is wrong with listening to standards? Just because I wear cowboy boots caked with manure doesn't mean I can't appreciate good music. The kind with melodies and voices that are real and not manipulated with a computer."

With a shake of his head, Chandler said, "I'm amazed, Trey. Truly amazed."

"Well, I'll bet if you ask Roslyn, she'll tell you that she likes standards, too."

Chandler rolled his eyes in Trey's direction. "And how do you know this? You asked her?"

"Shoot, no! I can just tell by looking at her," Trey answered confidently. "She's all class. Nothing trashy about that woman. She has good taste."

"Guess you can tell this just by looking at her, too, huh?" Chandler asked drolly.

"Well, yeah. She has good taste in men. 'Cause it's pretty obvious that she's gone on you."

Chandler sputtered, "What the hell are you talking about? Who's been spreading that kind of rumor?"

Trey shook his head. "Calm down, Doc. No one is talking about the two of you. This is my own opinion and I won't say anything to anybody. Unless you want me to, that is."

"I want you to keep your mouth shut. Period!" Chandler suddenly boomed. "Can you do that for one blessed minute?"

Trey glanced at him, then fastened his eyes back on the highway. "Hmmph! Guess I touched a nerve."

"No. You didn't just touch a nerve," Chandler barked at him. "You've stomped on about a thousand nerves."

"Well, pardon me, for being a friend," Trey said, managing to sound sarcastic and offended at the same time. "If you think about it for a minute, it'll dawn on you that I'm the only guy you can talk to about private things. Besides your brothers, that is."

Damn if Trey wasn't right, Chandler thought. As irritating as the man could be, he was more than Chandler's working partner. He was a friend. Someone who would give his very last penny to Chandler if he thought he needed it. And though he was a chatterbox from dawn to dusk, he never repeated anything Chandler had told him in confidence.

Wiping a hand over his face, Chandler said, "Don't mind me, Trey. Here lately I've had a lot on my mind."

"You always have a lot on your mind."

"Yeah. But this is different," he muttered as he looked out the passenger window at the passing landscape. The area was as raw and untamed as much of Arizona. The stark hills were covered with outbreaks of rock mounds and brushy vegetation. Thanks to the late-winter moisture, there was green grass on some of the lower slopes, along with bursts of red and yellow wildflowers. He really should drive Roslyn through this area, he thought. She'd think it was beautiful.

"You're talking about Roslyn now."

He didn't know how the guy was so perceptive. Or was it that Chandler was so transparent? "She's part of what's on my mind," he admitted.

A different song began playing on the radio and Chandler recognized it as one that had been sung at Blake and Katherine's wedding. His oldest brother was married and had three children now. His youngest brother, Joseph, had a wife and baby with plans to add more to their brood. Both men were happier than Chandler had ever seen them. And somehow they'd learned to juggle their jobs to accommodate their family life. In Chandler's eyes they were supermen and something he could never be.

"Why?" Trey asked. "You regret letting her work at the clinic?"

Chandler had to admit she'd surprised the hell out of him this past week. She'd been doing her part to help at the clinic without one complaint about being tired. In fact, she seemed to be thoroughly enjoying everything that went on with caring for the animals. Even scrubbing soiled examination tables and cleaning dog kennels. And he'd more than enjoyed having her near.

"What's there to regret? She's loving it. And every bit she does helps Cybil keep up. It's just that—"

"She'll be having the baby soon."

"I'm looking forward to that," Chandler admitted.

"Are you? Maybe you're thinking after the baby gets here, she'll be heading on to California."

"She will be heading to California," he said, unable to keep the hollowness he was feeling from his voice. "She has a little house and piece of property there. She'll make it her home and make a new life for herself and the baby."

"Without you. That's really what's on your mind, isn't it?"

Chandler squinted a sharp look at him. "Look, Trey, Roslyn isn't my business. And I'm in no position to try and make her my business. Even though I like her...a lot."

Trey's short laugh was mocking. "Hell, Doc, don't try to kid a kidder. It just won't work. You're making a bunch of excuses because you're too afraid to try and make her your woman."

Snorting, Chandler stared blindly out the windshield. "Afraid of what?"

"Plenty of things. Like how she might turn you down. How she might rather be in California or even go back to her rich daddy in Texas rather than stay on an isolated ranch with you. Or maybe the baby's daddy is still in her heart and she doesn't have room for you in it."

Chandler felt sick inside. Because no matter how dorky Trey could get at times, the guy somehow managed to put his finger on the crux of the matter. "If you think I've gone and fallen in love with Roslyn, you're all wrong, Trey. My life is full. Too full for a wife and baby."

Trey tugged on the brim of his battered straw hat, then shot Chandler a goofy grin. "I never mentioned anything about love. You're the one who brought that up."

"So I did," Chandler muttered. "Now see if you can build a fire in this thing. You're driving at a turtle's pace."

Trey cursed. "'Slow down. Don't get a speeding ticket.

Speed up. You're going like a turtle.' This'll be the last time I drive you anywhere, Doc."

"Other than crazy, you mean?"

"No. You're doing that to yourself."

Chandler started to give him a sharp retort, but promptly bit back the words. Trey was right, he suddenly concluded. He was driving himself crazy thinking about Roslyn and the uncertainty surrounding her future plans. Did he honestly want to be a part of them? Or in the end, would he be better off to let her go?

He'd never managed to maintain a lasting relationship with a woman. Trying with Roslyn might end up breaking both their hearts. He was half out of his mind with wanting her and needing to tell her just how deeply his feelings for her had grown.

But what would happen if he did tell her? Or maybe he should be asking himself, what would happen if he didn't?

Chapter Nine

The next evening, Roslyn was giving the last of the four beagle puppies its bottle of milk when Chandler walked into the room.

"Looks like he's enjoying every drop of his supper," he said as he stood next to her shoulder and peered down at the tan-and-white puppy she was cradling in the crook of her arm.

"He's certainly nursing like he feels good," Roslyn agreed.

"You're going to make a good mother, Roslyn."

The compliment warmed her, but it was the odd light flickering in his blue eyes that was creating a slow burn in her cheeks.

Clearing her throat, she said, "Hopefully I inherited my mother's nurturing instincts. It's not something you can learn from a book."

His eyes continued to study her face. "No. It comes from within."

This was the first quiet moment Roslyn had shared with him today and as always, just standing next to him, breathing in his scent and feeling the heat radiating from his body were enough to make her knees mushy.

Drawing in a deep breath, she looked back down at the tiny puppy. "He's nearly finished. Is there something else you need for me to do?"

"Have the other pups been fed?"

She nodded. "He's the last one."

"Good. I just finished treating the final patient for the day so we're closing up," he told her. "Loretta and Danielle have already locked the front. Cybil and Violet are going to stay here at the clinic tonight and take turns with feeding the pups until morning."

There were a pair of cots in a small alcove just off the recovery room for times Chandler or other staff members were needed at the clinic throughout the night.

"Oh, my. That's every two hours!" Roslyn exclaimed. "They'll be exhausted tomorrow."

"They're tough. They're used to doing overnighters. And by tomorrow afternoon, the owner can take mother and pups home. Then it will be her responsibility to care for the new little family. Hopefully she'll have someone there to help her."

With the tiny bottle drained of the specially mixed formula, Roslyn placed the pup back with his two brothers and one sister, then carefully latched the kennel.

"I think I've finished all the chores in here and I've put up the new medicines that arrived this afternoon," she told him. "All I need to do now is gather my things from my locker."

"Uh, before you do that, Roslyn, I have something to ask you," he said.

She turned to look at him and was surprised to see a

hesitant expression on his face. One thing she'd learned about Chandler, especially since she'd been working here at the clinic, was that he never seemed uncertain or indecisive. But something was bothering him now.

"Is anything wrong, Chandler?"

"Wrong? No. Not at all." He gave her a lopsided grin, then shook his head. "I'm really rusty at this, Roslyn. What I'm trying to do is ask you to join me for dinner, here in town—just the two of us."

It was a good thing there weren't any flies in the room because Roslyn couldn't stop her mouth from falling open. "Dinner? Just you and me—like a date?"

"Well, I guess it is a date," he answered. "Do you feel up to it? Or would you rather go on home to the ranch so you can rest?"

Actually, her back had been aching off and on since she'd eaten lunch, but she wasn't about to let that stop her from sharing a special evening with Chandler.

"Oh, no. I don't want to rest. I'd love to go." She looked down at herself. "Except I don't have any other clothes with me."

"I don't, either. But we don't care if we're wearing work clothes, do we?"

She gave him a wide smile. "I don't mind at all. Just give me a minute to freshen up."

"Take your time. I'll wait for you in my office," he told her.

She hurried out of the recovery room and down the hallway to a small room furnished with lockers and a private restroom for the staff.

After plucking her handbag from a locker space, she rummaged around for a compact and tube of lipstick. With a shaky hand, she applied both, then took down her ponytail and brushed through the shoulder-length tresses.

Even with the powder and lipstick she looked rather pale, but there wasn't much she could do about that tonight. Besides, it wasn't like Chandler hadn't seen her all day in her jeans and work shirt and very little makeup.

She was turning away from the mirror, when Loretta walked into the room, then stopped and stared. "Oh, Roslyn, I thought you'd already gone for the day."

"No. I only finished feeding the baby beagles a few minutes ago." She gestured downward at her shirt and jeans. "Do I look presentable enough to go into a restaurant?"

Loretta arched an eyebrow at her. "You're staying in town for dinner?"

Roslyn felt a blush sting her cheeks. "I am. Chandler's taking me out," she said, unable to hold back the rush of excitement in her voice.

Loretta's big green eyes were suddenly glinting with speculation. "Chandler? I didn't realize you call the boss by his given name."

Which was telling, Roslyn thought. Everyone here at the clinic called him Doc. But he wasn't actually her boss. Well, maybe he was in a technical sense. But that was only a small portion of what he was to Roslyn.

Turning, Roslyn thrust the hairbrush into the handbag she'd left lying on a shelf in the open locker. "Well, that is his name," she reasoned.

"Hmm. And you have been living with him and his family. I can see why he's Chandler to you." She moved closer to Roslyn and lowered her voice to a sly whisper. "Is this dinner a real date?"

Roslyn didn't have to look in the mirror to know that her cheeks had turned an even deeper pink. "That's what he called it. I'm not willing to call it that, though."

Loretta looked at her in disbelief. "Why ever not? Doc

means what he says. Unless he's teasing. And he's not nearly as much of a jokester as his brother Holt."

"You know Holt?" Roslyn asked with faint surprise.

Loretta chuckled. "There probably isn't a woman in all of Yavapai County and beyond who doesn't know Holt Hollister."

Roslyn had heard about Holt's numerous escapades with the ladies and yet since she'd been living at Three Rivers, she'd not seen him with even one woman. She was beginning to think Holt's reputation as a ladies' man was mostly just an overblown rumor.

"Well, think what you like," Roslyn told her. "But Chandler is just being nice and feeding me before we head home. He's not really taking me on a date."

Loretta pulled an impish face at her. "If he isn't, then he should be."

Stepping back, she gave Roslyn a closer inspection. "You look fine. Except there's some sort of stain at the bottom of your shirt."

"There is? Where? I don't see anything."

"It's below your belly. That's why you can't see it." She picked up the hem of Roslyn's navy blue blouse and pulled it up high enough to show her the large stain.

"Oh, drat. I spilled some of the puppy formula when I was mixing it. I guess it went on my shirt, too."

Loretta suddenly snapped her fingers. "Not to worry. I just now remembered I have something in my locker you can wear."

Roslyn laughed out loud. "Are you crazy? I couldn't squeeze myself into any of your blouses."

"You can this one. It's one of those flowy, filmy things that's way too feminine for me. My mother gave it to me as a gift. Her way of saying you need to look more alluring. I brought it to work thinking I was going to take it back to the store for an exchange. I never did. And here it still hangs."

She pulled the garment out of the locker next to Roslyn's and held it out for her to see.

Roslyn instantly gasped with delight at the coral-and-yellow printed blouse. "Oh, how pretty! And the way it's cut, maybe I could get in it. Are you sure you won't mind if I wear it?"

"I'd love it if you would. Here, let me help with the buttons. You don't want to keep Doc waiting."

Chandler was trying to keep his eyes on the street and the slow-moving car in front of him, but every few seconds he found himself glancing over at Roslyn.

How she'd instantly transformed herself he didn't know, but somehow she'd managed to make herself look particularly lovely tonight. And not just because Loretta had lent her a blouse. Her face seemed to be radiating a special light and her brown eyes were glowing with... what? Was that love? Happiness? Whatever it was, he wanted some of it.

"Is there a particular kind of food you'd like to eat tonight? Since Wickenburg is small there's not a whole lot of choices, but most of them are good," he told her.

"I like all kinds of food. You pick. This is your town. You know what's best."

Chandler had never dated what he'd considered snobbish women. But after Roslyn's agreeable comment, he realized that none of them had been as accommodating as she was. Not just about the choice of a restaurant, but about everything. All of them would've been insulted if he'd asked them on a date fifteen minutes ahead of time. And they would've definitely suggested he drive on down to Phoenix so they could have a *real* dinner served to them."

"Okay. I think I know a place you might like. We'll be there in five minutes."

"Town seems busy this evening," she remarked as she gazed out at the shops and businesses lining the street.

"It's Friday. Folks are getting ready for the weekend."

She glanced over at him. "I've never noticed you doing anything special on the weekend."

He shrugged a shoulder. "I used to do plenty of things on the weekend. Especially with my brothers. We'd go over to Lake Pleasant and fish. And once in a while we'd drive up to Cliff Castle. That's a casino up near Camp Verde. Holt usually made a killing at the blackjack tables."

She laughed. "That's not surprising. And what about you?"

He chuckled. "I mostly watched Holt. That way I saved my money."

She turned her knees so that she was facing him. "So what about now? You don't ever do those types of things anymore?"

He shook his head. "No. And I can't exactly tell you why. Except that after Dad died, I guess all of us began to change in some ways. So did the ranch. Suddenly everything turned serious and we all decided that making sure it remained in the black and keeping the Hollister legacy going was more important than anything."

"You weren't thinking in those terms when your father was alive?"

"Up to a certain point. Don't get me wrong, we all worked hard back then. But with Dad around we never doubted or worried about the ranch's solvency. He was our rock. Losing him shook all of us. And it hit Blake the hardest. He threw every bit of himself into the ranch and suffered a broken engagement because of it. For a long time Joe was driven to find Dad's killer. Every spare moment he had was spent on solving the case. And Holt, well, he just went a little wilder with the women and horses and whiskey."

"And you? What about you, Chandler?" she asked gently.

He rubbed a hand over his face. "These past six years since Dad died, I've tried not to think about my life too much. But now that you're here, I'm beginning to see there's more for me than the ranch and my patients." He reached over and clasped her hand in his. "I've told you this before, but I'll say it again. I'm very glad you decided to park in front of the clinic that first night you hit town."

As his fingers warmed her hand, she felt her heart melting into a helpless little puddle.

Smiling at him, she said, "I'm kinda glad I did, too."

Jose's, the restaurant Chandler chose for their evening meal, was located on the edge of town and far enough from the main highway to make it a quiet and cozy spot.

The building was fashioned in a sprawling, hacienda style with stucco walls painted a pale turquoise and a red tiled roof. A porch with arched supports ran the width of the front and at the top of each arch hung long strings of drying red peppers. At one end of the porch, a bougainvillea covered in yellow-gold blossoms grew all the way to the roof, while at the opposite end a single saguaro stood like a sentinel against the desert horizon.

Roslyn was totally charmed by the outside of the place and even more so when they entered the small restaurant and took seats in a quiet corner. All through the meal of avocado stuffed with grilled chicken, she continued to gaze around at the little round tables with orange-and-white checked tablecloths and vases of yellow marigolds.

"This is so nice, Chandler. Thank you for inviting me out tonight and bringing me to this beautiful little place. Don't tell Reeva, but the food is out-of-this-world delicious. And speaking of Reeva, I hope you called to let her know we wouldn't be eating at home tonight."

"I called. And she didn't even yell at me," he joked. "I suspect that after the big group she had for dinner last night, she was relieved to get a break."

Roslyn smiled as she sliced her fork into a piece of *tres leches* cake. "Last night was a surprise for me. No one had told me Joe and his family, and your sister, Vivian, and her family, were going to show up for dinner. I really enjoyed visiting with all of them."

Candler grinned. "I think you especially liked Little Joe."

Laughing softly, Roslyn shook her finger at him. "Tessa says everyone has to start leaving off the little part of his name or he'll forever be known as Little Joe instead of Joseph Junior."

"Hah! I have news for my sister-in-law. It's too late to drop the little. That part of my nephew's name has already stuck."

She swallowed another bite of cake. "You're probably right. But no matter what name you call him, Joe is adorable. And I'll tell you another thing. If my child is a girl, I hope she grows up to be as lovely and vivacious as Hannah. She and Nick are quite a pair together, aren't they?"

She probably wasn't aware of it, Chandler thought, but Roslyn had become a part of the family, too. But would she want to remain a part of it? She'd already left her home and her father back in Texas. What made Chandler think he'd be able to hold her at Three Rivers?

Not wanting to dwell on that question tonight, he tried to push it out of his head and focus strictly on her and this rare time of being alone with her.

"Hannah and Nick have a special bond," he answered. "From the first time those two kids met, they hit it off perfectly. Which surprised the heck out of me. Nick is about a year or two younger than Hannah and for a long time she tended to boss him around, but he seemed to like it. Now that Hannah lives on the reservation, they don't get to see each other every day. But their parents make sure the two of them still get to spend plenty of time together."

Roslyn nodded. "Katherine told me that one of the reasons Nick and Hannah clicked so much was that neither had a father."

"That's true. Kat's first husband died in a car accident and Vivian's ex never had any desire to be a father to Hannah. Fortunately, both kids have two parents now. Blake is a good father to Nick and Sawyer is a great dad to Hannah. So everybody is happy."

She let out a wistful sigh as her gaze drifted down to the last of her dessert. "When I first ended my engagement I didn't dwell too much on my baby not having a father. But here lately it's been on my mind much more. Now that the baby is nearly here I feel guilty. My child isn't even born yet and I've already failed him, or her."

He'd never heard her talk this way and it cut into him more than he wanted to admit. She'd been duped and betrayed by a man who'd never deserved her in the first place. Chandler didn't want her to carry around a load of guilt or hurt for any reason.

Reaching across the table, he wrapped his hand around hers. "You shouldn't be feeling guilty. Just think about it. Do you think your baby would be better off with a father who's a liar and a cheat? I don't."

Beneath the veil of her long lashes, her brown eyes studied his face until a glaze of tears suddenly threatened to spill onto her cheeks. Then she glanced away and swallowed hard.

"I know you're right about that. But that doesn't make me any less of a failure." She turned her gaze back onto his face. "I should've had better judgment. I shouldn't have wanted to please my father so much and followed my heart instead."

Her last words caught his attention. "You mean there was someone you loved before Erich, but your father didn't find him suitable?"

She shook her head. "No. Before Erich I never had any serious feelings about a guy. There were a few, if given a chance, I might've fallen in love with. But they were regular men with regular jobs. Being *regular* never stacked up good enough for Martin DuBose."

What did she consider Chandler? Just a mediocre country vet? Or was she thinking the Hollisters were too wealthy for her taste? Most folks would probably consider that to be a crazy question, but he didn't. He'd noticed that Roslyn never talked about her family's wealth, or the things it could get for her. He wasn't at all sure that she even liked being wealthy.

"You'll fall in love soon enough and give your child a father." The words coming out of his mouth sounded stiff and awkward. And why shouldn't they? Just thinking about Roslyn being in another man's arms made him sick, through and through.

She pushed aside the dessert plate and picked up her coffee cup. "We're always talking about me, Chandler. What about you?"

"Me?" He shrugged nonchalantly. "My life is already settled. There's not much to talk about."

Her head moved slowly back and forth. "I don't believe that."

"Which part?"

She grimaced. "The part about your life already being settled. I can't imagine you spending the remainder of your years without a wife, or babies, or time for yourself."

He cleared his throat. She was giving him the opportunity to make a statement. He could ease his hand away from hers and flatly explain that he didn't want any of those things. But the truth was, he'd be lying. Deep down he wanted to be like his married brothers. He wanted to experience that same joy and love that they were blessed with each and every day.

"To be honest, Roslyn, having those things used to be one of my main goals. While I was in vet school I came close to asking a woman to marry me. But that didn't work out. My studies took up too much of my time. Then later, after I'd started my own clinic, I met a woman I thought might be *the* one. She had her own career as a nurse. She understood about putting in long, irregular hours at work. And she was as dedicated to her profession as I was to mine."

"What happened?"

"Actually, I had driven to Phoenix to find the perfect diamond engagement ring to give her when she called and said we needed to talk. You know, the old phrase that basically means 'I'm dumping you.'"

"But why? Had she found someone else?"

"No. At least I didn't have to bear that humiliation. She was honest enough to tell me that she'd never be happy living on the ranch, making a sixty- or seventy-mile commute to work every day. She wasn't an outdoor girl. Nor was she an animal lover, so basically there was nothing at Three Rivers that appealed to her."

Her eyes softened and her fingers squeezed his. "There was you."

If the long room hadn't been filled with evening diners, he would have leaned across the table and kissed her. As it was, he could merely gaze at her and wish.

"Uh, well, I wasn't enough. You see, I don't think she ever really loved me. She dated me in hopes that I was the right one. But I wasn't."

She let out a long breath, then flexed her shoulders. "It's good that you didn't make a mistake with either of them. But time has passed and I think…"

A grimace wrinkled her brow as she pulled her hand from his and rubbed it against the small of her back.

"What's wrong?" Chandler asked with sudden concern. "Are you not feeling well?"

"I don't feel sick. This afternoon twinges started coming and going in my lower back. I thought that once I got off my feet the pains would quit. But to be honest, they're getting worse."

"I'd better pay out. I think the baby is coming," he told her.

Her mouth popped open, very nearly making Chandler laugh outright.

"The baby? But it can't be! It's still several days until my due date. And I just went for a checkup two days ago."

"Didn't he tell you the baby could come early or late?"

She bit down on her lower lip. "Well, yes, he did say that. But—"

She didn't finish speaking. Instead, she groaned and grabbed her back with both hands.

Chandler promptly signaled to the waiter and after explaining the situation gave him a very large bill to cover the meal and a generous tip.

With his arm around Roslyn's waist, Chandler helped her outside and into the truck.

As he steered the truck in the direction of the hospital, she gave him a wobbly smile.

"I'm so sorry I've cut our evening short, Chandler. It's the nicest date I've ever been on," she told him.

She was doing her best to smile through her pain and all of a sudden Chandler's heart was so full of feelings for this woman he wondered if it might burst.

"It's the nicest one I've ever been on, too," he said, his voice sounding like his throat had been sandpapered. "We'll do it again. After the baby gets here and you're back on your feet. Is that a date?"

Nodding, she clutched the front of her stomach. "It's a date, Doc."

Chapter Ten

Since Maureen had already promised Roslyn she'd be with her in the delivery room, Chandler gave his mother a quick call as he made the short drive to the hospital.

Unfortunately, the call went straight to her voice mail so he called the line in the kitchen, figuring Reeva would be sure to answer.

"Chandler, what are you doing on the phone?" She fired the question at him before he had a chance to get one word out. "You're supposed to be taking Roslyn out to dinner!"

"We've already had dinner. I'm taking her to the hospital. Is Mom in the house? She's not answering her phone."

"No. She's still out with the hands. They decided to move some of the cattle down from Prescott today. It'll probably be after midnight before she gets back," the cook explained, then practically shouted in his ear. "Did you say hospital? Is Roslyn having the baby?"

"Looks like it. And Mom was planning on being her labor coach," he explained. "Now it looks—"

"Coach, hell!" Reeva interrupted with a snort. "Roslyn doesn't need a coach at her side. She needs a man! Don't you think you fit the bill?"

Chandler had tended hundreds of animal births. Many had been easy, while a few had ended tragically. Throughout, he'd determinedly kept a calm, level head because he was the man who was responsible for helping the new little lives enter the world. But none of them had been human. None of them had been the woman who'd grabbed onto his heart and now held it in the palm of her hands.

"I'll try, Reeva. Leave Mom a message, will you?"

"She'll get the message. And I'll call upstairs right now and let Blake and Kat know what's going on."

"Thanks, Reeva."

Chandler ended the call and finished the short drive to the hospital in record time. By the time he wheeled the truck into the emergency-room entrance and parked beneath a wide overhang, Roslyn was already experiencing contractions.

He lifted her out of the seat and began carrying her toward the sliding glass doors, when a dark-haired nurse wearing navy blue scrubs met them with a wheelchair.

"Has she started labor?" she asked.

"It appears so," Chandler answered as he gently deposited Roslyn into the chair, then stepped out of the way.

The nurse wheeled Roslyn into the building while Chandler was left to follow. Along the way, the woman peppered Roslyn with pertinent health questions and Chandler was content to remain silent and allow the woman to take control. Until she parked the wheelchair in front of an admissions desk.

"What are you doing?" He was boiling over with frustration. "There isn't time for this. Roslyn is in labor! She needs care, not questions!"

"I'm sorry, Mr., uh— I don't believe you've told me your name," the nurse stated calmly.

He took note of the name tag pinned to the left shoulder of her scrub top. Mariana Reed.

"My name is Hollister, Ms. Reed. Dr. Chandler Hollister," he said with what little patience he could summon.

Most everyone in the area recognized the Hollister name. Along with owning and operating Three Rivers, the family donated large sums of money to different local causes in the community, including this very hospital. But the skeptical arch to Nurse Reed's eyebrows made him think she doubted he was actually a Hollister or a doctor.

Apparently she thought he should be dressed in a tailored suit and wingtips instead of a cowboy who'd been in one too many feed lots.

Nurse Reed loudly cleared in throat. "Well, Dr. Hollister, in your profession you should know the hospital has to have your wife's necessary information before we can treat her. If you can provide it and her insurance card, I'll be happy to take her on back to the labor room."

There was long list of things he wanted to tell the nurse. The main one being that if he waited around for paperwork to be completed, most of his patients would die before he ever got the chance to treat them.

Chandler opened his mouth to give Nurse Reed a sharp retort, but by then Roslyn had recovered enough to interrupt the exchange. She reached for his hand and squeezed it as though he was the one who needed reassuring rather than her.

"Chandler, it's okay," she said. "The last time I visited

the doctor, Kat brought me by the hospital so I could fill out preadmission papers. Everything should be ready to go."

The nurse promptly instructed an older lady sitting at the admission desk to check for the information. After Roslyn supplied her birthdate and social security number, the clerk confirmed that the necessary info had already been registered.

With a smug smile for Chandler, the nurse said, "Looks like your wife already has things under control. So if you'd like to follow us down the hallway, there's a waiting room on the left, where you can make yourself comfortable while we take care of your wife."

"Oh, but can't he come with me?" Roslyn asked anxiously.

"Not right now," the nurse answered with a shake of her head. "He may come back later on, after we get you settled in a labor room."

Roslyn glanced up at Chandler and the beseeching look in her eyes tore a hole right through his heart. "You will stay with me, won't you?"

"Wild horses couldn't drag me away," he promised.

Nurse Reed's stern expression softened with approval. "Now that's the way a husband should be talking to the woman who's about to give him a child."

Roslyn looked awkwardly from Chandler to the nurse. "But he's not my husband," she explained.

The confession caused the nurse to pierce Chandler with a look of real disappointment. If she was trying to make him feel like a heel, she was doing a great job of it, he decided. But he'd rather have the nurse thinking he was a jerk, rather than put Roslyn through the awkward explanation of her broken engagement.

"I should have guessed," Nurse Reed said bluntly. "Then you—"

"I'm the baby's father." The quick claim spurted out of Chandler's mouth before he could even think about the consequences. "And I want to be present at the birth."

If the nurse was surprised to hear that a member of the Hollister family was having a child out of wedlock, she didn't show it. Instead, she merely nodded.

"Certainly, Dr. Hollister, I'll let you know when you can join her."

Relieved, he bent down and placed a kiss on Roslyn's cheek. "I'll see you in a few minutes, darling."

A look of confusion filled her eyes, but pain quickly followed and before he had a chance to say more, the nurse was wheeling her away.

As Chandler watched her go, he felt a big part of himself going with her.

Five hours later, Roslyn gave birth to a perfect little daughter. Exhausted and exhilarated at the same time, tears streamed down her cheeks when the delivery room finally calmed and the baby was placed upon her chest.

"Oh, my," she whispered in awed wonder "You're so beautiful, my baby daughter. So utterly beautiful."

She kissed the top of the baby's damp head, then glanced up to see Chandler standing at the side of her bed, where he'd been ever since they'd entered the delivery room.

Smiling at him through her tears, she said, "Come closer, Chandler, so you can see her better."

He bent over the bed railing and touched a finger to a bit of hair stuck to the newborn's scalp. As Roslyn studied his reaction, she decided he looked as overwhelmed as she felt.

"Her eyes are squinted," she said. "I can't really tell what color they are. Can you?"

Her daughter was awake and squirming, but her face was squinched as though she was getting ready to let out a loud howl.

"I've heard all babies had blue eyes."

"I don't think that's true. But maybe they are blue. Like yours," she added impishly.

A sheepish grin twisted his lips. "I hope you didn't mind me telling Nurse Reed that I was the father. I thought it would make things easier for you—and me."

How could he think she would mind? Just hearing him claim the baby as his had caused her heart to swell with emotions she could no longer deny.

"I didn't mind," she whispered. "I was...very grateful."

His gaze met hers and for a brief moment she thought he was going to kiss her, but the nearby voices of the attending nurses seemed to remind him that they weren't alone.

His attention returned to the baby. "She's incredible, Ros. Just like her mother. And I told you it was going to be a girl, didn't I?"

The teasing smile on his face added to the warm emotions spilling from her heart and spreading to every corner of her body. "You most certainly did. I'll never doubt your diagnoses again."

He chuckled then lowered his head to place a kiss on her forehead. With one hand holding the baby securely to her breasts, she reached up with her free hand to touch the side of his face.

"Thank you, Chandler, for...being here with me. For—" Tears choked her throat and she struggled to swallow away the aching lump. "For caring about me... and the baby."

His blue eyes gentle, he stroked a tangled strand of hair back from her face. "You don't have to thank me, Ros. This is where I wanted to be. We just didn't know this was going to happen on our date night, did we?"

"No. It's a date I'll never forget." For plenty of reasons, she thought. Even before the baby had decided to suddenly make her appearance into the world, Roslyn had felt Chandler drawing closer to her. Now, going through five hours of exhausting labor with him holding her hand, wiping her brow and giving her soft words of encouragement, she knew for certain that she felt more than close to him. She loved him. Plain and simple.

But where was that love going to land her? Smack in the middle of a heartache?

No. She wasn't going to try to answer that now. At this moment she was the happiest woman alive. Her child was safely born and snuggled in her arms. And whether Chandler would ever love her or not, he cared enough to be at her side at the most important time in her life. For now, she couldn't ask for more.

Before the night was over, Chandler ended up grabbing a couple of hours of sleep on a couch in the waiting room. When he woke up just before daylight, he quickly slapped water on his face and hurried to the gift shop on the bottom floor of the hospital. After purchasing the biggest bouquet of flowers he could find, he took the elevator up to Roslyn's private room, which was located in the maternity ward of the hospital.

At the door he knocked lightly, then stepped inside to see Roslyn sitting up in bed with the baby in her arms.

And from the way she'd positioned the thin blanket, he had to assume she was breast-feeding her new daughter.

"Hello," he said. "Is it okay if I come in?"

She'd brushed her light brown hair and pulled it into a ponytail, and a bit of color had been dabbed on her lips. After the hard labor she'd gone through, he didn't know where she'd found the energy to do either. But this morning she looked amazingly beautiful and refreshed.

"It's very okay. Are those for me?" she asked, her gaze going to the vase of flowers he was carrying.

"They are. Congratulations, new mother." He deposited the vase in an out-of-the-way spot on the nightstand.

"Thank you," she said. "I've never seen daisies and roses mixed together. They're very beautiful."

"So are you." He lifted off his hat, then dropped a kiss on top of Roslyn's head. "How are you feeling?"

Her smile was like a beam of sunshine and Chandler realized that seeing her happy made his spirits soar.

"After all the pain and pushing and straining, I should feel awful, I suppose. But I actually feel wonderful. I want to sing and shout."

"And so you should," Chandler said gently. "You've been blessed with a beautiful daughter. How does that feel?"

She glanced down at the baby and Chandler couldn't miss the love and pride swimming in her eyes.

"I never thought it would be like this, Chandler. I didn't know I could love this much, or feel so fiercely protective." Her eyes glistened as they met his. "But to be honest, I'm a little scared, too. I'm responsible for someone other than myself now."

He reached over and squeezed her shoulder. "You're going to be everything this little girl needs."

Now that the baby was actually here, Chandler's protective feelings for Roslyn and her child had grown to enormous proportions. And in spite of being exhausted, he'd had trouble staying asleep for more than fifteen minutes at a time. And the problem hadn't been the hard couch or the freezing temperature of the waiting room. No, his mind had been whirling with thoughts of Roslyn, the baby and how much he wanted them to remain in his life.

At this moment, with her soft brown eyes delving into his, the idea of telling her exactly how he felt was pushing and prodding at him. Yet he held back. Too much had happened in the past twenty-four hours and far more needed to happen before they could talk about a future together.

Clearing his throat, he rolled up the brim of his hat with both hands and squeezed the expensive felt. "Have you decided on a name yet?"

"I have. That is, if you agree to it."

Confused, he shook his head. "Me? What I think shouldn't matter."

She reached beneath the blanket and straightened her clothing, then slipped it away from the newborn's face. Chandler's heart instantly squeezed with love as he stared at the baby. What little hair she possessed had dried to the same light brown color as her mother's. Most of the redness had left her face and now that her features were relaxed in sleep, he decided she resembled Roslyn.

"But it does," she said. "I'd like to name her Evelyn Kay."

His gaze flew up to meet Roslyn's. "Evelyn is mother's first name. You want to name her after Mom?"

Nodding, she said, "I hope she or none of the family will mind."

He suddenly smiled. "Mind? Mom will be thrilled. If you haven't already guessed, she loves you like a daughter. But how did you know that was her name? She's always gone by Maureen."

"I was in the kitchen one day helping Reeva and we were discussing names. She told me. Kay was my mother's middle name. So she's going to be named after two special women."

"Well, I think Evelyn Kay is perfect." It would be even more perfect if the name was followed by Hollister, but that was a different matter. One that would require a commitment he wasn't sure either of them was ready to make.

He made a point of glancing at his watch. "I better go. The girls have already opened the clinic. I need to get over there," he told her.

Nodding that she understood, she smiled. "You can announce Evelyn's arrival to everyone. And in case you don't remember the nurse telling us in the delivery room, she weighed six pounds and ten ounces and she's nineteen inches long."

"And she's very beautiful, like her mother," he added with a playful wink. "I'll be sure and spread the word."

He started to leave, but before he could turn away from the bed, she quickly caught him by the hand.

Arching a brow at her, he asked, "Was there something you needed before I go?"

"No. I, uh, I just wanted to tell you that...well, that you made Evelyn's birth very special for me. I'll never forget that, Chandler."

Was this the beginning of a goodbye? No. Somehow, someway, he couldn't let that happen.

Bending, he placed a kiss on her lips."

More than two weeks later, Chandler knocked on the door of his mother's office and without waiting for an answer, stepped inside.

She was sitting at the desk with the landline phone jammed to her ear. As soon as she spotted Chandler, she motioned for him to stay and he took a seat, while she finished the phone conversation.

"I know. Yes. I'm doing the best that I can," she said. "It's not something—"

She paused and Chandler noticed a mixture of sadness and frustration on her face.

"Okay. I'm going to try not to ponder on it too much. No. Don't do that. I'll call you. Tomorrow evening." She hung up the receiver back on its hook. "Sorry about that, son. Were you wanting to talk with me?"

He couldn't tamp down his curiosity. It was nearing midnight. Who could she be talking to at this hour? "Was that Vivian or Camille?"

Instead of looking at him, she studied the ink blotter on the desktop. "No. Just someone I'm thinking of doing cattle business with. Nothing important."

She glanced up, and though Chandler hated to think it, she wasn't being truthful. Which made no sense at all. His mother wasn't a person who lied about anything. Unless she believed the lie would save someone a heartache.

Deciding not to press her on the issue for now, Chandler said, "I see. Someone on West Coast time. Well, do you have a minute to talk?"

"Always," she said. "Is anything wrong?"

Chandler didn't waste time coming to the point. "Yes. Something is very wrong. I just left Roslyn's room and she tells me she's rented an apartment in town. She's going to be moving in by midweek."

Maureen leaned back and folded her hands together in her lap. "I already know about that."

"Surely you don't approve! She needs to stay here on

the ranch, where Reeva and Jazelle and Kat can all help her with the baby."

"And you told her all of this?" Maureen asked.

"I told her that and a lot more. She has no earthly reason to get an apartment. Not when she's more than welcome to stay right here."

"I've already made that argument with her, Chandler. I'm afraid she has her mind made up. And to tell you the truth, now that I've had time to think on it, I believe she's doing the right thing for herself and the baby."

Chandler jumped straight up and began to pace around the shadowy room. "How could you say that, Mom? I can see how close you've already grown to baby Evelyn. And I know how you feel about Roslyn. You can't want them to leave!" he argued.

She frowned. "I didn't say anything about wanting them to leave. I said it was probably the best thing for them."

"Hell, what's the difference? Either way, they'll be out of the house," he muttered.

"And that bothers you."

Maureen hadn't bothered to put her words into question form. She already knew how he felt.

Shaking his head, he crossed the room and sank into the chair he'd vacated moments ago. "Damn right it bothers me. She doesn't need to be alone."

"Lots of single mothers care for their babies alone. And Roslyn isn't a helpless person. In fact, I'm very proud of her. She's taken to motherhood like a real pro. Like she's already had three or four babies before this one. I have no doubt the two of them will be fine on their own. And even if she does need some help, all she has to do is pick up the phone and one of us will be there for her. It's not like she's moving to another state."

But this is the first step to making that big move, Chandler thought. The very one he didn't want her to make.

"I don't like it."

Maureen's smile was placating. "No. I don't expect that you do. All of us can see that you've—grown very fond of Roslyn. It's understandable that you want to keep her here—close to you."

He darted a sheepish look at her. "Are my feelings for Roslyn that transparent?"

Her smile deepened. "They aren't on your sleeve yet, but they're pretty darn close."

Chandler groaned. These past couple of weeks since she'd come home with the baby he'd purposely made time away from the clinic to be with her and Evelyn. With each day that had passed, he'd fallen more and more in love with them.

"I might as well admit it, Mom. I'm crazy about her and Evelyn. But I don't know what to do about it."

She shook her head. "A good start would be telling her how you feel. Have you done that?"

He pushed fingers into his hair and raked them backward. "Not exactly. I wanted to give her time—to adjust to being a mother. And to being away from her father and home in Fort Worth. Besides, I'm not keen on being rejected."

Maureen's chuckle was full of disbelief. "I can't see that happening. Roslyn thinks you're the grandest thing since the discovery of fire. But I do think she has her doubts about you."

Stunned, Chandler stared at his mother. "What are you talking about? I've always tried to be a responsible man."

"Depends on how you define *responsible*." She stacked several papers together, then slipped them into the bottom drawer of the desk. "Yes, you're accountable to your family, the ranch and your work. But what about Roslyn and baby Evelyn?"

He groaned. "Hell, Mom? I'm giving them all the time I can."

"Right now, you are. But Roslyn doesn't know if that will last. She's already had one man upend her life. Understandably, she's going to be cautious. You need to respect her wishes to be on her own and give her time to figure everything out for herself."

Chandler was about to retort that there was no need for Roslyn to be independent. That he'd be only too happy to take care of her. But it suddenly dawned on him that he was being an idiot. Roslyn had just run away from a controlling man. He didn't want to give her reason to run again.

"You're right, Mom. But I worry…"

Maureen walked around the desk to stand in front of him.

"You worry about what?" she urged.

Frustration put a curse word on his tongue, but he bit it back. "This deal with her father. Roslyn still hasn't talked to him. You'd think she'd at least want to tell him that the baby had arrived safely and he was now the grandfather to a daughter. But she's stubborn about it."

Surprised, Maureen asked, "You brought all of that up with Roslyn?"

Chandler blew out a weary breath. "Once. Not that it did any good. She quickly shut me down."

Maureen laid a hand on his shoulder. "Chandler, not everyone's dad is as loving and supportive as the one you had. Remember that and try to respect Roslyn's wishes."

He shook his head. "Mom, you always taught us kids

that bitterness was the same as poison. To carry it around made a person sick. Don't you still believe that?"

She slowly eased into the chair next to his and rubbed her eyes with both hands. The disenchanted gesture made Chandler want to put his arm around her shoulders and remind her that he and the rest of her children hadn't forgotten the loss she'd endured.

"Dear Lord, Chandler, sometimes it amazes me how much like Joel you are." She dropped her hands and gave him a battle-weary smile. "Ever since your dad died I've tried very hard not to be bitter. But sometimes when I forget to hold my guard up, the resentful feelings creep up on me. When that happens I'm not good and...well, perhaps you're right about Roslyn. Maybe it would be best if she confronted her father and cleared the air. I can't say. But I am sure of one thing. You'll regret it if you let her get away."

On that count, Chandler couldn't argue with his mother. Roslyn and baby Evelyn had become everything to him. And somehow, someway, he had to convince her that she needed him in her life as much as he needed the two of them.

Chapter Eleven

Leaving Three Rivers had been the hardest thing Roslyn had ever done in her entire life. When she'd driven away with Evelyn and all their personal belongings, she'd felt as though a part of her heart was being torn away. The Hollisters had become her family and Chandler… Just thinking about him put a lump of emotion in her throat and filled her heart with a longing that refused to go away.

Now, after more than two weeks of being gone from the ranch and living in her own apartment, she was still questioning her decision to leave a place where she and the baby had been totally surrounded by people who cared about her.

But from the very beginning, Roslyn had made an agreement with Maureen that she would only stay until she'd had the baby and was recuperated enough to move on. That time had come and she'd been determined not to stay longer and take advantage of the generous family, even though Chandler had put up an argument for her to stay.

But it hadn't been the kind of argument Roslyn had hoped or wished to hear from him. He'd never once mentioned the word *love*. He'd never once told her that he didn't want to live without her and Evelyn. That's all it would've taken to keep her there on the ranch with him. But he'd never spoken anything that could have been construed as a vow of love. He'd not hinted anything about wanting to make a future with her. Instead, he'd kept harping on the fact that she needed to stay on the ranch, where she'd have plenty of help with the baby.

Sighing, she glanced down at Evelyn to see she'd finished nursing and had fallen asleep. Roslyn eased her nipple away from the baby's slack mouth and readjusted her clothing before she rose from the wooden rocker and placed her in a white bassinet.

At the rate her daughter was growing, it wouldn't be long before the bassinet would be too small to accommodate her. But for now, Roslyn preferred to have the baby sleeping in the same bedroom with her, instead of across the hall in the nursery.

The apartment Roslyn had rented was in an older building complex located fairly close to the school where Katherine worked as a secretary. From a window at the back of her living room, she could see a portion of a small city park equipped with gym sets and bumpy slides. At the front of the ground-floor apartment, there was a cluster of Joshua trees and a small flower bed filled with native rocks and a variety of succulents.

It was a pretty place in a quiet neighborhood and Roslyn liked the way the rooms were coming together. Since she'd moved in, she'd been gradually collecting pieces of furniture and rugs and wall decorations to make the place feel more like home. And the nursery was turning out to be bright and cheery with all white furniture and bright yellow curtains.

Yes, she and Evelyn were in their own little home now, she thought, as she walked out to the living room. This was what she'd planned from the very beginning. And no, Wickenburg was still a far distance from Redding. But that would come later.

How much later, Roslyn? When Evelyn gets to be three or four months old? Or will it take a year for you to find the courage to move on from the Hollisters—mainly one Hollister? The gentle veterinarian with black hair and sky-blue eyes and a smile that melts your bones. You need to forget Chandler. Sure, he likes your company. But he's never going to be serious. He's never going to love you.

Doing her best to shake away the mocking voice in her head, she walked into the kitchen with the intention of preparing something for the evening meal. She wasn't hungry, but she needed to make sure she maintained plenty of milk for Evelyn.

She was rummaging through the packages and cans stacked on the pantry shelf when the doorbell jangled.

Thinking it might be Katherine stopping by on her way home from work, she hurried out to the tiny foyer at the front entrance and peered through the peephole on the door. But instead of Katherine it was Chandler standing on the small, concrete porch.

This was the third visit he'd made to the apartment and each time the sight of him never failed to shoot a beam of joy right through. Even if he didn't love her, even if it was impossible for him to make a commitment to her, she wanted to be near him for as much and as long as possible. Maybe that made her foolish, but she couldn't help it.

Swinging the door wide, she greeted him with a bright hello.

"Would you like an uninvited visitor?" he asked.

The lopsided grin on his face put a smile on hers and she reached for his hand and tugged him across the threshold.

"You never need an invitation," she told him.

He held up a large brown bag in one hand and a pink paper gift sack with handles in the other. "I brought Evelyn a gift. And dinner for us," he said. "I hope you haven't already eaten."

He handed the gift to her and she peered inside to see an adorable little dress of white-and-pink checks trimmed with white lace.

"Chandler, you shouldn't have bought Evelyn anything. The nursery is already stacked with stuffed animals and toys that you've given her."

He waved away her protest. "Little girls love clothes. She can't have too many."

Groaning, Roslyn shook her head. "She's only a bit over a month old. She doesn't know what she's wearing."

Chandler chuckled. "Years from now when she sees pictures of herself, she'll be glad."

The delicious smells coming from the bag made her mouth water. Now that Chandler was here she was suddenly very hungry and very happy.

"I was just in the kitchen wondering what I was going to make myself for dinner. You've saved me from the task." She motioned for him to follow her. "Let's take that to the kitchen. Or we could eat in the dining room. The view from the table there is much nicer."

"The dining table is fine with me. But I'm not going to eat a bite until I see my baby Evelyn," he said. "Is she asleep?"

"Yes. I just put her in the bassinet. But you won't disturb her."

After Chandler deposited the sack in the kitchen, the two of them made their way to Roslyn's bedroom. Along the way, she noticed his jeans and dark brown shirt were clean, telling her he must have changed at the clinic before he'd driven over here. This evening he looked even more handsome than usual, making it very difficult for her to keep her hands off him.

Inside the bedroom, he bent over the bassinet. "Look at her! She's growing like crazy!"

"It's only been three days since you've seen her," Roslyn pointed out. "She couldn't look that much different."

"She does to me. She's gaining weight and getting longer. Next thing we know, she'll be trying to climb out of this thing!"

Roslyn didn't miss how he'd used the word *we* in his statement. And ridiculous or not, it gave her hope that he was looking toward the future. A future with her and Evelyn.

Laughing softly, Roslyn said, "She won't be able to climb for months!"

"Who says? She might be a little superwoman." He straightened and slipped his arms around Roslyn's waist, which was growing slimmer every day. "Like her mom."

Although Chandler had been showing her more and more physical affection since Evelyn had been born, he'd always pulled back before things got heated. She wasn't sure if his reticence was because she'd been recuperating from giving birth, or because he wanted to keep a cautious distance between them. Either way, each time he touched her, she felt as if every cell in her body was glowing.

"Hmm. How does it feel to be in a house with two superwomen in it?" she asked.

A low, sexy chuckle passed his lips before he lowered his head toward hers. Anticipation hummed through her as she splayed her hands on his broad chest and tilted her face up to his.

His kiss was warm and left the taste of promise on her lips. When he lifted his head, she instantly wanted to pull it back down to hers and kiss him a second time. But she didn't want to press him. She wanted him to reach for her on his own.

With a hand on his arm, she said, "Our dinner is getting cold. We'd better go eat before Evelyn decides her nap is over."

She thought she saw a flash of frustration in his blue eyes, but then he smiled and nodded. "Right. You need to eat without interruption."

As it turned out, Evelyn woke before Roslyn finished all the food on her plate. But Chandler was only too happy to go fetch the crying baby for her.

He rose from the dining-room chair. "You stay put. I'll take care of Evelyn."

"But her diaper probably needs to be changed."

He feigned an insulted look. "Roslyn, if I can examine a hissing, clawing cat, I think I can handle one sweet little baby."

She laughed. "Sorry. I'd forgotten you have that special touch."

Inside the bedroom, Chandler gently gathered Evelyn up from the bassinet and carried her across the hall to the nursery, where a changing table was positioned between the crib and a matching chest of drawers.

He was fastening the tabs on the clean diaper when

from the corner of his eye, he saw Roslyn step inside the door. Knowing she was watching his every move, he finished snapping the baby's onesie back together, then wrapped her in a light blanket.

He scooped up Evelyn from the changing table and cradled her safely in the crook of his left arm. "See, not so much as a tiny whimper," he playfully bragged.

"Where did you learn how to handle a baby?" she asked. "And don't tell me at the animal hospital. There is a huge difference between animal and human babies."

"To be honest, I learned a little about baby care way back when Vivian gave birth to Hannah. Viv was terrified she was going to do something wrong."

"That surprises me about Vivian. The night she visited the ranch, she came across as a very confident woman to me."

"She is now. But years ago when that jerk of an ex-husband left the ranch like a scalded hound, it shattered Viv's self-confidence. Not only about caring for the baby, but about everything. Holt and I and Joseph all helped her with the baby as much as we could. Until she finally woke up and realized she wasn't helpless, she was just divorced."

"Hannah is thirteen now. That was a long time ago," Roslyn stated. "Obviously you've not forgotten how to change a diaper."

He grinned. "You know what they say. Once you ride a bike you never forget. Same with dirty diapers."

Laughing, she moved out of the doorway. "Let's go to the living room," she suggested. "I've made coffee to go with the Italian cream cake you brought."

"That means I'll have to put Evelyn down," he complained.

"She can lie on the cushion next to you on the couch," Roslyn suggested.

"That's not the same as holding her."

Roslyn playfully rolled her eyes. "If you keep this up you're going to spoil her."

Wasn't that what fathers were for? Chandler caught himself before he said the question out loud. He wasn't Evelyn's father. But he felt like he was and everything inside of him wanted to be. Yet to say something like that would imply a serious commitment. Was he really ready to do that? To expose his heart?

Well, hell, Chandler. What are you doing here? It's not like you needed to leave the clinic and come over here to see Roslyn just to have something to do. When you left the office earlier, Trey and Cybil were still dealing with patients. But they'd insisted they could handle things because even they can see you've fallen in love with Roslyn and need to be with her. Don't you think it's time you face up to the reality that she already owns your heart?

Clearing his throat, he said, "Evelyn isn't going to be a spoiled little girl. She's going to be loved and protected."

The baby's warm weight against his chest was a feeling like nothing else he'd experienced and as he bent and kissed the top of her little head, he suddenly realized why his brothers were so happy. Joe and Blake had everything a man really needed.

By the time they finished dessert, Chandler had related everything that had been going on at the clinic and the ranch since he'd last seen her. Just hearing him talk about both places made Roslyn homesick, but she did her best not to show it.

Above anything, she needed to show him that moving here to town hadn't been a mistake. Her father had raised her to be a sponge and to Roslyn that was unacceptable. Yet at times, when she was feeling lonely and isolated, she wondered if she'd carried the independent thing a bit too far. Had living with the Hollisters really been that much of a crutch for her?

Staying there as an excuse to be close to Chandler was wrong, she firmly told herself. Especially if he had no plans to take their relationship a step further.

"Evelyn has fallen asleep again," he said as he smoothed a finger over the baby's fine hair. "Maybe I should put her back in her bed."

He was so incredibly gentle with Evelyn. Just watching the way he cradled the baby in his arms, the way he hummed and talked to her, filled Roslyn with bittersweet emotions. Would her daughter ever have a father who loved her as much as Chandler seemed to love her?

Not wanting to dwell on that melancholy question, Roslyn rose from the armchair. "Okay. While you do that I'll clean up our dinner mess."

Moments later, she placed the last dish in the dishwasher and closed the door just as Chandler entered the kitchen.

"She's sound asleep," he announced. "Do you need any help in here?"

"No. All finished."

Awkward silence suddenly filled the room and Roslyn watched him jam his hands in the front pockets of his jeans and lean a shoulder against the doorjamb.

"Is something wrong?" she asked.

"No. I'm just wondering what it's like for you living here—with just you and Evelyn."

She shrugged and walked over to him. "I've already told you that I like it. The apartment is cozy and convenient and has all the space the two of us need."

His eyes narrowed as he studied her face. "That's not what I mean."

"If you mean, do I get lonely, I'd be lying if I said I didn't. After living at Three Rivers with lots of people around and things always happening, this little apartment is very quiet. But staying here is good for me," she reasoned.

"Your voice is wobbling, Roslyn. If it's so good for you, then why are you about to cry?"

Because she was feeling totally helpless, she thought. Because she was standing here looking at a man whom she loved with all her heart and he didn't love her back. And probably never would.

"I'm not about to cry," she lied. "I just get a little emotional when I talk about Three Rivers. While I was living there the ranch became very special to me."

And that was definitely no lie, she thought. No matter what happened with Chandler in the future, she would never forget the beautiful ranch or the Hollister family.

His nostrils flared slightly as he pushed away from the door frame. "I was hoping I had become special to you," he said quietly.

She wasn't expecting anything like that to come out of his mouth, and for a moment, she could merely stare at him and wonder what was going on behind those blue, blue eyes.

"You are," she admitted.

He moved close enough to wrap both his hands around her upper arms. Roslyn's heart began to pound with anticipation.

"That's hard to believe. I asked you to stay on the ranch. You refused."

Was that disappointment she spotted in his eyes, or simply frustration?

Shaking her head, she said, "I explained to you that I needed to stand on my own for a while. And why are you bringing this up tonight? It's not like we haven't hashed it out before I left the ranch."

He moved his hands to her back and drew her forward until the front of her body was touching his. "No. We didn't hash it out. Not completely. Because at that time I didn't…no, I couldn't tell you how I really felt."

She flattened her palms against his chest and savored the warmth of his hard muscles. "Why not? I was there for over two weeks after Evelyn was born. You had plenty of opportunities to talk—about whatever it was that you wanted to tell me."

The sound he made in his throat was something between a cough and a groan.

"Yeah, I could talk. But I couldn't do this." Drawing her closer, he nuzzled his lips against her ear. "I couldn't show you how much I want you. How much I've been aching to make love to you."

Just hearing him speak the words was enough to turn her knees to mush. The sensation caused her fingers to instinctively clutch folds of his shirt to support herself.

"You couldn't? Why?"

Her voice was slurred with desire as she tilted her head and exposed the column of her neck to the searching warmth of his lips.

His arms tightened around her. "You'd just given birth," he reasoned. "And I wanted to give you time."

She slid her hands upward to his shoulders and gripped them tightly. "You should have told me how you felt, Chandler."

Delving his fingers into her hair, he turned her face until their gazes melded and only a scant space separated their lips. The connection stole her breath and scattered her senses in all directions.

"Would it have made any difference?" he asked.

The helpless moan in her throat was more like a sob. "Yes! Just to know that I was important to you in some way would've been—"

"You're important to me in *every* way, Ros. If I didn't realize that when you were at the ranch, I do now."

He wasn't exactly saying "I love you," but at this point, he was saying enough.

"Oh, Chandler."

Bringing her hands up to his face, she began to rain kisses over both his cheeks, his chin and finally the corners of his lips.

With a needy growl, he fastened his lips over hers and kissed her so deeply and passionately that she was instantly and totally lost to him.

The fiery contact went on and on, until her lungs were crying for air and her body was aching to connect to his. When he finally lifted his head and gazed down at her, his breathing was hard, his eyelids heavy.

"As much as I want you, this can't go on," he whispered gruffly. "Otherwise, I won't be able to stop. And I don't want to hurt you."

Before she could reply, he turned and walked a few steps away from her. Confused, she stared at his back.

"Hurt me? Why—?" Suddenly it dawned on her and she closed the space between them and rested a hand against his back. "Chandler, I promise, you're not going to hurt me."

"I can't take that chance. I—"

"No," she interrupted. "Listen, I just had my post-birth checkup yesterday. The doctor says I'm in great shape— if I feel like being intimate it will be fine."

Still uncertain, he turned back to her. "What about birth control? You're breastfeeding—" He suddenly paused and shook his head. "I'm sorry, Roslyn, I sound like a doctor. When I should be talking to you like a—"

"Lover?" she asked.

"Yes," he said sheepishly.

Smiling coyly, she moved forward until her breasts were pressing against his chest and her hips were aligned to his. "You need to quit worrying, Doc. The birth-control issue was taken care of while I was still in the hospital."

A horrified look came over his face. "You didn't do anything permanent, did you?"

Chuckling, she hugged him tighter. "No. Later on I'm going to want Evelyn to have brothers and sisters. When that time comes I can have the birth control removed."

He let out a relieved breath. "Oh. I'm glad I—" His arms came around her as he buried his face in the side of her hair. "I'm acting like an idiot, Ros. But nothing about my life has been the same since you left Three Rivers. I've missed you so much. I want you...more than you could possibly know."

She eased out of his arms and reached for his hand. "Maybe as much as I've been wanting you."

Not bothering to say more, she led him back to the bedroom and over to the queen-size bed covered with a fluffy red-and-white comforter.

Chandler looked over his shoulder at the bassinet. "What about Evelyn?"

Smiling impishly, Roslyn said, "She'll never know we're in here. But if it will make you feel better, I'll move her to the far side of the room."

She left him long enough to roll the bassinet to the opposite corner of the room, then returned to his side.

Chandler promptly gathered her up in his arms and gently laid her in the middle of the bed.

Laughing softly, she said, "Don't you think I'm wearing too many clothes for bed?"

"I'm going to take care of that problem in due time," he promised.

Her heart was pounding with eager anticipation as she watched him quickly discard his boots, then strip down to nothing but a pair of black boxers.

His body was everything she'd imagined it to be. Starting with his arms and ending with his legs, he was all hard, sculpted muscle and golden-brown skin. She couldn't wait to touch him and discover how it would feel to have her body tangled with his.

He climbed onto the bed and, kneeling over her, began to unbutton her blouse. Once the two pieces of fabric fell away and exposed her bra, his fingers traced the lacy edge, then cupped around the fullness of her breasts.

"I'm not exactly looking my best," she murmured. "I still have a bit of weight to lose and my skin is marked in places."

Smiling, his fingers lingered on her breasts for a few moments longer, then slipped downward over her midriff and onto the zipper of her jeans. "You couldn't look more beautiful to me than you do at this moment."

"You don't have to say that sort of thing to make me happy, Chandler. It's enough that you want me...like this."

By now he was tugging her jeans over her bare feet. Once he'd tossed them to the floor, she raised up so he could remove her blouse. When it was out of the way, he eased her back to the mattress, then stretched out next to her.

"Do you think I'm just mouthing words?" he asked as he pulled her into the circle of his arms.

Giddy with desire, Roslyn wrapped her arms around his neck. "I don't know what you're thinking," she admitted.

"Then it's time I showed you."

His lips found hers and as he kissed her hungrily, his hands reached to her back and unclasped her bra. When he peeled the fabric away, his fingers traced the outline of each breast and then his mouth left hers to brush against the soft sensitive skin.

The teasing sensation caused the aching need in her to build and spread, until she was certain it was going to consume her.

Then just when she was sure he was going to take one of the budded nipples into his mouth, his head lifted and he reclaimed her lips with another heated kiss.

By the time his tongue invited hers to mate with his, the room was spinning and every inch of her was burning with a need so intense she thought her body would ignite into a thousand tiny flames.

The taste of his mouth was a delicious mystery that made her want more and more, while the hard warmth of his body lured her senses to a place she'd never been before. Somewhere along the way, she realized she was crushed so tightly in his arms, she could scarcely move, much less breathe. But it didn't matter. Nothing mattered except making love to him.

When he finally eased himself off the bed and removed the last of their clothing, Roslyn had to bite back the needy whimpers clawing at the back of her throat.

Back on the bed, he positioned himself over her, but instead of connecting their bodies, he looked down at her and his blue eyes gently searched her face.

"Ros, are you sure about this—about me?"

His voice was thick with desire and yet she could also

hear something else. Something that sounded incredibly like love. Was that possible?

No. She wasn't going to think about that now. Tonight was all about giving him what he wanted and taking everything she needed.

Reaching up, she cradled his face with her hands. "I'm sure, Chandler. Very sure."

He let out a long breath and then with his eyes locked on her face, he parted her thighs and lowered his body down to hers.

Roslyn had thought she was prepared for him, but she'd been wrong. The sensation of having him inside her was like a thousand cymbals crashing together in her head. It sucked the oxygen from her lungs and rocked her equilibrium.

With a helpless groan, her fingers latched onto his shoulders. "Chandler. Oh, Chandler."

Lowering his face to hers, he kissed her forehead, her cheeks and finally her lips. "I know, my darling. It's too good. Too good."

Yes, it was too good, she thought. Because now, after this, after him, nothing was going to be the same.

The thought very nearly caused her to sob, but she swallowed the urge and pleaded, "Love me, Chandler. Please love me."

He answered her imploring request, and in a matter of moments Roslyn was meeting his rapid thrusts with a fierceness that stunned her.

Long minutes later, Chandler stared at the shadowy wall of the bedroom and wondered what had just happened to him. Taking Roslyn to bed had been like walking into a tornado and he was still shaking from the aftermath.

From the very first night Roslyn had come into his life, he'd recognized that she was different from the women he'd dated in the past. He'd not understood exactly why she'd evoked such tender feelings in him, but she had. And because of her situation with the baby and her father, he'd tried his best to tamp down his emotions and think of her simply as a woman in need. But that hadn't worked. Now, more than two months had passed and he could no longer deny that he loved her utterly. But would the future take her and the baby away from him?

The soft touch of her hands against his back tugged his thoughts to the present and he rolled over so that his face was next to hers on the pillow.

"Is something wrong, Chandler?"

His hand trembling, he smoothed strands of tangled brown hair from her face and tried to give her an easy smile.

"Nothing is wrong, my sweet. I'm just trying to get my wind back." He rested his forehead against hers. "Besides, I'm the one who should be asking if you're okay."

She curved her arm around his waist and drew the front of her damp body next to his. The feel of her full breasts and soft thighs brushing against him made his loins ache to have her again. It was crazy how much he wanted her. How much he figured he would always want her.

"Mmm. I'm more than okay. I feel—"

He pulled his head back to see uncertainty swimming in her eyes. "You feel what?" he prompted. "Do you wish this hadn't happened?"

"Oh, no, Chandler. I'm not thinking anything like that." She touched her fingertips to the indentation in his chin. "I was just trying to decide how to tell you that... I love you."

He went stock-still and for a moment he thought his heart had quit beating. "Love...me," he said. "Roslyn, what just happened with us, it...was incredible, but—"

Her gaze dropped from his face and she pulled slightly back from him. "You don't have to explain or make excuses. Just because I love you doesn't mean I expect you to automatically feel the same about me. But I decided—" Sighing, she rolled to her back and stared at the ceiling. "After the huge mistake I made with Erich, I don't want anything hidden between you and me."

Propping himself up on one elbow, he gazed down at her soft features. "I don't want anything hidden, either," he said gently. "And if you hadn't stopped me a moment ago, you would've heard me say how much I love you, too."

Her gaze fluttered warily up to his face and she stared at him in stunned disbelief. "You...love me? Chandler, I—"

He waited for her to finish, but no words followed. Instead, a trail of tears slipped down her cheeks.

"Roslyn, why are you crying? What's wrong?"

Her head twisted back and forth on the pillow. "Because...this all has to be a dream. I'm afraid I'm going to wake up and you'll be gone."

Was she really that insecure? Couldn't she see how much he adored her?

"Oh, darling Ros, why would you think that? I'm here. And I have no intentions of leaving or letting you slip away."

Her brown eyes were still wet with tears and filled with doubt. "You already have a wonderful life, Chandler. A huge, loving family. A thriving business. Devoted friends. You don't need me and Evelyn. Especially when you can have any woman."

Groaning, he reached to pull her close. "Even if I could have any woman, I don't want her. I want you."

"I don't know why. I'm just a runaway with too much baggage and too many scars. My father tells me I need to grow up or I'll never be able to hold a man."

Wrapping his arms tightly around her, he said, "I think the man needs to work on his own problems before he gives out advice. But we'll discuss him later. Right now I don't want to waste this night with talk. Do you?"

She smiled at him and his heart swelled as he wiped at the track of tears on her face.

"No," she whispered. "I don't want to waste a moment."

He lowered his lips to hers and as he kissed her, he recognized, for the first time in his life, he was tasting real love.

Chapter Twelve

The next morning, Hollister Animal Hospital was overrun with patients, and to make matters worse Cybil was late getting to work because she'd been helping her sister tow her dead car to a garage to be repaired.

He hadn't fully expected to be finished with everyone on the appointment book, plus a few walk-ins, by the time lunch hour rolled around. But somehow he and the staff had cleared the place. Since he rarely left the building, other than to make a house call, Loretta had looked surprised when he'd told her he was going downtown and wouldn't be back until the clinic reopened at one.

Chandler hadn't told any of the staff where he was going. His plans were too private and special to share with anyone, except the woman he loved.

A few minutes later, when he walked up on the small porch of Roslyn's apartment, he could hear Evelyn screaming angrily. But by the time Roslyn opened the door to greet him, the baby had quieted to intermittent howls.

In spite of the noise, Roslyn didn't appear to be the least bit flustered. In fact, the smile on her face had to be the warmest, most inviting one he'd ever seen.

"Chandler! Come in before Evelyn disturbs the whole neighborhood!" She reached for his hand and tugged him over the threshold.

Chandler stepped past Roslyn and into the foyer. "She must be wanting her lunch."

Roslyn shook her head. "She's already had lunch. She's angry because I took her out of the bathtub and dressed her."

Chandler laughed. "So she's already a little diva and doesn't want her bubble bath to be interrupted. What a girl!"

"'What a girl' is right," Roslyn said with a chuckle. "I can already see her teenage years ahead. I'm not expecting them to be easy."

She raised up on her tiptoes and lifted her face to receive his kiss. The sweet contact of having his lips on hers brought the night before rushing back to him, and from the wash of pink on her cheeks, he figured she was remembering, too.

"This is a wonderful surprise," she murmured. "How did you manage to get away from the clinic at this time of day?"

"It must be the full moon," he said jokingly. "All my patients were cooperative this morning."

She linked her arm through his and urged him on to the living room. "Have you eaten yet? I'll fix you a sandwich and iced tea."

"I…don't have time to eat. I need to be back at the clinic by one. And I want to talk with you."

Both her brows arched coyly. "Just talk?"

Grinning, he pulled her close and placed a long kiss on her lips. "Yes, just talk for now. But later tonight might be different," he suggested.

"I'll take that as a promise." She gestured to the couch. "Grab a seat and I'll put Evelyn in her crib. I think she's beginning to see the mobile. That might keep her occupied."

Normally he would've ignored her offer to take a seat and followed her to the nursery so he could hold Evelyn. But with the few minutes he had quickly ticking away, he didn't want to get sidetracked.

"All right," he told her. "I'll wait right here."

While she was gone, he double-checked his pocket and sighed with relief as his fingers came into contact with the small, fabric-covered box. Damn it, he should've taken the time to stop and buy flowers, too. But those would have to come later tonight, he thought, when he took her to Jose's for dinner.

"Wonder of wonders," Roslyn said as she reentered the living room. "As soon as I put her in the crib, the crying stopped and her eyelids drooped. She's probably already asleep."

"I'm glad. Because I need your undivided attention."

He patted the cushion next to his and she obliged by sinking down close to his side.

"Okay, so what is this about? Returning to work at the clinic?"

He looked at her with surprise. "Why would you think that? Evelyn isn't two months old yet and I know you want to spend as much time with her as possible."

She shrugged. "I've been talking with Loretta. She says Cybil is running herself ragged and causing extra work for you. It's obvious you could use my help."

"Would you like to work at the clinic again? I mean, later on, after Evelyn gets a little older."

She reached for his hand and rubbed her fingertips over the back of it. Her touch helped soothe the anxious beat of his heart.

"I loved working at the clinic," she said. "But whether I go back later depends on how you feel about it."

He took a deep breath and let it out. "That's what I wanted to talk with you about—to tell you exactly what I want. For you and me and Evelyn."

Her lips parted as her gaze searched his face. "What are you saying, Chandler? Are you asking me to move back to Three Rivers?"

He clasped both her hands between his. "Yes, I am. I asking you to come back to Three Rivers as my wife."

"Wife."

She repeated the word as though she'd never heard it before and Chandler could see he'd shocked her.

"That's right. I want you to be my wife, Roslyn. I want Evelyn to be my daughter." Rather than wait for her to reply, he reached to his shirt pocket. As he pulled out the box and flipped open the lid, her brown eyes grew wider and wider. "Will you marry me, Roslyn DuBose?"

Shaking her head, she let out a sound that was something between a laugh and a sob. "I don't understand, Chandler. When did you decide this?"

"Probably when I carried you into the clinic that first night we met."

She groaned. "Be serious, Chandler."

"I am being serious. I wanted to wrap my arms around you and never let go. I still feel that way. I'll always feel that way." He took the ring from its velvet bed and pushed it onto the appropriate finger. "If you don't like the ring, you can change it for something else. And it might need to be resized. I guessed at the fit."

She gazed down at the large, emerald cut diamond flanked by two smaller round diamonds.

"It's unbelievably beautiful, Chandler. And the size is perfect. But I——" She looked at him and shook her head. "Are you truly certain this is what you want? Last night——"

"I've been thinking about this long before last night, Roslyn. I love you. I love Evelyn. You're everything I want. All I need now is for you to say yes."

She looked at the ring, then back up to his eager face. "I love you so much, Chandler. The only thing I can say is yes. Yes! Yes!"

Flinging her arms around him, she pressed her lips to his and as he kissed her, Chandler felt as if everything in the world had righted itself.

When their lips finally parted, he pressed his cheek against hers and held her tight against him. "I know you're probably wondering about my work and how I'll ever make time for you and the baby. But I will. I promise I'll make it happen. We're going to be happy—together."

She pulled her head back far enough to look at him and the joy he saw in her eyes made his spirits soar even higher.

"I'm not worried. Blake and Joe have managed to balance work and marriage. Whatever your brothers can do, you can do, too."

"Dang right," he said with a chuckle. "Now, when are we going to set the date? I'm sure you'll want enough time to plan a wedding and that's okay with me. As long as you make it quick."

Laughing, she squeezed his hands. "You mean, like a few-days quick? Or a few-weeks quick?"

"I'm thinking days, but I want you to be happy. Maybe with Mom and Vivian and Katherine and Tessa all helping with wedding plans, you can shave the wedding date down to a month from now."

She leaned forward and kissed him again. "Oh, Chandler, I don't need a fancy wedding. As far as I'm concerned I'd be happy to elope to Reno or somewhere. But then I'd feel badly about knocking your family out of the celebration. Maybe we can compromise with a simple ceremony on the ranch?"

He nodded. "That sounds perfect. Because I wouldn't feel good about leaving out family, either. And Roslyn, speaking of family—I really want you to contact your father and let him know about the baby, and me, and the wedding. It would be the right thing to do."

Like the flip of a light switch, her expression suddenly turned incredulous.

"You expect me to contact my father? After all I've told you? I can't believe I'm hearing you right, Chandler!"

Pulling her hands from his, she rose from the couch and walked across the room. Chandler stared after her. He'd expected her to be resistant to the idea, but not this vehemently.

"I don't think my suggestion is that outrageous, Roslyn," he reasoned. "This is an eventful time in your life. I'm thinking you should want to show your father that you're happy. That you're now the mother of a beautiful daughter and a wife to me."

She turned around and even at a distance he could see the anguish twisting her features. "I'm not inhuman, Chandler. It would give me great satisfaction to show him how much he misjudged me. I'd like for him to see I'm a capable person and can stand on my own without him dictating my every move. Trouble is, his interfering wouldn't stop there, Chandler. You see, happiness doesn't factor in to Martin DuBose's plans. Whether my mother or I was ever happy has never been his concern. He's only interested in having things his way. To put it bluntly, he'd cause us all kinds of hell."

Chandler left the couch and walked over to where she stood. Her hands were clenched and her breathing was coming in short bursts. The sight of her anger was contagious and in spite of his normally cool head, he was rapidly losing his patience.

"What exactly do you think I am, Roslyn? Just a bystander? A milksop who's afraid to come out of the shadows and defend the woman he loves?"

Confused, she stared at him. "No. Of course I don't think that. But—"

"There are no buts, Roslyn," he interrupted. "If I'm going to be your husband, then all of this affects me, too. Your problems become mine and vice versa. No matter what they are, we need to resolve them together. And the way I see it, you can't expect to move happily into the future until you resolve this thing with your father. My Lord, Ros, the man doesn't even know where you are!"

"And I'm better off for it!"

She practically yelled the words at him and as Chandler studied the fury on her face, disappointment welled up in him until he was practically choking on it.

"I can see this isn't going to work," he said dully.

"You're darn right it isn't going to work!" She stalked past him and didn't stop until she'd put a measurable distance between them. "I just got out from under one man's thumb. I don't intend to turn around and tie myself to another. Not a man who wants to dictate my life before I even become his wife! No! This isn't going to work for me."

The day had started like a beautiful fairy tale, Chandler thought. The sky had never been a more vivid blue and the breeze was as fresh as a spring flower. He was blessed with a job he loved and, even more importantly, the woman he'd prayed would come into his life and fill it with happiness.

Fairy tales aren't real, Chandler. And apparently the love Roslyn professed to feel for you wasn't real, either.

Chandler was sure something inside him was dying, yet somehow he managed to close the space between them. Her lovely features were defiant and so far removed from the woman he'd proposed to only minutes ago, that he felt he was looking at a stranger.

"There for a moment, I was beginning to question myself. I was wondering if I might be wrong and you were right. But that hardly matters now. You've just shown me that your father is the smart one in all of this. You're not mature enough to be a wife to me or any man."

She opened her mouth to make a retort, but Chandler didn't bother to stand there and listen. She'd already made it very clear how she felt.

As he started out of the room, she yelled at him, "Here. You can take your diamond and your oh-so-perfect ideas with you."

Chandler felt the ring hit his back and heard the ping as the piece of jewelry fell on the hardwood floor. The sound was like a gavel at the end of a trial, he decided. Everything had reached a conclusion and it wasn't a happy one.

"I don't want it," he said without a backward glance. "Keep it and add it to your collection."

Roslyn was in the kitchen, packing items into heavy-duty cardboard boxes, when the doorbell rang.

Wiping her hands on the seat of her jeans, she walked out to the foyer and wondered what she would do if the person on the other side of the door was Chandler. Which was a moot question altogether. More than a week had passed since Chandler had proposed marriage, then turned around and walked out of her life. No. He'd be the last person to be standing on the porch of her apartment.

To her relief the caller was Katherine and she quickly opened the door wide and invited her inside.

"This is a wonderful surprise," Roslyn told her. "Are you just getting off work?"

Katherine nodded. "I thought I'd pop by and say hello before I drove on home to the ranch. How's little Evelyn?"

"She's asleep in the nursery. Go take a peep at her while I make us some coffee," Roslyn told her.

Moments later, as Roslyn poured water into the coffee machine, Katherine entered the kitchen, then stopped and stared at the partially filled boxes.

"What in the world? Surely you're not sending these things to charity. It all looks new to me."

Roslyn bit down on her lip. "No. Not to charity. I'm getting it organized. Before I call a moving van."

Katherine made her way through the boxes on the floor to join Roslyn at the cabinet counter.

"Moving van! Have you found a different apartment already?"

Roslyn couldn't bring herself to look at Katherine. During her stay at Three Rivers, the woman had become like a sister to her. "No. I'm…leaving Wickenburg. I've decided it's time I move on to Redding and settle down on Mother's property."

"Oh. Gosh, I don't know what to say. Except that I wish you wouldn't go. Everyone here loves you so much. And actually…well, I'm not supposed to say anything, but given the circumstances, I think I'd better. Maureen has been very busy putting a baby shower together for you. I think she's planned it for next Saturday night at the ranch. She wanted to surprise you."

Maureen didn't have time to draw a deep breath much less plan a shower for Roslyn—a party that she didn't deserve. Especially now that everything had ended between her and Chandler.

Suddenly the anguish in her heart was too much to hold back and she pressed her hands over her face to hide her tears. "Oh, God, Katherine, this is terrible. Just terrible."

Taking her by the shoulders, Katherine led her over to the kitchen table and eased her into the nearest chair. "Roslyn, what's happened? Tell me."

Choking back her sobs, Roslyn related everything that had happened, starting with Chandler proposing, the engagement ring and ultimately the quarrel over her father.

"I ruined everything, Kat. But I didn't see that I had much choice. If I invited Dad back into my life, he'd make sure everything would be ruined, anyway. So Chandler put me in a no-win situation."

Katherine went to the cabinet and filled two cups with the freshly brewed coffee. After spooning powdered creamer into both, she carried them over to the table.

"Drink. It'll make you feel better."

"Thanks, Katherine," she said ruefully. "I'm surprised you still want to stay and have coffee with me. Now that you've heard the whole story. And you know that I've... well, probably hurt Chandler."

Shaking her head, Katherine said, "Don't be silly. Besides, I can see how all of this has hurt you, too. Frankly, I'm stunned. Chandler hasn't spoken a word of this to Blake or Holt. They would've already said something.

And Maureen certainly doesn't know. She's still planning the party as though nothing is wrong."

This news only caused more tears to sprout from Roslyn's eyes. "This is awful. Truly awful. I'll have to tell her. I can't go out to the ranch. Not now. Besides, Maureen is going to hate me once she hears what happened. And Chandler—I couldn't face him. Not for any reason."

"Maureen isn't going to hate you. But I can tell you this, she's going to be terribly angry if you up and leave Wickenburg like this."

Roslyn reached for the coffee and took several sips and tried to gather her composure. "I don't really see any point of staying here, Katherine. Yes, I love it here and, yes, I've made lots of great friends on the ranch and at the animal hospital. But being here—I couldn't forget Chandler."

"Is that what you really want? To forget him? You told me a few minutes ago that you love him."

"I do! I guess I always will. But he sees everything differently than me." She paused and sucked in a painful breath. "I don't think he ever understood the cold expanse between me and my father. Or the heartache I've endured because of him. If he had understood, he wouldn't have asked me to include him in my plans…our plans."

Smiling gently, Katherine reached over and patted Roslyn's hand. "Chandler probably doesn't understand you completely. But on the other hand, I don't believe you understand him, either."

Gripping her coffee cup, she looked at the other woman. "What do you mean?"

"Chandler is a born nurturer. He wants everything and everyone, human or animal, to be well and happy. There's not a vindictive or spiteful bone in his body. In fact, his brothers often complain that he's too laid-back and too easy with people that he should get angry with."

"He certainly got angry with me." The icy fury Roslyn had spotted in his eyes just before he'd walked away was something she'd never forget.

"Yes, he can get angry. But mostly he's a caring guy. And, in many ways, I think the death of his father was even worse on him than his brothers."

Surprised by the remark, Roslyn asked, "Why would you think that? I'm sure each of them was equally devastated."

"Yes. But Chandler carries the extra burden of resembling his late father and having the man's gentle personality. Everyone, even Maureen, expects him to always be like Joel."

"That's too much to expect from Chandler," Roslyn murmured. "Just like it was too much for him to expect me to throw my arms open to my father."

"You might be right. But Chandler has no father now. And I'm sure he'd tell you that he doesn't want that same emptiness for you. He wants every aspect of your life to be full and happy. That's just the kind of guy he is. A nurturer," she repeated.

"So you're trying to tell me that you think I'm wrong."

Shaking her head, Katherine reached for her coffee. "It's not my place to tell you what's right or wrong, Ros. But if you love Chandler, you shouldn't be running away."

"I'm afraid, Kat." Rising to her feet, she began to wander restlessly around the kitchen. "And though it probably doesn't look like it to you, I love Chandler too much to drag him into a family that was…never really much of a family. He deserves better. He deserves a father-in-law who would embrace him instead of reject him."

Katherine's cynical laugh brought Roslyn's pacing to

a halt and she looked over to the table to see a wry twist on her friend's face.

"Oh, Roslyn, when Blake and I fell in love I had all kinds of awful baggage. My first marriage was a disaster and I blamed myself for my husband's death. And Dad…well, I harbored plenty of bitter memories toward him. After he became disabled with a stroke, I questioned whether I was doing the right thing to move back to Wickenburg to care for him. But in spite of my misgivings, Nick and I moved back in with him."

Roslyn had to ask, "How did that go?"

A sad smile touched her face. "We had a little over two good years with him before he passed away. I didn't think I would be devastated over his death. He'd caused my mother and brother and me so much sorrow and humiliation. But I was devastated to lose him. And later, after I'd had time to think about everything, I regretted that I stayed away from Dad all those years. Because I realized that in helping my father, I was also helping myself."

More tears began to stream from Roslyn's eyes. "I'm not sure I'm capable of helping my father change. But I suppose it's never too late to try, is it?"

The somber expression on Katherine's face suddenly turned into a bright smile. "Never," she agreed. Then she jumped to her feet and carried one of the cardboard boxes over to the cabinet counter.

When she started pulling out the contents, Roslyn asked blankly, "What are you doing?"

"Unpacking. So hurry up and let's get this stuff back where it belongs before Evelyn wakes up."

Two days later, hours after the clinic had closed for the night, Chandler and Trey were still working at the barn.

"Is his leg mending, Doc? I sure hope so. His horns are as big as baseball bats. I want him to go home. Pronto."

Chandler made a thorough inspection of the stitches he'd sewn into the bull's back leg. "The laceration is healing. If he doesn't develop a fever I'll send him home tomorrow. Have you given him the shot of antibiotics?"

"Yep. All done."

"Good." Chandler motioned for Trey to move aside, then opened the squeeze chute to allow the black bull to move into the holding pen.

Without bothering to look back, Trey rushed past Chandler and out the nearest gate. "Better run, Doc! He's mad as hell!"

Unconcerned, Chandler walked through the gate Trey had just rushed through. Behind him, the bull had already turned his attention to a pile of alfalfa in the hay manger.

"He's not mad. He's hungry." Chandler secured the lock on the gate, then glanced over to where Trey was washing the manure off his boots with a garden hose. "How about me and you changing clothes and driving over to the Fandango? It's Friday night. The place will be hopping."

Dropping the hose, the lanky blond turned a disbelieving stare at Chandler.

"Doc, are you feeling okay?"

Grimacing, Chandler lifted the hat from his head and raked a hand through his hair. Actually, he felt like he'd been run over by a herd of stampeding cattle. But he needed something to blot out the miserable thoughts going on in his head.

"Hell yes, I feel okay. Why are you looking at me like I'm crazy? It might do us both good to have a few drinks and do a little dancing."

"Who are we going to dance with?" As soon as Trey

had asked the question, he laughed. "Dumb question, huh? Women take one look at you and it's all over for me."

As the two men began walking down the sloping ground to the back entrance of the clinic, Chandler said, "What are you talking about? You're the Romeo of Yavapai County."

Trey laughed. "Sure, Doc. Even if I was a Romeo I don't think going to the Fandango is a good idea."

Trey's negative response surprised Chandler. Normally the guy was always ready for any kind of entertainment. Especially a trip to the notorious nightclub.

"Why not?" he asked.

Groaning, Trey said, "I always end up getting into a fight. And I don't particularly like nursing a black eye."

Chandler said, "You wouldn't get a black eye if you'd lead with your left instead of your right."

"Oh, Doc, you don't know what I lead with," Trey complained. "And I don't believe for one minute that you really want to go to a honky-tonk. Yeah, it's Friday night, but we got to deal with that herd of goats over at the Tabor farm early in the morning."

"That'll be quick work."

Chandler opened the door and started down the hallway to his office. Trey clomped behind him.

"Sure," Trey said mockingly. "Three hours at the quickest. Besides, Roslyn wouldn't like it if she heard you were out carousing around."

The middle of Chandler's chest winced with pain. Nearly two weeks had passed since he'd walked out of Roslyn's apartment and, try as he might, he couldn't forget her or baby Evelyn. He couldn't push away the pain of losing them, much less look into the future. There was nothing there but a black, empty pit.

"What's Roslyn got to do with anything?" He picked up a stack of files on the corner of his desk, while cutting a glance at Trey. The other man appeared astounded by his question.

"Well, hell, Doc. She has everything to do with it. I thought you were crazy about her."

Dropping the files back to the desk, Chandler walked over and sank onto the couch where Roslyn had lain after her fainting spell. That night, like every other moment he'd spent with her, continued to roll through his head, reminding him that he was nothing more than a stupid fool.

"I don't really want to talk about Roslyn," he said bluntly. "She's moving on."

The crestfallen look on Trey's face made Chandler feel even worse, if that was possible.

"Dang. She told all of us here at the clinic that she wanted to come back to work after the baby got a little older. Did you tell her she couldn't work here anymore or something?"

Or something, Chandler thought sickly. "No. I didn't tell her that. We, uh, we just went our different ways, that's all."

"Well, you could knock me over with a feather. I got the feeling that the two of you were going to be permanent."

Chandler grunted cynically. "Trey, a man can't count on anything being permanent. Especially when it comes to a woman."

"Yeah," Trey mumbled in agreement. "Another good reason we shouldn't go to the Fandango."

"Hey, can't a guy get some service around here?"

Both men jerked their heads around to see Joseph sauntering through the door, and since his brother was wearing a deputy sheriff's uniform, Chandler figured he had to be ending his shift, or just beginning one.

"What's going on?" Chandler asked in the cheeriest voice he could muster. "Did you come to arrest us for bad behavior?"

Joseph chuckled. "Knowing you two, I should probably haul you in for lacking common sense."

"Nobody ever accused us of being geniuses, Joe," Trey joked. "'Course, Doc is pretty darned close to one."

Rolling his eyes at that, Chandler gestured to the empty end of the couch. "Have time to sit a minute?" he asked Joseph.

"No. I'm on my way home and I'm running late, as usual. I have something out in the truck for you. Better come get it."

The three men trooped outside to where Joseph's pickup truck was parked. When he opened the back door, Chandler immediately heard a cacophony of yips and whines.

"Is that what I think it is?" Chandler asked.

Joseph reached in and pulled out a black-and-white spotted pup, no more than three months old. He was scrawny and dirty and trembling with fright. Chandler's heart went as soft as a marshmallow.

"Where did you find him?"

"Take a guess. On the side of the road. Somebody didn't want him," Joseph said. "I told Connor you'd take him. You couldn't turn down a stray if your life depended on it."

Joseph handed the dog over to Chandler, who immediately turned around and handed the animal to Trey.

"You know what to do to take care of him," he told Trey. "The end kennel is empty. Put him in it."

"Right, Doc. I'll fix the little guy."

Trey left with the pup and Joseph shut the back door on the truck, then opened the driver's door and climbed into the vehicle.

Before he had had a chance to back away, Chandler asked, "How's Little Joe and Tessa?"

"Little Joe is just like his uncle Holt—he's turning into a mischievous rascal and he never shuts up." The grin on Joseph's face deepened. "Tessa's been throwing up. Don't tell anybody yet, but we think she's pregnant."

Pregnant. Another Hollister baby. For those few brief minutes Roslyn had worn his engagement ring, he'd believed Evelyn would be his child. Now some other man would eventually become her father. The idea left a sick, heavy feeling in his heart.

"Lucky you," he said with as much enthusiasm as he could summon.

"Yeah. Lucky me." His expression suddenly wistful, he looked at Chandler. "Tessa and I are truly blessed to have Little Joe and a baby on the way. But there's a bittersweetness about it, too. We can't help but wish our fathers, and Tessa's mother, were around to enjoy their grandkids. Mom is the only grandparent our children will have."

Chandler forced a smile. "Thank God for Mom. She'll be happy when you give her the news."

Joseph shut the door and put the truck into Reverse. Leaning his head out the open window, he said, "Gotta go, brother. Take care of that pup. I figure by the time Evelyn starts crawling, she'll need a furry playmate."

Lifting a hand in farewell, Joseph drove away. Chandler thoughtfully watched his brother's truck disappear into the darkness.

Their father, Joel, was gone. Tessa's father, Ray Maddox, had also died a few short months before she'd come to Arizona. And Katherine's father, Avery, passed away before he'd had a chance to see his daughter marry Blake and give birth to the twins.

It was too late for those men, Chandler thought. But Roslyn and her father could still have a worthwhile relationship, if they were willing to work at it. Still, that was something Roslyn needed to decide for herself, not because Chandler pushed her into it.

He'd been wrong to insist she contact her father. These past hellish weeks without her and Evelyn had taught him just how wrong. Instead of urging her to mend the broken bridges behind her, he should've been vowing his love and support. He should have been convincing her that she and the baby were the most important things in his life. Not her relationship with Martin DuBose.

But if Chandler went to her and admitted that he'd been stupid and wrong, would she be willing to forgive him? Would she give him another chance? He didn't know. He only knew he had to try. Otherwise, his chance at real happiness was going to be forever and truly over.

Chapter Thirteen

Early the next morning, after Chandler and Trey finished treating the goats and returned to the clinic, he changed into clean clothes and headed straight to Roslyn's apartment.

The sight of her Jaguar parked beneath the covered carport was a relief. At least she hadn't run away for a second time, he thought. But who was driving the black sedan parked directly behind Roslyn's Jag? The bar code on the license plate suggested it was a rental.

Had a friend come all the way from Fort Worth to visit? Or had Roslyn's father finally tracked her down?

He didn't care if he was interrupting. Roslyn was the woman he loved. He wasn't leaving until he'd talked with her and she understood how much he still wanted them to make a life together.

After parking the truck behind the sedan, Chandler hurried to the front porch and was about to punch the doorbell when he noticed the door was slightly ajar. What the hell was going on? Roslyn didn't leave her doors open.

He knocked on the doorjamb in hopes the sound would draw Roslyn's attention. After a few moments passed and she didn't appear, he decided to forgo manners. He entered the house and started down the short foyer toward the living room. Halfway there, he picked up on a man's voice. Low and gruff, it was as cold as a snow-capped mountain, and the sound caused Chandler to stop in his tracks.

"Do you have any idea of the embarrassment you've caused me, Roslyn? The shame you have brought on the DuBose name by your irresponsible behavior?"

As Chandler listened to the man's questions it was all he could do to keep from running into the room and knocking him flat on the floor. But he understood that Roslyn needed a chance to fight her battle with the man, before he stepped in to back her up.

She said, "I'm sorry that's how you see things, Dad. I called you, hoping the time I've been away might've softened your feelings. That you'd want to see me and your grandchild. But obviously I was hoping for too much."

"Soft. You can't get ahead in the world by being soft, Roslyn. And you would try to twist things around and make me look like the villain in all of this." The coldness in his voice turned to sarcasm. "Now I've got to try to explain to my friends and colleagues why my own daughter ran away from home. It's indecent. And I'm telling you one thing, when we get back to Fort Worth, you will do exactly as I say. Nothing more. Nothing less."

Chandler took a step forward with the intention of revealing his presence, but Roslyn began to speak and he forced himself to pause.

"You've misunderstood, Dad. I invited you out here because I thought as my father you had a right to see your granddaughter. But that's where it ends. I have no intention of going back to Fort Worth or living in the same house with you again."

The man let out a scoffing laugh. "And what do you think you're going to do? Are you thinking you'll take the money your mother left you and buy your own place? If so, I should remind you that I can find some sort of legal loophole to take every penny you have away from you."

"I suppose that would make you feel superior to take your granddaughter's financial security away from her," Roslyn said stiffly. "Well, go ahead. I honestly don't care what you do with any of the money. My life is here now. With the man I love. The man I'm going to marry. That's all that matters to me."

Joy flooded through Chandler, while Martin DuBose snorted loudly.

"Marry you? Who? Some blue-collar worker with a big heart and an empty bank account? I really think—"

Chandler had heard enough. He walked into the room and faced the man who was the reason Roslyn had run from Texas and straight into his arms.

Gasping with surprise, Roslyn stepped toward him. "Chandler! I...didn't hear the doorbell. Were you—?"

He moved to Roslyn's side and wrapped an arm around the back of her waist.

"The front door was open and no one answered so I came in, anyway," he explained. "I've been standing in the foyer."

Uncertainty pinched her features. "So you heard what was being said?"

He gazed down at her and hoped his eyes were conveying all the love he felt for her. "More than enough," he answered softly, then turned his attention to her father.

"I'm Dr. Chandler Hollister," he said, introducing himself to the tall, lean man with iron-gray hair. "And yes, I wear a blue collar. It's usually denim like the one I have on now. 'Cause it's tough as hell and hard to tear."

Suddenly uncomfortable, Martin DuBose cleared his throat. "Am I safe to assume you are my daughter's fiancé, Dr. Hollister?"

Roslyn reached for Chandler's hand and the sight of the emerald cut diamond on her finger told him everything he needed to know. She'd already forgiven him.

"I am."

"Chandler is a veterinarian," Roslyn said proudly. "He and his family own one of the largest ranches in the state of Arizona. But that's not why I'm marrying him. No, it's because he's the kindest, most hard-working and honorable man I've ever known. And I love him with all my heart."

For a moment her father appeared totally stunned by his daughter's statement. Then he straightened his shoulders and walked to the opposite side of the room. With his back to them, he stared out the picture window, but Chandler figured the man wasn't seeing anything except the empty life he'd created for himself.

After a moment, Martin said, "I see. So I guess you think you don't need me anymore."

Roslyn glance incredulously at Chandler before she replied to her father's comment. "I need a father who will love me even when I don't do the right or perfect thing."

Martin turned and the regret on his face proved to Chandler that Roslyn would eventually have the father she deserved. It might take months or even years for that to happen, but at least there was a chance.

Evelyn's loud cry suddenly broke the awkward silence and Chandler looked at Roslyn and smiled. "I'll go take care of our daughter. You and your father have plenty to talk about."

Epilogue

Roslyn peeked into the crib, then walked across the room to where Chandler was already settled between the covers of their queen-size bed.

"Our daughter was asleep before I got her pajamas on," she said.

Sliding next to her husband's side, she sighed with contentment as he switched off the bedside lamp and pillowed her head on his shoulder.

"I can't believe the ranch house is finally quiet," Chandler murmured against the top of her head.

Roslyn chuckled. "It was a great Halloween party. Evelyn worked hard to keep up with the twins and Little Joe."

At six months old, Evelyn had grown into a cheerful baby with big brown eyes, dimpled cheeks and a head full of light brown curls. Chandler adored their daughter and was already making noises to Roslyn about giving her a brother or sister.

He said, "Well, it won't be long before her crawl turns into a walk and then she'll really be able to chase after the big kids. If you ask me, Hannah and Nick had the best idea. They slipped upstairs with a bagful of candy and watched reruns of *The Munsters*."

"Just seeing those two cousins together makes me smile," Roslyn said. "It's so wonderful that Vivian and Sawyer are finally expecting a baby this spring. And with Tessa about to give birth any day now, we're going to have plenty to celebrate this Thanksgiving."

He nuzzled his nose against her temple. "Yes, the holidays are going to be very special this year. Hannah is finally going to get the sibling she's always wanted. Tessa and Joe are about to get their second child. And you and I are—"

"Happier than I ever thought possible," she finished dreamily.

Marrying Chandler five months ago and living here at Three Rivers had given her everything Roslyn had ever wanted. A loving, devoted husband and a home filled with a tight-knit family. Chandler's workload was still heavy, but he'd taken the step to lighten it by hiring another male assistant to help him and Trey handle the bigger jobs. And recently Roslyn had resumed working at the clinic on a part-time basis. Since the job gave her a chance to care for the animals, plus spend more time with her husband, it was a winning situation for everyone.

As for Roslyn's father, he'd relented somewhat and attended her and Chandler's wedding, which had been a beautiful outdoor ceremony on the front lawn of the ranch. Since then, her father had visited Three Rivers twice and though things were hardly perfect between him and Roslyn, they were slowly changing for the better.

Chandler's fingers gently turned her face toward his and the moonlight filtering through the windows illuminated the provocative grin on his face. "I was about to say you and I are going to add to our little family, God willing."

She whispered, "I have a feeling that our little family is going to turn into a big one."

As his fingers traced gentle circles on her bare shoulder, he went suddenly quiet and Roslyn glanced up at his pensive expression.

"What are you thinking?" she asked. "Are you worried I can't deal with more than one child?"

"Not at all. You're a wonderful mother, sweetheart. You could tie one hand behind your back and easily deal with six more babies. To be honest, I was thinking about Mom and all these new grandbabies she's getting. On the surface she acts like she's on top of the world. But when she believes we're not looking…well, I'm more certain than ever that she's hiding something from us."

His comment prompted Roslyn to lever herself up on one elbow and gaze down at him. "I haven't mentioned this, Chandler, because I didn't want to worry you needlessly, but the other day I went to Maureen's office to give her a message from Reeva and found her with tears on her face."

Frowning, he asked, "Mom was crying? Was she on the phone?"

"She wasn't doing anything, just staring out the window. Which is totally unlike her. I asked her what was wrong and she passed it off as nothing more than a blue mood. Chandler, did Holt or Joe tell her about those items they found? The piece of shirt fabric and the belt tip?"

He shook his head. "None of us have breathed a word about it. Joe has them locked away. No, I think something else is going on with her."

"Like what?"

A few silent seconds ticked by and then he answered,

"A man. I don't know if it's Uncle Gil or someone else, but I think Mom has fallen in love and doesn't want us to know that she's finally put our father in the past."

After a moment's thought, Roslyn reasoned, "Well, if that's the case, I wouldn't worry about it, darling. After all, look what falling in love has done for us."

Groaning, he pulled her back down and into the tight circle of his arms. "Yeah, just look. You can't wipe the smile off my face."

"You know, I think you deserve a Halloween treat tonight," she murmured coyly. "And it has nothing to do with candy."

Chuckling, he rolled her onto her back. "I couldn't agree more."

* * * * *